Praise for *Braking Day*

"Engaging, fast-moving, and inventive. The characters and the space environment feel totally real, as do the life and death challenges that never miss a step."
—Jack Campbell, *New York Times* bestselling author of The Lost Fleet novels

"Oyebanji crafts an amazing lived-in world aboard a sprawling generation ship, and a twisty mystery that'll keep you guessing to the very end." —Dan Moren, author of the Galactic Cold War series

"Adam Oyebanji's *Braking Day* blows the airlocks off the science fiction mainstay of generation ships with a vibrant world within bulkheads that's as convincing as it is fresh. The characters are fabulous, the world-building impeccable yet never in-your-face, and the plot is breathtaking. All I can say is this is the best SF novel I've read in decades and it may be the best I've ever read. This author is now a must-read for me, and I'm sure he will be for you. Bravo!"
—Julie E. Czerneda, Aurora Award-winning author of *In the Company of Others*

"Lovingly crafted characterization and world building, along with a satisfying twist, make *Braking Day* a worthy entry in the (space)shipboard thriller genre exemplified by classics such as Arthur C. Clarke's *2001.*" —*Booklist*

"The tension mounts as Ravi is determined to prevent mutually assured destruction while his ship's officers are equally determined to pretend all is well. This is a story of people who are their own worst enemies as groups fracture, danger ramps up, and options close in."
—*Library Journal* (starred)

"An outstanding debut novel that features exceptional world-building and a really well-realized generation ship society. Filled with twists and turns, it kept me guessing in the best way right up until the end."
—Michael Mammay, author of the Planetside series

BRAKING DAY

ADAM OYEBANJI

DAW BOOKS
New York

Cover illustration by Kekai Kotaki

Cover design by Adam Auerbach

Interior design by Fine Design

Edited by Leah Spann

DAW Book Collectors No. 1914

DAW Books
An imprint of Astra Publishing House
dawbooks.com
DAW Books and its logo are registered trademarks of Astra Publishing House

Printed in Canada

ISBN 978-0-7564-1854-0 (trade paperback)
ISBN 978-0-7564-1823-6 (ebook)

First Paperback Edition, April 2023

10 9 8 7 6 5 4 3 2 1

To Barbara, without whom nothing
is worthwhile.

And to Alex,
for his love of dragons.

Midshipman Ravi MacLeod, weightless and adrift in zero *g*, did what he often did. He barfed into his sick bag. With an ease born of long practice, he sealed it up and tossed the whole schmeer into the recycler. The little machine gurgled gratefully, adding its vibration to the gentle thrumming of the elevator. The car, he noticed, had finally passed the ten-kilometer mark. Less than five to go.

The elevator car—the only one that ran express to the engine rooms—was a blast from the past. Seldom used as it was, it was one of the few parts of the ship still in its original condition, right down to the bronze plate with its early version of the ship's logo. First Crew would have been right at home here.

He doubted First Crew would have appreciated being cut off from the hive, though. He didn't quite know when it had happened, but happened it had. At some point during his descent, the ebb and flow of data through his implants had died away to nothing. The nearest working routers would be in the docking ports, he reckoned, several kilometers "above" him and getting farther away by the second. His face twisted into a wry grimace. He would be offline for the duration.

An image of Chen Lai popped into his head. In his imagination, the engineer's stern, gray-haired visage looked both disappointed and annoyed.

Explain to me, Middy, the engineer would demand, *how you can be offline WHILE STILL ABOARD THE SHIP?*

Chen Lai would lean forward, peering relentlessly into Ravi's eyes. As the scene played out in his head, he could picture his mumbling response all too clearly. *It shouldn't happen, sir. No matter where you are, you should always be in range of a router.*

So, Chen Lai might respond, *what the hungary do you think is going on?* The old man would stand there, stone-faced. Waiting.

The routers, sir. There'd be the usual rush of blood to his face. *There are routers in the engine rooms. They're not working for some reason.*

And then Chen Lai would have nodded and sent him off to do something menial and humiliating. Ravi grinned to himself in relief. Thank Archie the pedantic SOB was nowhere in sight.

The grin faded as quickly as it had come.

There was something wrong with the routers.

He hung motionless in the middle of the elevator car. His face twisted with strain as his implants reached out to the engine rooms, feeling blindly for any sign of the silent equipment. The sudden beginnings of a headache stabbed at his temples.

Would he have to fix the routers before he did anything else? The headache, unpleasant to begin with, was intensifying rapidly. Did he even know *how* to fix the routers? He threw an anxious glance through the roof of the car. What if he had to go all the way back up without accomplishing *anything?* His mouth dried up at the thought of Chen Lai's disdain, the unspoken mockery of his well-bred classmates.

His jaw tightened with mulish determination. No way, he told himself. No sarding way. He'd space himself first.

A series of musical chimes rang through the cabin, and Ravi, without really thinking about it, pointed his feet at the floor. A minute or two later he was drifting downward. The elevator, after an hour-long journey to get there, was decelerating. A weak, ersatz gravity pulled him to the deck, only to vanish the moment the elevator slid to a halt.

"Engine rooms," the elevator announced. The airlock lights were all green, so he went ahead and opened the hatches.

Which was stupid. The whole module, unvisited since Archie knew when, was still warming up. It was barely above freezing. Ravi looked around in dismay. Every surface was covered in a thin layer of frost. White breath billowed in front of him, drifting lazily in the direction of the nearest filter. The air itself, stored away for far too long, tasted of metal. Its cold fingers slid effortlessly through the thin blue fabric of his fatigues and pressed against his skin. Ravi cursed silently. He'd been careful to bring his toolkit. He hadn't thought to pack a sweater.

His headache was still getting worse.

A sigh escaped from his lips in a puffy cloud. He followed it deeper into the compartment. The room was set up for thrust, which meant he was floating in through the ceiling. "Beneath" him, the monitors were in sleep mode, an iced-over landscape of dark screens and drowsy orange lights.

Ravi brushed the rime off one of the chairs, strapped himself in, and used his hands to fire up the boards. The switches burned cold against his fingers.

The boards lit up: green mostly and a bit of red, but nothing critical. The hive burst into life. He could feel the press of data against his implants, the quiet hum of information, the mindless chatter of systems. He breathed a sigh of relief. The routers were working after all. Left alone in the dark for maybe the best part of a decade, they'd simply turned themselves off.

Tap. Tap.

Ravi would have jumped out of his seat, but the straps held him back. He let out a nervous laugh.

Like there'd be anyone down here, he chided himself. *As if.*

His hands were still shaking, though. He tried to blame it on the temperature.

Creepy noises were only to be expected, he told himself. Until a few hours ago, the engine rooms had been deep-space cold. Sleepy, huddled molecules, newly energized by an infusion of heat, would want to fly farther apart. The materials made of those molecules, the switches, the consoles, the decks—*stuff*—would have to expand to accommodate them. There would be all sorts of creaking and cracking as the edges of things stretched into new spaces and fought each other for the right to be there.

Tap. Tap. Tappity-tap.

He ignored it. He unstrapped himself from the seat and floated free. He had work to do.

The last time the drive had been fired was nine and a half years ago—a minor course correction. Ravi had been a child at the time and incapable of understanding the details. But he remembered the excitement leading up to it, how parts of the ship had been broken down and turned through ninety degrees, the way his mom—less brittle then, with Dad still around—had checked and double-checked that his toys and belongings were properly stowed. He remembered how the ship's great habitat wheels had ceased their endless rotation, the way everything and everyone had floated. It had been awesome. And his young-boy stomach hadn't cared one bit. He and his friends had wriggled free of their parents' grasp and soared through the living spaces, bouncing off the bulkheads, playing tag on the ceilings, throwing stuff in impossible directions. *Flying.*

And then, finally, the drive had stretched and yawned and woken from its long slumber. He remembered the gentle but relentless way it flipped everything sideways, turning walls into floors and windows into skylights. It plucked at the whole enormous vessel like a guitar string, making her hum and rattle along in harmony. Every step he took was suddenly and unbelievably light. In a moment of carelessness, he would fly high off the deck, arms flailing, but the drive would always bring him back down, safe and sound, cradling him in soft hands. It was magical.

It lasted for three whole weeks.

At the end of it, with the wheels spun up again and everything returned to normal, the ghost of those soft vibrations lived on in his imagination. He couldn't let go of it. He needed to know how the drive worked, how to make it work, how to keep it working. He needed to be an engineer. An *officer*.

Tap. . . . Tappity, tap, tap.

Years later, when he'd nervously confessed this ambition to his parents, his father's reaction had been less than encouraging. "Who cracked your motherboard?" he'd asked. "You're a *MacLeod*, son, not some bastarding officer." There'd been laughter then; all bitterness, no humor. "You'll never pass the exam. And even if you did, they'd find some other way to sard you. Don't think for one second that that lot'll ever let someone like you near their precious sons and daughters. A MacLeod in officer training? Never gonna happen. They despise us. They're *afraid* of us. And don't you forget it!"

"Just because you never made it doesn't mean I won't," he'd said defiantly. "All I need to do is keep out of the brig."

He'd seen the flash in his father's eyes too late. But the backhand never landed. His mother had gotten in the way.

"No harm in a kid dreaming," she'd said, her smile fragile but firm. "Let it go, eh?"

He'd been packed off to his pod instead, where he'd lain in the dark, the ceiling mere centimeters above his nose, tears of anger pricking at his eyes.

And then the awful sol when they'd come for Ramesh MacLeod in the early hours of the morning, two ShipSec officers and a drone, escorting him away through corridors that were still night-cycle dark. They'd not known how awful it was at the time, of course. Ramesh MacLeod was no stranger to the brig. But this time was different. He never came back. Only his molecules returned, recycled into biomass and polymer and Archie knew what else.

In a unit that was suddenly too big, Ravi salved the scars of his grief with schoolwork and movies. Hour after hour of extra study, followed by something in black and white from the twentieth century. Anything to delay the onset of night-cycle and its tear-stained memory. He sat the officer's entrance exam. Passed it by the width of a transistor.

And now, despite the disdain of his betters and the disbelief of his family, he was well on his way. One more semester till graduation. He grabbed his toolkit.

Tap. . . . Tap, tap, tap.

The drive had been checked and triple-checked, of course. But Chen Lai was a past master at finding trainee-level grunt work for every possible system—including the ship's main engines. According to Chen Lai, this particular job, the inspection of a tertiary coolant mechanism, was so simple, it required little more than a moron in a hurry.

"Which is why," he'd said drily, "I chose you. Try not to break stuff."

Ravi unlocked the hatch to the next compartment. It swung open with a tired creak. Orphaned pieces of ice floated away from the broken seal.

After a moment's hesitation, he drifted through, his skin prickling with irrational goosebumps. Unlike the chamber he was leaving, most of the engine rooms had only standard shielding. If the drive were to suddenly burn, the radiation in there would fry him like an egg.

No danger of that, he reminded himself firmly. Braking Day was weeks away. *Weeks.*

He shook the feeling off and accessed the hive instead. A bunch of schematics flooded into his mind's eye. He cross-checked the data with his real ones. Sure enough, tucked away in one corner, was a small access plate. The label read ISV-1 ARCHIMEDES, followed by a string of numbers and the curvy, old-style version of the ship's logo. The numbers matched the schematics, so Ravi opened it up. The cover came away to reveal the insides of a dark, spiraling duct. A shot of sub-zero air puffed against his face.

Tap.

He really wished his head didn't hurt so much. It was hard to concentrate, and what he was about to do required thought and a bunch of coding. He closed his eyes to make things easier.

With his eyes shut, he could see only one thing: the back of his own knee in infrared. It glowed hot yellow against a cold, blue background. A drone's-eye view. This particular drone was staring at him from the inside of his toolkit.

Having linked himself to the drone, the rest of it was easy. He fired up the machine's tiny thrusters and let it fly into the ductwork. The drone dropped through a series of specially designed gates and into the coolant system proper. Then it went to work, scanning every which way to Homeworld and piping the results into Ravi's head.

Hands tucked into armpits, Ravi floated easily in the middle of the compartment and let the drone's readouts wash over him. Numbers and schematics coated the inside of his eyelids. Everything was green. Everything matched the remote diagnostics. The system, if it were ever needed, would do its job. The drone, inspection complete, headed for home.

Tap, tap, tap. Tap, tap, tap. Tap, tap, CLANG!

There were no straps to save him this time. Ravi jumped out of his skin. His body spun through the air like a wayward top. The compartment rang like a bell.

Tap, tap, CLANG!

Ravi's breath was coming in short, cloudy gasps. Beads of sweat prickled his forehead.

This wasn't creaking caused by heat. Something was banging against the hull. Right outside the compartment. Ravi held his breath.

Not something, he realized suddenly. Some*one*. There was nothing random about the noise outside. This wasn't a collision with some broken-off piece of ice or other accidental debris. There was cadence to it. Rhythm. The deliberate act of an intelligent mind. Someone was banging on the bulkhead. In deep space.

Aliens!

The word smashed its way into his head, an unwelcome guest. The spit disappeared from his mouth.

Then he laughed, sudden and hollow. Aliens were for kids. Stories for the pitch black. Halloween. This whatever-it-was was a trick. A stupid trick to scare him witless. Ansimov, probably, or maybe even Boz. He had to admire the trouble they'd taken. And the nerve. Fifteen kilometers—on the outside. They must have hitched a ride on the elevator running gear.

Tap, tap, tappity-tap, tap.

The sound was drifting away now, toward the next compartment. In which, so said the schematics, there was an airlock.

Ravi's lips twitched, animated by vengeful mischief. He was meant to think that aliens were banging on the airlock door. Maybe even sound the alarm and make a complete fool of himself. And then Ansimov or whoever it was would burst in and live-broadcast his stupidity all over the ship.

But not if the airlock was actually, like, *locked.*

Ravi's smile grew wider. With the elevator going nowhere and standard tanks, there was no way Ansimov had enough air to freestyle fifteen klicks to safety. He'd have to beg Ravi to let him in. And when Ravi spread his hands and said the lock was *jammed,* Ansimov would be the one panicking. Punker punked.

There was a small tightening in Ravi's right eye as he turned on the video camera. Technically, he was abusing the privacy laws. Only medics and engineers had a recording function, and it was for work use only. But Ansimov was similarly equipped, so . . .

Racing to beat Ansimov to the airlock, Ravi opened the hatch to the next compartment and flitted through. The compartment itself was little more than an anteroom. It was small and cramped, with starlight as the only illumination. The blue light of the Milky Way shone through the porthole in the airlock's inner door, making silhouettes of the ice-rimed emergency suits that lined the walls like an honor guard.

Ravi barely noticed. He rushed to open the inner door before Ansimov reached the outer one, and succeeded. The outer door deadlocked with a satisfying *thunk,* and Ravi gave himself a metaphorical pat on the back. So long as the inner door was open, the outer one would remain closed. That was how airlocks worked. There was nothing Ansimov could do about it.

Tappity-tap, tap.

Ansimov and whatever he was dragging across the hull were getting closer. Ravi floated through the airlock to the outer door and pressed his face against the porthole. He didn't want the camera to miss a thing.

The view, it had to be said, was spectacular. The porthole looked "up" toward the prow of the ship. He could see the gantry that formed the ship's kilometers-long spine stretching away from him, its crisscrossing struts coated with layers of icy, pinkish dust. And then, in the vacuum-clear distance, the habitat wheels, rotating about the spine in slow majesty, each one moving opposite to its neighbor, their walls dotted with lights. And beyond even the wheels, more than twenty kilometers from where he was floating, sat the vast disk of the ship's forward shield, a shadowed expanse of black against the white glare of Tau Ceti, the Destination Star.

There was a face at the porthole.

It wasn't Ansimov or even Boz. It was a young woman—a girl, really—no older than he was. Blonde. Blue-eyed. A friendly smile revealed slightly crooked teeth. Ravi stared at her in disbelieving horror.

She wasn't wearing a spacesuit.

2.0

And then what?" Boz MacLeod asked. She wasn't judging. Not yet, anyway. She was simply curious. She fished a cigarette and lighter out of her top pocket. Ravi's gaze flicked instinctively upward. Boz chuckled. "Sensors have been dead for years. No one's going to know."

Ravi had no doubt his cousin was right. This was Boz's bolt-hole, after all, long vanished from the ship's specifications and impossible to find unless you knew it was here. High up in the Fiji Wheel, it must once have been a control room. Charred deck plates spoke to some long-ago catastrophe. Control panels gaped empty, their innards gutted for parts. The seats that remained were just bolted-down frames, their upholstery burned away in whatever disaster had happened here. Various flavors of graffiti, much of it BonVoy, glowered from the bulkheads. The graffiti was old, though. Judging from the slogans, Fourth Gen. Maybe even Third. Crates of contraband that Boz had "acquired" through various trades were stuffed carelessly into the corners.

Boz pressed the tip of her cigarette against the arcing electricity of her lighter and took a long drag. The tobacco glowed red. A wisp of blue smoke spiraled toward the ceiling. Ravi thought about the overworked air filters and winced. His cousin, entirely unfazed by the damage she was doing, just stared at him, waiting for an answer.

"Nothing," he admitted at last. "I kind of freaked out, and when I looked out the porthole again, she was gone. Nothing there but vacuum. I fired up every external sensor I could find. Zip. Nada. Nothing."

The beginnings of a smile quirked at his cousin's lips.

"But you were in the middle of punking that handsome classmate of yours. So . . . what about the recording?"

Ravi cursed himself for all kinds of a fool. He'd opened up his camera and taped the whole thing, expecting to catch Ansimov in a full-on panic. He still had the data.

"Link me in," Boz demanded.

With a literal blink of an eye, Ravi flashed her a key. Inside his head, he could feel her settling in beside him. He played the tape.

Nothing. Well, nothing that showed the girl. There was a camera's-eye view painted across the inside of his eyelids. It floated to the outer door and looked out the porthole. Then everything blurred as he spun away. It was a full minute before the video stabilized and he returned to the porthole for another look.

But all the tape showed was an anteroom, an airlock, and a spectacular view of the ship. There was no sign of the girl.

Boz slid away, breaking the connection.

"Maybe you imagined it. You were all alone in the back of beyond. Easy enough to get freaked out, you know?"

Ravi nodded, reluctantly. The tape didn't lie, and there was no sign of the girl. And no one—*no one*—could live in hard vacuum without a space-suit. It couldn't have been real.

And yet . . .

"Have you told anyone else?" Boz asked.

"Not a soul. Apart from you, obviously."

"Good call." She looked at him hesitantly, touched a hand to his wrist. "Are you cool? Do you need to see someone, you know, *professional*?"

"I'm not mad."

"No. You're just seeing things."

A wry chuckle escaped into the open, despite Ravi's best efforts to restrain it.

"I think I'm just trashed," he confessed. "Chen Lai's riding us pretty hard. He's got Braking Day marked on his schedule with a big, giant *X*, and Archie help anyone who sards up his countdown." He flashed his cousin a brittle smile. "A good night-cycle's sleep and it's all good."

"Awesome." Boz stood up suddenly, with enough force to float off the deck.

"You know it's only half a *g* up here," Ravi mocked. "You need to keep your excitement under control. Unless, of course, you *want* to smack your head on the ceiling."

Boz, who had already drifted back down, spared him a pitying look.

"You need to live a little. Better to hit the ceiling now and again than spend your life welded to the deck." Her eyes took on a mischievous glint. "Besides, I *am* excited."

Boz was the proud owner of a scuffed brown jacket that pre-dated the Launch—or so she claimed. She also said it was made of a blood-soaked material called leather, which, knowing Boz, was a bare-faced lie. Eyes gleaming, Boz reached inside of said garment and pulled out a palm-sized metal sphere, lovingly hand-painted in yellow and black.

"What is it?" Ravi asked, suddenly curious.

"This is BozBall. My new little helper. It's why I asked you up here." She dropped the metal sphere onto the deck plates. "Go fetch," she ordered. She only used her voice, Ravi noticed. There was no accompanying burst of code.

For several long moments, the "BozBall" just sat there, a yellow-black lump of useless. A series of snarky comments arranged themselves on Ravi's tongue, ready to jump into the open. Before *that* happened, however, the little ball started to spin.

Ravi felt something tickling his implants.

"Is that thing *scanning* me?"

Boz said nothing.

The ball rolled across the deck until it bumped into a couple of crates. Ravi's eyes widened in surprise as the homemade drone sprouted a bunch of spidery legs and started to climb. It reached the top of the crates, jumped onto the ceiling, crossed a good chunk of it upside down, unscrewed a rusted ventilation grille, and disappeared inside.

Ravi turned to look at Boz and clapped appreciatively.

"Wow. That's pretty . . ."

His voice trailed off. He'd expected Boz to have that slightly vacant expression people wear when they're remoting a gadget, but Boz was just grinning manically. She was fully "present."

"Isn't it great?" she asked enthusiastically. Her grin, if anything, grew even wider.

Ravi stopped paying attention. His own expression, he knew, was not so much vacant as pained. He almost groaned with effort, peering into every corner of the nearby hive. Boz was there, her presence a small eddy in the current of data flowing through the ship. But the eddy should have been bigger. More complex. There should have been tendrils of information—of code—flowing between her and the BozBall. There weren't any. In fact, no matter how hard he looked, there was no sign of the BozBall at all.

It wasn't part of the hive.

He stopped peering electronically and used his eyes as nature intended. To glare at his cousin.

"What in Archie's name do you think you're doing?" he yelled at her. "This isn't a twenty-liter fine and a couple of sols' torpor, Boz! You could get recycled!"

Boz's only response was a dismissive wave of the hand.

"I'm serious," Ravi persisted. "That . . . whatever you call it, is a full-blown LOKI. ShipSec'll have your hide!"

Boz burst out laughing.

"It's just a bunch of algos, Rav. It's not like it can pass a Turing test or anything."

"And you think ShipSec will *care?* It's a machine. It's not part of the hive. It thinks on its own." He ticked off each charge on a slightly unsteady finger and gazed earnestly at his cousin. "It's a LOKI, Boz. They will mulch you."

A flicker of doubt surfaced briefly on Boz's face. Briefly. She was grinning again, reckless as ever.

"Yeah, well. First, they have to catch me." She glanced back up at the duct, where the BozBall had reappeared. There was a soft whirring as it re-attached the rusty grille. Boz's grin grew still wider. "And if they do, it'll be worth it."

Ravi was about to point out that nothing was worth getting mulched for, when BozBall arrived at its creator's feet. Delicate limbs held up a small, rectangular package wrapped in purple foil.

Ravi knew his mouth was hanging open, but he couldn't quite figure out how to close it.

"That cannot be real," he said at last.

"Oh, but it totally is. Stashed it here last week—*without* BozBall, mind you, and yet he found it in no time at all."

"Where'd you . . ."

"Don't ask. Eat!" Boz took the package from BozBall, tore it open, and handed half the contents to Ravi. The warm aroma of chocolate filled the room. And not the ship-made stuff that tasted like denatured cellulose. This was different; a cathartic symphony of syrupy fragrance, filling his head with half-octaves of sweetness and a complex, organic bassline. This was *real* chocolate. From Earth.

And it was 132 years old.

With trembling fingers, Ravi broke off a small square and took the tiniest of bites.

The flavors exploded in his mouth like a bomb.

3.0

He was staring at a plate. The old-fashioned kind: round, and without dividers, and made of baked soil. The sort of plate that smashed into a dozen pieces when Earth women hurled them at their husbands in the black-and-white movies. This plate wasn't black and white, though. It was ornate, and beautiful, and full of color. Blue, and yellow, and cursive black in an interlocking pattern he couldn't quite place.

The pattern began to disappear. Slowly at first, then ever faster under tendrils of green mold that spread across the surface until all that was left of the plate beneath was its shape. And soon, not even that. The mold kept growing. Thicker and higher, and thicker and higher, until it was reaching his face and forcing his mouth apart and putting roots down in his throat.

Ravi didn't know if it was the dream that woke him up or the splitting headache. The hammering in his skull was so bad, he couldn't face using his implants.

"Lights," he croaked.

If the system was surprised at receiving a voice command, it gave no sign. Gentle, early-morning illumination splashed across his quarters. *Quarters* was, admittedly, a fancy word for a cramped cabin that was barely three meters cubed with no window into the corridor, but it was low enough in Ecuador for the wheel to be turning at a full *g,* and it was his. Even if the fifty-five-liter rent was more than he could really afford.

Ravi waited until the chips in his head felt a little less raw before accessing the time: 0452. Early, but not early enough to go back to sleep. More from habit than desire, he opened his implants to the newsfeeds. Nothing unusual. Preparations for Braking Day. Spartans had beaten Cataphracts in overtime to represent *Chandrasekhar* in the Fleet Cup. Engineers on the *Bohr* had managed to print an old-time grand piano but were having trouble getting it to play. And closer to home, on *Archimedes*, Carmela Patel and Team NFR had run away with the last Formula EMU race before Braking Day— and possibly ever. There was video of the throne-like extravehicular maneuvering units, primarily designed for accessing the outside of the ship but stripped down here for racing, rounding the ship's stern and hurtling across the finishing plane, Carmela's suited arms raised aloft in victory. This, of course, was not news to Ravi. Ansimov moonlighted as a mechanic on Team Spike. They'd come in a very poor fourth. To say that Vladimir had been less than pleased failed to capture either how much he hated losing or his contempt for the pilots responsible.

What *was* news, sort of, was that the owners of Diner Seven had been fined a thousand liters for hygiene violations. Despite the pain, Ravi found himself shaking his head. Why people insisted on eating there was one of the ship's great mysteries. Anyone with half a chipset knew that a trip to Seven risked a subsequent one to the infirmary. And yet.

With a sigh weary enough to have come from his mother, he rolled out of his bunk, folded it against the wall, and got on with his sol.

His sol would probably have been easier without Sofia Ibori. Not that she'd ever done anything to him, mind you, which summed up the problem in a nutshell. Sofia was tall, and beautiful, and off-the-charts smart. And she was only faintly aware of his existence. He stared wistfully at the back of her neck from his usual position at the rear of the class. Her dark hair was gathered up in a thick, off-center braid that draped itself lazily over one shoulder. It gleamed like starlight when she moved.

Vladimir Ansimov nudged him in the ribs.

"Ask her out." There was more than a hint of mischief in his voice.

"Yeah, right. Like that'll ever happen. She's an officer, for Archie's sake."

"And so are you. It's a match made in deep space."

Ravi stared stubbornly at his feet. Ansimov's tone morphed into something approaching exasperation.

"Ask her out, dammit; don't ask her out. I really don't care. But don't let your background hold you back, amiko. You're as much of an officer as she is." A faint chuckle. "Which isn't much at this point, I guess, everyone being a trainee and all."

Lieutenant-Professor Warren took a sledgehammer to their conversation.

"So glad to see that Midshipmen MacLeod and Ansimov are giving us their *full* attention," she said archly. "After all, it would be such a waste of resources to spend time teaching trainees who don't want to learn, wouldn't it? Particularly when they come to us from such—ah—*non-academic* families."

The blood rushed to Ravi's face. Ansimov swore under his breath. Some of their classmates snickered.

"We were talking, as I'm sure you know, because you were listening *so* hard, about basic photosynthesis." Warren's gaze was fixed on Ravi now and unrelenting, like an arboretum reptile. "So, I'm sure Midshipman MacLeod would just *love* to give us a quick summary of the chemistry of carbon-dioxide reduction—*without* cybernetics."

Ravi could feel his heart hammering in his chest. Photosynthesis. The means by which plants turned sunlight into energy. The stuff of life, even here, in deep space. Everyone else would be accessing the hive for the relevant information, just in case the professor turned on them next. He, thanks to Ansimov's big mouth, was expected to do it the old-fashioned way. He licked suddenly dry lips.

"The . . . er . . . reduction of carbon dioxide," he began, his voice soft and hesitant, "is a process in which . . . er . . carbon dioxide combines with, um, a five-carbon sugar, ribulose one five-bisphosphate, to . . . um . . . yield two molecules of a three-carbon compound, glycerate three-phosphate, also known as three-phosphoglycerate."

Professor Warren looked displeased, which meant he was on track. Even better, Sofia Ibori was looking right at him. A good kind of butterfly fluttered in his stomach. His voice became stronger, more confident.

"Glycerate three-phosphate, in the presence of ATP and NADPH produced during the earlier, light-dependent stages, is reduced to glyceraldehyde three-phosphate." He allowed Prof Warren to see him smile. *Screw you and your my-family-isn't-good-enough crap,* he thought fiercely. "This product is also referred to as three-phosphoglyceraldehyde, 'PGAL' or, more generically, as triose phosphate. The vast majority of the glyceraldehyde three-phosphate produced, maybe five out of every six molecules, is then used to regenerate ribulose one five-bisphosphate so the process can start all over again."

He fixed Professor Warren with what he hoped was a look of insultingly false innocence.

"Way to go!" Ansimov coded, transmitting from his own chipset directly to Ravi's implants.

Professor Warren's lips pressed themselves into a thin line.

"Well done, Middy." The thin line took on a nasty curve. "I don't know how you managed to access the hive without anyone catching you, but well done nonetheless."

Ravi churned with anger. He wanted to protest his innocence, say something cutting, but the words wouldn't come. Not in time, anyway. And now Professor Warren was turning away, looking for some new victim. It didn't take her long.

"Midshipman Ibori: photosynthesis as we generally understand it is optimized for the light of the Home Star. More particularly, the light of the Home Star as seen from the bottom of Homeworld's atmosphere. At a basic level, what changes are being made to accommodate the different spectrum of radiation we can expect from the Destination Star?" A sour glance in Ravi's direction. "Implant-free, if you please."

Sofia leaned forward in her chair, smiling easily. To Ravi, it was as if the whole room had been lit up by an arc welder. Perhaps, if he hadn't been paying her so much attention, he wouldn't have noticed the thin trickle of code she'd dropped low-down in the hive. It started crawling upward, through a bunch of increasingly secure hierarchies.

With a small shock, it came to Ravi that Sofia had no clue about the professor's question. She was trying to download the answer without anyone finding out. He looked at the code a little more closely. It was a spiderbot, lines of programming designed to sneak past security and steal stuff. The sort of thing Boz might make—if Boz were still in kindergarten. This one was clunky and clumsy and at least a generation out of date. If it climbed much further, it was going to trip an alarm and put Sofia in violation of the honor code.

He dropped some code of his own. One of Boz's best: sleek, and undetectable, and *fast*. It latched on to Sofia's spider and essentially hacked its transmitter.

"We can see you," Ravi warned. To Sofia, the message would seem to come from the spider. Unless someone in the room was really trying, no one else would even hear it, much less pin it on him.

Sofia's smile barely flickered. The spider disintegrated in a wisp of ones and zeros.

"Before I get to that," she asked, "can you help me with something I don't understand? About Destination World?"

"Of course," Professor Warren replied. Ravi tried not to imagine what she'd have said if it was *him* trying to change the subject. First Crew's Chief

Navigator had been an Ibori, and there'd been an Ibori in the Officers' Mess ever since. Sofia was entitled.

"Why are we modifying plants at all?" she asked. "Why not just live off the land? Make the most of what's there, like the Mission Plan says?"

"Well, one reason is we don't know what the biosphere is actually like." Warren blessed Sofia with an indulgent smile. "Archie's hooks, we don't even know what Destination World *looks* like yet. The best we can do is a blue pixel in the telescopes. We know it can support life, and we know it probably *has* life because of the methane in the atmosphere, but we don't know anything about how that life works. Is it based on DNA? Does it make the precise proteins we need to survive? Is it laced with poisons?" Professor Warren shook her head. "We don't have a choice. We need to bring our own plant life—Homeworld life—and tweak it to thrive under a new star."

"But won't that mean crowding out the native plants? Even on Homeworld, people replaced plants and animals they didn't much like with billions of hectares of farms, didn't they?"

"Do you think she's a BonVoy?" Ansimov coded, only half seriously. *"Sounds like a lot of touchy-feely 'save their world' stuff to me."*

"Nah. She's stalling for time, is all."

Warren, meanwhile, was still considering Sofia's question.

"True," she agreed. "But Homeworld at its peak had, what? Eleven billion people? Even today, it's probably around five or six—or whatever the LOKIs allow them to have. Out here, the whole of humanity is thirty thousand souls and a gene bank. It'll be a long time before we're 'crowding out' anything."

Sofia opened her mouth to say something else, but before she could do so, the ship's clock chimed the hour. Mission accomplished.

"We'll take this up again next time," Warren said. New assignments flashed across the hive and into their implants. Ansimov, who must have taken a quick look before flicking them over to storage, let loose a groan. "We're also going to make a start on the chemistry of clays. If Destination World has them, we're off to the races. Class dismissed."

Ravi and Ansimov slouched out with the others. Ansimov cast a dark look at his classmates, his hands curled into fists.

"'Non-academic families,'" he mimicked bitterly. "'*Non-academic families!*' Why'd they let us train if they're going to throw it in our faces every chance they get?" He looked like he was going to spit on the deck, but a warning glance from Ravi stopped him. He spat into the nearest recycler instead, attracting guarded looks from those nearby. "They could at least not have us all in the same Archie-damned room for class. It's nearly all cyber-work, anyway."

"Saves energy," Ravi said. "And helps us bond."

"*Bond?* If you believe that, there's a habitat in Hungary I'd like to sell you."

Ravi didn't respond. His gaze had wandered back to Sofia. She was a little way ahead of them as they walked along Phoenix Circular, one of the wide passageways that went all the way around the wheel. Unusually for Sofia, she was on her own.

She'd looked at him, he remembered. The butterfly in his stomach woke up again. Maybe asking her out wasn't such a stretch. Maybe . . . .

The thought drained away. Sofia had reached an intersection. And in the intersection was a man: tall and slim, with a mane of wavy dark hair. He scooped her up by the waist and drew her to him, whispering in her ear. She giggled and pressed against him for a moment before pulling away, hurrying to catch up with the other navigators.

How could you be so stupid, he scolded himself. *Of* course *she has someone. People like that always do.*

By the time he reached the intersection, the man had sauntered off. But the damage had been done. And now his headache was back. He pressed his hands against his temples in a futile attempt at painkilling.

"You okay, buddy?" Ansimov asked. "You look like you're going to hurl."

"I'm good." Ravi, with some reluctance, made to turn left. Left was the quickest route to Engineering, but Sofia was going straight on, heading to Navigator Country. Despite himself, he took a lingering look in her general direction.

And stopped in his tracks.

"Man, you are just weird today," Ansimov muttered. "Hustle, amiko, before Chen Lai welds us to the bulkhead." He headed off, his boots thumping urgently on the deck.

Ravi ignored him. Sofia had caught up with her classmates, and they were already starting to disappear "upward" as the curve of the habitat wheel hid them from view. As they did so, however, they passed by a young woman leaning casually against the passageway wall. Her blond hair hung loose about her shoulders rather than braided back in the usual fashion. It would fly all over the place the moment she climbed up to the hubs and started bouncing about in zero g.

Or then again, perhaps not. It had looked perfectly normal the last time he had seen her.

On the outside of the ship. Without a spacesuit.

The girl waved at him and started walking away. Heart hammering in his chest, he ran after her.

4.0

So glad you could join us, Midshipman MacLeod."

Commander Eugene Chen Lai, it had to be said, did not look particularly glad. He glared at Ravi from under bushy gray eyebrows, daring him to explain himself.

Ravi knew better than to try. He was late, and that was that. Besides, even if Chen Lai *had* been minded to listen to him, no one would believe what he had to say. He wasn't sure he believed it himself.

"Apologies, Commander." He tried to make it sound sincere. Not that Chen Lai would care. Punishment would come in due course, regardless.

He took his usual seat at the back of the briefing room. Ansimov flashed him a puzzled *What happened to you?* look but said nothing. Which was sensible, because Chen Lai was speaking again, and the engineer did *not* like to be interrupted. His voice had the dry crackle of an electrical short.

"After yester-sol's checks, we can confirm that propulsion is nominal across the board, except for the L-three sequence control valves, which we'll swap out as soon as we get the authorizations back.

"What that means is we're good to go for any course correction the navigators decide to throw at us before Braking Day. Assuming we can fix the valves, of course." A wintry smile of encouragement pulled briefly at his lips before melting away.

"We need to get on with our survey of the habitat wheels. Most of these compartments haven't been rotated for thrust since Launch Day. Archie's hooks, some of these compartments didn't even *exist* back then. We need to make sure every single module can be turned through ninety degrees and that they can be secured and hooked up to the utility lines without any trouble." His face took on a menacing cast. "I do *not* want my teams run ragged during final countdown because someone didn't do the job right the first time. *Am I clear?*"

"Crystal!" the room shouted back.

Chen Lai nodded approvingly. Ravi felt a bunch of assignments hitting his implants.

"You have your schedules, people. Try not to break stuff."

There was a general shuffling as the room started to stand up, eager to get on with the sol's work.

"Oh, and one more thing," Chen Lai announced, his voice slightly raised as it climbed over the background noise. "Midshipman MacLeod?"

Ravi tried to ignore the sinking sensation in his stomach.

"Yes, Commander?"

Chen Lai's lips twitched into the fossilized outline of a smile.

"Once you've cleared your schedule, son, take a trip to Bermuda-four, deck twenty-five, Gunder's Passage. The sewage lines need cleaning out."

"Yes, Commander."

■■ ■■ ■■

The Gunder's Passage sewage lines were every bit as bad as Ravi feared. A second-stage recycler had gummed up, jamming the lines from no less than a dozen compartments. Cleaning out the lines was a soul destroying, messy business, leaving both Ravi and his drones spattered with what was euphemistically known as black water. But no matter what he did, he couldn't get the recycler itself to work right. Ravi fought to contain a rising sense of frustration. Beads of sweat on his forehead swelled to full-sized drips, winding darkly outlined paths across grimed skin.

"Keep doing it that way, Middy, and you'll be here all night-cycle."

Ravi had been so engrossed in his battle with the recycler, he hadn't noticed Melati Petrides standing behind him. Archie alone knew how long the engineering lieutenant had been watching.

"Ma'am?"

Petrides was not Chen Lai. The smile on her round face was open and friendly. The lieutenant inserted herself into his code.

"The knack, MacLeod, is to work *against* the impeller. That way, you'll build up enough pressure that when you open the c-valve like *this*, the gunk will vent itself. See?"

Sure enough, the stubborn jam Ravi had been struggling to remove was gone. A quick internal rinse and the whole mechanism was good as new—until the next time, anyway.

"Thank you, ma'am."

"Oh, don't thank me, Middy. I'm entirely self-interested. I need someone young and flexible, and the commander said I could have you—but only *after* you'd finished here." Her smile turned wry. "He did mention you'd be covered from head to foot in muck." She crooked a finger, indicating that he should follow. Ravi did as ordered, trailing the lieutenant into a maintenance stairwell and all the way down below deck thirty, Bermuda's deepest. A little-used hatch opened into a netherworld of pipes, cabling, and tanks. The infrastructure of existence, unseen and unthought-of by the thousand or so souls on the decks above. Sensing their presence, a few dim lights shimmered to life, bathing the whole scene in gray twilight. Cold air clung clammy to Ravi's skin, his breathing accompanied by streaming puffs of white. Overly strong gravity pulled at his knees.

Petrides led the way along a narrow catwalk, its grated deck plates hugging the broad curve of a water tank. The tank itself was at least a hundred meters long, bland and featureless, save for the occasional serial number stenciled on the side. But it was impossible to tell how deep it was. Both above and below, the tank's vertical extent was hidden by pipes and cabling and gloom.

Petrides came to a halt. It was no coincidence, Ravi thought, that she was standing beside a ladder built into the tank wall. It stretched up through a painfully small kink in the piping and vanished from sight. Petrides reached into her pocket and pulled out a small spool, the thread it contained attached to a small, clearly visible weight. Petrides patted the nearest rung. A small blueprint appeared on the inside of his eyelids.

"Right, MacLeod. According to the specs, this ladder will eventually take you to the top of the tank. At the top of the tank, there is an inspection cap." She tossed him the spool, the little weight digging into the palm of his hand. "Unscrew the cap, and unreel this plumb line through the opening until the weight hits the bottom of the tank, pull it back up and measure how much of the thread is damp—easy to do 'cause it'll turn bright red. Got it?"

He knew he must be staring at her like she was several transistors short of a circuit. Was this the lieutenant's idea of a joke? But then again, what if it wasn't? What if Petrides was serious and this was just more punishment? Blood burned in his cheeks. In the end, all he could do was stand at attention and utter one plaintive word.

"Ma'am?"

Petrides burst out laughing.

"I know, Middy, I know. It sounds like some kind of prank. But let me assure you: it isn't. We've read the sensors and run the diagnostics; we've had drone inspections and taken apart the drones. So . . . we're doing this old-school. Like dawn-of-time old-school. Wriggle your way up there, Mac-Leod, drop in the plumb line, and read off the depth. The line will tell us the truth once and for all. Hopefully, this is some bizarre software issue—a bug in the hive. If not, we've got bigger problems." She patted him on the shoulder. "Now get going. And stay flexible!"

Petrides wasn't really kidding about the flexibility. The tank wasn't a regular shape, and the ladder snaked and curved in cruel directions through ridiculously narrow gaps. By the time Ravi returned to the catwalk, his back, elbows, and knees had been scraped raw. He delivered the depth number to the nearest millimeter and tried not to wince with pain.

"You're sure?"

"Yes, ma'am."

It was clear from Petrides' expression that it wasn't the number she'd been looking for.

"Okay, Middy. You've been on duty long enough. Dismissed."

"Thank you, ma'am."

"And Middy?"

"Yes, ma'am?"

"Don't stint on the shower. That smell of yours is killing the filters."

— — —

"It's not funny," Ravi insisted. He struggled to make himself heard above the raucous noise of the diner.

"It's kinda funny," Boz replied, grinning from ear to ear. She batted away a food-thieving hand from an older cousin and wrinkled her nose. "Also: you still smell."

Ravi hoped to Archie she was joking. He'd burned forty liters of water, trying to wash away the aftermath of his battle with the sewage lines. Water he didn't really have. And it was a long way to payday.

He and Boz were facing across a table in Diner Nine. Although no one called Diner Nine, where the MacLeods had gathered to shoot the breeze and do business, "Diner Nine." They called it "Ansimov's," after the family that had owned it for at least two generations. Vladimir's mother, Khadija, was keeping a careful eye on them, Ravi noticed, her face pinched into its usual expression of mild disapproval, her body pressed against one of the out-of-date ovens the family refused to upgrade because the new ones, according to Vlad, "cooked like crap. A human could do better."

"The thing I can't get my head around," Ravi said at last, "is that she just disappeared."

"People don't just disappear," Boz pointed out. "You must have lost track of her."

"But I didn't! There was nowhere for her to go! She was in the circular, plain as day-cycle."

"And then she turned a corner. Easy enough to break into a run and give you the slip when you weren't looking." His cousin broke into a mischievous grin. "I've done it dozens of times. Turn a corner, sprint to the next one, turn into that, and *ta-da*! You've 'disappeared.'" She curled her fingers into air quotes to emphasize the point. No mean feat, considering she was holding a cigarette. The tip reddened with movement, sending a curl of smoke toward the filters.

"Roberta MacLeod!" Khadija yelled at her. "Put that thing out before it shows up on the sensors! You want ShipSec in here?" Various MacLeods piled on, adding roars of mock disapproval to the general hubbub.

Boz waved good-naturedly and smothered the glowing embers between thumb and forefinger. Ravi had no idea how she did it without burning herself.

"The only one running was me," Ravi explained. "And I'm not slow. She didn't have *time* to reach another corner." He could feel his face forming into a frown. "I'm telling you, Boz. She just vanished." He snapped his fingers. "Like *that*."

"Hmmm," Boz murmured, stroking her chin. "There *might* be another explanation, you know."

"Which is what?"

"That you're sarding crazy! No one just 'disappears' into thin air. It's not physically possible. You're the engineer, cuz. You *know* this."

Before Ravi could respond, their uncle Torquil slid into a seat beside him. He was accompanied by the tart aroma of hydroponics and a wide smile.

"How's it going?" he asked Ravi. "Still doing the officer-training thing?" Ravi nodded.

Torquil gave him a skeptical look. At least he hadn't spat on the deck,

Ravi thought. In MacLeod lingo, any sentence with the word *officer* in it almost *required* the excessive use of saliva. It was like a rule of grammar.

"You gonna be looking down on us after you graduate? Turn us in to ShipSec?"

"Don't be daft, Uncle Torq. I'm an engineer. The only thing I'll be looking down on is jammed valves and worn-out bearings. I'm still family."

Torquil stared at him a moment or two longer and then decided to let it go.

"Braking Day's coming," he said, as if Ravi was the only person in the fleet who didn't know. "This whole beast of a ship is going to turn around, point its ass at the Destination Star, and . . . *Boom!* The drive goes off for a whole sarding year!" His eyes glowed at the thought. A powerful, heavily tattooed arm wrapped itself around Ravi's shoulder, like some gigantic Homeworld snake. "We slow down. We drop into orbit around Destination World, and we land. Mission accomplished!" The arm began to crush him with merciless glee. "And you know what happens then?"

"No, Uncle." Ravi rolled his eyes. "I'm sure I haven't got a clue."

"*No more officers!*" Torquil roared, banging the table and laughing. "*No more officers!*" Others nearby took up the chant, banging tables in unison. "*No more officers! No more officers!*" Only when Khadija Ansimov made to move from the ovens did the chanting fade away to good-natured laughter. Torquil leaned back in his chair, chuckling quietly.

"I'm sorry to break it to you, Uncle," Ravi said, "but you're going to have officers up your ass for an eternity after Braking Day. Reconnaissance, surveys, preliminary expeditions . . . It'll be years—*years*—before anyone gets to go down." He poked a sharp elbow into his uncle's ribs. "You'll be an old man. I mean an *even older* man, obviously. . . . And all that time, you'll have to call me *sir*." He shook his head in mock sympathy.

"You're killing me, Ravi." Torquil loosened his grip on Ravi's shoulder. Turned to look him in the eye. "You really sure you want to be one of those stuck-up, inbred bastards? They treating you okay?"

"Yes," Ravi said. "And yes." He wanted very much to believe the second yes was as true as the first.

His uncle didn't look entirely convinced. For a moment, it looked like he was going to pursue it some more. Until, that is, his face broke into a sudden, mischievous grin.

"MacLeod's World," he said.

"What?"

"MacLeod's World. That's what we should call Destina—"

"Uncle, shut *up!*" Ravi hissed, scandalized.

"Why?" Torquil's grin grew wider. "It doesn't flow so well, I admit. How about New—"

"Not another sarding word from you!" Boz said, even more sharply than her cousin. "You know it's bad luck. We haven't gotten there yet. Don't sard it up for the rest of us."

"Okay, okay! Archie's hooks, you two: I'm kidding. *Kid. Ing.* It doesn't count if you don't mean it."

"Yeah, well, let's not take the risk, eh?" Ravi said. He allowed himself to smile. "If something goes wrong now, Vasconcelos will be all over you."

This time, Torquil didn't hold back from spitting on the deck.

"That bastard. Should have killed him when I had the chance."

"Like you'd ever kill anyone," Boz teased.

"For him, I'd make an exception. You turn out like him, Ravinder Mac-Leod, and I'll tan your hide from one end of Haiphong Circular to the other."

"It's a circular, Uncle. It doesn't *have* an end."

"You know what I mean."

"Yessir, Uncle sir. If I have to be an officer, don't be a bastard one." He replaced his grin with something more serious. "I won't be, Uncle Torq. Promise."

"Deal. And hey, if the officer thing doesn't work out, come see me." He favored Ravi with a crafty smile. "Engineers get to know all the nuts and bolts, don't they? I bet there isn't a compartment in this ship you couldn't get into if you put your mind to it." The smile became positively wicked. "I'm sure we could find a use for someone with your particular set of . . . *talents*, eh?"

"Mom would kill me."

"Yeah, well. What your mother doesn't know won't hurt her." He turned to his niece. "On the subject of which, Boz, my darling, let's get down to business and talk chocolate." He leaned toward her across the table, propped up by powerful forearms. "I can get you forty liters a quarter bar."

Boz's response was an incredulous laugh. "Seventy-five or nothing, Uncle Torq. I gotta keep the vacuum out of the airlock; know what I'm saying?"

Torquil grunted, entirely unsurprised by the response. Cheerfully calculating eyes scanned Boz's guileless expression for some kind of tell.

"Sixty?" he offered, at last. "And some lightly used inductors?"

"Done." They shook hands. Some sixth sense made Torquil look over his shoulder. He blessed them both with an impish grin and left, avoiding Ravi's mother by seconds.

"What did he want?" Fairley MacLeod asked. She was staring anxiously at Torquil's back, her slim hands clasped too tightly together.

His mother was, as ever, a pencil-thin bundle of nerves. She was still pretty, Ravi thought, but the cheerful woman of his childhood was long gone. He liked to think that losing his father to the recycler had dimmed the light in her, but truth was, Dad's constant clashes with ShipSec, his always-broken promises to fly right, had ground her down long before the ship had finally had enough. She turned from Torquil to Ravi, her expression freighted with worry.

"He didn't want much of anything," Boz assured her smoothly. "He lost a bet on the playoff game, is all. We were just settling up."

She might as well have said nothing for all the effect it had. Fairley MacLeod continued to stare at her son, willing him to speak.

"What she said," he mumbled at last. His stomach hopscotched into knots, the way it always did when he lied to his mother. He managed a weak smile. "Nothing to do with me," he added. That, at least, had the virtue of being true.

His mother relaxed a little.

"Good. You've come a long way, Ravinder. A *long* way. You're one semester from becoming an honest-to-Archie *officer*." Her eyes shone with pride as she said the word, followed by a troubled glance around the room. "Don't let anyone drag you off the circular, Ravi. Not now."

"No, Mom." Ravi couldn't bring himself to look her in the eye.

"All right, then." She reached out to adjust his hair, but Ravi swung out of the way, embarrassed. He got to his feet.

"I need to get going," he said, more abruptly than he'd intended. He gave her a brief hug, and a smile to make up for it. "Got to study if I'm going to be an officer and all." He let her go, kissed her lightly on the forehead, and headed toward the exit.

Boz caught up with him in the corridor.

"Not so fast, Middy." She gestured at Ravi to follow her. Curious, he fell in step alongside.

"Where are we going?"

"To the scene of the crime. I've been thinking about your, er, *sighting,* and one of two things is going to happen. Either we figure out how your mysterious girl did it; or you're making an appointment with the shrink."

"I'm not going to the shrink."

"*I* will be the judge of that."

Boz headed for the habitat wheel's nearest spoke. Her progress was rapid, and Ravi struggled to keep up. Not for the first time, it occurred to him that Boz walked quickly because she was always expecting trouble. And like most MacLeods, trouble stuck to Boz like a rash. How could it be otherwise when half of what she was involved in was sketchy—and the other half was worse? Unlike Ravi, *both* her parents had been sent to the recycler. Ravi worried every single sol that she would be next.

"Pick it up, Middy!" Boz ordered over her shoulder as Ravi started to breathe heavily. "All that extra sewage slowing you down?" She threw him an infuriating grin and started to move even faster. Ravi would have sworn at her, but he didn't have the oxygen.

At the spoke, Boz, impatient as ever, chose the hubward paternoster rather than the elevator. The endlessly moving ladder—this one rattling "up" toward the hubs—moved more slowly than the elevator, but there was never a need to wait. Boz jumped across without breaking stride and hung on nonchalantly, using only one arm and a leg. Ravi was having none of that. He stuck himself to the worn rungs with every limb he had.

They rode the paternoster in silence. As they climbed through the remaining, night-dark decks and the weight of his body against the rungs lessened to nothing, Ravi patted his leg pocket. It was a nervous habit. He had plenty of sick bags, and he knew it. Besides, he wasn't going to be weightless long enough to need one.

The paternoster was coming to an end, bringing them out of the spoke and into the weightless center of the wheel—of all the wheels. "Above" him, Boz bent her knees and pushed off. Ravi pulled down a gridded navigation screen over the inside of his eyelids. Arcing green lines of possible trajectories flickered across his vision. He picked one and jumped, launching himself into the cavernous expanse of the hubs.

Queasy stomach or not, it was a sight Ravi never got tired of. The hubs: the long, hollow tube around which the ship's enormous habitat wheels made their turns. The wheels had to spin in order to make gravity. And the hub of each wheel was here, spinning in contrarotation to its neighbor, each one pierced by round spoke holes with their elevators and paternosters, the means by which the crew traveled from the wheel's habitable decks "up" to the hub and vice versa.

To call the hubs a "tube," of course, failed to do it justice, seeing as it was over two hundred meters across and more than five kilometers long. It was the largest open space on the ship, bar none—and the only way to get from one wheel to another that didn't involve a spacesuit. Because the top of each spoke opened onto the inside of the hubs, crew routinely floated from the hub of one wheel to the hub of another. Unlike the wheel rims, the hubs spun too slowly to make gravity. Unless people were manhandling a load or were otherwise incapacitated, they simply bent their legs and jumped from hub to hub, hurtling across the voluminous expanse like unguided missiles.

There were eight wheels in all, named alphabetically from stem to stern with Australia at the front/top and Hungary at the back/bottom. In front of Australia, there was only the round disc of the shield, and behind Hungary, a mess of loading bays, and airlocks, and vacuum-rated elevators leading out to the ship's spine and, ultimately, the flared bulk of the drive. But those were strange, foreign places, exposed to space and accessible only to a few. All life, the whole point of the ship's existence, was in the wheels. He still remembered the chants in kindergarten as he'd learned their names for the first time. *First is Australia, second is Bermuda, third is Canada, fourth is Denmark, fifth is Ecuador, sixth is Fiji, seventh is Ghana, and eighth but not least is Hun -ga-ree!* Though in truth, Hungary was very much the least and had been for generations.

Over time, the hubs had evolved from an engineering necessity into a three-dimensional recreation area: a park, of sorts, at the center of the ship. The volume was dotted with the spherical outline of zero trees, and caged-off spaces for freeball, and dancing, and any number of null-*g* pastimes. And even though everything around him was night-cycle dark, it was easy to see the broad rings of the hubs, each of them rotating in ponderous, eerie silence, moving opposite to one another on near-frictionless bearings. Sunk into each hub were four large, softly lit circles, each one a slightly different color, each one marking the entrance to a spoke. They moved in quiet, precise circuits, creating slow-moving patterns of round light. A giant's kaleidoscope.

Heart pumping with excitement, Ravi soared weightlessly into the volume. Now that he'd kicked off, the nav screen flashed up the corkscrew curl of his actual flight path. It was a glorious green, matching his intended course almost perfectly. His jump had been better timed than Boz's. He was headed directly to the Denmark Wheel. She was going to miss by at least a couple of hundred meters. She knew it, too. He could see her grimacing as she drifted off to his left.

The hubs, for Ravi at least, were a lot more fun in night-cycle. Darkness was easier on his stomach. Less to see. Less to upset his sense of balance. It was why, despite his initial fears, he'd never been sick outside of the ship. Soaring over Ecuador, he could hear the pulse of freefall dance music from a nearby cage. He wondered distractedly if Sofia was there, flying in and out of the arms of the man he'd seen her with at the intersection. Farther off, a knot of bright lights and voices indicated a freeball game in progress. Remembering it was the *Archimedes'* playoff game, Ravi twisted his head ever so gently to see who was winning. The cage, however, was too far away to make anything out. A round, free-floating zero tree drifted across his line of sight, blocking the view and filling his nostrils with the scent of eucalyptus.

Some minutes after leaving Fiji, he twisted himself around to land feet-first on the Denmark hub. It was another two minutes before Boz caught up with him, looking distinctly cross.

"Show-off."

"It's not my fault you're getting old and your eyesight's shot," Ravi needled. He took a deep breath. "Let's do this."

They rode a paternoster all the way down. Like everything else on the ship, it had seen better sols. The rungs of the endlessly moving ladder were worn and cracked under his palms. Its chain drive wheezed and rattled with the grinding resentment of 132 years of thankless use. Ravi stole a quick glance "down" toward the wheel rim. The paternoster's narrow shaft, running arrow-straight through the inside of the spoke, plunged dizzyingly into the distance, its twilight gloom interrupted by splashes of light that marked openings onto the various decks. At the very bottom, somewhere below deck thirty and farther than he could see from this far up, the rungs would loop around a hidden mechanism of gears and cogs and start moving "up" on a separate but parallel shaft back toward the hubs. The whole arrangement had a Rube Goldberg feel to it, but it worked. So long as a person was sound of limb, halfway coordinated, and lacking the patience to wait for an elevator, they could step through an entrance that was little more than a hole in the side of the shaft, hop across a meter or so of open space, and grab on.

Of course, if they were *not* sound of limb, or just plain clumsy, things might not go so well. High up in the wheel, where gravity was minimal, missing a rung was embarrassing but no big deal: there was plenty of time to grab the next one. Closer to the rim, though, as gravity climbed toward a full *g*, slipping off a rung was much more serious. If the unfortunate crewman lacked the presence of mind to brace themselves against the shaft wall, they would drop like the proverbial Homeworld stone. Every year or so, someone died or got badly injured on a paternoster, and the senior officers would agonize about shutting them down. But it never happened. They were far too convenient.

The officers might have reached a different conclusion, however, if they had taken the time to ride the paternoster taking Boz and Ravi into Denmark. The deeper they got, the more the battered rungs bucked and whipsawed, as if desperate to throw them off. By the time the two of them had descended to a full *g*, Ravi was clinging on for dear life. Even Boz's grip had strengthened from carefree to slightly cautious.

Ravi hopped off the paternoster and onto solid deck just as quickly as he could.

"This way."

The intersection, as they approached it, was deserted. Phoenix Circular, which had been so full of people earlier in the sol, stretched ahead of them into the nighted gloom. A couple of cleaning bots, under the supervision of a bored-looking janitor, moved slowly past in the opposite direction. Neither the bots nor the janitor paid them the slightest attention.

"The girl came down this way," Ravi said, reaching the intersection. The walls here were covered in murals: modern, Sixth Gen stuff for the most part. Edgy, and mildly subversive. But it was just possible to make out the faded name of the cross corridor stenciled underneath the artwork: MANCHESTER PASSAGE. "And then she turned *here*," he explained, pointing. "There's no . . ."

He came up short.

Chen Lai was in the cross corridor, running a worried hand through close-cropped, gray hair. And he wasn't alone. Standing next to him was Commander-Inspector Vasconcelos, head of ShipSec; and standing next to *him* was Qadira Strauss-Cohen, fourth of her name, Chief Pilot, and adjunct professor of post-LOKI history.

Ravi took a deep breath. No one called Strauss-Cohen any of those things.

They called her Captain.

*K*eep walking before they see us!" Boz coded. Her cybernetic voice echoed in his implants.

She grabbed him by the elbow and marched him across the intersection to the other side. Ravi shook her off.

"What was that for?" Ravi coded back, making no effort to hide his irritation. "We haven't done anything wrong! We have every Archie-damned right to be here!"

"And they have every Archie-damned right to haul your ass over and start asking questions. Do you really want to explain to your boss, and the Captain, what we're doing here?" She grabbed him by the shoulder. "Also: that's Vasconcelos around there, Ravi. ShipSec. The man suspects everybody. You think he's here for giggles? You think you can walk around that corner, tell him you're on the path of some, like, phantom babe, and he'll just let you go home?"

"Yeah, well, maybe you have a point."

"Damn right I do!"

"But we don't actually know why they're here. Maybe it's just a coincidence."

"You believe that?"

Ravi hesitated a moment; shook his head.

"Good. I was worried all that engineer stuff was making you soft in the head." Boz's eyes twinkled with sudden mischief. "Let's see what they're up to."

She reached into her jacket and pulled out BozBall.

"Boz!"

"What?" Boz's arms widened in a mockery of innocence. "It's not as if I can just go hack their chips, is it?" She ignored the alarmed expression on Ravi's face and dropped the little drone to the floor.

BozBall sprouted legs and hit the deck plates without making a sound. Turning back into a sphere, it rolled quietly around the corner.

A little yellow light flashed on the inside of his eyelid, followed by a long string of letters: Boz's key.

"Are you coming?" she asked.

Ravi's stomach was tying itself in knots. Images of disgrace and expulsion floated across his mind.

Followed by that of a girl who couldn't be.

"*Sure,*" he sighed. "*Who wants to be an engineer, anyway?*"

He picked up the key and turned it.

Boz's hyperactive mind was bubbling away beside him, a constant stream of barely shielded data sloshing in and out of her implants. His biological vision faded into the background, replaced by the view from BozBall. A distorted, wide-lens representation of Chen Lai, and Vasconcelos, and the Captain loomed in the distance. BozBall rolled quietly closer.

"Stop!" Ravi whispered, aloud.

"But we're too far away to hear anything."

"How close do you think you're gonna get before someone notices a freaky-bright, yellow-and-black ball rolling across the deck?"

"I'm sure BozBall knows what it's doing." Boz didn't sound entirely confident. Alerted by her tone of voice, Ravi cursed himself for not noticing. There were no coded links between BozBall and its creator. Once again, the little machine was operating entirely on its own.

"You can't stop it?" He fought to keep his voice from rising in panic.

"Not easily. It's . . . well, it's a *teeny* bit like a LOKI. Once you let it go, it pretty much does what it wants."

Ravi was too horrified to reply. He listened to his heart thumping instead.

BozBall was climbing now. Ravi could imagine its legs skittering up the side of the corridor. He could only pray that the skittering was quiet.

From the feed, it looked like Boz's dangerously independent drone had found a niche in the wall and settled into it. The view from the camera steadied.

Chen Lai appeared to be doing most of the talking. BozBall was still too far away to hear anything, which spoke well of the LOKI's innate sense of caution but did little to satisfy Ravi's growing sense of curiosity. Whatever Chen Lai was saying, neither the Captain nor Inspector Vasconcelos looked happy to hear it.

Chen Lai produced a screwdriver from his pocket and bent down over the deck plates. Ravi didn't need BozBall's mikes to hear the high whine of an electric motor. With Vasconcelos's help, Chen Lai pulled up a deck plate and laid it carefully to one side. All three officers peered down into the exposed void.

Chen Lai said something more, shrugged his shoulders. Vasconcelos shook his head in violent disagreement. The Captain said nothing but looked worried.

Ravi could feel the bile rising in his throat. The Captain never looked worried about anything. Even when there was something to worry about. Boz must have picked up on it too. The chitter-chatter of data rattling through her implants had slowed to a crawl.

BozBall, meanwhile, continued its snooping. It watched Chen Lai disappear underneath the deck, followed by the Captain, while Vasconcelos stood watch. They were gone for several minutes. When they returned, their humor had not improved in the slightest. After some further conversation, Chen Lai replaced the deck plate and the three officers walked off—in the direction of Boz MacLeod's little black-and-yellow spy.

Ravi froze. The stream of data inside Boz's head came to a complete halt.

BozBall froze too. Whatever brain Boz had endowed it with understood its only hope lay in being as inconspicuous as possible. No mean feat, given its strident bodywork.

"We need to go," Boz coded. *"They're coming our way."*

Faced with the dueling realities of the BozBall feed and his actual eyesight, Ravi stumbled a little as he followed Boz farther along Phoenix and away from the intersection. His cousin dragged him into a narrow gangway that dead-ended in front of a battered-looking storage unit. In the dim light of the night-cycle, they were practically invisible.

BozBall, in the meantime, had held its ground. It watched in silence as the Captain and Inspector Vasconcelos marched past, tight-lipped and distracted, their faces distorted by the wide angle of the drone's lens. Chen Lai, walking a step or two behind them, glanced briefly in the LOKI's direction.

And stopped. Ravi looked on, heart in mouth, as the engineer stretched out an oddly foreshortened arm toward Boz's *very* illegal device. The lens darkened as the engineer's hand swallowed it up.

Suddenly, without warning, Chen Lai jerked his arm away, swearing. Light flooded the lens again.

BozBall was moving. It had dropped to the deck and was rolling away from the officers just as fast as it could go.

"Get it!" yelled Vasconcelos, breaking into a run. The others followed.

But BozBall was too swift. It quickly outpaced them, turned down a couple of narrow gangways, climbed a wall and disappeared inside what Ravi guessed was some open ductwork. Only then did it come to a halt. Had

BozBall been human, it would have been panting heavily. The view from its camera was shrouded in black.

Ravi cut the link.

"What just happened?"

"Wasn't that just *awesome*?" Boz's eyes were luminous with reckless energy. "Did you see how the algorithms kicked in the moment Chen Lai grabbed it? The way it balanced flight and fight? The smoothness of the transition? It was so . . ."

"*Boz!*"

Boz tried hard to look serious and responsible.

"BozBall has some defense mechanisms," she explained. Her voice trembled with ill-contained enthusiasm. "Its algos interpreted Chen Lai's grab as an attempt to capture it. So, it, er, electrocuted him." She rolled over Ravi's garbled expressions of horror just as quickly as she could. "Nothing much. Just a quick zap so he'd let go. Then it just ran away and hid. Which it did, like, *perfectly!*"

She was beaming again, her smile like a small sun. Her happiness, as ever, was irresistible. Ravi, despite his best efforts, was unable to hold on to his irritation.

"Maybe we should go see what they were looking at," he suggested.

Boz insisted they wait a few minutes, in case the officers returned. Satisfied they had the night-dark corridors to themselves, Ravi unscrewed the deck plate that had caused their seniors so much consternation.

The two of them peered into the hole they'd made. A narrow access shaft, just wide enough for a fully grown man, stared back at them. It dropped vertically into the gloom. A series of grubby rungs stuck out from one side.

"Doesn't look like much," Boz said, shrugging. "Let's see where it goes."

She stepped onto the rungs and started climbing down before Ravi had a chance to protest. He allowed himself a small sigh and followed her down.

The air got very cold very quickly. The rungs themselves were coated with droplets of water. He could see little puffs of his own breath and worried that the moisture would be lost forever, unable to make it to the filters for recycling. They were very close to the outside of the ship now. There were no more decks down here. They were dropping into a twilight world of pipes and chambers and thrice-redundant machinery, all dedicated to one purpose: keeping everyone in the habitat wheel alive. Ravi pulled up the schematics, but it was easy to see they were wrong. And not because some-one had built over the original, either. This was an error in the original specs, a prelaunch cock-up. The lines painted on the insides of his eyeballs showed a shaft that dropped all of three meters, less than twice Ravi's height. This one was much deeper. Ravi took another step down.

"*Ow!*" Boz yelled.

Ravi had stepped on her head. She was standing in the middle of a fair-sized chamber, scoping everything out. Ravi hopped down beside her and immediately felt it in his knees. He was noticeably heavier than normal. Down here, comfortably below the last of the decks, the wheel was making turns for more than one *g*.

A stream of letters and numbers scrolled across his eyesight.

"Did you see that?" Boz asked. There was a trace of anxiety in her voice. And no wonder.

"Yes. Best not to hang about."

The radiation warning had been stark. By Ravi's reckoning, they were only meters away from the outer hull, and the shielding here was thin, either worn down by the passage of time or because people were never meant to be here.

There were doorways in the chamber wall. Old doorways, each one stamped with the baroque curls of the ship's original logo. And stenciled with a warning.

AUTHORIZED PERSONNEL ONLY

KEEP OUT

Mute lines of switches clung tight to the instrument panels beside each door. Ravi and Boz exchanged puzzled glances. Ravi reached out with his implants, tendrils of coded data curling about the doorways, looking for a way in. He shook his head in bemusement.

"Dead as a dust cloud. It's like they're not even here." His glance returned to the instrument panels. "I think you have to operate them . . . *manually.*"

He stretched his hand out toward the nearest bank of switches. Boz batted it away.

"Don't."

"Why not?" His hand was stinging from the force of Boz's slap.

"The doors may be dumb, but those switches are *not*. See? They're keyed to someone's fingerprints: probably the Captain's. Touch 'em, and Archie knows what'll happen." She looked around speculatively. "Poison gas, maybe."

Ravi wasn't sure if she was joking about the poison gas. But she was right about the switches. He felt briefly embarrassed. The switches were clearly biometric, and he'd missed it. His father, if he'd been around, would have tanned his hide. He thrust the thought away, angry at himself now, for being embarrassed. His father had been a criminal. Only criminals noticed such things.

Like Boz.

Another radiation warning flashed against Ravi's eyelids. Boz's, too.

"Let's get out of here," she said.

Ravi nodded and started climbing, the excess radiation dropping away like cast-off clothing as he did so. But as he scurried up the rungs to the warmth and safety of the decks above, something else began to bother him. Boz, who had no training in such things, hadn't noticed. But he had. It was the radiation. Not all of it was interstellar.

Some of it was coming from the other side of those doors.

6.0

avi rolled into class the next morning more sluggishly than usual. He'd had trouble getting to sleep, and then woken up in the early hours with a splitting headache. He tried to access the newsfeeds, but it hurt too much. The only thing he discovered before shutting it off was that Imperials had won the *Archimedes* playoff game, and their first Fleet Cup match would be an away game on *Bohr*. Unable to lay still, he'd slipped out of his quarters at 0400 and tried to walk it off. He ended up circumnavigating the whole sarding wheel. By the time he was done, the lighting in the mural-lined circulars—Ecuador had the best artwork in the whole ship—had transitioned from dead of night into full day-cycle. Irony of ironies, he was finally ready to hit the sack, but it was too late. Off to class he went. Exhausted as he was, only an empty stomach prevented him from upchucking in the hubs between Ecuador and Denmark.

Safe now in the arms of Denmark's gravity, he cast a jaundiced eye over the soft faces of his classmates. He imagined his father staring at him incredulously. *What you falling in with that lot for?* he might have asked. *Stab the likes of you in the back, first chance they get.*

He banished the thought from his mind.

"Rough night?" Ansimov asked, grinning.

Ravi's only answer was a grunt. He perked up, though, when Sofia Ibori walked into the room. He smiled hopefully in her direction but, as usual, she didn't notice him. She was too busy laughing with her navigator buddies—although why was a mystery. As far as Ravi could tell, not a one of them was the slightest bit funny . . .

He was sobbing hysterically.

"They're all dead?" he wailed. "All of them?"

A woman's old, kindly face was looking down at him.

"Yes," said the teacher. "Every last one."

Ravi's vision was blurred by tears. But his little hands had tightened into fists. The teacher smiled encouragingly.

"Let's try again, eh?"

Ravi screwed up his eyes in concentration.

"Cebisa Akagi," he said, firmly. "Ibrahim Antonov, Jeannette . . ."

A giant packet of data smacked into his chipset. Ravi looked around, startled, unsure for a moment where he was. He must have dozed off. Lieutenant-Professor Warren was standing at the head of the class, hands on hips, her cool gaze sweeping across the room.

"Change of plan," she announced. "Plants and clays will have to wait for another sol. This morning, we're going to discuss LOKIs."

"What?"

For a horrible, terror-stricken moment, Ravi thought he'd spoken the word aloud. He was relieved to discover it was Hiroji Menendez, one of the trainee medics. Warren fixed him with a wintry glare.

"One sol, Middy, if you ever manage to graduate, you'll be landing on a brand-new world. A brand-new world means a brand-new start. A chance to make up for the mistakes of the past. A chance to get it *right*. How do you expect to avoid the mistakes of the past if you don't even know what they were?"

"The whole Menendez family, for a start," Ansimov coded, with a snort. *"That's a mistake right there."*

Ravi found himself grinning.

"Stuck-up bastards. Go around acting like Iboris and Strauss-Cohens when they're nothing of the sort. I know for a fact his grandfather was a loading tech."

"Vlad, everyone knows his grandfather was a loading tech. It's not exactly a secret."

"Yeah, well. Did you know his delinquent kid brother was back in the brig last week? Vandalism. That's what I heard, anyway. His old man had to smooth it over. Again. If that was you or me, they'd have mulched us by now."

Hiroji Menendez was tall and painfully thin. Even sitting, he reminded Ravi of the water-hungry reeds lining the edges of Canada's arboretum. Unlike the real thing, though, Menendez was not much given to bending.

"But Professor," Menendez was saying, "the whole fleet knows LOKIs are illegal. It's not like anyone's going to build one, is it? Why worry about a mistake no one's ever going to make?"

Ravi stared at the deck, trying not to look guilty. There was no way this sudden change of lesson plan was a coincidence. After his encounter with BozBall, Chen Lai would have been in no doubt about what he was dealing with. The officers were trying to nip this thing in the bud.

Warren's thin lips pursed thoughtfully, weighing up an answer to Menendez's question.

"You ever use an airlock?" she asked. "Outside of a drill, that is?"

Menendez shook his head. Ravi's eyebrows arched in surprise, and then lowered again. Menendez came from an "academic" family.

"But you know the inner door has to shut before the outer one can open?"

Menendez gave a short laugh.

"Well, yeah."

"And why is that?"

"Because you'll expose the inside of the ship to outer space." Menendez spoke with exaggerated slowness, as if talking with an idiot. "You'd have a catastrophic depressurization. There'd be no air. The temperature would drop, like, two hundred degrees. You'd *die*."

Warren nodded solemnly.

"And what if you didn't know any of that? What then?"

There was a shuffling of seats. A shared discomfort rippled across the class.

"But *everybody* knows that."

"Sure. But what if they didn't? What if they knew the *rule* about the inner door but they didn't know the *reason?*" Warren's expression was grim. "How long do you think before someone figured it would be easier to just override the safeties, leave the inner door open, and go straight to the outer one?"

The class was very quiet now. Sofia Ibori raised a slow hand.

"But they'd still have to be pretty stupid, wouldn't they, Professor?"

"Not *stupid*, Midshipman Ibori. *Ignorant*. Don't ever mistake one for the other. They may look the same, but they're not." Her gaze fell upon the medical insignia on Menendez's collar. "You go to the doctor with a problem today, and the first thing he'll do is jack you in and read off your diagnostics. But back in the sol, he'd have attached you to a bloodsucking leech because he *knew* it cured fevers, or drowned you in an icy bath because he *knew* it would drive away mental illness: treatments so stupid they might very well kill you." Her gaze shifted from Menendez to the rest of the class. "The *treatment* was stupid, but the doctor wasn't. He was every bit as clever as you or I. He was just *ignorant*. He didn't know any better. Imagine, people, what our descendants will think about what we know today, tomorrow."

She let the thought hang in the air and took a deep breath.

"Ignorance is the enemy here. The rule against LOKIs isn't just a rule; it's a rule that exists for a reason. And the reason is important." Her eyes skipped across the class. "You all remember what *LOKI* stands for, I hope?"

"Loosely Organized Kinetic Intelligence," someone said. Ravi was too busy skimming the professor's data dump to pay attention to who was talking. "It's a particular type of AI. Lightly programmed but capable of reconfiguring itself as it learns and remembers, a bit like the human brain."

"Didn't our brain chips start out as LOKI tech?" someone else piped up.

"Yes, and yes," Professor Warren agreed. "LOKI in its day was a game-changer. It allowed artificial intelligence to do a couple of things it had been really bad at." She ticked them off with her fingers. "One, deal with stuff it had never seen before; and two, even more importantly, use initiative in a way similar to humans. In less than a decade, LOKIs took over all aspects of human life, from surgical interventions to running the bureaucracy. Living standards went through the roof; people were freed to pursue their dreams. They called it a golden age. And maybe it was.

"But it also upended the power structure. The richer and more LOKI-dependent a country became, the more vulnerable it was to cyberattacks. A hacked LOKI surgeon could slit your throat; a hacked LOKI bureaucrat could bring down a government. And cyberwarfare is cheap: a few clever people working with a few clever LOKIs could immobilize a command HQ or melt the engines of an aircraft carrier. Size no longer mattered. A trade dispute between Tanzania and China brought China to its knees. And what Tanzania did to China, other countries did to the United States, and the European Federation, and India."

"The LOKI wars," Sofia breathed.

"Exactly. People died by the millions with hardly a shot fired: starved of food, or poisoned by their drinking water, or decimated by LOKI-designed infections. The Homeworld economy collapsed; golden age to stone age in less than a generation."

The professor grew somber.

"And what did humanity do then? Learn their lesson? Dumb down the machines that caused all this misery? Of course not. They took humanity out of the equation and built more LOKIs instead. 'Bigger,' 'better' LOKIs. LOKIs that did more than run the bureaucracy. They ran the governments. They abolished the privacy laws to allow for constant, 'benign' supervision. They told you what to think and what not to think. When to have children and when not to. What careers to follow and what jobs to avoid. All in the name of saving us from ourselves.

"And it worked, after a fashion. No more wars, cyber or otherwise. Just a planet of aimless, machine-dependent children. The end of humanity as we know it."

There was no mistaking the steel in Warren's voice.

"Destination World will be different. We're not making the same mistake again. Not now. Not ever."

A file hauled itself to the top of Ravi's eyelid and opened.

"We're going to start with the economic and societal pressures that brought about the transition from classical AI to early forms of kinetic intelligence. To look at that, there's no better place to start than Bangalore, India, in . . ."

Ravi leaned forward, spellbound.

▬ ▬ ▬

"You've got to get rid of it," Ravi hissed. "It's evil."

"Who gave you religion?" Boz asked, staring at him in surprise. "It's a machine, not the devil incarnate." Her derisive snort hastened a cloud of blue smoke into the air. "What's next, Rav? Burning screwdrivers at the stake?"

"It's a sarding *LOKI*!" He was so frustrated, he wanted to shake her. "We came all the way out here to get away from those things, and now you're bringing them back? No way."

He could feel his lips firming in determination. One way or another, nearly everyone aboard had gotten some version of the LOKI lecture—including his cousin. Incorrigible as she was, even she had to understand it was time for BozBall to meet the recycler.

Boz didn't answer right away. She scanned the walls of the abandoned control room instead, as if the old BonVoy graffiti were new to her.

"You planning on turning me in, Midshipman?" The emphasis on his rank was subtle, but it was there. *Officer's Mess or family, Ravi? Midshipman or MacLeod?* That's what she was asking.

Ravi's classroom-inspired determination drained away. If he squealed to ShipSec, he wouldn't just be turning his back on his family; he would be as good as turning his cousin into mulch. Boz's record was only one notch above Dead Weight as it was—an infraction like BozBall would finish her.

"Can't you—just for once—fly right?" he pleaded.

"Sure, I could. But where's the fun in that?" Boz reached into the folds of her allegedly leather jacket and pulled out a shining rectangle of purple foil. "Could someone who kept to the circular give you *this?*" She offered the chocolate to Ravi. He remembered the way the last bar had exploded in his mouth; the rich, subtle flavors of the Homeworld. His tongue moistened in response.

"Where are you *getting* these?"

"You do not need to know. All you have to do is enjoy." She waved the package in front of him.

Ravi grabbed it. Saved it for later. And returned to the subject of Boz-Ball.

"If you're not going to get rid of it, can you at least paint it a different color? Something not so black-and-yellow?"

"I was thinking blood-red with gold accents."

She leapt away before Ravi could punch her in the shoulder, sailing across the compartment with only a half-gravity to bring her gently back to the deck. She settled daintily beside a burned-out console, hand resting easily on the charred remains of an instrument panel.

"I'm serious," Ravi growled.

"I know it."

Ravi gave up. He glared at the painted-over walls instead.

Boz's expression softened.

"Look," she said, by way of concession, "I'll think about it, okay?" She took to the air again, landing gracefully beside him. "Besides, you got bigger problems."

"I do?" Ravi was genuinely puzzled. Boz burst out laughing.

"The ghost girl, you idiot! How are you planning to fix *that*?"

Ravi's shoulders slumped in defeat.

"I have no sarding idea."

Above him, one of the ancient, untended lights flickered uncertainly, but didn't quite go out.

He was staring at a plate. The old-fashioned kind: round, and without dividers, and made of baked soil. The sort of plate that smashed into a dozen pieces when Earth women hurled them at their husbands in the black-and-white movies. This plate wasn't black-and-white, though. It was ornate, and beautiful, and full of color. Blue, and yellow, and cursive black in an interlocking pattern that looked like molecules.

The pattern began to disappear. Slowly at first, then ever faster under tendrils of green mold that spread across the surface until all that was left of the plate beneath was its shape. And soon, not even that. The mold kept growing. Thicker and higher, and thicker and higher, until it was reaching for his face and forcing his mouth apart and putting roots through his tongue.

He was choking. But not from the mold. From something in his throat. Something hard. And round. And almost alive.

He coughed it up.

BozBall. Red now, with gold accents. It arced through the air and landed in a veined sea of green. The green closed around it, swallowing it from sight.

There was screaming.

Ravi wasn't sure if the screaming was part of the dream or something he'd actually done. It felt like someone had taken a chainsaw to his skull. He could barely move his head, it hurt so much.

"Lights," he ordered. The voice that reached his ears was light and frail. It scratched at his throat on the way out. The lights burst on, hurting his eyes. Still squinting, he swung his legs out of his bunk and onto the scuffed carpet that covered the deck plates. It took real, physical courage just to stand up. His head exploded in a starry constellation of pain.

"Archie's hooks," he muttered. And then, more firmly: "This has got to stop."

Still not up to the trauma of using his implants, he used voice commands to call in sick and then, of course, immediately felt better. Still, he'd done it now. Better follow through.

Ecuador's infirmary was several decks up on the other side of the wheel, so it took him a while to get there. He winced as he authorized a ten-liter deduction from his tank and watched the insides of his eyelids flash red: the purser's way of warning him he was down to subsistence. It was only a couple of sols to payday, he reminded himself. He wouldn't go thirsty for long.

"Hop up here while I plug you in," the medic suggested, with absent-minded kindness. He exuded a gray gentleness, born of many years on the job. Crow's-feet danced happily around his eyes.

Ravi did as instructed. He sat on the worn examination table while the medic slotted a jack into the small port at the base of his skull.

The medic's expression took on the slightly blank look of someone reading a data stream.

"So," he asked. "What seems to be the problem?"

"Headaches."

A soft sound escaped from the medic's lips. Meaningless and noncommittal.

"How often?"

"Every sol, it seems like."

The soft sound again.

"And how long has this been going on?"

"A few sols, I guess."

"Anything like this ever happen to you before?"

Ravi shook his head. He half-expected it to hurt.

"Banged your head at all, anything like that?"

Ravi shook his head again.

The doctor's eyes regained their focus. He blessed Ravi with a brief smile.

"I'm not seeing anything very wrong," he said reassuringly. The smile faded away. "You do have a bit of inflammation around your implants, though. When did you last have them serviced?"

"Year end."

The medic's eyes traveled to the insignia on Ravi's collar.

"Trainee, I see?"

Ravi nodded.

"Engineering?"

"Yes."

"Tough discipline. Very tough."

The doctor flashed over a prescription.

"You've been working too hard," he said confidently. "Lean forward, please." He removed the jack from the base of Ravi's skull. "All those files. All that processing. All those *tests*." He shook his head ruefully, as if remembering his own time of trial. "Enough to stress anyone's cybernetics." He unscrewed the jack with a gloved hand and dropped it in a receptacle for cleaning. "The brain's a very plastic organ, Middy. It's constantly rewiring itself, which is why your implants have adaptive connectors: so they can keep up. But *stress* the brain, make it learn new things constantly, and that rewiring goes into overdrive, particularly at night, when the brain is busy cleaning itself out. The connectors can't keep up, and you get microlesions and all sorts of inflammation around the interface, which is what you've got here.

"I've given you a prescription for CerebroLaxin. Once a sol, just before bedtime with food." He leaned forward, staring intently into Ravi's eyes to make sure he understood. "Always before bedtime," he emphasized. "The damage is done at night, remember. When you dream."

▬ ▬ ▬

Prescription in pocket, Ravi had intended to head back to his quarters to study, and maybe download a movie. But as he headed along Columbus Circular, past Third Gen murals of a Homeworld none of the artists had ever seen, he couldn't stop thinking about the girl. More specifically, he couldn't stop thinking of an *idea* about the girl. That the idea was criminal and exactly the sort of thing his father would have done gnawed at his conscience. But not enough to make it go away.

It's only a crime if you get caught, son. Which you won't.

He caught an elevator to the hubs and kicked off across the cavernous void. Instead of heading "up," which would have taken him in the general direction of Denmark and the forward habitat wheels, Ravi's lazy trajectory took him in the opposite direction. As he sailed past the gaping maws of the Fiji spokes, the wide, cylindrical walls that held them in place became scarred and pitted. Black stains from a long-ago inferno painted the surface in a memory of violence. And, as it always did when he came this way, his heart fluttered a little with anxiety. It was all too easy to imagine the meteoroid ripping through the ship's hull in a cacophony of molten metal and decompression. A quarter of the crew had lost their lives, he knew, victims and heroes both. The victims had barely known what hit them. The heroes had saved the ship. But it had been a close-run thing.

Even now, three generations later, Ravi was convinced he could smell burning. When he'd confided this to Ansimov once, Ansimov's reaction had been swift—and unsympathetic. He'd never mentioned it again.

While the smell of burning might have been the product of an overactive imagination, the groaning in his ears was not—a stertorous, metallic creak that waxed and waned like the wheezing of some asthmatic giant.

The Ghana hub: its buckled bearings grinding around and around in reluctant rotation. Ravi landed on it with surprising precision, only a few dozen meters from the twelve o'clock spoke. He gave himself a mental pat on the back. Landing on Ghana with any kind of accuracy was tough to judge. It turned so much slower than the others.

Ravi glanced farther aft, to where the hubs closed in on themselves in a brightly lit, complicated mess of platforms and cages and airlocks: stopping-off points for the various elevators that ran out along the ship's spine. Posses of dock workers were floating from one cage to another, wrangling bulging nets of weightless cargo, though whether coming or going was impossible to tell.

There was so much going on, he could almost ignore the cold darkness he'd have to cross to get there.

Creaking or not, Ghana still turned. Hungary had died in the disaster. The unlit hub of Ghana's once-twin was frozen eerily in place, the wide mouths of its spokes gagged with plating. The plating, Ravi knew, was freezing to the touch. The vacuum on the other side was colder still. Or perhaps it was cold for other reasons. Hungary, they said, was full of ghosts. If a person were brave enough to wander its hub in the dead of the night-cycle, so the story went, they might still hear the screams of the dying crew.

Ravi grabbed hold of one of Ghana's rickety paternosters and headed into the wheel. Even as the deck numbers headed into the teens, he hardly bothered to hold on. Gravity at Ghana's outer rim, below deck thirty, was barely a third of a g. Up here, it scarcely registered. He stepped off the paternoster as lightly as possible. He had no desire to fly headfirst into the ceiling.

The circulars here were a dull gray and devoid of decoration, the walls a patchwork of hasty repairs no one had bothered to tidy up. Once-working doors had been welded shut, and most of the minor passageways were closed off with grating. The whole space echoed to the groans and creaks of the wheel's hub, its circular agonies now far above his head. Ravi loped along in the sort of skipping motion that works best in low g, covering meters with every stride. If the ceilings had been just a fraction higher, it would have been fun.

The circular dead-ended in a large double door. Slightly buckled, it opened with reluctance. Once through, Ravi found himself on a catwalk that stretched across the top of a huge warehouse, maybe two decks deep and almost as wide as the wheel itself. A small army of machines hummed along between rack after rack of … stuff, mostly crated and numbered, moving it from one place to another. A small number of human beings kept an eye on them.

The catwalk's guardrail was so flimsy, it was little more than decoration. Ravi leaned over it and waved.

"Boz!" he cried out. "*Boz!*"

Boz looked up in surprise. Although she was looking in his general direction, it was as if she couldn't make him out. Which was almost certainly true, Ravi realized. She would be half-blinded by a scrolling stream of manifests and schedules.

"Over here! Eleven o'clock high."

Boz's face cracked into a smile.

"Gotcha. Hang on a minute while I log out."

She jumped up to meet him. Literally. Ravi had been expecting her to find the nearest set of steps, but she didn't bother. Ravi had to admire her eye. Ghana might not be spinning quickly, but it was still spinning. And the closer to the rim a person got, the more quickly it spun. Moving from the faster warehouse floor to the slower catwalk in one graceful leap was *not* straightforward. Boz managed it anyway, landing softly on the outside of the guardrail and swinging herself over in an easy, well-practiced movement.

"So," she asked, grinning. "What's up?"

"Can you hack the crew personnel files?"

Boz's grin vanished. She grabbed Ravi by the elbow, marched him back down the catwalk and out onto the circular. Only when the doors closed shut behind them did she bother to speak.

"Archie's hooks, Ravi! Are you *trying* to get me recycled?" Her eyes blazed with anger. "You *know* I'm on probation, right? That I'm, like, *monitored* at work?"

Even in super-low *g*, Ravi could feel the blood draining from his face.

"Oh, sard. I'm sorry, Boz. I wasn't thinking."

A faint smile quirked at his cousin's lips.

"No," she said drily. "You weren't." She poked him lightly in the chest. "You're lucky I'm not your dad, because right about now, I'd be giving you a smack."

Ravi grimaced. He could almost feel the cuff on the back of his head.

Boz leaned against a scarred patch of bulkhead and fished out a cigarette.

"And luckily for the both of us, they're not hooked into my eyes and ears right now." She allowed herself a look of mild distaste. "Once they know I've turned up, they generally leave me alone. Proves I'm not . . . Dead Weight."

Boz looked suddenly uncomfortable. She brushed the words away with a visible effort and moved on.

"You have a, ah, *project* for me?"

Ravi nodded.

"When are you done here?" he asked.

"Half an hour. Or as long as it takes me to get a thousand liters of soymilk nobody can find and route it to Canada. After that"—she gave the side of her head a knowing tap—"I'm, like, totally free." Her eyes were alive with curiosity. "I'll meet you in the Fiji bolt-hole. Don't trip the booby traps."

The missing Canadian soymilk couldn't have presented Boz with much of a challenge. She reached the abandoned control room high up in Fiji less than twenty minutes after he did.

"Don't talk" were the first words out of her mouth. Followed by "Let's have a look at your chips."

Ravi opened his mouth to protest and then thought better of it. With a certain amount of trepidation, he flashed her a key.

"*Ow!*" His hands flew to the stabbing pain in his temples.

"Oops. Sorry about that." To Ravi's way of thinking, Boz didn't sound nearly sorry enough. He grabbed on to a stripped-down console to keep from collapsing. Alternating waves of lightheadedness and nausea washed across his head.

"Will you *hurry up?*"

"Almost done." The unsettling sensation disappeared. "Your code is a bescumbered mess, you know that?" His cousin wiped a bead of sweat from her brow. "Who services your software?"

"Geppert and Johnson."

"The shop in Bermuda-nine? You can afford that?"

"Mom pays," Ravi admitted, uncomfortably. "A present for making it to the training program. Said she wanted me to have the best. Like my class-mates."

"I'm not sure 'the best' is how I'd describe the inside of your head right now. A LOKI cyber-warrior would have left less of a bootprint. On the *plus* side, I can confirm there are no ShipSec tracers in there. You are completely clean."

Ravi refrained from pointing out that ShipSec tracers were for criminals and scofflaws. Like Boz.

"And yours?" he asked delicately.

"Fast asleep." Her voice dropped to a prideful whisper. "I hacked them months ago. If they wake up, I'll know it. Not that they will." She walked across to the burned-out remains of a chair and slid into it. "My head's my own until curfew. Even scofflaws are entitled to their privacy." Bolted to the deck, the chair swiveled with a reluctant squeak. Boz forced it through a complete 360 before she spoke again.

"You really want into the personnel files?"

Ravi nodded, not trusting himself to speak.

"Why?"

Ravi's hands started to shake. *Officer or MacLeod?* asked the little voice in his head. *Officer or MacLeod?* The shaking wouldn't stop. He stuffed his hands as deep in his pockets as they would go. The bottle of CerebroLaxin pressed against his fingertips.

"It's the girl. I need to know if she's real."

Boz's only answer was a raised eyebrow.

"If she's real, she's on the ship," Ravi explained in a rush. "And if she's on the ship, she has a file. Find the file, find the girl."

"And if she's not real?"

Ravi gave a resigned shrug of the shoulders. His fingers curled around the cool plastic of his prescription.

"Then I've got bigger problems."

Why are we doing this?" Ansimov asked, aggrieved. "It doesn't make any sense." His voice sounded tinny and small in Ravi's helmet.

"Because," Ravi replied, "Chen Lai told us to. Have you checked the torsion?"

A space-suited figure drifted into view, looking for all the world like one of the fat caterpillars he sometimes saw in the arboretum. Ansimov. His tether was stretched behind him in a lazy ripple, weaving a dark thread between stars. Moving too fast, Ansimov thudded clumsily into the base of the sensor dish and swore. A shiny object flew rapidly from his hand, spinning end over end. His torsion meter.

Ravi eyeballed the little tool's trajectory and launched himself after it, hauling it back only seconds before his own tether ran out of line.

"Thanks, Rav."

Slightly winded from his exertions, Ravi had the sensation of looking "down" at his classmate. From this distance, Ansimov looked more like a caterpillar than ever, a tiny bug feeding on the endless stem of the ship's spine. It stretched away from him in both directions, habitat wheels at one end, drive at the other, fifteen kilometers long, maybe a hundred meters across. A lattice of ice-rimed polymer, studded with fuel tanks, and sensor arrays, and whatever else the ship needed to keep flying. The white glare of the Destination Star lit the ice into pink diamonds.

A sharp tug on his tether was enough to pull Ravi back toward the ship. Constellations shifted lazily between booted feet.

"Say, Rav?"

"Yeah?"

"Any chance I can borrow you this evening? I could do with a hand servicing the EMUs."

"Probably not. I've got a . . . thing on with Boz this evening."

"What about straight after the shift? I only need you for a couple of hours. And I'm totally slammed with class."

"I don't know, Vlad . . ."

"I'll give you a cut," Ansimov offered. "Ten liters."

"Make it twenty." He remembered the flashing red from the Purser's Office. Subsistence.

"That's day-cycle robbery! Fifteen. Not a milliliter more."

"Done." He landed next to Ansimov and the sensor dish, the knee joints in his suit wheezing a little with the impact.

"Awesome. Thanks, amiko." Ansimov took hold of the recovered torsion meter with exaggerated care and wedged himself against the base of the dish. "Still don't know why we're out here," he grumbled. "This is drone work." He tested the meter against one of the large bolts holding the array in place and then moved on, apparently satisfied. "If Chen Lai weren't such a sarding sadist, we'd have had this job done in twice the comfort and half the time."

"Yeah, but then he'd just have us doing something else. And this . . ." Ravi turned away to take in an unwinking panorama of stars. "This is awesome. They used to make movies about deep space back on Homeworld, long before they really knew how to fly. Not a one of 'em comes close to showing how spectacular this is. You gotta love it."

"Speak for yourself. Which reminds me: the next time we go to the Roxy, I get to choose the program. I swear, if I have to see one more black-and-white movie with you, I'm going to space myself." Ansimov continued to work his way around the base, making the occasional small adjustment. His voice, tinny though it was, took on a conspiratorial cast. "I don't think this job is on the up-and-up."

"Really?" Ravi wasn't really listening. He was using the suit's augmented vision to see if he could pick out the other ships of the fleet. Both *Bohr* and *Chandrasekhar,* he knew, were close by—within a hundred thousand kilometers—but he couldn't find either one of them.

"Yes, really," Ansimov insisted. "Think about it, Rav. We're not using drones—for training purposes, Chen Lai says, but it also means there's no log of what we're doing. And this thing"—he tapped the edge of the dish with a gloved hand—"won't do what Chen Lai says it does."

Ravi turned from the star field to look directly at his companion. Ansimov's expression was unreadable. All Ravi could see was the mirrored surface of his faceplate. A gold-colored reflection of the Destination Star gleamed in one corner.

"How do you know that?" he asked—more sharply than he'd intended.

"Did you *read* the specs?"

"Course I did."

"Then you'll know the range resolution is all wrong."

Ravi did not. But he *did* know that Ansimov had a thing for sensors.

"Enlighten me."

"Chen Lai told us we're installing a sensor to pick up close-in debris, yeah? Objects that have broken off the ship or been accidentally discarded but which might still be drifting alongside. He told us we need to know where this stuff is before we start braking—"

"So it doesn't slam into us when we slow down," Ravi interrupted drily. "I was sitting right next to you at the briefing."

Ansimov was unabashed.

"Yeah, well. You need a real narrow pulse width for a system like that. You need to be able to see things small and close in. But you don't need a lot of power, 'cause you're not looking very far—a few thousand klicks at most. *This* baby"—he patted the dish again—"is almost blind close in, but it's *real* powerful. It can see out millions of klicks." Even encased in a suit, Ansimov's body language radiated puzzlement. "This thing is designed to find something big, a long way away, not some old shoe your grandmother flushed out an airlock back in the sol."

Ravi found himself frowning. Ansimov was right. Now that he'd pointed it out, it seemed obvious.

"I'm sure Chen Lai has his reasons," he said doubtfully.

"I'm sure he does." Ansimov adjusted the last bolt. "I just hope they're good ones."

— — —

Unlike Ravi, who splashed way too much of his pay on single quarters, Vladimir Ansimov still lived with his parents and kid sister in a series of compartments attached to the far side of the family diner. Ansimov's was shift-change busy, and drones loaded with food were humming among the tables like oversized insects. Vladimir led the way across the diner floor and into the kitchen.

"Hi, Mom."

"Don't 'Hi, Mom' me, Vladimir Ansimov." Khadija Ansimov pointed angrily at a bulking oven, its various readouts a serried array of red. "You promised me you'd get this fixed yester-sol. And look at it. Comet-cold and dead as stardust!"

"I told you," Vladimir sighed. "I'm still waiting for the part. It's out of date and I need to get it printed specially—and at cost; otherwise, we can't afford it. Janine Ojukwu's doing us a favor, and she'll get it done by tomorrow, I hope, but I'm not really in a position to lean on her, am I?"

"Janine Ojukwu *lurves* you!" said an impish voice. "You can *lean* on her all you want!" Ansimov's thirteen-year-old sister, Irina, emerged from behind a drone loaded with freshly washed crockery. Her fizzy, adolescent code was only barely able to direct the lumbering machine toward storage.

"Shut up, vermin, before I squash you like the bug you are."

"You and whose fleet?" Wide, curious eyes looked up at Ravi in a way he found slightly uncomfortable. "And how are *you*, Ravinder?" The drone lurched to a halt as Irina played with the zip of her fatigues.

"Good, thanks." He hurried through the kitchen behind Ansimov's broad shoulders, glad to reach the private volumes beyond.

Ansimov's personal space, as with most family compartments, was a simple pod off the main living area. But, unlike most personal spaces, this one had two entrances. The second one, entirely nonregulation, opened onto the diner's storage unit, a utilitarian compartment of racks and freezers—but with a significant chunk given over to a chaotic mess of half-repaired mechanisms, detailed models of fearsome-looking LOKI-wars weaponry, and two racing EMUs.

The EMUs looked huge and out of place in a compartment given over to dining utensils and cooking ingredients. As always, they reminded Ravi of the medieval thrones of ancient Homeworld, gold and ornate wood replaced by vacuum-rated polymers and bell-shaped maneuvering thrusters. These two, owned by a couple of officers who raced together as Team Spike, had been stripped down to save mass. They were painted a garish dark blue and orange, the team's so-called racing colors. They were still sitting on the trailer of the delivery bot that had brought them here.

"Is the bot yours?" Ravi asked.

"Kinda. Dad bought it six or seven years ago for the business, but we have a newer one now, so he pretty much lets me use it for whatever."

"Don't let Boz see it, for Archie's sake. You'll give her ideas."

Ansimov chuckled. EMU schematics flowered to life underneath Ravi's eyelids. Red, pulsing script highlighted the areas that needed attention. Thus informed, Ravi reached into the hive, dragged a nearby maintenance drone out of its locker, and set to work. The quiet whirr of power tools did their job and opened up an access panel. Ravi peered critically at the exposed innards, his vision augmented by readouts from the drone's sensors.

"This fuel pipe needs stripping out," he said. "It's choked up with crud."

"It's that bastard officer, Huang. Couldn't pick a trajectory if his life depended on it. The gullgroper throttles back and forth like an alternating current and sards up the system every sarding time. Every. Sarding. Time." Ansimov made as if to spit on the deck but thought better of it. "More water than talent, like his pal, Koenig. Another bastard officer."

"At least Koenig came in fourth."

"A *poor* fourth. And he was lucky to get that." Ansimov had opened up the back of the other EMU—Koenig's, presumably—and was probing the interior with a flashlight. "Officers, amiko. Couldn't win a race if their sarding lives depended on it."

Ravi laughed. Raised his hand in an imaginary toast.

"To officers."

"To officers," Ansimov responded in kind. "Inbred, arrogant gullgropers who've been keeping the rest of us down since Launch Day. I can't *wait* to become one!"

Ravi and his drone had removed the offending fuel line. The drone selected an attachment from Ravi's toolkit and started reaming it out.

"So, why are we giving up our free time for a couple of officers you don't even like?" Ravi asked. "This is, like, totally voluntary. It's not like they can *order* you to be their mechanic, is it?"

Ansimov grinned.

"I like the water. Better it sits in my tank than theirs, yeah? I get paid to be their mechanic, and I charge them rent for storing their stuff here, *and* I charge them a shipping fee for moving their sorry-ass EMUs back and forth from the airlocks. It's a sweet deal. The only downside is I have to spend time with officers."

"And how are you going to manage when you're an actual officer and you have to spend every waking moment with them?"

"Only till we get to Destination World, amiko. After that, all bets are off."

— — —

Working a whole shift in a spacesuit, and an additional couple of hours inside the guts of an EMU, had made Ravi tired and sweaty. But even with Ansimov's fifteen liters in the bottom of his tank, he still didn't have enough to get properly clean. He made the best of it with an old pack of wipes and headed out to meet Boz.

She was waiting for him at one of the Ecuador-9 paternosters, bouncing from one foot to the other in nervous anticipation. The lights were dimming with the start of the night-cycle. The paternoster lobby was deserted.

"What kept you?" she asked. "It's not that long till curfew."

Ravi blessed her with a soft smile.

"You know I'm on time, right?"

Boz just scowled.

"Fine. Let's go." She made to grab a rung.

Suddenly anxious, Ravi held her back.

"Are you a hundred percent sure we have to go to Australia? Is there no way to, you know, do your thing from down here?"

Boz sighed.

"For the last time, Ravi: no, there isn't. Privacy laws, remember? Personnel records are stored on a physically separate system. In Australia. We've been over this, like, a dozen times. The systems I need aren't just in Australia; they're on hardwired consoles in Officer Country in Australia. And the only bit of Officer Country we have access to is the Tank because it's technically an Officers' Mess and you, Archie save us all, are an officer in training."

She gave him a long, searching look.

"We don't have to do this, cuz. Totally up to you."

Ravi placed both hands on Boz's shoulders.

"It's not totally up to me. If this goes wrong, they'll throw me off the program. *You*, they might recycle."

Boz's laugh had that reckless edge to it.

"They have to catch us first. Which is *not* going to happen." Her eyes glinted with mischief. "We doing this or not?"

By way of answer, Ravi stepped past her and onto the paternoster's fast-moving rungs. The two of them rode up in silence, feeling the weight drop away with every deck. Ravi patted his pocket to feel the reassuring bulge of his sick bags.

Emerging into the hubs, Ravi lined up his nav screen and kicked hard for Australia. His projected path flashed a judgmental amber. Ravi swore softly but without any real anger. Hitting the forward habitat wheel all the way from Ecuador always required more luck than judgment. As he sailed past Denmark, the round, green ball of a zero tree puffed out of his way, leaving the smell of eucalyptus in its wake. Ravi looked ahead, trying to gauge where he would land, only to discover that his route was blocked by a milling crowd of people. They were milling because they were equipped with jet packs and weren't simply jumping from one part of the hubs to another. And they were milling around something he couldn't quite make out.

They were also wearing masks. Not breathing masks or air filters: *masks*. For disguise. Ravi's heart sank.

BonVoys. And he was heading right into the middle of them. He spun slowly around, searching for Boz. She was a good hundred meters off his trajectory and drifting farther away by the second. She gazed back at him with a shrug of the shoulders. He was on his own.

The faint murmur of chanting reached his ears. He knew what they were saying long before he could hear the words.

"No landing! No pollution! Save! Their! World!"

"No landing! No pollution! Save! Their! World!"

Ravi sighed. First Crew must be bubbling in the recycler. The mass of BonVoys got closer. None of them seemed to notice he was on a collision course. He reached out to the hive in a vain attempt to get their attention, but they were off the grid.

"Hey!" he called. *"Hey!"*

With a collective whoop, the BonVoys scattered in all directions. For the briefest of moments, Ravi thought they had heard him, but they were getting out of the way of something altogether different. A rapidly expanding sphere that quickly resolved itself into a holograph of a habitable planet, maybe seventy-five meters across. It started out blue-green under a swirl of clouds but rapidly degenerated into an ash-gray devastation. Then it reset to blue-green and started again.

"NO LANDING!" it boomed. "NO POLLUTION! SAVE! THEIR! WORLD!"

A shadow sped out of his blind side.

"What the . . . *Ooof!*"

The fleeing BonVoy thudded into him, spinning him end over end. Hub walls blurred across his vision in a sick-inducing spiral. His stomach lurched and knotted. Bile bubbled into the back of his throat. Panicking, and somehow forgetting he was at the weightless axis of an interstellar vehicle, Ravi scrabbled to hold on to something, anything. Clawed fingers hooked the edge of the BonVoy's mask and gripped for all they were worth. The mask gave way.

"Sarding idiot!" the BonVoy yelled. "What do you think you're doing?" He jetted away on an angry puff of gas.

Ravi didn't respond. He closed his eyes, reached into his pocket for a sick bag, and filled it to bulging. He'd been knocked so far off course, it took two more jumps to reach Boz at the Australia-12 spoke. She was loosely attached to a handhold, watching a swarm of ShipSec officers trying to disable the BonVoy hologram. Her face radiated disapproval.

"What a bunch of clowns," she muttered. Ravi wasn't sure if she was talking about ShipSec or the BonVoys.

Boz's gaze dropped to the sick bag in Ravi's hand.

"You still up for this?"

"Totally." He tossed the bag into the mouth of the nearest recycler. "Let's get going."

They headed into Australia on an immaculately maintained paternoster. Ravi's stomach settled down with the returning weight, but he barely noticed. He was too busy thinking about the snarling face of the BonVoy who'd hit him.

He didn't know his name, but he knew who he was.

Sofia Ibori's boyfriend. The one she'd hugged at the intersection.

I should have waited till payday, Ravi thought miserably. *And bought myself a sarding shower.*

Australia reeked of water. And all the things that water could buy. Like soap. And perfume. And clean clothes. They had hopped off the paternoster at Haiphong Circular, one of the wheel's big ones, lined with boutiques, and nightclubs, and the Roxy, an honest-to-Archie replica of a Homeworld movie theater. Unlike most of the ship, which was preparing to go to sleep, this place was just waking up. It was full of people. And every one of them was staring at him like he'd leaked out of a sewer line.

It wasn't just that he was unkempt and malodorous. He was wearing plain, standard-issue fatigues. Everyone else was dressed in something . . . not. Suits copied from twentieth-century archives, body-hugging ensembles from the twenty-first. Even Boz, with her so-called leather jacket and nonregulation boots, stuck out far less than he did.

Boz walked down the circular like she owned the place, smiling and nodding at everyone she met. Ravi, for his part, stuck his hands in his pockets, kept his eyes down, and lumbered after her like some reeking servant. He kept a wary implant on the hive, looking for any sign of a ShipSec scan or a surreptitious probe from a passerby. Nothing came up.

The walls and windows on one side of the circular suddenly disappeared, revealing a delicate skeleton of struts and piping. Not half-finished construction work, this, but infrastructure as art. A spidery catwalk, modeled after a Homeworld footbridge, arced gracefully through the ship's innards toward a large, cylindrical structure at least three decks deep. Pipes erupted out of it like the legs of a crudely designed spider. Once used for water storage, it was now a decidedly upscale officers' club called, appropriately enough, "The Tank." An illuminated doorway punctured its curved wall.

Boz turned briskly onto the catwalk. Ravi followed, his steps slowing to a crawl.

"You really think they'll let us in?" he asked, more conscious than ever of how bad he looked.

"They'll let *you* in because you're an officer in training. I get to tag along

as your guest." She looped her arm through his and dragged him toward the
door.

The hive rippled to life as the portal scanned them, informed them they
were attempting to enter an Officers' Mess as defined by Ship's Regulation
261-3d, and required proof of authorization. Ravi transmitted his ID and
referenced Boz as his plus-one. A green light flashed inside his head, and
they stepped inside.

The interior was a bewildering mix of levels and sublevels sweeping
round a hollow core. There were multiple bars, a couple of dance floors, and
plenty of dark booths. Pounding music blared from hidden speakers.

"Cool!" Boz yelled above the din.

Ravi imagined blood running from his ears. He picked a booth that
might be marginally quieter than the others and led them toward it. Boz sat
across from him, her face alive with excitement. Ravi could feel her probing
the hive. But barely. And only because he was looking for it.

Boz glanced around, consuming everything there was to see with hun-
gry eyes.

"This place is something else!" she coded. It was easier than shouting over
the pounding bass. *"Order something."*

Ravi's stomach knotted in dismay.

"I'm out of water," he confessed, miserably. Having to say it only made it
worse.

Boz spared him a sympathetic smile.

*"I thought you smelled a bit ripe! Don't worry, cuz; I can afford one round. And if we
don't order, this whole plan's out the airlock."* She dropped an order into the hive.

A wait-drone flew across to them on whooshing fans.

"Drink?" it asked. The pitch of its not-quite-human voice cut effortlessly
through the noise. "Perhaps something to eat?"

"No food!" Boz yelled. "Two Pittsburgh lites!" She was leaning in to the
drone, as if to make herself heard above the music. But a shrewder observer
might have noticed she was only centimeters from the machine's serial number. A *really* shrewd observer (or Ravi, who was looking for it) would have
seen the mechanical glittering of her right pupil.

"Two Pittsburgh lites," the drone repeated. It flitted away, deftly avoiding the flailing arms of an excited patron, and jetted toward the nearest bar.

"Did you get it?!" Ravi asked.

Boz's pitying look was all the answer he needed. Her fingers rippled across the tabletop in time to the music. Her eyes wandered from one part of the bar to another, never lingering and mildly curious. She looked for all the world like a woman waiting for a drink. She did not look like someone committing a crime.

The wait-drone returned on a soft sigh of rotors. Boz reached out to grab the bottles, but the machine held on tight.

"Eight point two-five liters," it insisted. "Please."

"*How much?*" Boz seemed genuinely taken aback.

"Eight point two-five liters. Please."

"Day-cycle robbery. Shoot me a key."

With eyes closed, Ravi watched the drone transmit his cousin a line of code. Which his cousin promptly used to deposit 8.25 liters into the Tank's account.

Unfortunately for the drone, the 8.25 liters was accompanied by several lines of programming that shouldn't have been there. Having entered the bar's systems, they rapidly metastasized, breaking out of bookkeeping and forcing their way into drone management. An indicator light on the wait-drone's scuffed exterior cycled from green to red. Boz barely had time to snatch the beers before the machine headed off to a docking station for diagnosis. The moment it docked, the diagnostics kicked in and were immediately hijacked by ones and zeroes of rogue code. The rogue code rampaged through the entire docking station, and then through the hardwire network to which the docking station was connected. The Officer Country network.

The Tank, however informally, was an Officers' Mess. Technically, however informally, it was Officer Country. And it was connected to the rest of Officer Country—barely—by a handful of unimportant systems. For Boz, though, it was enough.

The hijacked drone, its indicator light still shining a lurid red, reached out to Boz across the general network, loaded with information . . .

"I want to do it," Ravi was insisting.

"I absolutely forbid it," Mother said, powerful arms folded across his chest. "They'll turn you into a monster."

Ravi's chin jutted forward in defiance.

"It's too late. I already signed the release . . ."

Boz thumped the table with excitement.

"We're in!" She dropped a key—a long, complicated one—into Ravi's head. "Come on over. Door's open."

What the sard? Ravi came to with a jerk. Still trying to recover from . . . whatever *that* was, he took the key Boz had given him, turned it in the lock, and linked implants with his cousin.

The bar faded away to dull background. In front of him was a large, virtual oak table piled high with equally virtual paper files that Boz must have copied from a nineteenth- or twentieth-century movie. Dreamlike, he could feel Boz at his shoulder, but he couldn't see her.

"This is every file of every person on the ship," Boz said. *"All eight thousand nine hundred and fifty-two."* She wasn't really speaking, of course; it was just a chipset simulation, deeper and huskier than the voice Ravi was used to hearing. This was Boz's voice as *she* heard it. *"We're looking for a woman, so we can ignore anyone who identifies with your lot,"* she continued. The mountain of files almost halved. *"And we're looking for a young woman, so let's toss everyone younger than fifteen and older than thirty."*

"Thirty-five. Just to be safe."

"Thirty-five, then. That leaves us with . . . nine hundred and twelve candidates." Still a lot, but just about manageable. Boz heaved a sigh of satisfaction. *"Over to you, cuz."*

Ravi took a deep breath—real, not virtual—and went to work. Linking the pattern-recognition software built into his implants with purely biological memory was never easy. This time, it was even more difficult than usual. It was as if his memory of the girl was stored in the wrong part of his brain. His head throbbed with the effort.

Slowly at first, but more and more quickly, he cycled through the files, looking for someone, *anyone*, who bore the slightest resemblance to the girl on the wrong side of the airlock. Nine hundred and twelve times.

Zip. Nothing. Nada.

"No dice," he began. It was as far as he got.

"Get out!" Boz hissed. She cut the link. Ravi was back in his own head. Dance music pounded in his ears.

"Move!" Boz said, aloud this time. She was shoving him out of the booth.

Ravi stumbled to his feet.

"What's going on?"

"Trouble." His cousin's eyes were fixed over his shoulder. Ravi looked behind him.

ShipSec. Two officers were at the entrance, dropping scans into the hive just as fast as they could generate them. The bits and bytes of Boz's hack had scattered to stardust, but the scans were hunting them down, trying to reassemble them, to trace them back to their creator.

"Nice and easy," Boz instructed, one hand on his elbow. "Let's lift from the sarding launch pad."

She led the way toward a back exit.

And a third ShipSec officer, one with a considerable amount of silver on his collar. He was leaning against the curve of the Tank's outer wall, beside the patched-over remains of an old pipe. Commander-Inspector Vasconcelos. Ravi's heart beat a drumroll on his chest.

"Good evening, Crewman MacLeod," Vasconcelos said amiably, looking at Boz. "What a pleasant surprise." His gaze traveled to Ravi.

"Who's the accomplice?"

Ravi jumped as a hand landed on his shoulder.

T here you are!" Sofia Ibori said. And then, to Vasconcelos: "Hello, Uncle. Fancy meeting you here!" She made an exaggerated show of looking around. "Crowd's a little young for you, don't you think?"

The inspector frowned, puzzled.

"He's with you?" There was no mistaking the skepticism in his voice.

"Oh, yes," Sofia assured him. "Been with us all evening, haven't you, Ravi?" The hand she had on his shoulder tightened its grip. As his dad might have said, *If someone offers you a way out, take it.* Ravi nodded, hoping he didn't look half as guilty as he felt.

"And this one?" Vasconcelos asked, pointing at Boz. Every fiber of his being radiated disbelief.

The flicker of calculation on Sofia's face was so brief, Ravi almost missed it.

"No, I'm afraid not. Ravi spotted her heading out and was going to introduce us." She looked quizzically at Boz, her head tilted to one side. "Roberta, isn't it? Ravi's cousin?"

"Most people call me Boz. Pleased to meet you." And then, with a glance at Vasconcelos: "Another time, maybe." She flashed the inspector a brittle smile. "Shall we go?"

"Yes," Vasconcelos agreed, but not before giving Ravi a long, troubled stare. Accompanied by his officers, he escorted Boz off the premises, dropping a message as he did so. It flared on the inside of Ravi's head, unnecessarily bright.

I am watching you.

Ravi tried not to shudder. He turned to face Sofia.

"Thanks," he said. "I . . ." The words dried up. He felt the blood drain from his face.

Sofia's expression changed to one of concern.

"What's the matter?"

"The portal!" Ravi gasped. "Boz isn't an officer. I had to book her in! The moment Vasconcelos checks the records, we're screwed. *You're* screwed." He grabbed Sofia's hands without thinking. They were slim, and soft, and burned at his skin. "I'll go to Vasconcelos right now. Say I forced you into helping me." The words were coming out in torrents. "If we're quick, it'll be okay. It's not like you've done anything wrong, really, and he *is* your uncle, which has got to count for something, hasn't it? I'll just tell him . . ."

A man's derisive laughter brought him up short. With a start, he let Sofia go. His hands dived for the safety of his pockets.

Sofia's boyfriend. He was looking at him with something approaching pity. If he recognized Ravi from their collision in the hubs, he gave no sign.

"Ship's Regs five dash zero one-A," the man said lightly. And when Ravi continued to stare blankly, added: "The privacy laws. The record was wiped as soon you stepped in here. Can't have the authorities prying into our every move like a bunch of LOKIs, can we?"

Ravi must have looked skeptical, because Sofia jumped in.

"Jaden's right," she assured him. "He's a ship's barrister."

"When I'm needed," Jaden demurred. "It's not like it's a full-time job." Even on Homeworld, Jaden would have been tall. Here, with his height, and his good looks, and his waves of dark hair, he gave off an air of effortless superiority. Ravi, for his part, was painfully aware he needed a good wash. He tried to keep his distance, but without success. Jaden was sticking out his hand, clearly expecting Ravi to take it. "Jaden Strauss-Cohen," he said, introducing himself. The handshake was firm and confident, like the man behind it. Not a surprise, perhaps, given he was related to the Captain.

Did the Captain have any idea he was a BonVoy?

Did Sofia? Probably. She had to have gotten that "save their world" stuff she'd thrown at Warren from *somewhere.*

"Ravi MacLeod," he mumbled. Compared with *Strauss-Cohen* or *Ibori,* his name didn't amount to much. "Thanks for helping me out."

"Thank Sofia. She couldn't stand to see you go down like that." The younger Strauss-Cohen gave him a look of frank curiosity. "What were you up to, anyway?"

Looking for a nonexistent, vacuum-breathing girl with blond hair and a really nice smile.

"Stupid stuff. Just poking around in some files."

"Typical Roberta." Jaden smiled indulgently.

Ravi tried not to bristle. Jaden had no right talking about Boz as if he knew her. But then it occurred to him that Jaden probably did. He was a ship's barrister, after all, and Boz had had more than her fair share of *them*. His cousin was nothing if not a sophisticated consumer of legal services.

"Will Boz be all right?" he asked, suddenly anxious. "She's only one notch above Dead Weight."

Jaden shrugged his shoulders.

"It depends. What did she do?"

Jaden lost interest before Ravi could answer. He reached out and grabbed Sofia by the wrist, slid an arm around her waist. Ravi's stomach churned as Sofia nestled into him.

"Forget about your cousin. She's a loose thruster. Always was, always will be." He put a hand on Ravi's arm, as if to emphasize the point. "Join us for a drink?"

"Of course he will," Sofia said before Ravi could refuse. "You may have to order them the old-fashioned way, though." She flashed a knowing glance in Ravi's direction. "The drones don't seem to be working too well."

Jaden unhitched himself from Sofia and sauntered toward the nearest bar. As he did so, he was intercepted by a woman heading in the opposite direction. The two leaned their heads together, sharing some small joke before the woman moved away, her hand lingering on Jaden's shoulder. She looked vaguely familiar, Ravi decided. The name came to him after a moment or two: Ksenia Graham. A couple of years his senior, and a junior botanist. She was a looker, he admitted to himself, albeit in a curvy, obvious way. She lacked Sofia's slim elegance.

Sofia, he noticed, was eyeing Ksenia suspiciously. Aware of Ravi's gaze, she smoothed her features into something approaching playful.

"You're lucky you're not in the brig."

"I know." Ravi suddenly remembered how dirty he was. He took a step back, trying to keep his distance. "And I'm really grateful. Really. I am. I totally owe you one."

Sofia's smile was laser-bright.

"That's great, because I totally need a favor." Her hips were swaying in time to the music, stretching the fabric of her clothing, emphasizing the shape of her.

Ravi's heart fluttered in his chest.

"Sure. Name it."

"Prof Warren's chemistry class is killing me." Sofia's eyes were round and wide and luminous, teasing and pleading in equal proportion. "Can you help me study?"

For a giddy moment, Ravi thought she was asking him out, albeit in a twisted, ass-backward kind of way. At the end of the sol, when it came to school, Sofia sailed along effortlessly. What possible need could she have of Ravinder MacLeod, the guy who came from a "non-academic" family?

But then he remembered the crappy piece of code she'd dropped, trying to cheat her way to an answer. The way she'd distracted the professor with little more than an entitled name and a smile.

The same smile she was sending him right now.

It didn't matter. The fact she was smiling at all was enough.

"I'd love to. Just name the place."

"Awesome! How about the Canada arboretum? Sol after tomorrow? About eighteen hundred?"

"Deal." Ravi's eyes crinkled with anticipation. The return of Jaden, drinks clutched in both hands, barely dented his mood.

▬ ▬ ▬

He was staring at a plate. The old-fashioned kind: round, and without dividers, and made of baked soil. It was ornate, and beautiful, and full of color. Blue, and yellow, and cursive black in an interlocking pattern of organic molecules. Oxygen, and nitrogen, and lonely sulfur, wrapped in clanking chains of hydrocarbon.

The molecules began to disappear. Slowly at first, then ever faster under tendrils of green mold that grew thicker and higher, and thicker and higher, until it was reaching for his face and forcing his mouth apart and putting roots through his tongue.

He was choking. But not from the mold. From something in his throat. Something hard. And round.

He coughed it up.

BozBall. Black now, and white, with flecks of gray. It arced through the air and landed in a veined sea of green. And somehow, the green had become a Homeworld lawn and BozBall was a Homeworld sprinkler, and wherever the sprinkles landed, the lawn turned to brown and died, and the brown of the lawn turned into the brown of a tree trunk, growing apples that dropped onto the grass. But that couldn't be right. If there was no lawn, how could there be grass?

"Lights," Ravi mumbled.

There was pressure against the back of his eyeballs but not much pain. Ravi lay back in his bunk and offered up a silent prayer of thanks. The prescription, at least, seemed to be working.

And that wasn't the only good news. Payday had arrived. His tank was bulging with water. He rolled out of bed and skipped the two steps over to the shower, drowning himself in warm steam and soap. He overdid the steam thing. The mirror above his basin was clouded over. He wiped it clear with his hand.

And saw the girl standing behind him. He'd have jumped out of his clothes if he'd been wearing any. A panicked hand stretched for a bedsheet.

The girl didn't move. She simply stared at him.

Ravi stared back, his mouth dry.

"Wh . . . who are you?" he stammered at last. "How'd you get in here?"

The girl didn't reply. Her stare was direct but not threatening, her lips curved in something close to a smile. She was petite, he realized, with a boyish figure, and clad in fatigues that seemed a darker blue than normal. With a small shock, he realized her hair wasn't blond at all. Not really. It was . . . *dyed*. Artfully highlighted as if she'd just stepped out of a Homeworld salon. Ravi stared at it, transfixed. Hair dye, like chocolate, had run out long ago. But unlike chocolate, no one had attempted to replicate it. It messed up the recyclers.

Fascinated as he was, it took him a moment to realize she was speaking. At least, he thought she was. Her lips were moving, but Ravi couldn't seem to hear what she was saying.

"I'm sorry. I can't . . ."

His head exploded. Jagged white stars flashed across his vision. He collapsed to his knees, hands pressed against the agony in his temples. Then, all of a sudden, the deck rushed up to meet him and the world went black.

He came to stretched out on the floor, the worn carpet of his quarters rasping against his cheek. His head felt like someone had scraped the inside of his skull with a teaspoon, but it was an okay sort of agony, the kind of pain a person feels after the really bad stuff has stopped.

The girl was gone. He stumbled groggily to his feet; reached out to his bunk for support.

He'd heard her voice, he remembered. Through the pain, and the dazzling shards of light, and the falling to the ground, he'd finally heard it. Sweet, and pleading, and strangely accented.

"Ravi," she'd whispered. "We need your help."

Distracted as he was, it took Ravi several moments to get a handle on what Ansimov was trying to tell him.

"Say that again?"

"Amiko, what is up with you? It's like you're in another wheel." Ansimov peered into Ravi's eyes, as if to assure himself there was someone in there. "I *said:* some idiot has blocked off Manchester Passage. I was almost late today. Chen Lai would have had my *ass.*"

"Uh-huh." It was as much interest as Ravi could muster. He had bigger things to worry about.

"You'd have thought someone would have thought to post the work permit, but *nooooo.* Just block off a cross corridor without warning and force people to climb two decks just to get around."

"Bummer," Ravi said, still not listening.

"You're a gravity well of compassion; you know that?" Ansimov slumped back in his seat as Chen Lai walked in. Ravi's eyes twitched under the weight of data hitting his implants. Ansimov swore. He wasn't the only one, either.

"Today's assignments," Chen Lai announced. "We're falling behind on our survey of the habitat wheels. The navigators are close to signing off on a final approach, which means Braking Day can't be far behind. We *will* be ready to flip every chamber through ninety degrees come the sol, even if I have to kill every last one of you to do it. Understood?"

The room responded with varied flavors of enthusiasm. Chen Lai's focus on Braking Day made perfect sense, but getting there was going to be brutal.

"One more thing," Chen Lai said. He dropped a grainy video into their skulls. Ravi tried very hard not to gasp.

BozBall. As an engineer, Chen Lai had a recording function. He must have had the presence of mind to record it as he gave chase. The video was poor quality, to be sure, but there was no mistaking what it was.

"If anyone sees this device, or anything like it, report it to me. Do not approach it. Just log its location and wait for assistance."

"What is it?" Ansimov asked.

"We think it's a Third Gen maintenance drone," Chen Lai lied. "It must have been dormant in a crawl space somewhere until something woke it up." His face cracked into the faintest imitation of a smile. "It's wandering about the ship, trying to follow a fifty-year-old repair plan. Let's haul it in before it fixes something that ain't broke. Questions?"

The silence was deafening.

"Then you're dismissed. Try not to break stuff."

— — —

If trainees got overtime, Ravi thought, he'd be swimming in water. As it was, he was standing under the shower, trying to use no more than absolutely necessary. It was still more liters than he'd have liked, though. It had been a dirty day. His survey of living quarters in Denmark-7 turned up a bunch of compartments that had come off their runners. He'd logged it and tried to move on, but Chen Lai had insisted he fix them. All of them. Even with half a dozen drones to help out, he'd had to get between the compartment walls to figure out what was going on. He'd emerged hours later and covered from head to foot in 132 years of grease and grime. And *then* he'd had to finish the rest of his assigned tasks before the bastard would let him go. By the time he washed the last of the filth off his skin, night-cycle had begun in earnest.

Emerging from the warm embrace of the shower, he glanced longingly at where his bunk was folded up against the wall. After a moment of hesitation, though, he pulled on a clean set of fatigues instead. No rest for the wicked. Or, more accurately, no rest *because* of the wicked. He headed out the door.

The brig was the only part of Australia that reeked of neither water nor privilege. There was, however, a faint smell of disinfectant. Ravi knew, because Boz had once told him, that back in the sol there'd been no such thing as a brig. First Crew had been outbound less than a year when the need for one became apparent. The first brig had been in Hungary and had been lost in the disaster. As Boz told it, the replacement had been put in Australia so the senior officers could keep an eye on the rabble without having to leave home.

Of course, there were worse things than the brig. No one wanted convicted criminals sitting idly in cells, consuming precious resources. If an infraction couldn't be dealt with by fines or community service, the convicted

crewman would be dragged down to the medical facilities and put into torpor, a waking nightmare of suspended animation. Boz, who'd had a dose or
two, described it as being locked inside her body, conscious of everything
that was happening to her but unable to do an Archie-damned thing about it.
And if torpor wasn't enough, there was always the option of last resort: the
recycler. For Dead Weights. Ravi wiped suddenly sweaty palms on the front
of his fatigues.

"Thanks for coming," Boz said as she stepped into the visiting room. She
was escorted by a security drone, the stubby barrel of its dart gun sweeping
the chamber as it entered. The drone made no attempt to leave, positioning
itself stiffly by the doorway. There would be no privacy for MacLeods visiting MacLeods. It was a rule almost as old as the brig—and completely illegal.

Not that anyone cared.

Boz sat down at the compartment's single, bare table. She seemed to not
know what to do with her hands. They twisted around and around like dis-
engaged gears. It took a second or two for Ravi's understanding to catch up
with all the spinning. They'd taken away her cigarettes—and most likely
added a possession charge to her rap sheet. She must feel naked without
them.

Ravi's gaze went from Boz's hands to her face. Her expression shocked
him. His cousin was *scared*. The woman he knew was reckless and cynical
and joyful—often all at once. Sometimes, on very rare occasions, she was
rageful.

Scared? Never.

"How much trouble are you in?" he whispered.

"A lot, cuz. A *lot*." Her hands stopped spinning for a moment. "They're
talking about the recycler. For real."

She leaned across the table, her dark eyes boring into Ravi's.

"I had a visitor today. Strauss-Cohen."

"The barrister?" Ravi tried to keep the jealousy out of his voice.

"No. The *other* Strauss-Cohen. The *Captain*."

"The *Captain*?" Ravi was dumbstruck. "Why?"

"She wanted to know who I was working for."

The spit fled from Ravi's mouth. Conscious of the drone's looming presence, he chose the few words he could get out with care.

"And what did you tell her?"

A knowing smile flitted across Boz's face.

"The truth, of course. That I was nosing around for the hell of it. Not that it helped, though. She still didn't believe me." The smile evaporated. "But here's the thing. She wasn't that interested in the files. What she *really* wanted to do was talk about a, *ahem*, new kind of *drone*. From somewhere in Denmark. At Phoenix and Manchester, I think she said." Boz had been every bit as careful as Ravi in choosing her words, but Ravi totally understood what she was telling him. Strauss-Cohen was interested in BozBall because Chen Lai, having seen it, had pegged it for what it was: a LOKI in all but name. And the number of crewmen with both the ability and the thrusters to build one could be counted on one finger. He hoped to Archie his eyes were not as saucer-sized as they felt. "She's convinced someone asked me to build it," Boz added. "Demanded to know what it was for and why I'd be helping our enemies to take down the ship." Boz's expression was bleak. "That's when she mentioned the recycler. I don't think she was kidding." The hands started spinning again. "I'm Dead Weight now. For sure."

Ravi was scrambling to keep up.

"Enemies? What enemies?"

Boz shrugged.

"She didn't say. BonVoys, I guess?"

A snarling Jaden Strauss-Cohen floated across Ravi's memory.

"Bon Voyagers are idiots," he snapped, using the derogatory label in full. "Pie-in-the-sky ideas about 'saving their world.' As if we could just wander through deep space forever." He allowed his irritation to subside a little. "But that's all they are. Idiots. Apart from a bunch of stupid demos and a whole bunch of graffiti, it's not like they're a threat to the ship, is it?"

Boz, he realized suddenly, wasn't listening. Which was hardly surprising. BonVoys were the least of her worries. He reached over and touched her on the wrist.

"Look," he said quietly. "If there's anything you want to tell them that'll help you, like the names of any, er, *accomplices*, I think you should do it. No one wants you to go to the recycler."

Boz's face took on an expression he'd never seen before. Tenderness, maybe? He was strangely touched.

"There's nothing to tell," she lied with a wan smile. "You know me. I don't have any accomplices, and I didn't build any fancy new drone. As for the rest of it, my troubles are all my own." Her face took on a hint of frustration. "Besides, I can't give the Captain what she wants. I don't know anybody who's planning to take down the ship. That would be, like, totally insane."

There was a small, uncomfortable silence.

"Is there anything I can get you?" Ravi asked, trying to fill the hole. "Anything they'll *let* me get you?" He hadn't the slightest idea where Boz got her cigarettes from—not that they were allowed in here, anyway.

"Nope. If this thing goes the way I think it will, they'll bail me out tomorrow." The wan smile again. "It's not like I'm going to run anywhere, is it?"

"Maybe you could hijack a lifeboat and make a break for the *Bohr*."

He was rewarded with a small chuckle.

"Nah. *Chandrasekhar*'s more my speed. I hear those guys will take *anybody*." It was Ravi's turn to smile.

"Tomorrow, then," he said, rising to his feet. "If you're not out by the end of my shift, I'll go see the Captain myself."

He kept smiling until he was safely out of the brig. But all he could think about was Boz, and the recycler, and how his stupidity was forcing her down the same corridor as his dad.

12.0

The next sol, as Ravi headed out of class, Ansimov's complaint about his commute finally hit home. Phoenix Circular and Manchester Passage were completely blocked off. A giant plate had been welded across the circular from deck to ceiling, its bland gray face livened up by splashes of stenciled lettering. TEMPORARY CONSTRUCTION, they announced. NO THROUGH ROUTE.

This latter pronouncement was not quite true. The plate had a large hatch built into it. To get to the hatch, though, he had to get past a bored-looking ShipSec officer. A hulking security drone stood solidly at her side. Ravi cast a wary eye at the robot's dart gun. It didn't seem to be active, but a person could never be too careful with dart guns. The last thing he needed right now was a long, involuntary nap.

"I'm an engineer," he said, as pleasantly as he could; another pronouncement that wasn't quite true. "Can I get through, please?"

"Nope. Go around like everybody else." The officer pointed back the way he had come. "Nearest circular's on twenty-six."

Like he didn't know. Ravi swallowed his irritation and turned around. As he headed away, though, he dipped into the hive. Ansimov was right about that, too. There was nothing there about construction. Not a word. The schematics showed the intersection as clear.

He turned into the next passageway and found a set of steps that climbed up to the next few decks. The wheel was making turns for a full *g*, so by the time he'd hauled himself all the way up to twenty-six, his heart was pounding. His head was pounding too. But not with effort. With anxiety.

They'd clearly been working on the intersection for a couple of sols: more than enough time to post an announcement. And more than enough time to complete all but the most complicated of jobs. If the job was complicated, then Chen Lai would know all about it. Which also meant he knew the work wasn't posted. Which must also mean he didn't *want* it posted.

Chen Lai was hiding something. He'd bet water to widgets it was something to do with the cross corridor and the compartments under the deck. The ones that shouldn't be there. The ones that Chen Lai, and Vasconcelos, and the Captain had been so interested in—and unhappy about. Ravi worried about what Chen Lai was hiding all the way to Canada. After that, though, he pretty much stopped. Except for the sky, it was hard to worry about anything in Canada. Mainly because of the arboretum.

The arboretum took up fully one-third of the wheel on the lower decks, a shocking expanse of verdant green dotted with flowers and blossoms and the occasional bird. Back in the sol, there had even been streams running through it and a small lake. Those sols were long gone, of course, but there were still some reeded strips of wetland around the edges.

Ravi stepped onto the arboretum's thick grass with a certain amount of hesitation. It was still day-cycle, if only just. A blazing facsimile of the Home Star had not yet vanished from the artificial sky. The sky had been there since before Launch, an identical copy of the one above Homeworld. He could never look at it for more than a second or two, though. At least, not now, not during the day-cycle. The flaring starlight made him uneasy. For Ravi, born five generations into space, the star in First Crew's sky was too close. Too dangerous. He could almost *feel* the radiation coming off it, and it was a constant surprise that the arboretum had not been bleached to a brittle, lifeless white, himself along with it. Far better to venture out after dark.

Once the Home Star was safely below the horizon, Luna, the Homeworld moon, would come up and the arboretum would be alive with people taking in the sights. For now, however, it was almost deserted. A few intrepid toddlers weaved crazily between the trees in a madcap game of chase. Seventh Gen, Ravi thought suddenly. If all went according to plan, they would be the last cohort to walk the decks of *Archimedes*.

Sofia was sitting on a park bench, slim legs crossed in the shade of a tree. Ravi sat down beside her, happy she'd chosen a spot out of the starlight. By complete coincidence, the time display in his head flipped to 1800.

"You couldn't have been more punctual if you'd tried!" Sofia said, grinning. "How was your sol?"

"Brutal," Ravi said, thrilled simply to be talking to her one-on-one. "Chen Lai is really wielding the laser. We're still behind schedule and he's driving like crazy to catch up."

"Well, he's running out of time. We got near-final calcs of Destination World's orbit today. To be honest, we could plug in a final approach right now. We have more than enough fuel for the margin of error."

"So, what's stopping you?"

"The fact that my great-uncle's a perfectionist." Sofia's tone made it very clear she was not paying him a compliment. "He wants to get it right on the money—and he's still not convinced we won't smash into something fatal on the way in. Compared with Sol, Tau Ceti is a real dirty system."

"It would be a shame to come all this way just to crash."

"That would be bad," Sofia agreed, smiling. "We also got more information at the nav briefing this morning. About the planet." She stared out into the arboretum, her eyes focused on the toddlers.

"And?" Ravi prompted.

"When we get there, we'll definitely be able to stand."

Ravi just stared at her. Sofia burst out laughing.

"Do you know *any* history?" she asked.

"I passed the exam." History was not his strong suit.

"Then you have no excuse." Sofia's smile pulled some of the sting. "The fleet started out as an international government project, remember? But the LOKIs pulled the plug at the last minute. First Crew were able to acquire the whole enterprise on the cheap."

"Right," Ravi said, determined to redeem himself. "But they weren't called First Crew then, were they? They were the Liberty Foundation. One of a bunch of organizations fed up with Homeworld and determined to head for the stars." He raised an ironic fist above his head. "'People before LOKIs.' 'Freedom from bondage.' That sort of thing. We must have been a right royal pain in the ass. I bet they were delighted to see the back of us. Plus, we offered the most water for the ships."

Sofia nodded.

"And do you remember *why* the LOKIs pulled the plug?"

"Sure. The same reason LOKIs stop everything: they thought it was too dangerous. Too many variables they didn't like. No way to calculate the odds of success."

"Right. And one of the variables was?"

"Scalene plague," Ravi answered, parroting one of his old exam answers. "There was an outbreak at the time and no good way to screen the crew. The LOKIs didn't much like the idea of an incurable disease in a confined space, so they scrubbed the mission."

Sofia's eyes didn't roll, exactly. But Ravi got the distinct impression that if *she'd* been marking his history exam, he'd have gotten an F.

"Let's put out-of-control LOKI bioweapons to one side. Think about variables affecting the Destination World itself. About whether we could actually live there."

She was staring hard at him now, as if willing him to find the right answer. After far too long an interval, the water finally dropped from the faucet.

"Mass," he breathed. "Even if we got here plague-free, the LOKIs worried Destination World might be too heavy. We couldn't land without getting crushed to death."

"Exactly. They had an upper estimate of two point eight Earth masses. Way too much for people to live on—unless you want to have shattered knees and a heart attack at forty. But First Crew was dead set on leaving. They were willing to roll the dice." She shrugged her shoulders. "Anyway, it looks like they won. The system mass is barely one point five."

"Still sounds pretty heavy." Ravi didn't much like the idea of being fifty percent heftier than he already was.

"That's the *system* mass. The planet itself weighs in at about one point two and it's bigger than Homeworld, so gravity at the surface is about one point one *g*. We can live with that, apparently. The rest of it is moons. One huge one and maybe three or four others." She was staring out at the Seventh Gen toddlers, her face expressionless. "We'll weigh a little more, and the tides might be stronger than Homeworld, but nothing to stop us going down."

Ravi was looking at her curiously.

"For someone carrying incredibly awesome news, you don't look very excited."

"Don't I? I guess I'm still processing." Her gaze never wavered from the children. A couple of chaperones, both of them wearing broad-brimmed hats, were venturing out of the shade to round them up. A soft sigh escaped her lips.

"Do you really want to go down there?"

The question caught him off guard.

"I don't know," he confessed, after a moment's thought. He stole a wary glance at the setting red of the Home Star. "It's not like we have a choice, is it? Braking Day's an actual, like, *thing,* you know? And it's a one-way trip. Once we brake, we're done. By the time we enter orbit, we'll be running on fumes."

Sofia looked across at him, her expression unreadable.

"But if there was a choice: would you go?"

"Would you?" It seemed easier than answering.

"No." Sofia was staring intently into his eyes. "If it were up to me, I'd keep on going." She looked away. "I'd push on into the dark. Just to see what's out there."

"You sound like a BonVoy." Ravi tried to keep the tone light, but he wasn't sure he succeeded. An image of Jaden, unmasked and snarling at the BonVoy demonstration, floated across his mind.

Sofia's lips quirked in what might have been amusement.

"I know a few. And enough of the lingo to annoy the sard out of my family. But it's not really my thing. We Iboris are all about the Mission." She reached out a hand and brushed his cheek. The contact burned like fire. "You're lucky, you know that? Being a MacLeod.

"I'm serious," she added, seeing the expression on his face. "Your family's past is, as my uncle would say, 'entirely lacking in achievement.'" Ravi stiffened in sudden anger, his face burning. "So, there's nothing to shape your future. You can be whatever you want." A calming hand rested lightly on his wrist. "Being an Ibori carries . . . expectations. There have been three Chief Navigators who were Iboris, you know, and one Chief Navigator *and* Captain. Plus a Deputy Chief of Astronomy." She allowed herself an ironic smile. "The black sheep of the family." The smile drifted away, light and ephemeral. "So, here I am. Sofia Ibori, trainee Chief Navigator and maybe Captain."

There was no hint of irony in her voice, Ravi noticed. Just the settled recognition of a predetermined future.

"Doesn't sound so bad to me."

An image of his father popped into his head. *Sarding officers,* he'd snarled, spitting on the deck. *Think the ship owes them a living.*

"Doesn't it?" Sofia sounded like she was far away, perhaps trying her future on for size. "Navigating a ship that's going around in circles? Captain of a vessel that's being broken down for landing equipment?"

She reached out and gave his knee a sudden, friendly squeeze. "Forget it. We're not here to talk about Earth two point oh. We're here to talk about the chemistry of clays." She threw a pout in Ravi's direction, setting his heart to skipping. "This whole thing about cation-exchange capacity: I'm still not getting it." She tossed a key into his head. "Come over and show me."

Ravi was so excited, he almost fumbled the lock.

13.0

When Ravi awoke the next morning, news about Destination World's mass was all over the ship. Even though little was truly known about the planet beyond its chemical composition, its apparent surface temperature, and now the strength of its gravity, excited speculation filled the corridors about what it would be like to live "down there." When someone at the engineering briefing eagerly asked if the habitat wheels would be spun up to 1.1 g, just so the crew could get a taste of what was coming, Chen Lai's response was tart.

"Great idea. Let's take a super-huge, one-hundred-and-thirty-two-year-old mechanism that's grinding through its last bearings and *increase the loadings*! What could possibly go wrong?" He glared around the room, as if daring someone to answer. Nobody took up the challenge.

Chen Lai's acidity notwithstanding, the only people not thrilled by the latest discovery were the BonVoys. Hacked drones spewed smoke and slogans all over Australia—including Officer Country. Rumor had it the Captain herself had laid into one with a wrecking bar just to shut it up. In the meantime, Ansimov and Ravi were dispatched to Bermuda to clean up a sudden rash of graffiti.

"What a bunch of gullgropers," Ansimov complained. His drones were wiping down the front of an expensive-looking café. "'Save their world,' my ass." He washed away the offending words. "It's no one's planet till we get there. And then it's ours." The drones hummed and swished as they stored the recovered paint for recycling.

Ravi didn't look up from his work, but he could sense Ansimov's presence in the hive, the way his no-nonsense code flashed back and forth among his little coterie of robots. Ravi's own code was sparser, more elegant—like Boz's, really. But it lacked Ansimov's robust brutality. His partner's drones were moving through the assigned tasks significantly faster.

"Do you really want to go down there?" Ravi asked. He was thinking of Sofia and the arboretum. Fireball images of the Home Star charred the edges of his memory.

Ansimov's response was an incredulous laugh.

"Are you kidding? Of course I want to go down there! You think my great-great-grandparents boarded this tub so I could have the chance they literally died to give us and then *choke*?" He shook his head. "No way, amiko. The moment we're cleared to go down there, I'm on my way."

Ansimov's code slowed down a fraction.

"Are you thinking of *not* going down?" There was a distinct hint of disapproval in his voice.

"No. Well, not exactly. I mean, it's not like moving quarters to a new wheel, is it? We'll be clinging to the outside—the *outside*—of a giant ball of rock, tumbling through space right next to a sarding *star,* with no shielding, no bulkheads, and no life support, just a random layer of gas that could be stripped away at a moment's notice." Ravi shuddered at the thought. "Admit it, Vlad. Doesn't some part of that give you the creeps? Just a little?"

"Archie's hooks, Rav! You know the human race began on a planet, right?"

"So did malaria. Just because it happened doesn't make it a good idea." He took a deep breath. "Anyway, it's years away yet. We'll be orbiting and observing for the best part of forever, and then there'll be survey expeditions, and test camps, and quarantines. And after all *that,* the wheels will have to be broken down and turned into landing craft." He smiled mischievously. "Mark my words: Seventh Gen'll be fully grown before anyone has to live down there for real."

"They'd better not be. My family's been taking crap from bastard officers since Launch Day. I'm going down there with a bunch of drones, carving out some land as far from anybody else as is humanly possible, and never taking orders from no one ever again." Ansimov spread his arms expansively. "I'm going to have more land than I could possibly use in a lifetime," he bragged. "I'm thinking, like, fifty square meters."

Ravi gave a low whistle. When it came to personal space, no one could accuse Ansimov of dreaming small.

"Hey, amiko," Ansimov asked suddenly. "Do you think . . ."

Whatever Ansimov was going to ask was interrupted by a soft *pop*. Then a loud, liquid hiss. The blood drained from Ravi's face. Ansimov looked stricken.

Somewhere, somewhere close by, the ship was leaking water. Ravi didn't need to see it to imagine it, the precious liquid spraying into compartments and flooding them to ruin before dropping into the dark, secret places from which it could never be recovered. His mouth ran dry and thirsty at the thought. His heart thudded in near-panic.

Snap out of it!

"This way!" he yelled, heading down the corridor at a near-sprint. His flotilla of drones lurched along in his wake. The wheel here was only 0.8 *g,* so he made quick progress, reaching the nearest circular in a matter of seconds. He paused a moment at the intersection, pulling down virtual schematics and listening with real ears before scrambling off to his left. Ansimov's heavy tread thudded behind him. The back of Ravi's neck prickled with electricity. Ansimov was hurling giant chunks of code into the hive. A scream for help, stat.

A little way ahead of him a small group of people was standing at the entrance to a cross corridor. They were damp and panicky. When he arrived at the intersection, it was easy to see why. A line had burst under the corridor decking, releasing a geyser of water that had ripped up three deck plates. A foaming column of fluid lashed the ceiling, bouncing back in a cold, stinging spray that threatened to take out an eye. Water ran in uncaring torrents along either side of the corridor, pooling briefly in doorways before draining through the deck and into the bowels of the wheel.

Ravi looked on in dismay. There was too much of it for the ship's recycling system to handle. Some of it would be caught in the sumps, he knew, but the sumps would overflow and the rest of it would simply disappear. They would never get it back.

He found the line on the schematics, identified the nearest shutoff valve, and frowned. The valve was automatic. The moment the line burst, it should have slammed shut and cut off the flow. The live feed on the inside of his head was crystal clear. The valve was shut. It was working as intended.

But the geyser was blasting away undiminished. The relentless, near-freezing spray sucked the heat out of the air, turning it to chill. Ravi's skin prickled with goosebumps. Using a couple of drones to shield him from the worst of the spray, he waded down the corridor. The drones were not waterproof, apparently. They faded and died in a shower of sparks. Drenched to the skin, and cursing himself for an idiot drone-killer, Ravi plowed on. He bent over double as he squeezed past the geyser's roaring pillar. The sound of it was deafening. Behind him, Ansimov lost his footing on the slick deck plates. Ravi kept going. Ansimov scrambled clumsily to his feet.

Twenty meters past the blowout, the deck plate above the misbehaving shutoff valve was almost dry. Ravi pulled out his screwdriver and started loosening the bolts. Wordlessly, Ansimov joined him. They pulled up the plate and peered into the trench below. Then they peered at each other.

"Archie's hooks!" Ansimov muttered. "That *cannot* be right." Ravi could feel him checking and rechecking the specs. "This is sarded up, amiko. Sarded up." Both of them turned on their eye cameras, recording for future reference.

Someone had spliced in an extra line. And not well. The main water line, the one that showed on the specs, ran toward the now-closed shutoff valve, exactly as designed. But the second line looped around the valve in some kind of bypass before rejoining the pipe downstream. And the bypass itself had a couple more lines—cheap-ass, jury-rigged pieces of hose, really—that branched off it in the direction of the nearest compartments.

Behind them, the escaping roar of water continued unabated.

Ravi stared at the mess of piping, trying to get his head around it. Whoever had done this had used a makeshift Y-junction to split the original pipe into two. One arm of the Y ran "normally" toward the shutoff valve, while the other marked the beginning of the bypass. It made a crude kind of sense, Ravi thought. After all, if a person were going to divert water from one line into another, how else would they do it?

What was odd, though, and what Ravi couldn't figure out, was the contraption built into the top of the Y-junction. He frowned, trying to make sense of what he was seeing. It looked like—there was no other way to describe it—a wheel. A wheel on top of a pipe. What was it for? His eyelids flickered with the effort of trying to pick up a signal from it. Nothing. If he couldn't see it with his own eyes, it would have been utterly invisible. And yet, for all that, it looked strangely familiar. He'd seen something like this before. But for the life of him, he couldn't think where.

Ansimov scratched his chin, his camera eye glassy and opaque as he recorded what he was looking at. Ravi could tell from the flow of code that he was busy transmitting it elsewhere.

"There's a team on the way," Ansimov announced. Then winced. "But they're at least ten minutes out."

Ravi listened to the sound of the water and despaired. At the rate it was leaking away, ten minutes was an eternity.

"Do they have any advice?"

Ansimov shook his head.

"They're as flummoxed as we are," he said, pointing at the wheel. "And pissed as all hungary. The only thing they're certain about is that someone's been stealing water."

Ravi nodded somberly. Water theft would certainly explain the Rube Goldberg setup snaking under their feet. He choked back a sudden surge of anger. Every generation had some, he knew: antisocial gullgropers who thought it'd be a good idea to steal other people's personal stuff. But *water*? His lips set into a firm and unforgiving line. Recycling was too good for people like that.

Like Ravi, Ansimov was busy trying to scan the wheel. But unlike Ravi, he was clumsy. His code was skidding all over the place—and some of it was bouncing against Ravi's own implants. A stabbing pain shot through his temple.

"Hey, Vlad, knock it off! You're not going to find anything—and you're busting my head open."

The wild spray of data died away.

"Sorry, amiko." Ansimov pointed sheepishly at the wheel. "I thought it might be buried too deep to see."

Ravi shook his head in sympathy.

"It's not there. And believe me, I looked. Whatever that thing is, it's not part of the hive."

Ansimov bent down for a closer look. He reached out a hand to touch it but pulled away at the last minute.

"Do you think it's like a LOKI or something?"

Ravi thought about BozBall. The way it could roll, or walk, or climb. The quality of its sensors. Its scary ability to think for itself.

"No," he said, flatly. His eye ran over the makeshift tubing. "This is all too primitive. If it were a LOKI, it'd be more, you know, *together* than this." He frowned, searching for the right words. "This thing looks . . . stupid. You can't always see a LOKI, because it doesn't need the hive. You'd only notice it if it hooked itself in." He prodded the wheel with his toe. "But this thing doesn't even know what a hive is. It's like something from the Steel Age."

And then, suddenly, he knew what it was.

Because it really was from the Steel Age. And in every Homeworld submarine movie they ever made.

He bent down, closed his hand around the wheel, and tried to turn it.

The wheel surrendered to the pressure with a sharp little squeak. Ravi kept at it until the wheel tightened under his grip and refused to go any further.

Back down the corridor, the roar of water died away to nothing. Ansimov looked at him in amazement.

Ravi shrugged, suddenly embarrassed.

"Lucky guess."

There was a splashing of footsteps in the corridor. Chen Lai, with Lieutenant Petrides, a couple more engineers, and a small army of bots, their fat, rubber wheels shiny with water. Linked into Ansimov's feed, they didn't bother to ask for an explanation. They'd seen the whole thing for themselves. A sharp blast of code jerked the robots into action. Hoses rippled out of their housings accompanied by the thirsty whine of pumps. With startling efficiency, they gulped down liter after liter of vital fluid before it could slide away to oblivion.

Chen Lai surveyed the devastation with a grimmer expression than usual. He stared at the jury-rigged bypass, his face stony with anger.

"Get ShipSec down here. And trace these Archie-damned lines to the bescumbered cretins who laid them!" He glared down at the little beads of water huddled against his boots. Without spilling a drop, he placed them under the passing hose of a robot for collection. "Someone is going to pay for this."

"I'll see to it," Petrides said, voice tight. The lieutenant's normally good-humored expression had been replaced by something approaching rage. Her livid gaze took in the entirety of the deluge before sweeping across the two midshipmen. Ravi, worried that he was somehow the cause of Petrides' fury, flinched. "MacLeod, Ansimov: with me."

The makeshift lines were as dumb as the now-closed wheel and every bit as invisible. But under Petrides' relentless directions, Ravi and Ansimov used drones, repurposed sensors, and old-fashioned, knuckle-scraping tugs of the hand to follow the hoses all the way to the end. It took them three and a half hours, tracing a serpentine course along corridors, through bulkheads, and down, always down, past deck after deck to the very bottom of the wheel, to the uninhabited spaces of mechanisms and machinery that lurked between human warmth and the wheel's ice-cold outer rim.

"I don't sarding believe it," Ansimov said. He sucked absent-mindedly at a small cut on his little finger, his fatigues—like Ravi's—filthy with assorted types of muck. Puffs of white breath steamed into the gray, dimly lit air.

All the pipes terminated in a large, makeshift water tank. Ravi gave a low whistle. There was capacity for at least ten thousand liters here, he reckoned. Nowhere near the size of the ship's official tanks, but huge for something clearly thrown together on the sly. The tank's construction, though effective, was crude, its various parts clumsily glued together by someone with more enthusiasm than skill, the parts themselves warped and irregular, produced, no doubt, by lightweight printers far too small for the task. Needless to say, it did not appear on the specs.

"Well, at least we know why the water level in the official tanks is too low," Petrides murmured. "Someone's been siphoning it off."

Ravi's mind flashed back in time: the lieutenant tossing him the prehistoric plumb line. Her dissatisfaction with the amount of water.

She frowned briefly.

"I don't see any outlets, though. This tank isn't big enough to account for what's missing. They must be bringing it here for temporary storage and then moving it somewhere else, so there's got to be a way to pump it out."

"Maybe the outlets are on the other side," Ravi suggested. The tank was tightly wedged amidst a small forest of pipes and a couple of large pumps. The catwalk they were standing on didn't allow them to see all of it, and there were no nearby sensors for their implants to access. Petrides cast a speculative gaze over the two midshipmen. Ravi had no doubt what was coming. Between him and Ansimov, he was very much the smaller.

"Think you can wriggle to the other side and take a look?"

"Yes, ma'am." Conscious that gravity down here was slightly more than normal, he clambered through the piping with exaggerated care. Ancient grime, undisturbed since Launch Day, slimed its way onto his hands and face and fatigues. He managed to get across the top of the tank and peered down the other side. It was a very long drop. There was a catwalk down there, maybe three or four meters below the level of the one they'd arrived on. Ravi could just make out what looked like a spigot.

Feeling more and more like one of those large, human-like animals from the Homeworld forests, he slid from pipe to pipe until he could jump down onto the new catwalk. He landed with a thump, breathing hard from the exertion. Glancing down through the walkway's grated surface, he could see nothing but more pipes and darkness. He very much hoped he could find some way to walk around to the other side. He didn't much fancy climbing back up.

"There's a tap here," he coded, sending them a visual as he did so. *"No outlet pipes."* He glanced along the walkway. It was broad and sturdily built,

curving out of sight behind a series of rumbling sluice tanks. Wide enough and strong enough for a wheeled vehicle. *"I'm guessing they bring in a water tender and just take it to wherever it needs to go."*

"Sounds about right," Petrides replied, using her voice. "See if you . . ."

She was cut off by the wheezing sound of an elevator door opening somewhere close by. Very close by. The fat-wheeled bulk of a cleaning bot lumbered into view from behind the sluice tanks, accompanied by an effervescent fizz of code. And behind the cleaning bot, just visible over the stubby curve of its main tank, was a face. Long; narrow; young. Definitely familiar. And every bit as shocked as Ravi himself.

"Sard!" The boy's code, buzzy and ill disciplined, kicked the cleaning bot into overdrive. The pitch of its motors rose to a scream. Hundreds of kilos of mechanism charged down the catwalk in Ravi's direction, intent on smashing him to pulp.

And came to a screeching stop, brakes smoking from the sudden deceleration. The boy's childish algorithms were no match for Ravi's. He'd lost control of the machine. And now he was running: hurtling toward the unseen elevator, his frightened boots clattering on the walkway gratings.

It was the work of less than a second for Ravi to move the cleaning bot in the opposite direction, though in doing so, he discovered the cleaning bot was not at all what it seemed. It had been modified to carry water—a *lot* of water. Fortunately, the tanks were empty and the unburdened machine had a real turn of speed. The bot hurtled after the kid, swerving left and right as the walkway chicaned through the sluice tanks on its way back to the elevator. The bot followed him through the elevator doors before they had a chance to close and pinned him against the far wall, motors whining against every attempt he made to squirm free. Ravi held him there until Petrides and Ansimov could find a way around to them. By the time they did so, Chen Lai, Vasconcelos, and a detachment of ShipSec officers had already arrived on site. The Inspector gave no instruction to release the cleaning bot's bruising pressure, so Ravi held it in place. The boy had tried to run him over. Ravi had no compunction about applying slightly more force than was necessary. The kid's breathing came out in short, shallow gasps.

"Cadet Menendez," Vasconcelos drawled. "How very nice to meet you. *Again.*"

Only now did Ravi realize why the kid looked so familiar. Willem Menendez. Hiroji Menendez's kid brother. Hiroji, the trainee medic who was too upscale for an airlock but whose grandfather had been a loading tech. The younger Menendez was what Sofia would call a "disappointment," an idiot child whose dad was always bailing him out of one scrape or another. If he'd been a MacLeod, young though he was, his rating would already be dangerously close to Dead Weight. As it was . . .

"Screw you, ShipSec. I got nothing to say to you. Nothing."

Vasconcelos's eyes narrowed dangerously.

"This isn't 'youthful high jinks,' son. This is *stealing water*." He glanced briefly at Ravi. "And quite possibly attempted murder. Daddy isn't getting you out of this one. So, you'd better talk, and talk fast."

"Or what?"

"You'll be mulched."

The words hit home. Hemmed in by a massive drone and unfriendly, grown-up faces, Menendez's adolescent defiance collapsed. His eyes moistened uncontrollably. Ravi eased the pressure on the boy's chest.

"I don't know much," he sniffed. "Went to a BonVoy demo a few months back. Got a handwritten note asking if I'd like to do more."

"*Hand*written?"

"Yeah, like something out of the Steel Age. But not traceable, see? No records."

Ravi had to admit it was clever. But he couldn't imagine using his hands to "write" anything. If you had to, fingers were perfectly okay for punching keyboards. Wrapping them around thin sticks of ink in order to draw words was a different vat of protein altogether.

"And you agreed to get involved?"

"Yeah."

"And after you agreed to get involved, whom did you meet with?"

"No one. Honest to Archie, it was all done on paper."

"Do you have the paper?"

Menendez shook his head. Vasconcelos sighed.

"This is not looking good for you, son. What *can* you tell me?"

"Every now and then, I get a message to go collect a cleaning bot"—he tapped the drone in front of him—"bring it down here and load it with water. Then I take it back where I found it."

"And where's that?"

"Bermuda-seven, deck three, at the janitor station next to the hydroponics."

"And did you see who picked it up?"

"No."

"You weren't even curious?"

"Well, yeah. But I didn't want to sard things up, know what I mean? I want to save their world."

An angry muttering filled the elevator. Vasconcelos glared everyone into silence.

"And do you know what the water is for?"

The boy hesitated. Licked his lips.

"I'm not going to ask you again."

"Look, I don't *know* know. But you kinda hear things sometimes. The water's for paying people off. People we need to make things for us."

"Devices?"

The boy nodded.

"What sort of devices?"

"No idea."

Ravi did, though. He remembered the BonVoy demonstration in the hubs, the massive hologram. *No landing. No pollution. Save their world.* Whoever had done that had serious skills. Made sense they wanted to get paid.

Vasconcelos pursed his lips.

"We'll talk about this some more. In the brig." At the inspector's curt nod, ShipSec officers cuffed the boy and marched him away, taking the cleaning bot with them as evidence. The engineers, meanwhile, stayed behind, waiting for Chen Lai's instructions. The commander's cold expression swept across the trainees. Ravi tried very hard not to quail.

And then Chen Lai did something odd. Very odd indeed.

He broke into a grin.

"Well done," he said. "Sarding well done." He clapped them both on the shoulder and stalked off to examine the makeshift water tank.

Ravi and Ansimov just stared at each other, too confused to speak.

A ctions have consequences. Chen Lai's remarkable good humor extended into the following sol. So much so that a message squirmed under Ravi's eyelids just as he was about to knock off his shift.

"Good job with the water leak. Report to the boat elevators, 0430 tomorrow. Five-credit training run to Bohr: prep boat for launch, load cargo, test out a new sensor array—and front-row seats to the playoff game. Task list attached."

Despite his fatigue, Ravi found himself grinning. Tomorrow's run would be carrying the Imperials, the newly crowned ship champions, to the first game of the Fleet Cup. Ravi wasn't a big freeball fan, but that hardly mattered. Everybody else was. There were people out there who'd give their motherboards to swap berths with him. He was about to become one of the coolest kids in class—for a sol or two, anyway. Not bad, he thought, for someone from a "non-academic" family.

Another message hit his implants.

"ARCHIMEDES BRIG—FOR YOUR INFORMATION—CREWMAN 6-7864 MACLEOD, ROBERTA J., RELEASED PENDING FURTHER INVESTIGATION."

Ravi shut down his drones and stowed his gear with a tuneless whistle. Shift over, he reached out into the hive.

"Hey, Boz!" he messaged. *"Kudos on getting sprung. Want to meet up? Usual place? Usual time?"*

There was no reply. Ravi didn't think much about it until after supper, when he messaged her again. Nothing. He sent out a tracer and watched it disappear into the hive in a welter of bits and bytes. Still nothing. Ravi, who'd been eating alone at Ansimov's, dropped off his scraped-clean plate and headed home with a frown.

"You all right?"

Boz, he reminded himself firmly, wasn't a child. If she didn't want to talk to him, she didn't have to.

And yet.

Boz *always* wanted to talk.

He paced the cramped expanse of his quarters until it was time to turn in, and then, instead of hitting the sack, he slipped out into the night-cycle dark, a small gremlin of worry sitting on his shoulder.

Boz's quarters were on a run-down deck in the Fiji mid-levels. Ravi found himself shivering. Climate control here had never worked properly—some weird quirk in the wheel's plumbing—and while the deck *technically* satisfied the 0.8 *g* minimum for residential habitation, it didn't pay to look at the gravity meter too closely. It was a crappy part of the ship—but the rents were cheap . . .

"Switch it on."

Ravi did as he was told. A faint headache ground at his temples. On the other side of the room, a small cursor appeared on the monitor, blinking expectantly.

"Good. Move it left, please."

Ravi moved the little dot across the screen, pleased that his eyelids were still this time.

"And right? . . . Good. Excellent, in fact."

He could feel himself smiling. *Nailed it*, he thought.

A voice behind him, one he wasn't meant to hear, said, "Congratulations, doctor. It looks like our little freak is ready to go . . ."

Ravi stumbled into a bulkhead, disoriented. Swearing softly, he closed and opened his eyes, trying to clear his head. Everything seemed normal: the night-dimmed lights, the garishly painted corridor, the quiet hum of the hive. Only the thumping in his chest told him otherwise.

What the sard was that? he asked himself. No way had he dozed off just walking. No way.

His teeth ground in frustration.

I'm not mad, he told himself, fiercely. *I'm not mad.*

But what if I am?

Turning into the cramped little corridor where Boz had her quarters, Ravi pushed the whole, stupid episode aside. The corridor provoked a small smile of recognition. Boz insisted the walls were covered in avant-garde murals, but she was kidding herself. It was graffiti, pure and simple. A particularly crude sentence caught Ravi's eye, making him wince.

He flashed some code at Boz's door, setting off the buzzer. No answer. He let a couple of cold breaths mist the air before he tried again. Same result.

He was frowning now. Boz was already under curfew for a previous infraction. She was *required* to be in her quarters. With a sigh of frustration, he turned on his heel and headed for home.

He took all of three steps and stopped.

You know, his father had once said, *it's not that hard to break into a compartment.* Which was true. But he was an officer, almost. Officers didn't do things like that. On the other hand, his cousin was a MacLeod. She would understand.

Ravi looked around. The corridor was still deserted. He probed the local bandwidth. Data trickled past in a desultory flow. So far as the hive was concerned, there was nothing the least bit interesting going on here.

Satisfied no one was watching him, Ravi opened a link to Engineering Services. He used his own authorization to enter a work order for the inspection of a broken faucet at a certain location in Fiji-4. Having created the order, he immediately volunteered to take it on. It was a simple job, perfect for a trainee, and the algorithms at Engineering Services saw no reason to stand in his way. They added it to his schedule for the following sol.

The schedule came with an access code. The moment it hit his eyelids, Ravi used it to override the locks on Boz's door. There was a cascade of soft clicks as they let go. Ravi quietly let himself in.

It took all of half a second to see that Boz's quarters were empty. Her unmade bunk was rumpled and cold, the shower unit was bone-dry. Wherever she'd gone after leaving the brig, it wasn't here.

"Where the hungary are you?" he asked out loud. The face looking back at him out of Boz's grimy mirror was lined with worry.

No one answered.

— — —

He was staring at a plate. It was ornate, and beautiful, and full of color. Blue, and yellow, and cursive black in an interlocking pattern of organic molecules.

The molecules began to disappear. Mossy tendrils grasped at the edge of the plate, squeezing the roundness out of it, making it jagged and ugly. An irregular triangle of green.

The triangle replicated itself. Unfolding and unfolding into a vast, poisonous lawn.

And on the lawn, there was a man in a long coat, and buckled shoes, and an enormous white wig. He was holding BozBall in his hand. The little

LOKI was black now, and white, with flecks of gray. The man tossed it through the air and watched it land and roll across the grass that was really mold. And wherever BozBall rolled, the lawn turned to brown and died, and the brown spread and spread and turned into the brown of a tree trunk, growing apples that dropped onto the grass. But that couldn't be right. If the lawn had died, how could there be grass?

"Lights," Ravi mumbled.

His head was splitting. He'd been so worried about Boz, he'd forgotten to take his prescription. The little bottle of CerebroLaxin was sitting untouched on top of his cabinet.

"Sard it," he muttered. He risked opening his implants to the hive. The early morning newsfeeds were agog with news that *Archimedes* ShipSec had made a number of arrests. Water-thieving BonVoys, allegedly, many from well-regarded families. The suspects, all of whom were described as "hardened ideologues," were refusing to cooperate, and ShipSec, as yet, had no idea where the stolen water had gone.

It was all too noisy. Wincing, he shut the whole thing off and rolled gingerly out of his bunk. Time to get up.

By the time he reached the boat elevators, his headache had dropped down from excruciating to merely painful—helped, no doubt, by the fact it was still night-cycle. The shadowy corridors and cavernous hubs had gone easy on his pupils.

Not as easy, though, as Sofia Ibori. Her slim frame and braided hair were waiting for him at the elevators. She was hanging in the middle of the loading cage with her usual loose elegance. He found himself grinning like an idiot.

"You running this show?" he asked.

She grinned back at him, a little bleary-eyed.

"Sure am." She touched him playfully on the wrist. "I'll try not to get us lost."

"And I'll try to keep us in one piece," Ravi promised, with mock solemnity.

"Not without me, you won't."

It was Ansimov, kit bag floating ahead of him, his face beaming with anticipation.

Ravi swallowed his disappointment. For a few, glorious moments he'd thought he was going to have Sofia all to himself. He berated himself for his stupidity. Of course Ansimov was coming. Ansimov had been at the water leak too. And while the Chief Navigator might be prepared to trust one of his trainees—and grand-niece—to go solo on a simple milk run, the Chief Engineer would not.

He bumped fists with Ansimov and grinned gamely.

"Try not to break anything," he said.

The pylons that attached ISV-1-LB-03 *Spirit of St. Petersburg* to the ship's spine were 3,500 meters aft of Hungary, so the elevator ride down was a long one. And, for Ravi, hellish. He looked around desperately for a place to be sick in private. The elevator was huge and full of cargo secured for transshipment in shabby-looking nets, so there were plenty of places for Ravi to float out of sight. But floating out of sight wasn't enough. No matter where he secreted himself, the sound of his retching would reach Sofia's ears. And she would totally know it wasn't Vladimir Ansimov.

"How's it going?" Ansimov asked, keeping his voice light. His expression, however, was full of sympathy. He had a pretty shrewd idea about the state of Ravi's stomach.

"Okay." He tapped one of the nets. "We're running soy over there?"

"Rumor has it their hydroponics are failing."

Ravi nodded. His unsettled stomach found another way to knot itself. If *Bohr*'s hydroponics failed completely, no amount of extra soy would keep them going. They would starve.

The elevator ride came to a merciful end. Ravi floated over to the lifeboat, found a quiet compartment, and threw up.

The rest of morning was spent prepping for launch. For Sofia, that meant sitting on the flight deck, running nav simulations and playing around with the lifeboat's new sensor array. For Ravi and Ansimov, it meant loading cargo and crawling over every square meter of the lifeboat, checking for defects. Even with drones, it was hard, sweaty work—and he'd had to wriggle through the guts of the aft port cooling pipes to double-check some old welding. By the time the passengers arrived, Ravi's fatigues were soaked through and he was covered head to foot in grime. He thought seriously about taking a shower. But the boat's shower operated at a 100% surcharge. He couldn't afford it.

"Take first watch," he told Ansimov. He tucked his hands in his armpits. It was the easiest way to stop his weightless upper limbs from springing out to the side. "I'll do the back shift."

"You take it," Ansimov offered. He was hanging loosely from the cargo-hold bulkhead. The muffled cheering of Imperials could be heard on the other side. Their passengers were still settling into the living spaces. Ansimov gave Ravi a sly smile. "You'll have Midshipman Ibori all to yourself. Soft couches, the warm glow of the instruments, the light of a billion stars shining through the window. How could you possibly fail?"

Ravi shook his head.

"No interest," he lied. "She has a boyfriend. And I'm whacked. I could do with some shuteye."

Ravi imagined being in the cramped confines of the flight deck with Sofia, couches side by side, close enough to be touching. The thought made him ache.

But he was a filthy, reeking mess. And she was . . . not.

Ansimov shrugged.

"Suit yourself. I'm going to check out the new array. See what all the fuss is about." He gave a brief frown. "Stupid waste of water, if you ask me. What are they hoping to see, little green men?" He opened the bulkhead door and disappeared.

■■ ■■ ■■

Ansimov was right about the stars, Ravi thought. *There really are a billion of them.*

The lifeboat's nose was pointed right at the Milky Way. A speckled blue river of dust and crowded stars stretched across the window from one corner of the sky to another. Cool, unblinking light trickled gently into the flight deck. There was no other illumination, not even from the instruments. Ravi had switched off the readouts. He stared out into space, letting his mind wander.

"Beneath" him, on the other side of the floor separating the flight deck from the rest of the boat, everyone was fast asleep. Sofia and Ansimov in the tiny cabins reserved for crew, the Imperials in the communal spaces used by passengers. Sofia had shut down the boat's modest motors hours ago. They were in cruise mode, drifting along in thrustless silence. Somewhere "above" them, *Bohr* would be waiting: twenty-five kilometers of habitat wheels, and trellised spine, and massive, bulbous engines. But she was still too far away to see, an invisible speck against the vastness of the Milky Way. For the moment there was just Ravi, and the boat, and the river of stars. Nothing else mattered.

A readout flickered to life on the inside of an eyelid.

The instrument lights may have been off, but the instruments were not. And he was jacked in, a thin cable running from the port in the back of his neck and into the couch. The entire control panel was connected directly to his head.

Normally, he wouldn't have noticed. So long as everything was nominal, the readouts were quiet. But the sensor array was suddenly awake, little signals pinging anxiously against his implants.

There was something out there. Running alongside and less than a hundred kilometers away.

Less than ninety now. Eighty. The array was going crazy. Jacked in as he was, he could feel the quick, nervous swing of the dishes, the sudden focusing of long lenses. Data washed against his mind's eye like a tide.

The object was small, and dark, and despite the array's best efforts, damn near invisible. As near as Ravi could tell, it was shaped like a slim, blunt-nosed tube. There was a slight flare at the rear. A housing, probably. For propulsion.

Ravi frowned. Whatever it was, it was too small to have come far. Not much room for fuel, even less for life support.

Assuming, of course, the people who made it were human. Ravi tried to laugh away the paranoia. But his heart beat faster just the same. The distance closed to fifty kilometers.

He was so busy with the readouts, the brushing of a hand against his wrist made him start.

"I'm sorry," he said, letting his eyes adjust to the real world again. "I didn't . . ."

The words curdled on his lips, frozen.

It was the blond-haired girl. She was stretched out on Sofia's couch, face toward him. She smiled and opened her mouth to speak.

Ravi had no idea what she said. He was too busy screaming.

▬ ▬ ▬

"I banged my knee," Ravi said sullenly. "It was an accident."

It wasn't a complete lie. He'd been only loosely belted to the couch. In his panic, he'd smashed his knee against the underside of a control panel.

He'd also ripped out the jack in the back of his neck. When the blinding pain had subsided, the girl was nowhere to be seen, and the object outside had vanished. And now Sofia and Ansimov wanted to know what the hungary was going on. Down below, confused, drowsy chatter filled the passenger spaces.

Ravi bit his lip. If he told them the truth, he'd be off the program for sure. No one wanted a nut job for an officer. Of course, a story that involved shrieking like a murder victim on account of some minor injury wasn't exactly elevating his rep, either.

The flight deck was too small for three people. Sofia was crammed into her couch. Ansimov was floating halfway through the hatch. He grinned wickedly.

"Amiko," he chuckled. "You scream like a girl." He ducked back through the hatch to avoid Sofia's swinging arm. "You've woken up the whole sarding boat." When his face reappeared, it was still grinning. "You able to finish your watch, or do you need medical attention?"

"Shut up, Vladimir."

Ravi and Ansimov swung around in surprise. It was Sofia speaking. The words were said quietly, without malice, as if she was distracted. She had relit the instrument panel and was staring at the readouts.

"Why did you retarget the array?" she asked.

"I didn't," Ravi said, "the array moved on its own." No sooner had he said the words than he regretted it. What if he *had* retargeted the array? What if the logs showed that he had? He'd clearly been hallucinating like crazy. What if the blurry UFO was just a figment of his imagination—like the girl? He could quite easily have fired up the sensors in some illusion-induced funk. Questions would be asked. Questions that would send him to the psych ward.

The chipset in his head started buzzing with interference. Sofia was directing a stream of code at the instrument panel and using way too much power. She hadn't bothered to jack in. Before he could complain, however, the instructions died away. Readouts flickered to life under three sets of eyelids. Sofia and Ansimov gave a small gasp. So did Ravi. But where Sofia and Ansimov were expressing shock, Ravi's was more like a sigh of relief.

Sofia had activated the sensor logs. The UFO was there on the replay, just like he remembered it. So that, at least, was real. The three of them watched its faint shadow approach to within fifty kilometers, and then, at about the time he smashed his knee, it drifted away again. The array tried to track it and failed. There was a faint reading at 125 kilometers and then the data stream went mute.

"Sarding hungary," Ansimov swore. "What in Archie's name was *that?*"

"It's why I banged my knee," Ravi said, seizing an opportunity to reha-bilitate himself. "That thing out there just *appeared.* One minute, I'm staring at the Milky Way; the next, *bam!*"

"You didn't think to lead with that?" Sofia snapped. "You know: 'I banged my knee because we got jumped by an *unidentified* flying object?' In deep space? What kind of bescumbered idiot are you?"

Ravi could only be grateful she was talking rather than transmitting. His chipset would have fried.

"I wasn't sure it was real," he said, sheepishly. "I wanted to double-check before I said anything."

That, at least, had the virtue of being mostly true.

Sofia's expression softened a little, though not as much as Ravi would have liked.

"We need to call it in," she said. "I'll contact *Bohr.*"

They docked with the *Bohr* some thirteen hours later. Live newsfeeds showed a couple of reporters and a small crowd of freeball fans waiting to greet the Imperials. Ravi, Ansimov, and Sofia had work to do, however. Cargo had to be unloaded, the lifeboat had to be powered down, flight re-ports needed to be filed. By the time the three of them floated out of the elevator and into *Bohr's* loading bays, the crowds had long since gone.

Someone was waiting for them, though. A petite woman, with close-cropped graying hair and a friendly smile, was hanging easily in front of them. Apart from the "ISV-2 *Bohr*" on her shoulder flashes, her uniform was identical to those found on *Archimedes.*

"I'm Keiko Svenson," she said, drifting over to meet them with an out-stretched hand. "Ship's Security. Welcome to *BoBo.*"

She had the strange, slightly singsong accent he'd heard on the news-feeds. It finally hit him: for the first time in his life, he was off the ship. The ShipSec officer grabbed Ravi's hand, bracing herself against the elevator to keep them both stable.

"Pleased to meet you," she said, pleasantly. "Midshipman MacLeod?"

Ravi nodded and introduced the other two.

"Wonderful. Now, if you'd care to follow me . . ." She kicked off, head-ing in the general direction of the habitat wheels.

"Are we under arrest?" Ansimov blurted out.

Svenson chuckled. She spun deftly in the air to look back at him.

"Have you done something arrestable?"

Ansimov hesitated longer than he should.

"No."

"Then you've nothing to worry about." But she gave him a slightly appraising stare all the same.

The ShipSec officer led them through the *Bohr*'s hubs and into the nearest habitat wheel. It took a while for Ravi to log himself into *Bohr*'s hive, but once he did so, it took only a moment or two to download the wheel's name: Haiti. Unlike *Archimedes*, *Bohr* still had all her wheels in operation. Ravi found himself wrestling with a weird sense of *déjà vu*. Everywhere looked like home, but it wasn't. If this were *Archimedes*, they'd be heading straight for Hungary. But Hungary was a closed-off, gutted hulk. Haiti was very much alive.

They descended to a full-*g* deck. Once there, Svenson took them on a brisk walk that ended in the most luxurious quarters Ravi had ever seen, with no fewer than *four* separate compartments. Two twin-bunked spaces for sleeping, some kind of shared communal area, and a self-contained shower and head. Even Sofia looked impressed.

"Do all your guest crews get treated this well?" she asked.

"Only the ones we like," Svenson joked. "Make yourselves at home."

Sofia picked her sleeping quarters without even pretending to give anyone an option. In the other, Ansimov beat Ravi to the top bunk.

When they returned to the communal living area, Svenson was sitting quietly on a sofa, waiting.

"Can I ask you," she began delicately, "about this, ah, *encounter* you reported?"

The three of them exchanged a quick glance. Primo quarters and a ShipSec officer playing tour guide suddenly made sense. After a moment's indecision, Ravi, who had, after all, been the trainee on duty, retold the story. He did not mention banging his knee. He did not mention waking the whole boat with this screaming. He most definitely did not mention the blond-haired girl.

Although Svenson nodded at all the right places, it was clear to Ravi she was thoroughly acquainted with the lifeboat's logs.

"Did you see anything that wasn't picked up by the sensors? Any markings? Any hint of a transmission interfering with your implants?"

They all shook their heads.

"Any idea why it didn't come any closer than fifty klicks?"

"Nope," Ravi answered, speaking, once again, for all of them.

"Did you do anything that might have warned it off? Tried to hail it on the radio, something like that?"

Only if you count hallucinating like crazy and screaming like a frightened child.

"No," he said stolidly.

"It's a damned shame," Svenson sighed. "It looks like he's going to get away with it. Again." The ShipSec officer clenched her fists and pounded her knees in frustration.

"Who?" Sofia asked curiously. And then: "This isn't the first time?"

"Not by a long shot. The object you saw was a test probe. A prototype. We're going to use them to scout out Destination World and its moons. There are half a dozen of them out there right now, being put through their paces. Someone—and we think we know who—is hacking them and taking them for joyrides. Usually, they just buzz the ship. This is the first time they've picked on a lifeboat."

The ShipSec officer rose to her feet.

"I'm sorry you've been troubled by all this. In some ways, it's just a prank. But it's a really expensive one." She broke into a friendly smile and headed for the door. A data packet buzzed its way into Ravi's implants. "Guest privileges for the ship, including free drinks at Da Gama's. You can use 'em to drown your sorrows when we spank your Imperials tomorrow night-cycle." She slipped out before anyone could fire off a reply. Her tinkling laugh faded away down the corridor.

"At least the natives are friendly," Sofia observed. "Nicest ShipSec officer I've ever met!"

"Yeah," Ansimov agreed. "They really know how to show you a good time." He gave Ravi a good-natured punch in the shoulder. "Plus, we know the sensor array works. Extra credit for sure. Just think: if they hadn't installed it, that probe could have been sitting right outside the airlock and we'd never have seen her. Crazy, huh?"

Ravi started to speak, but the words died on his lips.

"Something bothering you?" Ansimov asked.

"No. It's nothing."

"Good," Sofia said briskly. "Because these guest packages are *very* generous. We should hit the bars, like, *now.*"

Ravi and Ansimov trailed her out the door. Ansimov chattered excitedly about what they were going to do and when. Sofia explained that she had it all planned out and everything would go much more smoothly if they just followed her lead.

Ravi kept pace but said nothing. He was still mulling over what Ansimov had said about the sensor array. Eventually, with Sofia distracted by a circular full of high-end retail, he tugged on his partner's elbow.

"What that ShipSec officer told us: do you think it makes sense?"

Ansimov dragged his attention away from a display of large, brightly colored hats, breathlessly advertised as the future of fashion on Destination World.

"Sure," he answered. "Why wouldn't it?"

"Because, if Svenson is right, our brand-new, super-duper sensor array barely managed to detect some *Bohr* ne'er-do-well joyriding a probe."

"That's what the lady said. So?"

"So, engineering-wise, a probe's like a pretty ho-hum thing. All it has to do is loop around a planet, circle a few moons, and take a couple of pictures."

Ansimov's attention was wandering back to the hats.

"I'm not sure where you're going with this, amiko. We're here to have a good time, not relive Astrogation one oh one."

"It's a *probe*, Vlad. Why build something so dark, so near-invisible, that even a brand-new, super-duper sensor array can barely see it?"

Ansimov stared at the hats for some time, lost in thought.

"No idea," he said at last. "I just hope that the bastard officers know what they're doing. 'Cause it's beginning to look like they're an implant short of a chipset."

15.0

*B*ohr's guest privileges included a stunningly generous water allowance, so Ravi entered the lifeboat for the trip home clean enough to share a watch with Sofia. Outbound, he'd have fried his motherboard to be lying where he was now, smelling halfway decent, lightly strapped in, and with Sofia only centimeters away, running through the last phases of the countdown. Now, however, he couldn't care less. Truth was, he was terrified of another "episode." He didn't want Sofia to be around if he were to have another hallucination, but the alternative, standing watch alone, seemed even worse. At least if he went crazy with Sofia lying next to him, she would be able to stop him from doing something truly stupid, like blowing up the boat.

Between unclamping from the *Bohr*, orienting the lifeboat's blunt nose, and firing up the drive, Sofia had directed a stream of friendly, mostly mindless chatter in his general direction, to which he had responded barely, if at all. Trapped in his own head, he simply didn't have the energy.

That he was nutso, there could be no doubt. There was no girl. She had simply appeared on the couch beside him and vanished in a flash of unjacked agony. It would have been impossible for her to flee the flight deck in that amount of time. And even if she *had* somehow, she would have floated into Ansimov and Sofia coming the other way.

All of which led to one inescapable conclusion. He would have to drop out. Get treatment before he killed somebody. Find something else to do with his life. His heart pumped lumpily in his chest. More than once, he fought back the urge to cry.

"Ow!"

A jab in the ribs brought him back from the brink.

"What's wrong with you?" Sofia asked. "You've hardly said a word all shift."

"Nothing." And then, slightly more honestly: "I'm just not sure I'm cut out to be an engineer, is all." The thrum of the lifeboat's engines pushed him gently into his couch. Which was nothing compared to the wheel-load of misery pressing down on him at the same time. *This is what happens,* his father might have said, *when you try to be something you're not.*

"Don't be silly. Everyone says you're doing great. Even Warren." She chuckled quietly. "At least when she's not going on about your lowlife family."

"There's nothing wrong with my family," Ravi bristled. But in his mind's eye he could see his mother trying to look presentable in front of the ombudsman. Begging him not to sentence Dad to another bout of torpor. "And even if there was, it'll be different after planetfall. New start for everybody."

"You think so?"

"You don't?"

Bored with using implants, Sofia reached out a slim arm to adjust the instruments.

"Different? Maybe. But probably not better." Sensing Ravi's resistance, she turned in her couch to look at him directly. The glow from the control panel threw soft shadows across her body. "Look," she said. "The fleet's been out here for one hundred and thirty-two years. Thanks to the LOKIs, we're the *only* human beings in deep space, and we've become like our own little civilization, you know? A civilization with only a handful of murders, almost no crime—a few delinquents notwithstanding"—she didn't quite meet Ravi's eye—"and everyone pretty much gets along with everyone else. When, in all of human history, has *that* ever happened?"

Ravi nodded in reluctant agreement and stared out the flight-deck window. The star-speckled black gazed back at him.

"Landing on a planet's not going to change any of that," he countered after a moment's thought. "We'll still be the same people."

"No, we *won't.* Destination World is going to change us because planets aren't starships. Planets sard you up. We'll end up like Homeworld, with murders and crime and everyone looking out for themselves." She was fully animated now, her eyes gleaming with passion. "It's the *ship* that keeps us together. The ship that makes us our best selves. If people don't do their jobs here, other people die. Crappy engineering repair? People die. No-good botanists? People die. Incompetent purser? People die. *And everyone knows it.*" She put a hand on his wrist, the grip firm, insistent. "Up here, we're all in this together. Down there? Well . . ." Her voice trailed off. Indescribably sad and more than a little angry.

Ravi could see from the readouts that the soft push of the lifeboat's engines was beginning to pile on velocity. But for all that, the bright stars remained nailed in place, like lampposts in the dark. They didn't give a cracked lining about Sofia's worries. Or his own, for that matter.

"Yeah, well. It's not like we can do anything about it, is there? Come Braking Day, we're all going down, whether we like it or not."

Neither of them spoke much after that.

— — —

Profound misery, Ravi discovered, did have one upside. He lacked the mental energy to be sick. He made it all the way back to *Archimedes* without a single incident. Once aboard, he had thought about going straight to Chen Lai and getting it over with. Instead, though, he had simply headed to his quarters. Looking around the tiny space, he was once again teary-eyed. After tomorrow, he wouldn't be able to afford it. With a sigh, he slipped out of his fatigues, pulled his bunk down from the wall, and crashed out.

He was staring at a plate. Blue, and yellow, and cursive black in an interlocking pattern of organic molecules.

Mossy tendrils squeezed the roundness out of it, making it jagged and ugly. An irregular triangle of green, replicating itself into a vast, poisonous lawn, across which walked a man in a long coat, and buckled shoes, and an enormous white wig. He was holding BozBall in his hand, plain, and black, and without features. He tossed it into the air and watched it soar into skies seared by a frightening ball of fire. Up and up it went, until the sky blackened, and the ball of fire went away, and a dusty-blue river of stars wound across the universe.

BozBall, blacker than black, continued to climb, reaching for the smoky ribbon of lights far above it. And as it climbed, a little star detached itself from the others and dropped down to meet it. A star that acquired shape, acquired substance. A blunt, rounded nose. A flared stern. A grit-stained hull covered in huge, stenciled numbers. ISV-I-LB-03.

The lifeboat, *Spirit of St. Petersburg.*

BozBall fell toward the lifeboat, bounced against the hull, and grabbed on with spidery legs. It scuttled forward, toward the prow, where a girl with dyed-blond hair and a slightly crooked smile was waiting for it. She scooped it up with one hand and placed it on a panel only centimeters from the thick, tinted window of the flight deck. Her mouth moved out of sync with her voice, which came from far away, whisper-faint.

"Come get it," she said.

Ravi woke with a start, tensed against the eye-stabbing impact of a headache. Except the headache didn't come. Still, he didn't quite trust his implants.

"Lights," he croaked.

It was barely 0130. Technically morning, but not really. As he opened up his chipset one channel at a time, it was easy to tell that the ship was fast asleep. The flow of data through the hive had slowed to a trickle, just an automated system or two whispering in the night-cycle.

Come get it.

The voice echoed in his head as if the girl were beside him, breathing in his ear. He glanced around, startled. There was no one there.

He settled back on his bunk, uneasy. *This,* he thought to himself, *is what it's like to go crazy.* He closed his eyes, determined to go back to sleep. Might as well get a few more hours of peace before admitting to the whole world he was a nut job.

Come get it.

He screwed his eyes tight shut and forced himself not to react. Crazy was a state of mind. A bad state of mind, to be sure, but a state of mind nonetheless. And it was *his* mind, no one else's. *He* got to decide what went on in there. If he ignored the voice, pretended it wasn't speaking, it would have to go away. He unclenched his eyelids, forced himself to relax, to take deep, even breaths.

Come get it.

Come get it.

Come get it . . . .

"Shut up!" he shouted, unable to take it anymore. "Shut up, shut up, shut UP!" He was sitting on the edge of his bunk, yelling at an empty room. He caught an unflattering glimpse of himself in the sink mirror, slack-jawed and deranged. He lurched to his feet, scrambled over to his space chest, and dragged on some fatigues.

"Sard you," he said, still talking out loud. He pulled on his boots. "You want to see crazy? I'll show you crazy, you bescumbered SOB." He stumbled out into the darkened corridors, still talking to himself. "I'm not crazy. *You're* crazy. And you know what? I'm going to prove it."

He caught a paternoster to the hubs and jumped viciously "down" in the direction of the boat elevators. He blasted one with a furious stream of code and made it open for him. Only when it started rumbling down the spine on its 3,500-meter journey to the pylons did he realize he'd forgotten to bring any sick bags. As it happened, however, he didn't need one. He made the trip without incident.

The elevator thudded and hissed as its various airlocks and connectors linked up with *Spirit of St. Petersburg*. Fortunately, he was still registered on the lifeboat's system as crew, so he didn't have to hack the security. The vessel let him in without a whisper of complaint.

Ravi floated into a black void of cold, gasping for breath. The lights and the heaters had been off for hours, and the air was dizzyingly thin. Ship's Regs required that lifeboats be "habitable" at all times, but heating an empty vessel wasted energy, and air left alone in the compartments would find a way to leak. Most of it had been sucked back into the tanks. Entering a dormant lifeboat wouldn't kill him, but it wasn't exactly fun.

Ravi forced himself to calm down and breathe slowly. He reached out with his implants and turned on the lights. Synced to the ship, they were only night-cycle bright. Even so, it was plain to see that the boat's surfaces were beginning to ice up. They greeted the sudden illumination with a reluctant glitter.

Wishing he'd thought to bring gloves, Ravi drifted "up" through the hold, guiding himself with numb fingers. He flitted quietly through the passenger compartments and the crew spaces, all the way to the flight deck. Once there, he didn't bother to jack himself in. He didn't need to fire up the whole boat. All he needed was one little drone. He reached out with his implants until he found it.

The inspection drone was nestled in its usual compartment, midships, in the outer hull and close to a secondary airlock. The flight deck faded into the background as the drone's sensors flooded his mind's eye with imagery. The insides of his eyelids were suddenly awash with starlight as the compartment doors cycled open. The drone pushed itself out on a little puff of gas and floated toward the lifeboat's nose. Distorted by the wide angle of its camera lens, the hull appeared to curve away on all sides like an enormous, convex plain. Sensors sent strings of green numbers across Ravi's vision. Released from captivity, the drone was doing its job: inspecting. The hull was fine, it kept saying. Everything was nominal.

The curving plain suddenly steepened and fell away as the drone reached the nose. Parts of the flight-deck window floated into view, looking far bigger than it actually was. The drone hovered stoically in place while Ravi got his bearings. It took a few moments, but he managed to find the corner of the window he was looking for. The drone moved slowly now, in parallel with the window's edge. As it drifted along, Ravi counted the panels. One. Two. Three.

Attached to the fourth panel, only centimeters from the window, was a little black ball.

C hen Lai was speaking, but Ravi was having real trouble concentrating on what he had to say. He was thinking about the little black ball stuffed in the bottom of his space chest. Too cold to touch when the drone had first brought it in, he had waited for it to warm up in the frigid confines of the lifeboat, and then attempted to scan it, without success. It was shielded from easy examination and was making no attempt to communicate with the hive. Like BozBall, the imitation wasn't completely smooth. If he looked closely, there were a number of fine joints on the surface. Proof, if proof were needed, that it was capable of changing shape, perhaps even to the spider-legged form he had seen in his dream.

Ravi was painfully aware of three things. One: he should never have brought an unknown object aboard the ship. Two: having brought it aboard, he should have reported it straight away. But, three: the object was proof positive he wasn't completely crazy. Yet it was a proof he couldn't use. If he handed the object in, they'd ask him how he knew it was there. And after *that*, they'd either psych him off the program or toss him in the brig. So, the little black ball lay quiet at the bottom of his space chest, burning at his conscience.

Everyone in the briefing room was staring at him.

"Something on your mind, Middy?" Chen Lai was asking sarcastically.

"N . . . no, sir."

"Oh. I guess that's because there's *nothing* on your mind! Pay attention!"

"Yes, sir."

Chen Lai was staring at him, expression unreadable, perhaps thinking about loading punishment on top of the reprimand. He stared a moment more and turned away. Ravi let loose a quiet sigh of relief.

"As I was saying," Chen Lai began pointedly, "the navigators are telling us the system we're dropping into is full of dirty space. Way dirtier than Home System, apparently. In any event, they don't want anything getting in the way of the radio telescopes. So, as of 0200 this morning, the fleet is on radio blackout. All communications from here on in are by message laser only."

"There go the newsfeeds," Ansimov muttered mutinously. "How in Archie's name is anyone going to know what's going on around here?"

Maybe he spoke louder than he'd intended.

"For those of you wondering how life can go on without radio," Chen Lai added, "the answer is more message lasers." Ravi's eyelids twitched under assault from a data packet. "Which means more receiving dishes. Which *means* . . . you lot are going to get your sorry asses out onto the spine and start installing them, stat. Teams and schedules as assigned. Try not to break stuff."

The fact he would still have his precious newsfeeds did nothing to improve Ansimov's mood.

"They've had a hundred and thirty-two years to think about this, and they only figure out they need more message lasers *now?* They should have started installing 'em years ago instead of having us floating around on some insane fire drill."

"Aw, come on," Ravi joshed. "A shift and a half in open space? It'll be great. No classes today—and think about the view. The Milky Way? The Destination Star? You know you love it."

"Sard the view. It's a shift and a half. I want my bunk."

By a shift and a quarter, even Ravi had to concede that the view had lost its allure. He and Ansimov had been working flat-out the whole time, with no time out for meals. Refreshments had consisted of sucking nutrients and water out of tubes whenever a short respite presented itself. The rest of the time was spent in a fuzzy cloud of coding and drones, assembling and bolting and aligning dishes.

He was probably imagining it, but the Destination Star seemed brighter than the last time he'd been outside. Its pale light cast stark shadows on the ice-rimed gantry, throwing the delicate trelliswork of the spine into stark relief. The ice itself broke off in pinkish-brown lumps as the drones cleared it away to make anchor points. The pieces drifted slowly away from the ship, strobing bright and dark as they spun end over end in the starlight.

"Done," Ansimov muttered. Suit radios, to the relief of all, had not been banned. "Last one to the elevator's a LOKI." He unhooked his tether and pulled himself hand over hand through the trellises, a swarm of drones puffing along in his wake. His reckless progress made him uncatchable. He reached the elevator minutes ahead of Ravi—and everyone else, for that matter.

Back in his quarters, Ravi spent longer in the shower than he should have, but he figured he deserved it. Besides, he'd had over fifty liters of free water on *Bohr*, so his account was fuller than usual. He could actually afford it for once.

Washed and changed, he reached out into the hive, looking for Boz.

You there? he messaged. *Call me back. I'm worried about you.*

It was early evening. The hive was popping and crackling with data. But none of it was Boz's. Ravi sighed and headed off to Ansimov's for some real food.

— — —

Sofia had wanted to meet earlier than usual to go over Warren's chemistry assignments, so Ravi had picked the biggest tree in the arboretum to hide under. Even so, the faux Home Star could still be seen blazing between the leaves. Ravi couldn't help himself: he checked his radiation counter.

Sofia was really struggling with clays, and the frightening blue sky had darkened to a more comforting black before she'd finally gotten it. With the coming of darkness, the paths were beginning to fill up with people taking a stroll. Sofia arched her back against the tree trunk to stretch out a muscle. Ravi tried not to stare.

"Why'd you miss class yester-sol?" she asked. "Big job?"

"Chen Lai had us installing message lasers. To compensate for the radio blackout."

"Idiot."

"Say what?" Ravi could feel the heat rising in his face.

"Not you, silly. I'm talking about the cretin who thought shutting down the radios was a good idea. It's, like, a total waste of time. I use the radio telescopes every day, and they can see perfectly well, thank you very much. Always have, always will."

"But the interference . . ."

"Not a problem. There's a whole suite of algorithms designed to filter it out. You could have every radio in the fleet broadcasting at the same time, and the telescopes wouldn't even notice."

Ravi felt himself frowning.

"Then why do it?" He absentmindedly rubbed an ache in his shoulder. "It was a lot of work."

Sofia shrugged apologetically.

"It's my great-uncle. I love him to death; really, I do. But he's just an old fusspot when it comes to stuff like this. Everything has to be 'beyond nominal.'" She raised her fingers in air quotes.

"Then maybe your great-uncle should come outside and 'beyond nominally' bolt on some hardware," Ravi grumbled, though he was smiling just a little. "It'd give him a 'beyond nominal' sense of perspective."

Sofia rewarded him with a giggle.

"It wouldn't do the slightest bit of good. Sure as water is wet, he'd find something to complain about, and demand that it be fixed, like, *immediately*."

Ravi grimaced. Sofia's great-uncle sounded an awful lot like Chen Lai. It took him a moment to realize that Sofia was staring at him, a soft smile playing on her lips.

"Say, Ravi? Can I ask a favor?"

"Of course. Anything." There was a warm feeling in the pit of his stomach.

"Could you show me the drive? Vladimir told me you've been all the way down there, and I'd really like to see it before it's too late. I mean, it's carried us all this way, this amazing distance, and I'd just like to take a look before they fire it up for the last time." She looked wistful. "Something to tell the kids, maybe. You know?"

Ravi did know. The very idea of the drive, its sheer power, its . . . *relentlessness*, had haunted his dreams since childhood. He understood the hold it could have on a person, the magnetism of it, this thing that had so effortlessly hurled them between stars. And yet.

"It's a restricted area. You can't just go down to the engine rooms, Sofe. You need clearances. Access codes. And that's just for the elevator. The rooms themselves are asleep: no air, no heat, which means more clearances to power them up." He shook his head reluctantly. "It can't be done."

"Can't you just ask Chen Lai? Everyone says he really likes you. I'm sure he'd do you a favor."

A small jolt of surprise set Ravi to blinking. The idea that Chen Lai liked *anybody*, let alone him, seemed absurd. He gave Sofia a piercing, slightly distrustful look. She returned his stare with wide-eyed interest, her lips parted in a soft smile. Even if he didn't believe it, she surely did—and Sofia was connected. She would know what she was talking about. He felt suddenly warm and more than a little giddy. Maybe Chen Lai liked him after all. Which was great, he thought soberly. But he was still Chen Lai.

"Chen Lai won't go for it," he said, with genuine regret. "The guy is by-the-book." He looked curiously at Sofia. "Unless your uncle could . . ."

Sofia shook her head with a smile.

"Eugene and Uncle don't get on." Her voice dropped to a conspiratorial whisper. "They both wanted to marry my aunt back in the sol. Eugene lost"—a playful roll of the eyes—"*obviously.*"

Ravi was surprised yet again. The engineer was beginning to sound surprisingly human.

Sofia reached out and placed her hand on his wrist. It was soft, and warm, and it was suddenly difficult for Ravi to think about anything else.

"Surely, there's *some* way? I can't believe a little thing like a trip to the engine rooms is really so difficult. Is it?"

The hand on his wrist was very, *very* warm.

"Let me see what I can do." It was like someone else speaking, from very far away.

"Thank you!" Sofia squealed. "Thank you, thank you, thank you!" She flung her arms around his neck and hugged him. For a moment, it felt to Ravi as if the wheel had stopped spinning.

Sofia stepped back.

"Well," she said. "I guess I'd better get going. Busy day tomorrow. A *lot* of calculations."

She stepped out from under the tree, its leaves black shadows against the night sky, and headed to the path. Ravi stared at her retreating back until a strolling couple blocked it from view.

"*That* was interesting," Boz said.

Ravi practically jumped out of his skin.

"You are totally wrapped around her finger." She seemed more amused than disapproving. She was standing in front of him, hands in pockets, wearing her trademark allegedly leather jacket. In deference to the public nature of the space, there was no cigarette.

"What? Where?" Ravi was painfully aware that he was incoherent, but he couldn't seem to do anything about it. All he could do was grin at her stupidly. Boz sat down on the grass, back against the tree trunk, and made herself comfortable.

"I got your messages about an hour ago." Curious eyes drank in the arboretum crowds. "You and your girlfriend were spilling enough code for a newsfeed channel, so I just followed the breadcrumbs till I found you. Thought I'd give you a surprise."

"Heart attack, more like. And she's not my girlfriend."

Boz raised an eyebrow.

"You sure about that? Mind if I have a go?"

"She's out of your league. Besides, she's spoken for." The words left a sour taste on his tongue. He quickly changed the subject. "Where have you *been?* I've been trying to get hold of you for the best part of a week."

"Australia," Boz said delphically.

"Since you *left* the brig, you gullgroper! I got the message you'd been released, and *poof!* Nothing."

"Australia." The smugness was so thick, you could cut it with a knife. Ravi stared at her in rank disbelief. It took a while for the water to drop from the faucet.

"You were in Officer Country," he said slowly. "Cut off from the hive. That's why I couldn't reach you."

Boz nodded. Her eyes sparkled with excitement.

"I was rotting in the brig, wondering if they could drop me down to Dead Weight without a trial, when the guards tell me I've got visitors." Her voice dropped melodramatically. "What they didn't tell me was the visitors were Commander-Inspector Vasconcelos *and the sarding Chief Navigator!*"

"You're kidding!"

Boz pressed a hand against her chest.

"Honest to Archie, it's true. Anyway, I'm thinking Vasconcelos would recycle me soon as breathe, but what's Niko Ibori doing here? Who needs a navigator for an execution?"

She paused to let the scene sink in.

"So, Vasconcelos asks me how I'd like to have the charges dropped and my crew status upgraded to Satisfactory? Well, who wouldn't? I said yes— like . . . *DUH!* But what's the catch? And then Ibori starts talking, going on and on about needing probes to figure out Destination World and the inner system, and how they need better software, and would I help out with the programming because I'm, well, I'm the best they have."

Boz's expression was distinctly immodest. Ravi was staring at her, mouth agape.

"They *want* you to code?" he asked, scarcely believing his ears. He reached back into his cousin's past. "Aren't you barred from coding jobs? Like forever? Didn't the ombudsman say you were a loose thruster who couldn't be trusted with anything important?"

"What the ombudsman said was that I was a coding genius."

"Whose love of mischief, general disrespect for authority, and three previous convictions precluded you from being trusted with anything important or, in fact, *anything* to do with coding."

"He might also have said that. But bygones are bygones, apparently. Ban's lifted." Boz was literally shaking with excitement. "They really need me. These probes have got to . . ." The words dried up without warning. Boz had raised a hand to her mouth, as if to stop any more coming out.

"These probes have got to what, Boz?"

A small sliver of worry wormed into Ravi's stomach. Vasconcelos was ShipSec, and Niko Ibori didn't know Boz MacLeod from a hole in the hull. They were not friends or family, and they owed her no favors. He could picture his father spitting cynically on the deck. Vasconcelos and Ibori were *officers.* He very much doubted they had Boz's interests at heart.

"*Boz!* What have these people gotten you into?"

"Nothing. Well, *everything*. But nothing bad. This stuff's really, really cool; I just can't talk about it yet. That's why I've been hidden away in Australia. They don't want the stuff I'm doing leaking into the hive, not till everything's in place." She looked far more earnest than usual. She reached out for his forearm, squeezing it in emphasis. "This stuff is important. You'll see."

Ravi took a deep breath and tried to let it go.

"Good for you," he said as cheerfully as he could manage. "Maybe you can stop that mischief-maker on the *Bohr* from hijacking 'em in mid-flight."

"Hijacking what?"

"Probes." Ravi filled her in on the buzzing of the lifeboat, the way the probe had closed to within a hundred klicks before they'd even seen it. But Boz, if anything, looked even more confused than before.

"That can't be right. They haven't even built a hull yet. They're still working on the architecture. And like I said"—she tapped her head—"no software."

"Yeah, well, *Bohr* ShipSec would beg to differ. They told us the probes were up and running. Plus, I *saw* one. Brand-new sensor array, remember?"

Seeing Boz was about to argue, he changed the subject.

"Sard that," he said quickly. "There's more important stuff to talk about." His face, he knew, had become very, very serious. "I need to tell you something—show you something—totally weird." He looked deep in his cousin's eyes, searching for the old Boz.

"Can you still keep a secret?"

The air filters in Boz's Fiji bolt-hole were beginning to fail. Cigarette smoke gathered about the vents in an idle blue cloud, reluctant to move farther. Ravi wondered distractedly if he could patch them up. He gnawed at his lower lip, stopping only when the skin started to split.

Cigarette in one hand and Ravi's retrieved object in the other, Boz tossed the little black sphere into the air. Gauging the low gravity to perfection, she threw it to within centimeters of the ceiling. It drifted down again, far too slowly. An easy catch.

"Well, you can't be completely insane," Boz admitted, frowning. "But I don't see how a drug-addled hallucination can direct you to something as . . . real as this." She tossed the BozBall lookalike again, getting it even closer to the ceiling.

"I'm not drug-addled," Ravi said hotly. "Or insane." Of the latter, though, he was much less certain.

"Well, what, then?" Boz challenged. "There's no girl, is there? She's just a mirage. Girls with, with *dyed hair* don't materialize on flight decks or breathe hard vacuum. And yet you see her—all the time—plain as day-cycle. If it's not insanity and it's not drugs, I don't know what it is." She shook her head in frustration and stared hard at her cousin. "Is it drugs?"

"No!" The denial echoed off the graffiti-daubed walls.

"But it has to be *something*, right?"

Ravi looked down at his feet.

"I've no sarding idea. I've been to the medic, and he didn't find anything wrong except for some inflamed implants. I'm not on drugs, except for the one prescription—which I got for the inflamed implants. All I know for sure is I saw her with that thing"—he pointed at the black ball—"and it was right where she left it when I went to look for it."

Boz took a long drag on her cigarette.

"I have the answer," she said suddenly. Ravi gave her a sharp look. Boz stared back, her expression grave. "You must be psychic," she declaimed. Her voice dropped to a whisper. "The girl's First Crew—has to be, with dyed hair and all. She was horribly murdered by someone's great-great grandmother, and her long-dead ghost wants you to avenge her death."

Just for a moment, Ravi thought Boz was being serious. Then she burst out laughing, peals of merriment bouncing off the graffitied bulkheads.

"It's most likely you're nuts," she said, wiping a tear from her eye.

"Har sarding har."

Boz had moved on. She was peering intently at the BozBall lookalike. Her right eye, Ravi noticed, had the strange glitter that came with enhanced vision. It took him a little longer to realize that she was also dropping bursts of code into the hive, seemingly at random. The bursts disappeared into the data stream, only to return moments later, transmogrified into something very different. A fuzzy, one-way filter of bits and bytes. Data from the hive could come in, but it couldn't go out again. Whatever Boz and Ravi did next, no one would hear them.

Safe from prying tracers, Boz directed a stream of interrogatories at the fake BozBall, trying to find a way in, a way to make it talk. The code was coming so thick and fast, Ravi could barely keep up. The code was inventive and variable, and most amazing of all, she was doing it on the fly. When it came to his cousin and coding, no one in the fleet could touch her.

But she was still not good enough. The fake BozBall just sat there, like some polymer pudding. Code kept bouncing off it, going nowhere. Boz's cigarette died to ash in her hand. She rummaged around in her pocket for another one and lit it up. The cloud of smoke in the room grew thicker.

"Maybe I'm going about this the wrong way," she said, slowly. She turned a thoughtful gaze in Ravi's direction. "Ask it what it wants."

"What?"

"Ask it what it wants. Nothing complicated or threatening. Just ask it what it wants, straight up."

Ravi cleared his throat, feeling like a fool.

"Er . . . what do you want?" he asked.

"In *code*, you idiot!"

Ravi took the time to shoot Boz a vile look. Then he did as she demanded, interrogating the silent sphere on a number of wavelengths.

One of those wavelengths evinced the merest flicker of a response, like the opening of a tiny doorway. Boz pounced, crashing through the entrance with code of her own.

"Got you!" she murmured, followed by, "Hey, little guy, how's it going?"

In answer, the fake BozBall sprouted legs and changed color, switching from black to bright yellow in the blink of an eye. Like someone just out of earshot, Ravi was aware of a stream of data flowing between the little machine and Boz, but he couldn't quite make it out. The fake BozBall backed away a few steps.

"Don't do that," Boz crooned. "We just want to talk, is all. Nothing to worry about." The flow of code eased as she took a long drag on her cigarette. "Now, then. Let's see what you're made of." She reached out a hand, as if to stroke it, the gesture accompanied by a snaking ripple of data.

The drone stiffened on its legs and turned red. A burst of white exploded across Ravi's vision, accompanied by a sharp, stabbing pain in his temple.

"Ow!" he yelled.

Boz didn't hear him. She was too busy screaming. She drifted to the deck, clutching her head in both hands. Ravi stumbled toward her, vision returning, tears streaming from both eyes.

Boz was out cold. The fake BozBall was a ball again, black and passive. It lay on the deck a couple of meters away, looking like just another piece of control-room debris. If someone other than Ravi had happened upon the scene, there was no way they'd have connected it to the unconscious crewman.

Ravi put two fingers against Boz's neck, feeling for a pulse. To his immense relief, he found one without trouble. Moments later, his cousin's eyelids fluttered open.

"Sarding hungary," she breathed. "*That* was a trip!"

"Are you okay?"

"Yeah." Boz rubbed at her temples. "Mostly, anyway." She reached out a hand for Ravi to pull her to her feet. Once upright, she directed a piercing glance in the strange machine's direction. But she was careful not to send it any more code. She fished in her pockets for yet another cigarette. Her legs must have been shaky, because she didn't light up until she'd settled herself into the burned-out remains of a swivel chair. Her face, when she turned to Ravi, was thoughtful.

"I can tell you three things," she said. "First: that thing's complicated. Like seriously put together." To Ravi's surprise, she looked despondent. "It makes BozBall look like a five-year-old's toy. I couldn't code anything like that if I lived to be a hundred. It was like . . . like it was alive, you know? Like it knew what it was. *Who* it was. And second: it definitely didn't want to be talking to the likes of me." She shook her head ruefully. "It made that very clear."

She took another, deep puff of her cigarette. The tip glowed red in the gloomy light of the compartment.

Ravi waited for her to say something, but she didn't. She just sat there in a halo of smoke, lost in thought.

"And?" he prompted, at last.

Boz looked at him blankly.

"And what?"

"You said there were three things. 'The little black ball's real complicated' and 'It doesn't want to talk to me' is only two."

"Oh, yeah." Boz pulled herself together with visible effort. "Thing three: no one on the ship could have made it. *No one.*"

Ravi could feel his heart thudding uncomfortably.

"*Bohr?*" he suggested. "*Chandrasekhar?*"

Boz shook her head.

"I know a couple of gals on *Bohr* who could make something maybe half as good as BozBall," she said, with more than a touch of conceit. "And maybe one guy on *Chandra.* That's it."

"But there's no one else out here. We're literally in the middle of sarding nowhere."

"Not as sarding nowhere as we used to be. In case you haven't noticed, the whole ship is preparing for Braking Day." She stared earnestly into Ravi's eyes. "We're almost there, cuz. Deep space is getting shallower by the millisecond. Once we fall in-system? Who knows what's waiting for us."

"Not *aliens,* for sard's sake," Ravi scoffed. Or, at least, he tried to. The blonde girl and her crooked smile floated across his mind's eye. "Nav has been staring at the Destination Star for a hundred and thirty-two years—and the LOKIs were looking for fifty years before that. Nobody's seen a thing."

Boz raised her hands in an I-don't-want-to-fight kind of gesture.

"I'm just saying. You got a better explanation?"

"Yeah. There are thirty thousand crewmen in the fleet. And *one* of them is a lot better at coding than you are."

But the image of the blonde girl wouldn't quite go away.

— — —

If he hadn't been so worried about the fake BozBall, Ravi would have been more than a little pleased with himself. Conscious of her shiny new Satisfactory rating, Boz had refused to help him worm his way into the engine rooms. But that hadn't stopped her from telling him—hypothetically, of course—how such a thing might be done. With a series of fake permissions buried in an unused section of the engineering logs, everything he needed to get all the way to the drive and back again was in place. It had taken several heart-pounding evenings of hacking to get it done, and he'd nearly been caught by the security software Boz had tried to warn him about. But, in the end, he'd managed it. Everything was set. He should be feeling triumphant. Or guilty. Or both.

Instead, all he could do was worry about the black sphere at the bottom of his space chest. The fact it had knocked Boz out cold showed it was potentially dangerous. But short of giving her a thumping headache, it hadn't actually done any lasting harm. And when all was said and done, it was only defending itself against an attempted hacking. Once Boz had stopped, it had reverted to type: a bland, unremarkable ball of nothing. All it seemed to do was sit there.

But Ravi had locked it inside a sealed, armor-plated box just to be safe. Then, MacLeod that he was, he'd taken the armor-plated box and rigged it to a makeshift alarm, just to be safer. He should report it, he knew. But not yet. Not until he could find out more about it. Not until he could come up with a better story than "I had this really weird dream, activated an inspection drone, and found it." He did *not* want to be carted off to Psych. Or the brig.

It was late, and he was floating in darkness at the aft end of the hubs. Full night-cycle had just kicked in, and the very few lights between Ghana and the boat elevators had mostly winked out, hiding the scarred, sloping walls at the bottom of the ship. He could feel the cold reaching out to him from long-dead Hungary, though. Hear the arthritic creak of Ghana's slow turns, like a groaning of ghosts. Ravi suppressed a shiver. The ship was *old*. Even with a Chen Lai running the show, she wouldn't last forever. Sooner or later, something that couldn't be fixed would break, like *Bohr*'s hydroponics. They were reaching the Destination Star just in time . . .

"I can do it better," Ravi was saying. His chin jutted forward in stubborn deter-mination. "A machine is never going to figure it out. It's too chaotic. You need more feel."

He was strapped down to a couch, he realized, surrounded by a wall of moni-tors. Just beyond the corner of his eye, someone was shuffling around, emitting a tuneless whistle. The whistling stopped.

"You don't have the horsepower," the unseen person objected. "You can have all the *feel* in the world; it won't mean anything if you can't process the inputs."

"The machine can do that for me. I just need *control*."

There was a long pause.

"Maybe," the voice said, at last. "Maybe . . ."

His eyelid twitched under a clumsy load of data, bringing him back to the here and now. Sofia was looking for him. He responded with the cyber-netic equivalent of a wave while struggling to get his panicky breathing under control. *I'm not mad,* he told himself, fiercely. *I'm not mad. . . .*

Sofia's shadowed silhouette was drifting in toward him. He anchored himself to a handhold and grabbed her by the arm to stop her overshooting.

"Thanks," she said breathlessly. Even in the darkness, he could see the glitter of excitement in her eyes. "Are we good to go?" Her whole body was trembling with anticipation. Ravi struggled painfully to ignore it.

"Yes," he said, managing to keep his voice businesslike. He pointed to a series of handholds built into the wall, some original, some replaced after the meteoroid strike. "This way."

The handholds led to a little-used airlock. Even though he'd followed Boz's hacking instructions to the letter, Ravi was still relieved to discover that the airlock was expecting them. It cycled open in response to a short burst of code. Moments later, they were floating into an elevator. Sofia looked around appreciatively.

"This is definitely old-school."

"It's the express car to the engine rooms. It's basically unchanged since Launch Day."

Sofia ran a thoughtful hand over the old bronze plaque with the ship's logo. The design had become simpler over the years. Easier to make. More plain. This was the original in all its baroque, curlicued glory.

"Cool," she murmured.

The elevator set off with a soft shudder. The gentle acceleration set them drifting toward the ceiling.

"How long will it take?" Sofia asked.

"About an hour." He shrugged his shoulders. "It's a long way."

Code washed up against his implants as Sofia probed her surroundings. He laid a warning hand on her arm.

"Don't. We're not meant to be here, remember? Best not to leave a trail."

Sofia pouted but did as she was told. With nothing to code, download, or analyze, her fingers drummed an impatient tattoo against a safety rail.

"You're right," she said, with mock despair. "It's going to be a *long* trip."

Ravi grinned. In fact, the trip seemed to take no time at all. His stomach behaved itself for once, and Sofia chatted up a storm the whole way down. Only when the elevator began to brake did she fall silent. The elevator came to a halt, latching on to the engine rooms with a soft *thunk*.

This time, Ravi waited until the rooms had warmed up before cycling the airlock. They floated in through the ceiling, looking "down" on the circular console and its five chairs. The space was still cool but not uncomfortable. There was no sign of any ice.

"This is the auxiliary control room. When it's running, the drive is operated from Engineering, but we have people down here to keep an eye on things in case something goes wrong."

Sofia looked around with wide, curious eyes. The control room was like the elevator: vintage. It was full of quaint touches long since abandoned in the more lived-in parts of the ship. She glided down to one of the seats and strapped herself in, letting her slim fingers run over the controls.

"I wonder what it felt like," she mused, "to be sitting here on Launch Day." She spread her palms out against the console, her face vibrant. "You know? To feel the drive firing under your feet for the very first time? To start a journey you would never see the end of?"

Ravi said nothing, imagining instead the slow, building rumble of engine thrust. The way the vast bulk of the ship would have shifted only reluctantly under the awesome assault of energy, moving from slower than a walk to tens of thousands of kilometers per second under months of ceaseless, unrelenting pressure.

Followed by shutdown. By decades of silence. He drew a deep, tremulous breath, overwhelmed by it all.

"What about radiation?" Sofia asked. "Is there extra shielding down here?"

"Yes. But only in the control room. The rest of the compartments are only used when the drive is off, for maintenance and inspections, that kind of stuff." He gave a wry smile. "You do *not* want to be in there when the drive fires up."

Pushing off from the nearest bulkhead, he floated across to a heavy-looking hatch on the other side of the room and opened it.

"This way. Let's see what there is to see."

He led her through the rest of the space, mostly storage with racks of spares and various sorts of specialized drones. He swallowed hard when they reached the external airlock, half-expecting to see the blonde girl waving at him through the porthole again, but nothing happened. Sofia took it all in in respectful silence, asking questions when she had to but mostly just listening to what Ravi had to say, which was far more than he'd intended. He found himself talking about the drive, and how it worked, and its various pipes and valves and nooks and crannies with an almost lyrical intensity. Sofia hung on his every rushed word.

It was intoxicating.

"Last stop," he said. He double-checked the specs in his mind's eye, projecting them against the bulkhead in front of him. He floated up to where the bulkhead met the ceiling and peered through the grill of an air filter. He put a hand against it and smiled. It was warm.

"What are you doing?"

"Just wait," he said delphically. He wedged himself between ceiling and wall so he wouldn't spin, pulled out his screwdriver, and disconnected the filter. A sharp tug was enough to get it loose. He left it hanging in the air, a floating box of tissue-thin membranes.

"Come on up," he suggested with a wave of his hand. Sofia drifted across to join him. She peered into the dark hole left behind by the filter.

"So, what am I looking at?"

"Put your hand in," Ravi whispered. "Far as it'll go."

For a moment, Sofia looked hesitant, as if expecting an unpleasant trick. Ravi grinned at her and thrust his hand in first. With an expression somewhere between curiosity and a grimace, Sofia followed his lead. Her eyes widened in surprise.

"Feel that?" Ravi asked. It was an unnecessary question. She was feeling exactly what he was. Her hand was beside his, pressed against the far side of the air vent. The surface was almost hot, and he could feel a faint tremble of vibration against his fingertips.

"What is it?" Sofia's voice was soft, almost reverential.

"The drive. It's never really off, only asleep. The reactors rumble away with nothing to do, and the excess energy is bled off as a power supply." He tapped the far side of the vent with a fingernail, striking a hollow echo. "This is the closest you can get to it from inside the ship—from anywhere, really. The Q-seventy-six sub-coil—the plumbing, basically—is just a few centimeters away."

"Isn't it dangerous?" Sofia did not, however, move her hand away.

"No. It's just a tiny slice of energy and plenty well shielded. At least until you fire up the drive for real. Like I said before, you don't want to be anywhere near here when she cuts loose." He gave her a cheerful grin, the trainee engineer in his element. "To be honest, we're more of a danger to the drive than the drive is to us. The shielding isn't very thick here, so if we stove it in or something like that, we'd damage the piping on the other side and the drive wouldn't like that at all. She'd shut down completely and it would take us months to start her up again."

He would have said more, but something very odd was happening.

He was falling. Slowly, to be sure, but falling nonetheless. So was Sofia. She looked over at him, suddenly alarmed.

This can't be happening, he thought. *We're not in a habitat wheel. There's nothing spinning and no gravity. How can I be falling?*

Flashing red script scrolled across his vision. Sofia gasped in alarm.

"The control room!" Ravi snapped. "Now."

The data burned at the inside of his eyelids, stark and uncompromising. The compartment was awash in radiation. Not yet lethal but climbing rapidly. They scrambled into the control room, the hatch slamming shut behind them.

"What's going on?" Sofia asked.

Ravi's brain orbited the question in rapid, panicky circles. Radiation and the sudden onset of gravity could mean only one thing, but he didn't want to say it.

"*Ravi!*" Sofia screamed. "What is it?"

He licked suddenly dry lips.

"The drive is on. It shouldn't be, but it is."

his makes no sense," Sofia said. Safe inside the control room, her alarm had transmogrified into irritation. "It's not *time* to fire up the drive. Uncle hasn't signed off on the calculations, nothing's been secured for thrust, and the sarding ship is *pointing the wrong way!"*

Ravi looked at her sharply. She was right, of course. The front of the ship was still aimed at the Destination Star. Turning on the drive would simply make the ship move faster. She was speeding up, when the whole point of Braking Day was to slow down. It made no sense.

And yet it was happening. Sofia was *standing* on the deck. The force the drive was exerting was very weak, but it was strong enough to hold her down. So long as she didn't wave her arms about, anyway, which is what she was doing now. The motion dragged her off her feet in the direction of the ceiling.

"Archie's hooks!" she muttered.

Ravi half-floated, half-fell into a couch. The console in front of him was part of a backup control system, designed to operate independently if something went wrong on the flight deck. It took only the flicking of a few switches to cut it off from the hive entirely. Anonymity protected, he grabbed a data jack and plugged himself in. Bits and bytes flooded through his implants, swamping his biological senses. It was as if he was floating inside the drive itself, surrounded by swirls of white-hot energy.

Part of him was terrified, the other part exhilarated. He wasn't ready for this, he knew. He didn't have the training. He was blinded by light, deafened by the raw output of power. But he needed to understand. Preferably without blowing out his implants.

Even though he felt outside of it, he made his body take slow, deep breaths. He forced his mind to make sense of what it was seeing, to remember it was just data, just a simulation. Slowly, through the sheer exercise of will, the light became a little less blinding, the noise more manageable. Patterns began to emerge. Flow and counter-flow, eddies and weirs, valve gates and choke points. A seething river of energy trammeled by banks, and dams and channels. Except in one place. An overflow pipe. A sluice gate in the dam. Energy, errant and angry and curious, had found it and was pouring through, screaming its rage into the blackness beyond.

From somewhere out of sight, behind him maybe, a small, distant voice. Worried.

"Ravi? You okay?"

With groaning effort, Ravi choked off the flow of data until he could dimly see and hear the world around him. He reached around to the back of his neck and disconnected the jack. The sudden silence was deafening.

Sofia was staring at him, her face pinched. She gave him a weak smile.

"You looked like your head was going to explode," she said, her voice heavy with relief.

"It felt like it," Ravi admitted. "Next time, I'll just fire up the monitors. Do it the old-fashioned way."

"Was it worth it, at least? Did you find anything out?"

"Yes." He didn't bother to hide his mystification. "The drive is firing, all right. But barely. That's why the gravity's so low."

It was Sofia's turn to look puzzled.

"How's that possible? I thought the drive was either on or off. All the nav calculations have been done assuming a single number for thrust." She looked mildly put out. "You could get a lot more creative with a variable."

Ravi shrugged.

"The drive *is* designed to be on or off. When you're blasting zillions of tonnes of starship across twelve point four light-years' worth of interstellar space, you don't really need to be subtle. But even though we call it 'the drive,' it's really nine thrusters bundled together. Mechanically, each one of them is independent. It's the software that links them together. Rewrite the software, and each thruster could take on a life of its own." He looked carefully at Sofia, to make sure she was following him. "Right now, one is on, eight are off." He laid a careful hand on the console. There was no hint of vibration. "You know what? If you were up in the wheels, you might not even notice. Even in the hubs, you might just think you'd overcompensated or something. As thrust goes, it's pretty pathetic."

"Are the thrusters all the same size?"

Ravi nodded.

"Then why are they doing this? What's the point? Burning fuel just for the hungary of it? The math makes no sense! They make us go a tiny bit faster only to have us slow down again on Braking Day?" She sat down on the edge of a couch, suddenly disconsolate. "This whole thing is sarded up."

"You know what else is sarded up? Whoever's doing this is doing it in secret."

Sofia threw him a sharp look.

"Think about it. This isn't like turning on a light. You can't just press a button and *ta-da!* the drive is on. There are interlocks, systems to prevent an accidental firing. The whole thing is surrounded by protocols and proce-dures. There are simulations, and tests, and warmups, and warm downs, and launch teams, and committees, and warnings to the crew, *and none of that has happened!* Almost no one knows this is going on. Except us. And we're not meant to be here."

Sofia looked thoughtful.

"Could we have done this? You know, by accident? Like you say, we're not meant to be here. Is it possible we tripped a switch or something?"

"No," Ravi said patiently. "Interlocks, remember? You can't just turn the drive on. There are too many safeguards. You could do a crash startup in an emergency, but even then, you'd need three officers, with three separate keys, to access the system simultaneously." He shook his head firmly. "This has nothing to do with us."

Sofia stared up at the ceiling, as if she could see through it to the icy ki-lometers of gantry on the other side.

"Uncle must know about this," she said quietly. "And the Captain." She sprang up again, agitated, and flew off the deck. She had to brace herself against the ceiling to get back down. "But why would they do it? This is just . . . just *stupid.*"

"What about BonVoys?"

Sofia was staring at him like he had two heads.

"It makes sense," Ravi insisted. "Isn't the whole point of being a Bon Voyager for the journey to go on forever? Maybe they hacked the drive. Maybe they want us to go so fast, we can't slow down in time to make plan-etfall. Or maybe they want to burn off so much fuel, there isn't enough left for braking."

Sofia shook her head.

"The BonVoys I know would tell you that the whole point of being one is to protect an innocent world from people. Not stopping is one way, sure, but it's not the only way. And if they're clever enough to hack the drive,

which they are, they're clever enough to know this is never going to work."
She pointed emphatically at the ceiling. "Sooner or later, someone up there
is going to wake up and realize something is wrong. They can't accelerate
the ship fast enough or burn enough fuel to make a blind bit of difference
before that happens. If this is a BonVoy plan, it's the worst plan ever, which
means it can't be BonVoys. But I've got no clue what the Captain thinks she's
doing. This whole thing is . . . pointless."

Ravi wanted to argue with her, but Sofia was right. Any BonVoy smart
enough to hack the drive would be smart enough to know it wasn't worth
the effort. He opened the airlock in the ceiling with a quick burst of code.

"Time to go."

There was a retractable ladder folded into the ceiling by the airlock door,
clearly meant to be used when the ship was under thrust. But the gravity was
so weak, it wasn't worth the effort.

Sofia made to jump up and then stopped.

"The radiation," she asked. "Is it safe?"

"Totally. The elevator's designed for this. It's even better shielded than
the control room. Your radiation alarm won't even twitch." He jumped
ahead of her, soaring effortlessly through the hatch. "Whatever's going on,"
he said, "we won't find the answer down here."

19.0

The plate and its colorful decoration had been crushed and warped into an irregular triangle of green, unfolded, like origami, into a vast, poisonous lawn.

The man was there, in his long coat, and buckled shoes, and enormous white wig. Except it wasn't the man somehow; it was the girl. She was sitting under a tree. An apple fell from the fruited leaves, dropping softly into the girl's hand. The girl laughed and rolled the apple across the poisoned lawn, which suddenly became grass. It rolled to a stop against the leg of a bathtub. A bathtub that, even in the black-and-white movies, would have been old-fashioned. The bathtub was filled with a king's ransom of warm, soapy water that slopped over the side because he was *sitting* in it. He tried desperately to get up, to stop the precious liquid from overflowing, but he couldn't seem to manage it. And the harder he tried, the faster it flooded over the edge. And now the girl was at the side of the bath, leaning over him, a familiar, slightly crooked smile playing on her lips. Her strange accent was crystal-clear.

"We need your help," she said.

But he was naked in the bath and needed to cover himself up. . . .

He was sitting upright in his bunk, breathing heavily, a slight sheen of sweat on his forehead. It was pitch-black.

"Lights," he said, using his voice just to be safe. But there was no headache. The prescription was doing its work—finally. He thought about going back to sleep, but it was 0527. His implants were about to wake him up anyway. He stepped into the shower and watched the curved path of steaming water as it made its way down to the recycler. Half-dozing in the moist warmth, he thought about shower scenes in the Homeworld movies and the unnatural way that water fell to the ground, as if all it wanted to do was drop straight down with the least amount of effort. Planetary gravity, he supposed. Homeworlders didn't need a spinning wheel to keep their feet on the deck.

Gravity. He snapped awake as surely as if the shower had turned cold. There was a gravity meter a little way down the corridor outside. He reached out into the hive until he found it. It was reading 1.003 g, boring and normal. He dug a little deeper, running an engineering diagnostic, digging up more-nuanced data about force vectors. Also boring and normal. There was nothing even slightly off. No outside acceleration to throw the readings off kilter. The only thing acting on the sensors was Ecuador's slow, endless rotation. Whoever had activated the drive in the middle of the night-cycle must have shut it down again.

Or had Chen Lai put a stop to it?

But if Chen Lai knew anything about the drive, he wasn't saying. Ravi even broached the subject at the end of trainee briefing, asking if there were any thrust tests scheduled, only to be met with a blank stare and a curt no. His classmates seemed equally ignorant. Unable to tell them what he'd been up to the previous evening, Ravi had tiptoed up to the subject sideways. But once he did so, no one he spoke to admitted to feeling anything unusual. And then, when Ansimov flat-out asked him why he was so interested, he'd had to let the matter drop.

In the arboretum that evening, neither he nor Sofia could concentrate on schoolwork. They huddled under a tree, waiting for the evil eye of the Home Star to set.

"No one in Nav knows anything about it," Sofia muttered. "Or they're not telling. I asked Uncle straight out—"

"You did *what?*"

"—and he said it was news to him, but he would look into it. He said Engineering might have been having an issue with one of the thrusters."

"If that's true, nobody told us."

"I'll tell you something else. The ship isn't pointing in the same direction it was yester-sol morning. Either firing on one thruster pushed her off-axis, or someone turned the ship through about thirty degrees." She gave him an amused smile. "We're kinda traveling sideways."

"What about the shield?" Forward of Australia, the shield was a two-thousand-meter-wide disc of super-dense, impact-resistant polymer. It was meant to protect them from ship-killing meteoroids. So long as it was in front of them.

Sofia's smile disappeared.

"I didn't think about that." She looked more than a little worried. "The ship's got to be exposed. Most of it, anyway."

Ravi's mind flashed to long-dead Hungary and its plated-over spokes.

And that was with the shield in place. He could almost feel the dust particles ripping through the hull. The blasts of flame and decompression.

"We've got to tell someone," he said.

Sofia just laughed at him, the sound mixing with the rustling of leaves overhead.

"You think you can turn the ship through thirty degrees and the navigators wouldn't *notice*?" She had to catch her breath for a moment. "*Everybody noticed!* Their instruments were pointed the wrong way! You think they're blind?"

"So, what did 'everybody' have to say about it?" Ravi demanded, not the least bit amused.

Sofia managed to look serious.

"Uncle said the ship had been turned to get a better look at the surrounding space, in case we needed to come up with alternative trajectories."

"And people bought that?"

Sofia nodded.

"It's probably true. This is a *very* dirty system we're dropping into. Uncle will want as many options as possible."

Hurtling into a dirty system unshielded didn't strike Ravi as very sensible. "Someone's risking an awful lot of lives for a look-see."

"I'm sure the Captain knows what she's doing."

"Sure." Ravi didn't push it. He watched the fake Home Star set below the fake horizon instead.

▬ ▬ ▬

"You have got to be kidding!" Ravi hissed, staring under the table at Boz-Ball. "Why haven't you destroyed it already?"

Nursing a bottle of the cheap beer that made Abell 386 a favorite MacLeod hangout, Boz was fishing in her pockets for a pack of cigarettes and failing miserably. BozBall, now a muted and inconspicuous gray, lay silently at her feet. Twentieth-century music, a vain attempt to add a touch of class, blared out of period-looking speakers, masking their conversation.

"Sard it," Boz muttered. "Must have left 'em in my quarters." She peered mischievously at Ravi. "Why would I destroy it? At least *my* piece of forbidden tech is home-grown. Who knows where yours came from?"

Ravi pictured the black sphere locked in an armor-plated box at the bottom of his space chest, and winced. But he refused to back down.

"I'm not the one flirting with Dead Weight," he pointed out.

"Neither am I. I'm Satisfactory now, remember? I have room for a screwup or two—and no curfew."

"Boz! Ravi!" Uncle Torquil yelled from a neighboring table. "Shut the sard up!" He lurched to his feet, clearly the worse for wear. "I want to say something!"

Boz and Ravi did as they were told, as did half the tables in the place, populated as they were by members of the family. Ravi stole a quick glance at his mother, who was sitting immediately to Torquil's left. Her eyes were unnaturally bright. "To Ramesh MacLeod," Torquil said, raising a bottle. "The best brother a man could hope to have. He sarded nobody that didn't deserve it, and nobody sarded him." Torquil paused, frowning. "'Cepting the officers, of course. Who sarded him real good. And for what? Trading merchandise acquired through . . . *entrepreneurial* hard work, that's what!"

"And decking a lieutenant," Ravi and Boz murmured together.

". . . and decking a lieutenant," Torquil added. "Who deserved everything he got!"

A quiet tear was sliding down his mother's face.

"Happy birthday, brother," Torquil finished. "The bastards may have mulched you, but we'll remember you forever! To Ramesh MacLeod!"

"To Ramesh MacLeod!" the family yelled. If some of the other tables looked distinctly uncomfortable, not a single MacLeod gave a broken circuit. Uncle Torquil sat down to thumping applause. Ravi's mother threw him a brittle smile and touched his sleeve in apparent appreciation.

She hated this whole thing, Ravi knew. But the family insisted. To them, his dad was some kind of under-deck hero. But Ravi and his mom knew Ramesh MacLeod for what he truly was. A sly, opportunistic crook who would still be with them if he could have kept to the circular. Stupid bastard. Stupid, *selfish* bastard.

He cut himself on a blade-sharp memory: flying along on his dad's shoulders, laughing high and reckless as they weaved through the corridors.

He took a slow swig of his beer.

"If they find you with that thing," he told Boz sternly, "they'll bust you back down so fast, your head will spin." He failed to keep the worry off his face. "And then they'll mulch you."

Boz just grinned.

"No way. I'm too important to them. They need me." Her eyes were alight with excitement. "You know my . . . *encounter* with your little black bot?"

Ravi nodded, remembering how pale and fragile Boz looked after it had knocked her out cold.

"Its software is . . . different. It got me to thinking about a different way to code. More like what I saw when I hacked into it. And before it hacked into *me*." Boz was bouncing in her seat now, barely able to contain herself. "I think I've cracked it, Ravi. The coding problem with the probes. If I'm right—and I am—we can hit every spec on the navigators' wish list and then some."

Boz's joy was infectious. Ravi found himself grinning alongside her.

"Way to go, cuz." His grin evaporated into a sigh. "Maybe when you're done with the probes, you could code me back to sanity."

Boz looked concerned.

"More crazy hallucinations?"

"And dreams. They're getting nuttier by the sol. If I'm not unglued already, I'm getting there fast." He told Boz about the latest installment, right the way through to being naked in a bathtub. Boz being Boz, he thought she would laugh at that, but she didn't. She was staring at him curiously.

"Do you ever look at the ship's logo?" she asked him. "Not the modern one: the old-style, First Crew version?"

"Sure. They're all over the place if you know where to look. The engine rooms elevator, the . . ."

Boz cut him off with an impatient wave of the hand.

"And what's it a picture of?"

"No idea," Ravi shrugged. "It's just a lot of curvy lines. The modern one's a lot cleaner-looking."

There was a mischievous smile tugging at the corner of Boz's mouth.

"You've lived on this ship your whole life, *and you don't know what our logo is?*"

"Like I said. It's a bunch of lines. If they're super-curvy, it's old. If they're straighter, they're new. End of story."

"You are such a sarding engineer," Boz laughed. "Head's so far up your own ass with equations and repair schedules, you can't see what's right in front of your nose. Except, maybe, more of your ass."

"So, enlighten me, O Wise One."

"Our ship," Boz said with exaggerated slowness, "is the ISV-one *Archimedes*. Its logo is *a man sitting in a bath.*"

Ravi just stared at his cousin, blinking slowly. And feeling like a complete idiot. *Of course it is,* he realized. Now that Boz had said it, the stylized lines he'd been staring at since the day he was born suddenly made sense.

Boz's smile had turned wry.

"The fleet's three ships are named after important pre-LOKI physicists," she reminded him, "Archimedes being far and away the most ancient of the lot. There's a famous but probably made-up story about him, involving a royal crown that was meant to be made of gold. The king suspected that it wasn't and wanted Archimedes to find out for sure. It was a crown, so he couldn't melt it down or cut it up for testing or anything like that. He knew what it weighed, of course, and he knew the volume of pure gold he needed for the same weight. What he didn't know was the volume of the crown. It was ornate and complex, and he hadn't a clue how to measure it, and the king was getting impatient.

"But Archimedes lived on the Homeworld, remember. He apparently had more water than he knew what to do with." Even though she was telling the story, it was clear from Boz's tone that this was the bit she believed the least. "Anyway," she continued, "because Archimedes was a zillionaire, he could literally sit in a giant tub of water to get himself clean. And he put so much in that when he hopped in himself, some of it slopped over the side." She shuddered at the thought. "It was then that he realized the volume of the water he displaced was equal to the volume of his body in the bath. He could do the same thing with the crown: put the crown in a container filled to the brim with water and measure the volume of water that slopped over the edge. He was so excited at solving the problem, he got out of the bath and ran through the streets, shouting '*Eureka!*' which means 'I have found it!' in whatever his native language was." Boz's expression became positively wicked. "In fact, he was so excited, he forgot to put his clothes on first."

"No way!"

"Yeah, well, it probably didn't happen. But the point is, the story's been around for literally thousands of years, and it's why the ship's logo is a man in a bath." She allowed herself a smug chuckle. "Not a lot of people know that."

"I never really thought about it," Ravi said, staring at the deck. He looked up again, frowning. "But what does it mean? Why, in Archie's name, would I be dreaming about being part of a logo I never even knew about?"

Boz fumbled once again for her missing cigarettes and swore softly.

"Let's take a real big leap and assume you're not crazy." Her fingers drummed a nervous tattoo on the tabletop. "And let's take an even bigger leap and assume your discovery of the little black drone wasn't some insane coincidence. Which means someone *wanted* you to find that device. Which means your dreams aren't dreams, and your hallucinations aren't hallucinations. They're messages."

Ravi's heart thudded heavily against his ribs.

"Messages from whom? And why don't they make sense?"

"Let's not worry about who's sending them. Let's see if we can figure out what they're trying to say."

Ravi remembered the woman's accented words, repeated more than once.

"She said she needs my help." He thumped the table in frustration. "But I don't know how or why or where."

"We need to take this slowly," Boz suggested. "Treat it like a coding problem. Let's start with what we know. In the dream, you are the man in the bath. The ship's logo is a man in a bath, so our blonde gal is connecting you with the ship."

"If you say so."

"Do you have a better idea?"

He meekly shook his head. His cousin, at least, was *trying,* which was more than he was.

"So, what does the girl represent?" Boz asked, more to herself than Ravi. "Someone old? No one's dyed their hair since First Crew, but they've been in the recycler for decades. Second Gen, maybe?" Even as she said it, though, she was shaking her head.

Ravi shook his head, too. For the same reason. The math didn't work.

"She'd have to be at least a hundred and seven," he pointed out. "It's not possible."

"Waivers, maybe?"

Ravi shook his head again.

"Everyone turns Dead Weight at seventy-five. Even with waivers, I've never heard of anyone making it past eighty." An old lesson floated unexpectedly to the top of his head. "Come to think of it, wasn't it Second Gen that made the rule in the first place? Crew numbers were totally out of whack back then, and it was, like, the most humane way of stopping the support systems from crashing." He found the sudden influx of knowledge perversely pleasing. "I don't know much history, but I know *that*. If anyone from Second Gen was still with us, it'd be all over the newsfeeds."

"Fair point." Boz took a thoughtful gnaw at her bottom lip. "Forget about the dyed hair. What else about her? You said in the dream she was wearing old-time clothes, not fatigues?"

Ravi nodded.

"How old-time?"

"I've no idea. *Old*. Pre-LOKI for sure. Maybe even pre-industrial."

Boz raised a skeptical eyebrow.

"Well, how the hungary would I know?" Ravi exclaimed, more frustrated than anything else. "When did they stop wearing giant sarding wigs? When did they *start* wearing giant sarding wigs? I'm not a historian, am I?"

"No," Boz said, with a soft smile. "What you are is a fan of old Homeworld movies. Have you seen any where they wear stuff like that?"

"I'm not sure. Maybe? *Yes*." He brightened considerably. "Let's access the movie library. Now I think about it, there's a ton of 'em." He fastened a key and flashed it over to Boz. "You'd better come in."

Boz crowded into his head, watching, as he reached out into the hive and looked for movies with really big wigs. It didn't take long.

"*Amadeus*," he breathed. "*The Three Musketeers. The Draftsman's Contract*."

"*Saucy*," Boz giggled, racing him through the images. The giggle was echoey, coming from both inside and outside of Ravi's skull at the same time.

Ravi ignored it, trying to find links between the movies and actual Homeworld history. Normally, history put him to sleep, but this was kind of interesting.

"Okay," he said after a while, "we're talking the seventeen hundreds for sure, and maybe the sixteen hundreds. There aren't wigs before then, and after that they're too small—and mostly worn by lawyers."

"*Lawyers?*" Even though she was laughing, Boz sounded faintly shocked. "In Archie's name, *why?*"

"No idea. The point is, our girl is dressed in stuff that's beyond ancient."

"And from . . ." Boz hesitated, scrambling to find the name. "From *Europe*. That should help too."

"I don't see how. What's some long-recycled gal from . . . *Europe* got to do with what's going on here and now?"

"It's got to be *something*. Whatever's going on in your head isn't random. We *know* that."

"Yeah, well, it's got nothing to do with ships' logos. I may not have been able to recognize a man in a bath, but *Bohr*'s is easy. It's an old-style atomic nucleus with a bunch of electrons whirling around it. And *Chandrasekhar*'s is—"

"Totally boring," Boz interjected.

"A white dwarf orbiting a black hole. Neither of which has anything to do with a giant Europian wig."

They were interrupted by a sharp *click* from the deck. BozBall had shot out a couple of legs, as if it needed to steady itself.

"That's odd," Boz said.

Ravi wasn't listening. BozBall was trying not to roll—and he had a shrewd idea as to why. He reached out to the hive. Somewhere nearby, there ought to be a working gravity meter. It took a while, but he found one, a couple of decks down. It took much less than a while to discover the readings were off kilter.

"We're accelerating again," he told Boz. "Just like last night."

"Last night? What are you talking about?"

"When Sofia and I were in the engine rooms, the drive came on—part of the drive, anyway. It's happening again, right now. The ship is under power. It's real gentle, but it's there."

He laid a hand against the scratched surface of the table, hoping to sense some kind of vibration. But his hand, threaded with forty-eight named nerves and upgraded by implants, was no match for BozBall's sense of balance. He couldn't feel a thing, just the thumping bass of a Steel Age orchestra called Nirvana.

I 'm telling you," Ravi insisted, slumped, as usual at the back of the class. "Someone is firing the drive—part of the drive—every night-cycle."

"Yeah, right." Ansimov, it was clear, was not in the mood to be taken for a fool.

"I'm serious."

"Sure you are." Ansimov broke into a grin. "I don't know what you're trying to pull, Rav, but it's not going to work."

Professor Warren entered the room, ending the discussion.

After class, and on the way to the engineering briefing, Ravi was going to have another go at him. Before he could bring the subject up again, however, a heavy, gloved hand landed on his shoulder.

"If you'll come with me please, Midshipman."

Ravi found himself staring into the eyes of a ShipSec officer, an older type with iron-gray hair and a professionally neutral expression. Ravi tried valiantly to ignore the sudden lump in his throat.

"Am I under arrest?" he asked, trying to keep his voice light.

"Do you want to be?"

Conscious that half his classmates were staring at him, Ravi shook his head. The faintest of smiles flitted across the officer's face.

"Then this way, Middy. If you would."

The press of engineers and other trainees moved hurriedly aside, as if Ravi's sudden trouble was contagious.

"Bound to happen," Hiroji Menendez said, making sure Ravi could hear him. "He's a MacLeod, after all."

"Hey, Hiroji," Ansimov shot back. "How's Willem? Brig treating him well?" Ravi was gratified to hear a couple of snickers in response. He kept his eyes resolutely to the front.

The local ShipSec office was halfway around the wheel and five decks up. By the time they got there, Ravi was breathing hard. Even at full gravity, the officer was a fast walker and clearly not minded to give him a break. Determined not to show weakness, Ravi had matched him step for step, but now he was paying for it. He could feel the faint sheen of perspiration on his forehead, the quickened pace of his heart. There was more to his condition than too much exercise, however. He was about to step into a ShipSec compartment under guard. He took a deep breath and stepped through the hatch . . .

He was curled up tight on the deck, but the boot still found its way into his stomach.

"Freak!" the voice was shouting. "You don't belong here! Get back to the lab! You're a *freak!*" The boot landed again. Ravi wanted to scream in pain, but he was too busy gasping for breath.

"Get off her!" a voice roared. Older. Male. "Or I'll jinting well kill you myself! *Git!*"

Ravi's mother was looking down at him, pistol in hand. His lined face was a mixture of anger and concern.

"You okay?" he asked. Strong arms hauled Ravi to his feet.

Ravi buried his face in his mother's chest and bawled his eyes out.

"Why won't they leave me alone?" he cried. "I'm just as human as everyone else." He looked up at his mother, seeking reassurance. "I am, aren't I?" His voice was querulous. Insecure.

His mother hugged him with a bone-crushing ferocity.

"Course you are, lass . . ."

"You okay, Middy?"

The ShipSec officer was looking at him strangely. Probably because he was frozen in place, one foot on either side of the hatch.

"Yes," Ravi replied, his voice shaky. He passed across the threshold. "Totally."

With a raised eyebrow, the officer escorted him past the reception counter and into a tiny office. There was just enough room for a desk and two chairs. The fact that one of those chairs was already occupied only increased his sense of foreboding.

"Good afternoon, Middy. Sit. Please."

Commander-Inspector Vasconcelos was all smiles. According to Boz, that was never a good sign.

Trying to keep his knees from buckling, Ravi did as he was told.

"Thank you for coming," Vasconcelos said graciously. "I know you're very busy."

Ravi shot a surprised glance in the direction of the now-departed ShipSec officer.

I didn't think I had a choice.

He didn't have the nerve, however, to say it out loud. Vasconcelos, meanwhile, was giving him an appraising look.

"So, Midshipman MacLeod, how is the training going?"

"Okay, I guess."

The inspector allowed himself a small chuckle.

"There's no need to be modest, Middy. I'm told your training is going very well, indeed."

"That's news to me, sir. But I'm happy to hear it."

In other circumstances, Vasconcelos's words would have given him a jolt of pride. But this was ShipSec. He wanted desperately to be somewhere—anywhere—else. The office walls were completely bare. There were no murals or posters or any form of decoration. Apart from the usual vents and air filters, there was nothing to occupy the eye. One of the filters was making a faint fluttering sound. A sure sign it was about to fail. Maybe that was why the air seemed to be stuffy and pressing in on him. Or maybe it was his imagination.

"You're on track to graduate with your class in . . . what?" Vasconcelos asked. "Another hundred and eighty sols?"

"Yes, sir."

The inspector's smile acquired a slightly harder edge.

"And I imagine you'd like to stay on that track?"

Ravi stiffened in his seat.

"Sir?"

Contrary to regulations and common sense, Vasconcelos's chair was not bolted down or attached to the deck in any way. This did, however, allow him to tip it backward on two legs until it was leaning against the wall. He stared affectedly at the ceiling, as if talking to himself rather than a half-terrified midshipman.

"The Chief Navigator tells me that you and Midshipman Ibori are peddling some rogue-planet story about the drive firing in the middle of the night-cycle."

Ravi's heart thudded in his throat. Did ShipSec know about the trip to the engine rooms? Was he about to get thrown off the program? Or worse? The tininess of the room was no coincidence, he realized. The bareness of the walls not an accident. The cramped space was oppressive, designed to throw him off balance, to bend him to Vasconcelos's will. And it was working.

What would Boz do? Ravi asked himself. And then, chillingly: *What would my dad have done?*

"*You're not caught till you're caught, son. Don't help 'em get you there.*"

He stared straight ahead and said nothing.

A dry chuckle escaped from the inspector's lips.

"A MacLeod to the core, I see. Your family should have a cell block named after it." The smile vanished from his face. "Non-cooperation with a ShipSec inquiry is grounds enough to get you thrown off the program," he snapped. The chair tipped forward under his weight, the front legs landing on the deck with a metallic crash that made Ravi jump. "Have you or have you not been telling people the drive is firing at night-cycle?"

"Yes, sir."

"Why?"

"Because it is."

"And how do you know that?"

Ravi hesitated, unsure of what Sofia might have already said. If she'd told them about the engine rooms, he was done anyway. But if she hadn't . . . Well, either way, he wasn't going to do the inspector's work for him.

"The drive fired night-cycle before last while I was in a lo-grav area," he said. "It had a noticeable effect. I checked out a nearby gravity meter, which showed we were accelerating. Slowly, to be sure, but the only thing capable of moving the ship like that would be the drive."

It was, strictly speaking, almost true.

Vasconcelos was looking at him from under hooded eyes.

"You are to cease and desist from this nonsense with immediate effect," he said brusquely. "The drive isn't firing. And if anyone tells you otherwise, you are to deny it. Understood?"

"The drive *is* firing," Ravi heard himself say. The words were cold, and deliberate, and felt like they were coming from someone else. His more usual self was already starting to panic again, the urge to jump up and flee almost overwhelming. But he forced himself to see it through. "Why are you asking me to lie?"

Vasconcelos looked genuinely angry. He leaned across the desk until his face was mere centimeters from Ravi's.

"Just do what you're told," he snapped. In that moment, that close, he looked just like Ravi's father.

"Or what?" Ravi snapped back, the MacLeod temper surfacing at long last. "Telling the truth isn't a crime, and you can't order me to lie . . . *sir*. The drive is firing. The gravity meter logs will *prove* the drive is firing. And if I want to tell people the drive is firing, there's nothing you can do to stop me."

Vasconcelos sat back with a short, barking laugh.

"A truth-loving MacLeod? That's a new one." He took a deep breath and stared at the wall behind Ravi's shoulder, as if looking for inspiration. When he spoke again his voice was icy calm. "Take a look at this."

Ravi's eyelid twitched under the impact of a data packet. It was short and easy to read.

SHIP'S SECURITY: ISV-1 ARCHIMEDES

SUMMARY COVER SHEET

CREWMAN 6-7864 MACLEOD, ROBERTA J.

MOST RECENT CHARGES: CONDITIONALLY
SUSPENDED

SHIP'S STANDING: SATISFACTORY (PROVISIONAL)

As Ravi watched, however, the last two lines changed.

MOST RECENT CHARGES: VIOLATION OF SHIPS
REG 3-111(a) ET SEQ.

SHIPS'S STANDING: DEAD WEIGHT

"You can't do that!"

"Actually, I can. Your cousin's status is entirely at my discretion. The Chief Navigator would like to keep her around for her, ah, *skills*, but I can rescind her status at any time. And believe me, if you think the consequences of Dead Weight are going to be waived in her case, think again. Unless, of course . . ."

He paused delicately.

"Fine," Ravi mumbled. "No more talking about the drive."

He got up and left the office before he could punch the smile off of Vasconcelos's face.

— — —

"He said *what?*"

Boz looked horrified. Her hands, Ravi noted with alarm, had started to shake. So would his, he thought, if a trip to the recycler depended on the whims of the Chief of Ship's Security. The glowing tip of her cigarette jittered frantically back and forth. So much so, Ravi thought, it might actually fly out of her fingers. To guard against the possibility, she jammed it back in her mouth. Ravi tried not to cough. The air filters were on their last legs. Even without the cigarette smoke, the atmosphere in the abandoned control room, high up in Fiji, had become dangerously stuffy. The air reeked of damp.

"Point is," he said, trying to calm her down, "no one is going to do anything. Vasconcelos wanted me to shut up about the drive: I'm going to shut up about the drive. Case closed."

"Are you kidding?" The cigarette in Boz's mouth muffled her words but not her incredulity. "This is *Vasconcelos* we're talking about. Soon as this probe project is done with, he's going to have me mulched."

"I don't think he can do that," Ravi said, but without much conviction. And then, more firmly: "I'm *sure* he can't do that. It's has to be against regs. Has to."

"Yeah, well, if you were a ship's barrister, I might believe you," Boz said cynically. "But as you're not . . ."

She let the words trail off, the silence pregnant with despair.

"We could get a barrister's opinion," Ravi suggested. "At least we'd know where we stand. We shouldn't let that bescumbered gullgroper push us around without a fight."

"Who has the water for a barrister?" She shot him a weary smile. "We'd need enough to fill that dream bath of yours."

"I thought barristers were free."

Boz just laughed at him.

"Ship pays for your defense if you're charged with a crime." She took the cigarette from her mouth and blew out a long plume of smoke. "Otherwise, you're on your own."

A sudden, sour taste filled Ravi's mouth. Not because of the problem. Because of the solution.

"Sofia's . . ." He could barely say it. "Sofia's *boyfriend* is a ship's barrister."

"Jaden?"

Ravi nodded.

"Sofia owes me. Maybe she can persuade him to do us a favor."

"Maybe," Boz agreed. She brightened a little. "Jaden's full of himself, but he knows what he's doing. He got my last set of charges dismissed." A small smile crossed her face. "You know, for a Strauss-Cohen, he really has it in for the authorities."

"Probably because he's a BonVoy," Ravi said dourly.

Boz must have thought he was joking until she caught sight of his expression.

"Seriously?"

"Seriously." He told her about the BonVoy demonstration in the hubs, his encounter with the masked Jaden.

Boz shook her head in wonder.

"That," she said, "would explain a lot. The Captain must be horrified . . . Unless she's one as well."

Ravi had to smile at that.

"You know what's bugging me?" Boz went on. "The fact that this whole drive thing is a secret. Why? Why bother? There's got to be a dozen really good reasons for firing the drive, so why all the shielding?"

"The Destination Star is filthy with dust and meteoroids," Ravi agreed, remembering what Sofia had told him. "Maybe it's just a minor course adjustment?"

"Or not. No one gets madder than when they're caught doing something wrong, you know. Officers are no different. And the way you tell it, Vasconcelos was mad as hungary." She pointed the glowing tip of her cigarette at him. "You mark my words, Rav: whatever they're firing the drive *for*, we're not going to like it."

Boz's suspicions rolled around the inside of Ravi's skull long after he'd made it back to his quarters, pulled his bunk out of the wall, and killed the lights. He didn't remember his dreams when he awoke the next morning. But he was certain they hadn't been happy ones.

▬ ▬ ▬

Ravi and Sofia stood awkwardly under the large tree at the center of the arboretum, waiting for the fake Home Star to go away. As it turned out, only Ravi had been interrogated by ShipSec. Sofia had had a pleasant meal with her great-uncle, the Chief Navigator, who had suggested that it would be better if the subject of the drive were not raised again. The Captain had her reasons, apparently. Sofia had agreed.

"Why wouldn't I?" she'd said, when Ravi had challenged her about it. "If they don't want me talking about it, what's it to me—or to you, for that matter?"

Ravi didn't have a good answer to that.

The fake Homeworld sky was starting to darken.

"He's late," Ravi muttered.

"No, he's not." Sofia pointed toward the nearest entrance, her eyes sparkling.

Jaden Strauss-Cohen was striding confidently in their direction, his luxurious hair hidden under a wide-brimmed hat, clearly modeled after the ones people wore in the old-time Westerns. Ravi was even more jealous than usual. The hat, which protected Jaden's eyes from the searing rays of the arboretum's day-cycle starlight, probably cost a river's worth of water. Way more than Ravi could afford, anyway. And that was just the beginning. Nothing Jaden was wearing was standard. And nothing he was wearing was cheap. Ravi glanced down at his fatigues and sighed. Even Boz had her blood-curdling leather jacket. All he had was a collection of ship's-issue fatigues, mostly scuffed at the knees, and a couple of sweaters, both scuffed at the elbows. He picked distractedly at a piece of lint. As if removing it would make his clothing suddenly elegant . . .

It was hard to ignore the tight knot of officers in the corner of the lab, but he did his best.

Take the cake, he suggested. *You know you want it, and it tastes so good.*

On the other side of the workbench, the boy was staring at the slice of cake, his scalp dotted with electrodes, his expression conflicted. He shook his head, but there was no force in it.

C'mon, it's cake. It's delicious. What if they take it away and you never get to taste it?

Impulsively, the boy grabbed for the cake. The moment he touched the plate, he yelped and swore as a tiny jolt of electricity zapped his hand away.

"Incredible," one of the officers said. "And she's the only one of them who can do this?"

"Yes, sir." An unseen voice from behind him. "With a subject like this, fully mapped, she has a ninety-three percent success rate. Even though he knows he's going to get zapped, he can't stop himself reaching out."

The boy nodded in rueful agreement.

The officer strode over to the workbench and leaned onto it with widespread arms. He looked Ravi in the eyes, his expression one of naked curiosity.

"You, young lady, are going to help us kill our enemies. How do you feel about that?"

"I'm eager to do my duty, sir."

But he wasn't eager. Not even a little bit . . .

"Jaden!" Sofia cried, running over to him. "So glad you could make it!" She led him excitedly by the hand until he was standing next to Ravi under the broad boughs of the tree.

Jaden, for his part, looked slightly bored.

"Sofe tells me your cousin's in trouble with ShipSec. Again." He sounded more amused than anything else. The fact that Boz was a wave of the hand from getting mulched didn't seem to be bothering him at all.

Disoriented as he was, Ravi didn't have enough bandwidth to be annoyed.

"We just want to know where we stand," he said, groping his way back to reality.

Jaden stretched out on the ground, back against the tree trunk, pulling Sofia down with him. She followed him with fluid grace, happy to be kept close. Ravi stayed standing, staring into the distance and waiting for an answer. Tiny Seventh Gen children were playing on a nearby stretch of meadow. He closed his ears to their shrieks of laughter.

"If I've understood what Sofe told me correctly," Jaden said languidly, "Roberta's been given the benefit of a provisional reclassification. Senior officers have the discretion to do that if it's in the ship's interest. Usually, there's some sort of quid pro quo. Do something for the ship, and you get reclassified to a higher grade." He played idly with Sofia's hair, stroking it with long fingers. "If that's right, Commander-Inspector Vasconcelos can't just reclassify Roberta back down to Dead Weight and send her to the recycler. There has to be a hearing. And Vasconcelos would have to satisfy the ombudsman that Roberta had failed to keep her end of the bargain." He looked up at Ravi and grinned. "So, so long as your cousin does what Sofia's uncle wants, she's golden."

There had been a tightness about his chest Ravi realized, because it lessened a little at Jaden's words. But only a little. They were talking about Boz, after all.

"But what if—*ow!*"

He'd been going to ask what happened if Boz *didn't* do as she was told, or if the Chief Navigator and Vasconcelos simply lied about her work. But he was rubbing his head instead.

The tree had dropped a fruit on his head. The offending object, already bruised from its encounter with his skull, rolled to a stop at his feet.

"Are you okay?" Sofia asked, not bothering to stifle a laugh.

"Yeah," Ravi said ruefully. "It did hurt, though."

"Now I know what Newton looked like when he was hit on the head with an apple," Jaden joked.

The girl was sitting under a tree. An apple fell from the fruited leaves, dropping softly into the girl's hand. The girl laughed and rolled the apple onto the poisoned lawn . . .

"Are you okay?" It was Sofia again. But this time with a hint of worry.

Ravi forced himself back to the real world.

"I'm fine," he assured her. He gave her a weak smile before turning his attention to Jaden. "What's Newton got to do with apples?"

Jaden raised an eyebrow, as if surprised by the question.

"Newton's theory of gravity, silly," Sofia said, before Jaden could answer. "The story is that he got the idea when he was hit on the head by a falling apple. Just like you."

Sofia kept talking, but Ravi wasn't really listening. He wasn't much for history or stories, but he'd heard of Isaac Newton. Ancient physicist, and inventor of many of the equations that Ravi had wrestled with at school—and which the navigators used to steer the ship. Quietly, so as not to appear rude, he reached out into the hive.

Isaac Newton, born Earth Year 1643 CE in the British Isles, just off the coast of Europe. Died, same place, EY 1727 CE. Pictures, or rather old-style drawings, of Isaac Newton flooded his head. A narrow, harshly chiseled chin that changed little as he aged. Intense, staring eyes that changed not at all. Eyes that, as often as not, stared out at him from beneath an enormous white wig.

The man from his dreams.

I t doesn't make any sense!" Ravi snapped. He stepped out of the way as Boz unloaded a small delivery bot. Inside a couple of bland looking crates were some second-hand inductors, presumably from Uncle Torquil, a bunch of electronic equipment that had vanished from the manifests, and packs of freshly manufactured cigarettes. Boz stuffed the crates in one corner of her Fiji bolt-hole and reloaded the machine with discreetly packaged chocolate.

"Archimedes was a physicist," she pointed out, not for the first time. She slipped some code into the bot's routing software, altering its memory. "He has an apocryphal relationship to bathwater, and there's a bath in your dreams. He's also the name of this ship." She paused a moment, as if to examine her handiwork, before sending the bot on its way. When she spoke again, she spoke slowly and with exaggerated care, as if speaking to a child. "Newton was a physicist. He has an apocryphal relationship to apples, and there's an apple in your dreams. He *has* to be the name of a ship."

"But he isn't! The fleet has three ships, *Archimedes, Bohr,* and *Chandrasekar.* None of them was ever called *Newton,* and no one even suggested Newton as a name. I checked. The ships were just hull numbers when the Liberty Foundation bought them from the Deep Space Commission. They had a variety of nicknames, like 'the Dreidels,' or 'the Hula Hoops,' or 'the White Elephants,' but no one ever, *ever* called them '*Newton.*'"

He bent down and reached into a kit bag he'd brought with him, pulling out a collapsible stepladder, a hulking cylinder of nitrous oxide, and some grimy-looking air filters he'd "liberated" from Bermuda. Ravi had intercepted them on their way to the recycler. They weren't really fit for the purpose, but they still functioned, after a fashion. Which was more than could be said for the ones in the abandoned control room. He set up the stepladder and got to work, replacing dead filters with the nearly dead. The recycler wouldn't be able to tell the difference. If anyone was interested, its logs would show an unusual delay between the official repair work in Bermuda-7 and the beginning of the recycling process, but it wouldn't show anything missing. And once he'd finished, the air in the bolt-hole would be slightly less stale.

Boz watched him from the dubious comfort of a burned-out chair. There was no sign of the usual cigarette, presumably out of respect for the soon-to-be unprotected vents.

"I didn't just check the ship's names," Ravi complained, as he removed the first of the old filters with a well-practiced tug. "I checked the *crews*. There were no Newtons in First Crew. Not one. And no one's taken the name since." He slammed the replacement into place and opened a panel labeled NOBOSS to one side of the vent. He switched out the old nitrous cylinder for its younger replacement.

"What's a NOBOSS?" Boz asked.

"Nitrous Oxide–Based Oxygen Supply System. Emergency life support, basically."

"Ugh. Five seconds of my life I'll never get back. There's a bunch of Newmans on *Chandra*."

"Not the same thing. And you know it." He closed up the NOBOSS panel and moved to the next filter.

Boz favored him with a careless shrug.

"Let me go over your searches. Maybe you missed something."

"I didn't 'miss something.'" But he fashioned a key anyway and tossed it over. Boz grabbed ahold of it and crowded into his head. Link established, he could feel the restless churn of his cousin's mind, the flow and eddy of digital information. It was a constant burble in the back of his skull. Being Boz, he thought, had to be exhausting.

He pulled up his search history for Boz to see. Even though he was standing on a stepladder and Boz was across the control room in the wrecked remains of a chair, it felt like she was pressed against the back of his eyeballs. The data flickered to life in front of them, pictures, and video, and text.

"*See?*" Ravi said, or rather thought, communicating with his cousin in code. "*Absolutely nothing.* Newton, starship Newton, ISV Newton, First Crew Newton, Liberty Foundation Newton, Deep Space Commission Newton, interstellar colonist Newton, Tau Ceti Newton—"

"Wait!" Boz hissed. "Wind it back!" She was using her real voice, low and urgent.

Ravi did as he was told. Boz forced her way into his data stream, making him feel slightly nauseous. She peeled back the underlying code, then peeled it back some more. She reached into the depths and grabbed on to seemingly random pieces of programming, pulling them closer to the surface and fitting them together in a tightly interlocking pattern.

"What does that look like to you?" she asked quietly.

Ravi's heart thudded heavily in his chest.

"It's a tracer," he said, speaking aloud. "A really good one." He felt sick to his stomach. "I never noticed it. It never occurred to me—"

"That someone might be watching you?" He didn't need to see the cynical half-smile shadowing her face. He could feel it. He started to say something.

"Stop talking. And try not to think. I need some quiet in here."

There was a faint tickling sensation in his head. Boz was tiptoeing through his implants, picking away at the search data and reaching out to the hive at the same time—all while using his chipset. It was a breathtaking demonstration of technical skill, but Ravi was too traumatized to appreciate it. Someone had been *following* him, for Archie's sake.

With exaggerated care, so as not to leave footprints of her own, Boz followed the path of Ravi's earlier searches, pursuing his various bots and queries deeper and deeper into the hive.

Ravi looked on, fascinated. He could barely bring himself to breathe.

Boz wasn't just watching where the bots and queries had gone; she was looking at how those bots and queries had affected the hive. It was like following a stone thrown into the depths of a pond while also looking at the ripples, both on the surface and below. She went through them all in excruciating slow motion.

It was the strangest thing. Not one of Ravi's searches had got to where it was going. Each one had been hijacked by lurking pieces of code and turned away, diverted into a desert of useless information. And rising back up with that useless information, wrapped in it, in fact, was the tracer. A poison pill of programming, sending information on every single search to . . .

Vasconcelos.

"Are you sure?" Ravi asked. He used his real voice again, worried his cybernetic conversation might be monitored.

"Yes." Boz had jumped up from her wreck of a chair and was taking elongated paces about the control room. The half-gravity barely held her to the deck. "Whatever this Newton thing is, it can't be something you just dreamed up. It's got to be real. Real enough for Vasconcelos to protect it with bots and sic a tracer on you."

"Am I in trouble?" The words came out unbidden, an anxious blurt. What would he tell his mother if he got thrown off the program?

"For what?" Boz asked, laughing. "Archie's hooks, Middy, you carried out a *search*. It's not a crime!"

"But what about all this?" He gestured around the room. "It's not something you'd want ShipSec to know about, is it?"

"Not a problem. First, the tracer isn't geographical; it's monitoring your search activity, nothing else. Second, even if it was, this space vanished from the schematics years ago. If Vasconcelos was trying to track you physically, your present location would look like a glitch. *It doesn't exist.*"

"Yeah, well." He thought back to his interview in the cramped little office, the ease with which the inspector had bent him to his will. "I don't like the idea of Vasconcelos keeping tabs on me, is all. It creeps me out." He slammed the replacement air vent into position as if to mask his apprehension. He picked up the stepladder and moved on to the next one.

"Pass me the filter," Ravi asked, pointing to his kit bag. Boz pulled out the replacement and handed it up to him.

"You know what?" she said. "We should screw with Vasconcelos for a change. Let's find out what he's trying to hide and rub his stupid, smug face in it."

From his perch atop the stepladder, Ravi looked down at his cousin. Her face was alive with mischief. *No,* he decided to say. *I'm not messing with that guy, and neither are you. He'll throw me off the program and send you to the recycler.*

His mouth, however, belonged to a MacLeod.

"Sure," it said. He could feel the mouth spreading into a reckless grin. "You got any kind of a plan?"

"Maybe. But first, we should do something about that tracer."

Ravi could only look on, awestruck, as Boz wormed into the hive through Ravi's implants and tweaked the very edges of the tracer's code. To Vasconcelos, it would look like the tracer was still doing its work, but Ravi could block it off whenever he wanted. And when he did so, the tracer would send a made-up feed back to its master. The Commander-Inspector would never know it had been messed with. And if, by some miracle, he *did* find out, Boz had done all the work through Ravi's chipset, something she'd once compared to picking up food with two-meter-long chopsticks. Vasconcelos would think Ravi had sarded up the tracer, not Boz. He might be pissed at Ravi, but he'd have no reason to go after Ravi's cousin.

Despite Jaden's assurances, Ravi wasn't sure Vasconcelos couldn't find a way to turn Boz into Dead Weight. Ravi, on the other hand, was as close to respectable as any MacLeod could be. Vasconcelos would need all his sensors in a row to do Ravi real harm. Given the tracer was illegal, he was perfectly within his rights to destroy it. And if Vasconcelos wanted him off the program, he would have to present Chen Lai with actual evidence, which he didn't have. All things considered, odds were that Vasconcelos would do no more than give him the stink eye. *That,* Ravi could handle standing on his head in full *g.*

Subtly crippled, Boz let the tracer drift away, disguising itself once more in the ebb and flow of the hive. Job done, Boz jumped out of Ravi's head and back into her own.

"That," Ravi said breathlessly, "was sarding amazing." He meant it, too. Every word.

For someone who loved attention, the praise left Boz surprisingly unmoved. She was staring at Ravi with a look of frank curiosity.

"It was easier than it should have been," she told him. "Chip sets are . . . personal. They're full of nooks and crannies and strange little corners that shouldn't be there. Yours is . . ." Words failed her for a moment. And as she struggled to pull the right ones together, she began to look less curious and more troubled. "Yours is . . . mapped out. It's like someone has put a signpost at every twist and turn your implants have to offer. For someone like me, every possible obstacle, every trap, has been smoothed over. Making use of your implants was real simple. *Too* simple."

She grabbed him by the wrists and stared deep into his eyes, determined to force the point home.

"Do you remember the last time you let me do a sweep of your implants?"

"Sure. When I asked you to hack the personnel files." He smiled ruefully in remembrance. "It hurt like hungary."

"Exactly. And do you remember what I told you about the inside of your head?"

"Yes," he said, grinning. "You said my code was, and I quote: 'a bescumbered mess.'"

Boz didn't grin back.

"Yeah, well. The mess is all gone. Tidied away like it was never there. Someone has been playing house in your skull. A lot."

22.0

"T his is not a good plan," Ravi insisted. The faceplate of his spacesuit was pressed against Boz's so they could communicate without using the radios.

"It's a great plan." Boz's voice sounded tinny and far away. "It's the best plan ever in the history of plans, so shut up and get with the program."

He wished he could see her face, to get a better gauge on whether she believed a word of what she was saying. But the mirrored glass of her visor hid everything, reflecting back only the muted lighting of the airlock. The airlock itself, already depressurized, was cramped and little used, high up in the six o'clock spoke of Ghana. The whole compartment juddered to the wheel's crippled rotation. To Ravi's fevered senses, the vibrations seemed worse than before. He had a sudden, irrational worry that the wheel was about to break.

"Couldn't you at least have chosen a better airlock?" he complained.

"We've been over this," came the tinny—and slightly exasperated—reply. "This is Ghana, where everything is sarded up." She patted the airlock wall with a bulkily gloved hand. There was no air, so the sound didn't carry. "This little beauty is off the grid because someone back in the sol repaired it but never called it in. As far as the schematics are concerned, it doesn't exist anymore, so we don't have to hack it. Plus, there's next to no gravity this far up the spoke, which makes it a real easy jump."

"Yeah, about that," Ravi started to say, but Boz was no longer listening. She'd pulled her helmet away and was busy opening the outer door. It cycled open to reveal a blue-black sea of stars. Small particles of ice broke away from the seals and danced off into the dark. Ravi caught his breath, drinking in the view. He was bathed in the cool light of the Milky Way. An entire galaxy beneath his booted feet.

Boz had already swung herself outside and was perched against a handhold. With a certain amount of hesitation, he pulled himself after her. He knew what came next. His heart was thumping in anticipation.

The lock cycled shut behind him.

Boz tapped him on the shoulder and pointed. Although he could still feel

the vibrations from Ghana's shattered bearings, it felt like they were station-
ary and that the entire ship was moving around them. Even Hungary, a
mere few hundred meters away, seemed to be turning. Unlike the other
wheels, Hungary was almost completely dark, just a handful of nav lights to
ward off the unwary. Most of it was in deep shadow, but part of the circum-
ference was exposed to the cold glare of the Destination Star. In its faint
light, it was just possible to make out dust-scoured paintwork, interrupted
by the dark gashes of the meteoroid strike. Portholes were blown out, airlocks and access hatches hanging open, far too buckled to ever close. A des-
olate ruin.

But Hungary was precisely where Boz was pointing. At a spot on the
wheel's inner rim, not far from where it merged with a spoke. Without a
word, she pulled herself into a tuck, somersaulted for show, and kicked off.
Her unlit suit vanished from sight within seconds.

Ravi was alone, heart pounding harder than ever.

This was the worst part of Boz's plan. Jumping across open space without
a tether and with the added mass of a kit bag. If he got it wrong, he'd miss
the wheel entirely and go hurtling into the black. At best, he'd be picked up
by a lifeboat and thrown off the program. At worst, he'd be lost in space
until his life support ran out or, if he was really unlucky, fried by the drive
when it fired up in the night-cycle. His stomach, prudently empty in anticipation of this exact moment, tried to throw up.

"Why don't we just use the safety lines and walk?" he'd asked her.

"'Cause it'll take too long," she'd said crisply. "We'd have to climb half
the length of the Ghana spoke, rappel along the outside of the hubs, and then
climb all the way down to the Hungary rim. We don't have that kind of
time. Besides, it's a real rush." She'd smiled at him recklessly. "What are
you? Chicken?"

Ravi's heart continued to hammer. Hungary looked an awfully long
way down. And the rim looked painfully thin against the blackness of space
beyond.

But the spot Boz was aiming for was continuing to move. If he didn't go
now, he'd have to wait for another rotation. With a muttered imprecation,
he pulled down a guidance grid, watched the trajectories spiral across the
inside of his eyelids, picked one, and jumped, diving headfirst for Hungary.

Nerves cramped his style. He wouldn't have thought twice about it in
the hubs. But out here . . . He'd pushed off too hard. Hungary's shattered

inner rim was rising up to meet him far quicker than he expected. His biological eyes and his implants were telling him the same thing. He was too far to the left and headed for the aft edge of the rim. He had maybe a meter to play with, no more, and the rim's surface was cambered away from him. If he didn't stick the landing, he was going to slide right off the rim's edge and into space. Assuming, that is, he didn't rip his suit open first. There were jagged tears everywhere. Buzz saws for the unwary.

Think like Boz, he told himself breathlessly. *Think like Boz!*

Boz, he reminded himself, didn't think: she just *did*. With gusto. He took one last look, closed his eyes, and plastered a grin on his face.

Then he flipped himself over.

His boots were touching the inner rim. He bent his knees to absorb the impact. The suit's mechanicals wheezed and clicked in an effort to assist. The boots started to slide. He dug them in before they could really get going. The soles did their work. The movement stopped.

Done, he told himself, with grim satisfaction. *Done.* He turned slowly around, looking for the nearest anchor point.

He was about 200 meters away from where he needed to be. Wrapped in the ship's deep shadow and with her running lights off, Boz was still invisible. But he was as certain as he could be that she was already there. With a wry smile, he set off for the rendezvous point, a dark spoke towering "above" him in the near distance. He stayed tethered every step of the way.

— — —

"I don't believe it." The words rushed out between the collar of Ravi's spacesuit and his helmet, not waiting for him to get it fully detached. The air that rushed in to meet him was bitter cold and acrid with the smell of burning. "I don't believe it," he said again.

Boz's helmet was already off, floating a few centimeters from her head. Misted breath drifted lazily from her lips.

"You can't tell anyone I brought you here. And I mean *anyone*. If your mom finds out, she'll chop me into little bits and feed me to the recycler."

Ravi had to smile at that.

"I'm serious! You're the *good* MacLeod, remember? The one who's going to make officer. You're not meant to know about this. Not now, not ever, because what you don't know can't hurt you." She unclipped one of her gloves, sending it spinning carelessly through the air. Her bare hand flicked the switches of a makeshift heater. Like most of the compartment, it was an ungainly collection of ill-fitting and illegally acquired parts. But it worked. A blast of heat washed against Ravi's face.

"This is amazing," he said, and he meant it. The engineering was crude but effective and, if Boz was to be believed, had been running the best part of twenty years. It was, Boz assured him, the MacLeods' biggest secret. It must have been. Until a couple of days ago, he'd no idea it existed.

A bolt-hole. A small, habitable space in the middle of Hungary. Ravi's father had built it, cobbled together as a base of operations, allowing him to spend more time exploring and pillaging the wreckage instead of shuttling between the dead wheel and Ghana on a single tankful of air.

He ran a hand across a patched bulkhead, freezing to the touch, thinking of how his father must have done the same; how, even now, some of his DNA might still be clinging to the uneven surface.

They could have shared this if he'd followed his father's corridor. He'd still been in grade school when his dad had started taking him out on "jobs." Showing him how to reprogram a delivery drone to drop its cargo in the wrong place and "forget" where it had been; how an assistant quartermaster could be persuaded to lose track of inventory; how equipment heading for the recycler could be intercepted and repurposed. And then, the "job" done, his dad would take him to the movies. Old-style. At the Roxy in Australia. With popcorn and soda. There'd be a warm arm around his shoulder and his father would laugh and cry and just be . . . kind.

Until it all went sideways.

"I won't do it," he remembered saying. His voice had started to break by then, and he was beginning to grow into his body, but he was still terrified at the changing expression on his father's face.

"I didn't get you a part-time job in Recycling so you could hang around and do nothing all sol. Just do what you're told. It's not even hard. Just make sure the A-seven hatch is left open at the end of your shift and walk away: end of story."

"You didn't get me the job, Dad. Mom did. And I promised her I'd do it right."

"You *are* doing it right. Except for the hatch, which no one will care about."

"*I'll* care about it. It's wrong."

"'It's wrong,' the boy says. 'It's *wrong*.' Spare me the buggy code, kid. It's only wrong if you get caught—which you won't. And even then, it's only wrong 'cause some bastard officer said so so as to fill their own water tank instead. I should never have let your mother fill your head with this nonsense. You'll do what you're told, or I'll know the reason why."

"No."

"*What* did you say?" His father had advanced on him then, fist raised.

"I said no." It came out like a whimper, and he cowered away from the oncoming blow. But when it landed it was little more than a hard slap, easily shaken off compared with its predecessors. His father had stalked off then without a word. Looking back now and reexamining his father's expression, what he remembered was that his father had looked not angry but upset.

Betrayed.

There had been no more "jobs" after that. His father had let him be. Let him have the normal life he craved. But there had been no more sharing of the family secrets. No father-son trips to a bolt-hole in Hungary.

That was then, of course. His father had been mulched. One fight, one scam too many for the ship to tolerate. An image of his father's face, blurred behind thick glass on his way to the recycling chamber, rose up to torment him. He pushed it roughly aside.

Of those MacLeods who still knew about the bolt-hole, only Boz had the thrusters to use it. The trip was too nerve-wracking, the destination too hazardous for anyone else to venture here. In the stygian blackness of Hungary's interior, Ravi had lost count of the number of times Boz had stopped him from shredding his suit on some sharp-edged piece of ruin.

A splash of color in one corner of the chamber caught his eye, drawing out a smile of recognition.

"At least I know where you're getting the chocolate from," he said wryly. The netting was bulging with purple and loosely anchored to a piece of pipe. There had to be a hundred bars in there.

Boz favored him with a quick grin.

"There's more where that came from. *Deep* frozen—and designed to last basically forever." She grew thoughtful for a moment. "I think they were being saved for a special occasion, planetfall maybe. First Crew would have scarfed them down otherwise."

"And what about . . ."

"Bodies?"

Ravi nodded.

"There's a few. More than a few, actually." She looked somber. "I won't lie. The first time you see one, out there in the dark, it can totally freak you out. But you get used to it after a while." She drifted across and touched the shoulder of his spacesuit, keen to make a point. "If you do see one, try not to scream, and treat it with respect. This is their place, not ours. We're just visitors." She gave him a slightly embarrassed smile. "I kind of think of them as friends. So long as we don't sard with them, they'll let us out of here alive."

She pointed at his kit bag.

"Is everything ready?"

Ravi nodded.

"If you've got me a frozen computer, I've got you what we need to wake it up."

"Great." Boz floated across to a bulky set of valves. "Let's get your air tank topped up and get the sard out of here."

Minutes later, they were once again making their way through Hungary's dark interior. The suit lights were bright, but that only made the surrounding darkness blacker. Shadows jumped and lurched at every turn, fearful night shapes that stretched and bent against blasted bulkheads and torn-up decks. Hatches floated incongruously against the remains of shattered hinges, bits of pipe hung lonely in the vaulted spaces, and everywhere there were layers of ice. Not just the frosted white of water but the somber sheen of frozen gases, molecules of atmosphere turned to snow and captured before they could escape through the outer hull.

Perhaps, Ravi thought dully, someone's last breath.

The nav system was useless here. Ravi's implants had no idea where he was. The reference beacons they relied on didn't exist, either blasted away or drained of power long ago. He tried using his biological sense of direction but was soon completely lost. Deck-wise, they'd started out in the mid-teens and headed "down" into the twenties, he thought. But the twists and turns since then had left him hopelessly confused. They could be anywhere. He prayed fervently that Boz actually knew where she was going . . .

Ravi was perched on his bed, arms about his knees, rocking slowly.

"Why'd you do it?" Mother asked. He had a cup of tea in his hands. Ravi took it from him gratefully, swallowed hard.

"I was curious," he confessed. "I wanted to know what it felt like. To be one. To fly, yeah?" He took a quick, ragged breath between sips. "It was . . . horrible, Mum.

There's no joy in them. There's no love. No *humanity*. They just want to kill." He hesitated, licked his lips nervously before adding, "I think they dream, though. Sometimes, anyway."

"Dream?" Mother was trying not to sound skeptical. "What about?"

"Burning . . ."

He came back from whatever *that* was to find his cousin pulling them through the remains of a paternoster shaft. Ravi was glad she couldn't hear the ragged breathing in his helmet or feel the sweat prickling on the inside of his gloves. She stopped suddenly, bracing herself against a loom of exposed wiring and making a warning motion with her free hand.

There was a body hanging in front of them. A woman's, Ravi thought, although he had no idea why. It was shriveled almost beyond recognition, every trace of moisture leached out of it. A skeleton covered in shined-leather skin. Its fatigues, bleached and brittle from radiation, looked far too big for it. But the name stenciled against the chest pocket was easy enough to read: ANSIMOV, A.M.

Ravi's eyes skipped hurriedly away. The name tag was too much information, too personal. A great-aunt of his friend, Vladimir? His great-grandmother? Everyone had lost people in the meteoroid strike. Once he got back to the rest of the ship, it would be easy enough to figure out who she was, to find some way of telling Ansimov he'd met one of his ancestors. But he knew he wouldn't. It didn't seem right, somehow. And anyway, the fewer the people who knew he'd been over here, the better.

Boz, apparently satisfied that he wasn't having a meltdown, was already bending herself around the body, taking great care not to touch her. Ravi followed suit. She disappeared into the blackness behind them, one arm outstretched as if in farewell.

His suit radio burst into life.

"It wasn't here, last time I came this way. The drive must have dislodged it."

"I thought you said we weren't to use the radio," Ravi replied, still distracted by what he'd just seen.

"Suit-to-suit? This deep in the wheel? No one can hear us now, even if they were trying to." Boz was moving slowly along the shaft wall now, clearly looking for something.

"Do the . . . bodies move much?"

"Not usually, no," Boz replied. "But they *do* move. They're never quite where they were the last time you saw them." She'd found the remains of a small access tunnel and was pulling herself in. "The drive will be sarding with them, though. You and I might not notice a hundredth of a *g,* or whatever it is, but these guys will." She grunted as the space ahead of her narrowed. "Our frozen friends are floating around in here with nothing but time on their hands. Given enough time, a hundredth of a *g* could move them a real long way."

It was now Ravi's turn to grunt. Something had kinked the tunnel, bent it out of shape. He was bigger than Boz. The tunnel walls pressed against his tanks, pushed on his knees and elbows. His kit bag dragged like an anchor. His breath came in short little gasps. He worried about getting stuck. He worried about ripping open his suit. He worried about turning back and getting lost in the dark.

And then he was through. Boz was drifting at ease in the middle of a small but outwardly undamaged compartment. A frosted console and a couple of bucket seats were hanging upside down "above" her head. Racks of inert boxes lined the walls.

Ravi rapidly reoriented himself and let out a low whistle.

"Backup servers. Just like you said. Are you sure they're in one piece?"

"You tell me. You're the engineer."

Ravi pulled himself around the room, giving the racks of boxes a visual inspection. He opened his kit bag and released a drone. It puffed along beside him, augmenting his biological eyesight with X-rays and electronic scans.

There were little armor-plated compartments like this all around the ship, insurance against one type of disaster or another. Emergency supplies, spare parts, that sort of thing. The idea being that if the ship suffered some kind of catastrophic failure, there'd still be places a person could go, caches of stuff they could use, to at least stabilize things until the rest of the fleet could come to their aid.

This one was a backup, or partial backup, to the hive. If the computers and networks that kept ship and crew humming along as a unified whole ever went down, there should be enough information stored here to boot up some kind of replacement. A half-hive. A way to carry on.

Neither Boz nor Ravi cared about any of that. What they cared about was this: the backup servers had been cut off from the hive since the catastrophe. Their stored data was old and out of date. But what was there stretched all the way back to the Launch. And it was unguarded by any of Vasconcelos's codes. If there was information about Newton, it would be here.

If, that is, they could make it work. Ravi and the drone circled back to where they had started.

"Well?" Boz asked.

"I think we can do this," Ravi said. "The power cells are dead beyond hope of recovery, but that's it. And the power cells"—he tapped his kit bag, sending it into a spin—"the power cells, we can replace."

"Awesome. And to think I was going to break this whole thing down and sell it for parts."

With Boz being more hindrance than help, Ravi and the drone stripped out and replaced enough of the power cells to get the system to work. Then, with painful slowness, they warmed everything up so it wouldn't crack with use. As Ravi had to explain to Boz more than once, the components were designed to work in vacuum, and designed to work in the extreme cold of deep space. But they were *not* designed to operate with their internals caked in nitrogen ice. It didn't take a lot of heat to boil everything off, but it took longer than Boz wanted. They needed to get back to the living part of the ship before night-cycle ended; otherwise, someone was bound to notice they were missing.

"Come on," she kept muttering. "Come *on!*"

Ravi ignored her. He pulled himself into a bucket seat and strapped himself in. With Boz floating "above" his head, he reached out and stabbed a button on the console.

Lights flickered to life. Row after row of green, a couple of yellows, no reds. All good. Boz strapped in beside him. Ravi hesitated.

"What are you waiting for?" Boz asked, impatiently.

"It's the keyboard," Ravi confessed miserably. "This suit has the wrong sort of gloves. They're for outside work. I don't think I can hit the keys."

"What is this? The Steel Age? Jack yourself in! We don't have time for the keyboard, anyway. It'll take forever." Before Ravi could stop her, she pulled a wire from the chest of her spacesuit, reached out to the console, and plugged in.

Ravi flinched. A person never, *ever* jacked themselves in to an untested system. If something went wrong, a person could fry their implants—and a lot more besides. He waited for the sound of Boz's screaming.

It didn't come. Feeling foolish, he unspooled his connector cable.

His senses were flooded with cybernetic input, jaw-dropping in its immediacy, like he was actually there. He'd seen it before, of course, or thought he had. The Homeworld newsfeeds of Launch Day. Video of the fleet's majestic, if creeping, departure from lunar orbit. Interviews with First Crew. Puzzled and slightly mocking commentary from the news organizations, with words like *quixotic*, and *ill-advised*, and *doomed to failure*. The LOKIs, after all, had pronounced the mission unacceptably risky. What more need be said?

Archimedes had departed first, her paintwork gleaming in the too-strong glare of the Home Star, not yet scarred by dust, or dulled by radiation, or coated with ice. Shadows played against the long latticework of her spine as the angle of the ship began to change. The vast bulge of her thrusters was already pushing her forward, centimeters at a time, then meters, then kilometers. Gaining velocity, the ship began to grow smaller, despite the best magnification the newsfeeds could buy. She was on her way, climbing doggedly toward interstellar space, her habitat wheels locked and unmoving, their first rotations still more than a year away.

Bohr had launched next, identical in every way. Then *Chandrasekhar*, subtly different, sleeker. The result of lessons learned in the building of her older sisters.

This was where the feed ended. Where it *always* ended, on a snarky note from Adriana Onovo, the preeminent journalist of her day: "See you," she'd joked. "Wouldn't want to be you."

But the joke didn't come. The feed didn't end.

Another ship was tilting regally away from the cameras. Vast and majestic, compared even with what had gone before. Bigger, more magnificent, with habitat wheels at least a third wider and one, two . . . *ten* of them. She was climbing away from the Home Star in pursuit of her smaller siblings. And Ravi had the strangest impression: that she was holding herself back, lest she catch up with them too soon.

ISV-4 *Newton*.

"See you," the journalist joked. "Wouldn't want to be you."

"Y ou tired, Middy?" Chen Lai asked.

"No, sir," Ravi lied. Truth was, he was exhausted. By the time he and Boz had got back from Hungary, there'd been no time for shuteye. He'd simply showered and reported for duty.

"Then pay attention!" Chen Lai snapped. "You think I'm up here giving a briefing so you can go to sleep?"

"No, sir." Ravi was cringing with embarrassment, all fatigue banished. Chen Lai doused him with one more glare before turning back to the task in hand.

"As even the doziest crewman knows by now, Braking Day is almost upon us. And to do that, the ship has to be turned around so the drive is pointed forward. When it fires, it pushes us backward, we start to slow down. Simple."

"A Seventh Gen three-year-old knows that," Ansimov coded. Ravi rewarded him with a quick grin.

"What's not so simple is the shielding," Chen Lai continued. "Once the navigators swing us around, the forward shield will be pretty much useless. It'll be facing the wrong way. So . . . we're going to throw up a new shield, aft of Hungary." A faint smile crossed his lips. "Which will soon be forward of Hungary."

A soft muttering ran around the briefing room. Ansimov stuck up a hand.

"I thought the plan was to let the drive be our shield, sir. Let it vaporize or deflect anything coming at us?"

"That *was* the plan. But the navigators are still concerned about the amount of garbage floating around the Destination Star. There's more dust than they thought. We have enough remaining spare parts to cobble together a second shield, so that's what we're going to do." He held up a cautionary hand. "This is a highly technical and difficult operation with way more extravehicular time than usual. We will *not* be using trainees. Qualified engineers and techs *only*," he finished, riding roughshod over a small chorus of groans. "There'll be plenty of other stuff for you guys to do. I can assure you of *that*." Eyelids twitched under the impact of schedules.

"Huh," Ansimov grunted. "Looks like we have a real short walk on our hands today."

Ravi looked at him curiously.

"Those plates they put up at Phoenix and Manchester?" Ansimov prompted.

"The ones that add ten minutes to your sarding commute?"

"The very same. Guess who gets to take 'em down?"

Even with an extra contingent of drones to do most of the heavy lifting and cutting-up, getting rid of the plates was heavy, sweaty work. And the need to avoid damage to the plethora of pipes and wiring that ran through the circular's deck and walls made the work slow. They were at it for most of the shift.

When the last of the plates was down, however, and on its way to the recyclers, Ravi and Ansimov had a chance to look around.

Phoenix Circular, one of Denmark's main thoroughfares, was once again open. But the cross corridor, Manchester Passage, was not. On one side, anyway. What had once been a wide-open gangway was now the entrance to a brand-new series of compartments. A rectangular-looking security drone and an equally rectangular ShipSec officer were standing guard outside. Ravi groped about in the hive, looking for the schematics.

"Hey," he murmured to Ansimov, "any idea what's in there?"

Ansimov shook his head, his search for blueprints as fruitless as Ravi's. Ansimov, however, took it a step further and sauntered over to the guard.

"Say, amiko. What are you and the box guarding? Anything interesting?"

The officer rewarded him with a slightly sour look.

"If you don't know, you don't need to know."

For a moment, Ansimov looked like he was going to say something he might regret. Before he could do so, however, the heavily guarded door cycled open. Ravi felt his eyebrows arching ceilingward in surprise.

"Well, well," said Boz. "Fancy meeting you here."

▬ ▬ ▬

In Boz's bolt-hole, high up in Fiji, his cousin heaved a contented sigh, wreathed once more in cigarette smoke.

"So, are you going to tell me what you've been doing in Manchester Passage or not?" Ravi demanded. Boz had been stalling him all sol, insisting that she couldn't talk about it in public. Ravi had barely been able to keep the lid on his curiosity, and Boz was driving him nuts. She'd refused to tell him at a quiet table in Ansimov's, she'd brushed him off in a deserted gangway in Ecuador, and she'd *shushed* him in the hubs. Now they were hidden away in a forgotten corner of the ship and all but invisible to the hive. Short of the bolt-hole in Hungary, Boz's graffitied hideaway was about as nonpublic as it got.

Boz took another drag on her cigarette, prolonging the agony. At least, that's what Ravi thought she was doing. It took him more than a moment to notice that she was scanning the hive for surveillance and surrounding them both in a web of virtual trip wires. Even BozBall was dispatched to guard the physical way in. His cousin was leaving nothing to chance.

She breathed out a streamer of blue smoke.

"We're assembling the probe," she said simply.

If gravity in the control room had been anything more than half a *g*, the disappointment would have been crushing.

"That's *it*? You lead me on for half a sarding sol for *that*? Everyone on the ship knows you're working on the probe! It's not exactly a secret, is it?"

Ravi half-expected to see his cousin's reckless grin, proof of a prank well played. But Boz wasn't grinning. She was looking absently at the BonVoy graffiti. The BonVoys who had once come here had long since moved on. The slogans were Fourth Gen rather than Sixth. Maybe older. VOYAGE FOREVER, one of them read, TRAVEL IS DESTINY, said another, STARS NOT DIRT, demanded a third. In another corner, a skillfully painted rendering of the Destination World had an equally skillful red line slashed across it. Ravi's mind drifted briefly to the BonVoy demonstration in the hubs. The one Sofia's boyfriend had been so actively involved in. *"No landing!"* they'd screamed. *"No pollution! Save! Their! World!"* BonVoy slogans for the modern age. *What will they do after planetfall?* Ravi wondered. *Demand that we leave?* As if.

Boz's voice cut across his thoughts.

"Have you ever thought about Manchester Passage? About what a great location it is for assembling a probe?" Her lips quirked into something approaching amusement.

Ravi started to answer, to explain in no uncertain terms that he'd never thought about it and didn't care to. The words, however, were stillborn on his lips. New ones formed in their stead.

"It's a really *stupid* place," he said slowly. Puzzled teeth bit down on his lower lip. "In fact, it's almost the dumbest place I can think of. You're building it attached to the outside of a spinning habitat wheel. In a full gravity—more, actually, 'cause you're way deeper than the last deck—so everything has weight. You drop a wrench, it's going to go flying off into space so fast, no one's going to see it again. Or it smashes into something delicate. Or a spacesuit . . ."

His voice trailed off. In his mind's eye, he was looking at a smashed faceplate, a sudden puff of crystallized gases, the unnatural stiffness of the body within.

"Space probes aren't designed for gravity," Boz pointed out. "So, why would you go out of your way to build in it? It'd be like manufacturing one on a planetary surface. On the, ah . . ." She hesitated, reaching for the word. "On the *ground*. Like a Steel Age rocket scientist. What kind of bescumbered idiot would do *that*?"

"It *is* kind of insane," Ravi agreed. "So, why are they doing it?"

Boz took another drag on her cigarette.

"It's something to do with those compartments Chen Lai opened up with Vasconcelos and the Captain. The ones that don't show up in the schematics. Your boss was real particular about how the whole construction envelope had to be built on the outside of it. He got into a heated discussion with what's-her-name, Lieutenant Petrides. She wanted to know why they couldn't do the work in the lifeboat maintenance dock." Boz gave him a whimsical smile. "It wasn't really a discussion. It was more like Chen Lai snarling her down."

Ravi nodded thoughtfully. Petrides' question made sense. The maintenance dock was purpose-designed for the task. It was on the spine, so everything was at zero *g,* and it was accessible by boat elevator, so a person could drag in some really big pieces of equipment directly from the hubs. If they wanted to fix up a lifeboat or build a probe from scratch, the maintenance dock was the place to get it done.

Why cling to the rim of an endlessly rotating habitat wheel? Try as he might, the answer eluded him.

"And here's the other thing," Boz added. "This probe is *huge*. It's carrying enough fuel to do a grand tour of every planet in the system. And they're using Mark Nine thrusters."

Ravi raised a skeptical eyebrow.

"Honest to Archie. Mark Nines. They ferried them over from the *Chandra* last night-cycle. If this thing opens up, it'll be halfway across the galaxy before you can say 'Nice to see you.'"

Ravi frowned, trying to make sense of it all. Thrusters like that seemed like serious overkill for a probe. And they were incredibly difficult to make. Even with *Chandra*'s specialized printers, the tolerances were brutal.

"Maybe they don't want to take any chances," he suggested. "Sofia says the Chief Navigator's a paranoid perfectionist. And she should know. He's her uncle, after all."

"Maybe." Boz didn't sound wholly convinced. She carefully extinguished the remains of her cigarette, lit up another one, and settled back into the skeletal remains of a seat.

"So," she said. "From one mystery to another. What are we going to do about *Newton*?"

Ravi, at a complete loss, shrugged his shoulders.

"We could bring it to the Captain," Boz suggested. "Demand an explanation."

"Like *that* will go well."

"The newsfeeds, then." Boz brightened at the thought. "That's even better, actually. What better way to stick it to Vasconcelos?"

"The *newsfeeds*? No sarding way." A vague anxiety, something he couldn't quite pin down, was uncurling in the pit of his stomach. "We should let the wheels turn for a while. Just till we know what we're dealing with."

"We already know what we're dealing with. We spent all night-cycle pulling it from the records."

Ravi's exhausted body didn't need reminding.

"Sure, we did," he agreed. "But what is it you think we know, exactly? That the fleet used to have four ships and now it has three? And she wasn't part of the fleet, anyway. Not really. The Liberty Foundation—First Crew— they didn't buy her. We know that for a fact. It was 'Human Heritage,' whatever the hungary that was. For all we know, they got cold space boots and went back home."

"Doesn't seem very likely, though, does it? That's an awful lot of water for a return trip to the Kuiper Belt."

"Whatever. Point is, she's not here now. And the truth is, beyond knowing that *Newton* was a ship, that she launched the same day as the fleet, and that she was crewed by something called Human Heritage, we know sard all."

"I'm pretty sure *I* know what Human Heritage is," Boz said.

"Really?"

"Yeah, really. I know the newsfeeds were kinda vague, but the only thing that fits is they were some kind of 'preserve the species' outfit. You know, doomsday types who believed natural disaster would overtake the Home Star some sol and humanity would be wiped out. If it had the water, an organization like that would totally jump at the chance to buy an inter-stellar project."

"Maybe."

"You got a better idea?"

"No," Ravi conceded. "But Human Heritage—and First Crew, for that matter—they all lived on Homeworld. And Homeworld means LOKIs. And if there's one thing LOKIs are meant to be good at, it's evaluating risk. If LOKIs thought Human Heritage was right, they wouldn't have pulled the plug in the first place, would they? They'd have greenlighted the whole sard-ding project."

"Okay. So?"

"*So* . . . if the LOKIs didn't think it was a good idea, why did Human Heritage take the gamble? *We* left to get away from LOKIs, for the freedom to make our own decisions, to be human again and all that. But from what I can tell, Human Heritage had no beef with LOKIs at all. All those clips of them we looked at? Not a single one of 'em said anything even mildly criti-cal about Homeworld being controlled by AIs. Quite the opposite, in fact. I'd bet you water to widgets that Human Heritage and LOKIs got along just fine. Which leaves us this little problem: if Human Heritage was pro-LOKI, and if LOKIs had written off the interstellar project as far too risky, why would an organization that trusted them insist on going through with it?"

Boz shrugged her shoulders.

"Don't look at me, cuz. I've no sarding clue."

"Which is exactly why we need to know more," Ravi said firmly. "We can't go public with what we have. It doesn't make sense."

"You are such an engineer, you know that? It doesn't have to make sense. It just has to be *true*." An exasperated blue jet escaped from Boz's lips. "Besides, there's nothing more to know. We've got as much information as we're ever going to get, short of shaking it out of the bastard officers. And the only way we're going to do *that* is to confront them with what we know already, preferably in a way that embarrasses Vasconcelos as much as possible. One of those bescumbered gullgropers knows something, and the only way to make them cough it up is to plaster it all over the newsfeeds and shock them into telling us."

Ravi's vague anxieties crystallized into something real.

"And what happens if you shock them into something else?" he asked.

"Like what?"

"Like the recycler." He stuffed his hands in his pockets to stop them from shaking. He was back in the ShipSec office, remembering. "Vasconcelos was totally prepared to mulch you if I didn't stop talking about the drive firing at night-cycle. What do you think he'd do over this? He'll have you busted to Dead Weight in the flick of a transistor."

"*You* said that Jaden said he couldn't do anything to me without a hearing," Boz pointed out. "And I'm doing exactly what Niko Ibori wants me to do. So, it's all good."

"And what if Niko Ibori lies? What if Vasconcelos puts him up to it?"

"He wouldn't!"

"Do you want to bet your molecules on that?"

Boz stared thoughtfully at her cigarette, twisted it in her fingers.

"I'll think about it," she said, with obvious reluctance.

"Great. Just don't rush into anything, okay?"

A wry smile tugged at Boz's lips.

"Me? Rush into stuff? I think you've got the wrong gal."

More relieved than anything else, Ravi made his way back to Ecuador. He opened the door to his quarters, his body dragging with fatigue.

He took a step inside and stopped. There was a faint smell of burning.

"*Lights,*" he coded.

His quarters looked like they usually did. His bunk was folded against the wall, the shower unit bone-dry and spotlessly clean, his desk and chair neatly arranged. His space chest . . .

It took him a minute to figure it out. It was closed, and locked, and apparently undisturbed.

Apart, that is, from the small, circular hole reamed out of one side. Heart thudding, Ravi tore it open, strewing his few clothes and fewer belongings left and right in his race to the bottom.

The armor-plated box was still there. Still locked. But it, too, had a hole cut in its side, the edges flawless and mirror-smooth.

Fake BozBall, his dirty little secret from beyond the ship, was gone.

The plate and its colorful decoration had been crushed and warped into a scalene triangle of green, unfolded, like origami, into a vast, poisonous lawn that the girl, in her long coat, and buckled shoes, and enormous white wig, had somehow turned to grass.

He was sitting in his bathtub, in a king's ransom of still water, dark and deep to the very edge of the enamel. The girl was at his side now, leaning over him, a familiar, slightly crooked smile playing on her lips. Her strange accent was crystal-clear.

"We need your help," she said.

"Why?" He was shocked to hear himself speak.

The girl's eyes were startlingly blue, he realized, and a little sad. She trailed a finger through the top of the water, brushing against his skin. Except it wasn't the girl anymore; it was the man. The man who looked like Isaac Newton. Intense, staring eyes burned at him like a sun.

"I am coming for you," he answered in her place. "And when I get there, I'm going to kill you."

— — —

"I'm going to the Captain," Ravi said. "This is way out of my league."

He was still bleary-eyed and sitting smack in the middle of Ansimov's. He pressed his fingers against the chipped surface of a dining table to stop his hands from shaking. The place was empty, which was unsurprising, given the earliness of the hour. The day-cycle had barely begun. A late-running maintenance bot was rushing through its allotted tasks, giving the scuffed deck a hopeful polish.

"Are you cracked?" Boz coded. If anything, she looked worse than he did. Her hair was an uncombed mess, her skin had a waxy look about it, and dark circles orbited her eyes. Her implants, however, were in full working order.

"You're going to fess up because you had a bad dream? That's not just nuts; it's suicide."

"You know as well as I do that this is more than a bad dream," Ravi coded back, leaning across the table. He paused while a server drone delivered a liter of ice-cold water and the first breakfasts of the sol.

"This is on you," Boz grunted. "Least you can do, seeing as I don't have to be up for at least another two hours."

Ravi spared his cousin a slightly sour look and sent over the payment with the blink of an eye. The drone flashed back a receipt and retreated toward the galley. Ravi waited till it was safely out of range before speaking out loud.

"Someone or some*thing* is sending me messages in dreams. They showed me how to find that little black LOKI. Which is now missing. And they led us to *Newton*. And now a guy who looks exactly like Isaac Newton is threatening to kill me. That's pretty sarding serious."

"Sure, it is," Boz agreed, between mouthfuls of fruit and tofu. "But what are you going to tell Vasconcelos? That you're being threatened by a man in a dream? You think he's going to buy that?"

"He will when I tell him about the LOKI and what we know about *Newton*. Then he'll have to believe me."

"What he'll *believe*, cuz, is that you're several implants short of a chipset. A delusional psych case, who's let loose a full-blown LOKI bent on destroying the ship and everything we stand for." Boz leaned across the table and grabbed him by the wrists. "You tell him any of this and one of three things will happen." She ticked them off on her fingers, pressing down on his bare skin as she did so. "One: the medics will rate you criminally insane. Two: the ombudsman will find you guilty of sabotage. Three: you'll be found guilty of sabotage *and* criminally insane." Her voice dropped to a whisper. "What do you think will happen next?"

Ravi felt his mouth go dry. The rules had been in place since Second Gen, and they were very clear. Second Gen, first to be born in space, and with nothing in front of them but the Mission, had, by all accounts, been a clear-eyed, cold-blooded bunch. When everyone's life hung by a thread, there was no room for sentimentality. Being mentally ill was one thing, but being criminally insane—a danger to the ship—was something else altogether. The criminally insane were Dead Weight. Same with saboteurs.

"But what about the ship?" he asked. "If I don't say anything, we could *all* be dead, not just me."

Boz spared him a strange look. Respect, maybe? Grudging admiration? Whatever it was, being on the receiving end of it made him feel distinctly uncomfortable. Boz, meanwhile, helped herself to another forkful of breakfast.

"They'll recycle you," she said conversationally. Fruit and tofu continued to vanish from sight. "They won't believe some boogeyman is coming to get them. Whatever you tell them isn't going to 'save the ship,' so let's not martyr ourselves to no purpose, eh?"

Ravi's own breakfast lay untouched on the plate. He gave it a fitful stab, pushing the contents from one divider to another. Much as he hated to admit it, Boz had a point.

"Perhaps I could tell Sofia . . ."

"She's an *Ibori,* Rav. Being an officer's, like, wound into her DNA. She'll rat you out before you can say *entitled brat.* Or have you forgotten how *chatty* she gets with her great uncle?"

Ravi swallowed hard. His cousin wasn't wrong. He was already on the wrong side of Vasconcelos. He remembered the cramped little compartment, the inspector's threats. If she told her uncle what he'd done . . .

He fought hard to suppress a shudder.

"Okay," he said at last. "What do you suggest I do?"

"Nothing," Boz said, finishing off the last of her breakfast. "For now. If I'm right—and I am—these dreams are messages from *Newton.* We need to see if she's still out there. If we can prove that, at least, maybe you'll have a decent story to tell the Captain. One that doesn't end with your molecules degenerating into compost." Her eyes lit upon Ravi's still-full plate. "You want that?"

"Knock yourself out." He pushed the rectangle of food across the table. "How are we going to find a ship that's managed to stay hidden for a hundred and thirty-two years?" he asked. He could feel the doubt creeping into his voice. "Maybe she isn't there." An image of the launch footage from Hungary filled his mind. *Ten* gigantic habitat wheels. "That was one big-ass ship."

"Not out here. *Space* is big. Everything else is a pinprick. Particularly if no one's looking." Her eyes widened in sudden thought. "Do you think you can get your upscale navigator friend to give you a tour of Main Navigation?"

"I guess. Why?"

"Ask me no questions and I'll tell you no lies. But you'll need to take this with you." She reached into her pocket and dumped it on the table.

BozBall.

— — —

Sofia was eyeing him curiously.

"Why'd you bring the kit bag?"

"Habit," Ravi lied. "I was late off shift and forgot to leave it behind." There was a lump in his throat as he said this. It felt almost as big as BozBall, which was nestling at the bottom of the kit bag. He hoped to Archie it didn't do anything to bring attention to itself. Confident Sofia wouldn't see him, he quietly probed the hive, looking for signs of illicit activity. So far as he could tell, BozBall was still fast asleep.

"Okay," Sofia said. She seemed to find it amusing. "Come on in. Welcome to Main Navigation." She stepped away from the doorway with an outstretched arm and ushered him in.

Ravi caught his breath. Main Navigation was huge, almost cavernous in appearance. Everything was darkened to night. All the better to read the screens and monitors that lined the walls or glowed up from the workstations. Late in the sol, it was mostly empty. A couple of young heads bent over some readouts, an older officer pacing back and forth in one of the corners, surrounded by a coded swarm of calculations. Asteroid trajectories, Ravi guessed, but he didn't want to probe too closely. What he looked at instead was the main screen, almost five meters across, that dominated the entire space. It depicted a vast, blurry disc, almost entirely devoid of detail except for some blotchy shading. A couple of small white circles hung off to one side.

"Is that it?" he asked. "Destination World? The moons?"

Sofia nodded.

"Two of the moons, anyway. The others are hidden right now. It's still mostly guesswork," she said, pointing to the planet itself. "But we think this is an ocean. Bigger than Homeworld's Mediterranean, smaller than the Atlantic. We *think*. And this may be an impact crater. Two hundred, maybe three hundred kilometers across. A lot of argument about whether it is or isn't, of course, but the smart water's on the thing being real."

As Sofia reached out into the hive to manipulate the display, he could tell by a prickling in the back of his neck that BozBall had woken up. He tried not to look, worried that a wayward burst of code would alert Sofia to what was going on, but he couldn't help himself. Thin strands of tracer were attaching themselves to Sofia's transmissions, stealing the keys she was using to access the Main Navigation programs. To Ravi's alarm, they were spreading web-like across the whole Navigation architecture, snaring information and access codes from everyone and everything in the compartment.

"Is it recent?" he asked, desperate to keep Sofia distracted. "The crater?"

Sofia shrugged.

"Define *recent*. Recent enough not to have been eroded away. Not so recent that the planet's still devastated. Hundreds of thousands of years to some millions, I guess."

Ravi let out a sigh of relief.

"I was thinking it might be, like, yester-sol." When Sofia shot him a slightly pitying glance, he felt compelled to add, "Everyone keeps telling us the system is dirty. You can't blame a guy for worrying that his new home is getting pounded by big-ass rocks."

He was delighted to see the condescension vanish from her face.

"The risk isn't zero," she conceded. "And you're right: the system *is* dirty. But it's all relative. The chances we'll get a hit in the next thousand years or so is pretty close to zero. And we have the tech to protect ourselves from anything other than a direct hit." She flashed him a grin. "We've survived in space to the seventh generation, Ravi. I think we can handle a nuclear winter."

Ravi nodded absently, still staring at the blurred disk. The thought that he would have to leave the safety of the ship to stand on *that* made him queasy. To live in a place where the only thing protecting him from the ravages of the universe was a thin skin of colorless gas felt deeply unnatural. He was struck by a sudden thought.

"When we live down there," he murmured, "the floor's going to curve down instead of up, isn't it?"

Sofia giggled.

"Not so you'd notice, silly. The floor's so big, it'll look flat."

"I guess. But there'll still be a horizon, even if it's kilometers away. And when you go over it, you'll disappear from the bottom up, not the top down, yeah?" He shook his head in baffled wonderment. "Weird."

"The whole thing will be weird." Sofia placed a soft hand on his elbow and pulled him gently to one side, until they found themselves in the shadow of a quiet bulkhead. The faint *tick-tick-tick* of some automated system murmured at them from a nearby console. Sofia leaned toward him until her mouth was only centimeters from his ear. Her breathing tickled his skin. "You know what?" she whispered. "I keep telling myself it's not too late." Light fingers fluttered against his wrist. "We can just . . . not brake. Keep on going. Forget about the whole thing."

She took a step back and looked up at him, eyes shining. Ravi's stomach twisted itself into a strange knot. He almost found himself nodding in agreement. He *wanted* to nod in agreement.

And yet.

"We can't. Even if we wanted to, we can't." He knew the expression on his face was far too earnest, but he desperately wanted her to understand. "The ships are *old,* Sofe. Things are breaking down almost faster than we can fix 'em. Even now, *Bohr* can barely feed herself, and the whole fleet is running out of water. Another generation of this and we'll be a convoy of ghost ships." He tried to lighten the mood. "Maybe, in a hundred thousand years, some alien archeologist would find our frozen remains and wonder where the hungary we came from."

His attempt at levity fell flat.

"We could reduce the population," Sofia suggested, apparently serious. "Stretch our resources. Make ourselves more efficient. You're an engineer," she added with an encouraging smile. "You could totally make that happen."

Ravi shook his head.

"It'd never work. And even if it did, you'd only be postponing the inevitable for a generation or two." He found himself looking at her strangely. "You know, Sofe, this is BonVoy talk."

"It is, isn't it?" Sofia said, shocked at herself. "Forget I said it. I didn't mean it. Not really." She let out a long, tremulous sigh. "It's just . . . *weird,* is all. Braking Day. Living on the outside of a big ball of rock, like, forever. It gets inside my head sometimes." Ravi was startled to see tears in her eyes, but she forced herself to smile. "It'll all work out in the end. I'm sure of it."

Out of the darkness, a shadow loomed. The officer who'd been pacing. He was looking curiously at Ravi.

"Who's your friend?" he asked Sofia. He extended a hand to Ravi in greeting.

"This is Ravi MacLeod, Lieutenant. We're classmates."

"Are you indeed?" At the mention of his last name, the navigator's hand had dropped away. Ravi could feel the man's suddenly critical gaze taking him in, from the worn fatigues all the way down to the scuffed, standard-issue boots.

"Well, don't keep him up here too long. We wouldn't want anything to go missing, now—or get hacked—would we?"

For a heart-stopping moment, Ravi thought the navigator had picked up on the tracers.

The officer sauntered off, leaving Ravi rooted to the spot, a toxic mix of embarrassment, and fury, and no small amount of guilt welling up inside.

"Nice guy," he said at last, through gritted teeth.

Sofia, at least, had the decency to look distressed.

"We're not all like that, you know. The guy's a total gullgroper." She gave him an apologetic look. "Still . . ."

"Yeah, yeah." He said it more bitterly than he'd intended. "I'll clear your precious deck. I wouldn't want to mess it up any more than I already have."

He turned on his heel and left before Sofia had a chance to say anything further.

He stormed off in the direction of the nearest spoke, desperate to get back to Ecuador. He didn't know which was more hurtful: the nav officer's prejudice or the fact he was right.

— — —

"Do you have what you need?" Ravi asked anxiously.

"Yeah." Boz's face was slack, her eyes unfocused, but her voice was distinctly irritated. "You keep asking like you expect a different answer. Shut up and mind the door."

Ravi did as he was told. The door he was minding wasn't physical, though. It was in the hive. Ravi's software was standing lookout, keeping them safe from other people's prying eyes. Which mattered because what he and Boz were up to was totally worth the prying.

Thanks to Sofia's access codes, data was leaking out of the navigation servers, taking a long detour through the hive, and slipping unobserved into an abandoned control room high up in Fiji. The data was arriving out of order and still encrypted, but it was arriving. And Boz was busy beating it into something she could use. She was engulfed in a swirling dogfight of code, counter-code and hackbots, and it was clearly taking a toll on her. Her brow was dotted with beads of sweat, her breathing was shallow and irregular, and her complexion was waxy and sallow.

But she was winning. A slow smile spread across her face.

"Got you," she said. She tossed a key into Ravi's chipset. "Come on in."

Ravi linked implants with his cousin, sliding into the edge of her mind. He was floating in a sea of stars.

"What am I looking at?"

"A compilation of sensor logs," Boz explained. "Five years' worth." The scene started to shift. "There's *Bohr* and *Chandra*. The Destination Star is up there, obviously, and back down the other way is Home Star."

Ravi had never seen Home Star. Not knowingly, anyway. The Destination Star was easy, a cold searchlight at the top of the sky, striking light and shadow across everything it touched. The Home Star was different, because it wasn't. It was a star like any other. One among the countless millions shining through the visor of his spacesuit. An anonymous backdrop to hard, dangerous work. Inside the ship, on the star maps, it was easy. The Home Star was smack bang in the middle of Boötes, the Herdsman. Find Arcturus, they'd told him at school, and a person can't go wrong. It's practically next door.

But outside the ship, nothing was as simple as the maps. There was a whole galaxy out there. A billion billion stars, each one clamoring for its place in the universe, breaking the easy patterns of the astronomers, dissolving their straight edges into unbounded mist. Even with nav assist from his implants, he'd never been sure he was looking at it.

But now he was. A bright little star was staring up at him from the back of the ship, its swiftly speeding light barely twelve years old. He tried to feel something, to imagine the billions of people sheltering in its warmth, the LOKIs, the cities, the hurly-burly of interplanetary traffic.

His imagination failed him. It was just another star . . .

The meeting room was emptying out, but the speaker was still at the dais, answering questions. Ravi waited nervously, one hand sliding back and forth over the other. Behind the speaker, a larger-than-life hologram of a woman holding a baby and a scepter glowed down at them. The construct was labeled Εἰρήνη.

"What does that say?" he asked, when he finally got the speaker's attention. "I can't read it." Silently, he cursed himself for his cowardice, for asking a question he already knew the answer to instead of coming straight to the point.

"It means *Irene* in an old Earth language," the speaker said, smiling. "And *Irene* means?"

"*Peace*," Ravi said without hesitation. "Which, for us, means the abandonment of vengeance."

"Glad you've been listening." The speaker looked at him shrewdly. "You've been to our meetings before, I think. Several times."

After a moment's hesitation, Ravi nodded.

"And can I help you with anything else?"

Ravi could feel his heart thumping in his chest. He took a deep breath before taking the plunge.

"Actually, it's how I can help you . . ."

"Homeworld to Ravi. Come in, Ravi."

Boz was waving a hand in front of his face.

Ravi swallowed hard, trying to shake off his confusion.

"Sorry, cuz. Must have zoned out." A deep breath. "Let's do this."

The sensor logs shifted ever so subtly as Boz wound the clock back.

"Okay," she said. "This is Sol forty-six five seven one, oh-one thirty hours. Let's see what there is to see."

Even with both of them linked together, the work was exhausting. They moved forward in time and then back again, getting rid of anything that was meant to be there as they did so. They edited stuff out: easiest first, hardest last. *Bohr* and *Chandra* vanished, stars and galaxies disappeared, background radiation and gamma-ray bursts were quietly wiped away. Ravi's head felt like it was going to split open.

"There's nothing left," Boz coded disconsolately.

They were floating in a formless void of their own creation. They were moving forward in time, passing through Sol 47,432. Ravi could tell by the smell that Boz had lit up a cigarette, but he didn't have enough processing power to open his biological eyes. He ached from the pressure of broken furniture against his body. He didn't think he'd moved for hours.

"Let's get to the end," he replied, trying to sound cheerful. *"Maybe . . ."*

A little flash of something sparked in the void.

"Wait!" he signaled. *"Go back!"*

"It's nothing, just a glitch in the programming. I'll—"

"Go back!"

The faint echo of a sigh managed to reach his ears. Boz rolled the clock back.

A star popped into existence, dimmed, brightened, and then vanished.

"*See?*" Boz said. "*It's just a star. I must have missed a frame or two scrubbing it out.*"

The dimming star had Ravi's heart thudding, but he tried to keep his coding steady.

"*Run a diagnostic. See what you did.*" He tried not to hold his breath while she did so.

"*I can't find anything wrong,*" Boz said, puzzled.

"*That's because there isn't,*" Ravi replied, relieved and excited at the same time. "*Not with the programming, anyway. The star's in these frames because it's not meant to do that,*" he explained. "*We're looking at an anomaly.*"

"*We are?*"

Somehow, Ravi found the energy to open his eyes and winced. Everything was far too bright. Boz was staring at him curiously, waiting for an answer.

"Yes," he replied, meeting her gaze as best he could. "*This is a totally normal Class G star. They don't suddenly dim, unless—*"

"*Something passes in front of it!*"

"Right," Ravi agreed, running some numbers. "*And the pattern's all wrong for one of its own planets. Whatever did this is much closer. Too small for us to see but still big enough to dim a star.*"

"*Like an interstellar vehicle,*" Boz said.

Ravi's stomach lurched as Boz twisted his frame of reference. He closed his eyes again, fighting off a wave of nausea. The formless void returned, empty but for the single, solitary star.

"Okay," she said. Her coded voice boomed inside his skull, suddenly enthusiastic. "*Now we know which direction to look in, let's see what there is to see.*" Ravi's head ached even more than before. She was riding his chipset hard, using it to recalibrate the software. He gritted his teeth against the pain and did his best to keep up.

The results did nothing to ease the banging in his skull. There was something out there. Whatever it was lay in the same general direction as the *Bohr*, but it had to be much farther out. Point a telescope at *Bohr* and she would leap into view, a tiny model of a starship, her habitat wheels spinning against a backdrop of stygian velvet. But someone in Main Navigation had pointed the ship's biggest 'scope at the very spot Boz and Ravi were looking at and seen nothing. And the logs were very clear. That same someone had pointed the 'scope in that same direction every sol for more than a year, without success.

"They know she's out there," Boz said, aloud this time. "They sarding *know!* Why else would they be looking?"

Ravi didn't even try to disagree.

But even without a visual, there were anomalies. Flashes of energy that might have leaked from a heavily shielded drive, stray bursts of electromagnetism that might have been a radio signal, a possible splash or two from a laser.

And all from the same direction. All from somewhere past the *Bohr.* Ravi could feel the moisture leaving his mouth.

They were still moving forward through the logs: Sol 48,311, just weeks ago.

"Stop," Ravi croaked.

There was a faint whisper of energy, barely enough to notice. But it was there, and it was coherent, and it kept coming back in the same, insistent patterns.

"That's code," Boz said. "Super complex, for sure, but code all the same." She paused for a moment, apparently in thought. "If I didn't know better, I'd say it was a hack."

"It *is* a hack." Ravi's throat was so dry he could barely speak. "That's the sol Chen Lai sent me down to the engine rooms. The sol I started getting the crazy headaches." He pointed Boz in the direction of the nav log time stamp, matched it to where the pattern was particularly intense. "You see that?" He didn't bother to wait for an answer. "That's when I first saw the girl."

Y ou can't hack a human being," Boz said. "It's not possible." She was trying to light a cigarette, but shaking hands were getting in the way. The thin cylinder of tobacco slipped from her fingers and dropped lazily to the deck. Boz dived after it with a muttered curse.

Despite himself, Ravi could feel a small smile tugging at his lips.

"Just because you don't know how to do it doesn't mean it can't be done. Besides, you're the gal who said someone had been playing house in my head, remember?"

Boz looked up from the deck plates, her expression sour.

"Yeah, but I was thinking of the medics or the chipset maintenance techs. About some gullgroper messing about with the coding to your implants. I wasn't thinking about someone taking over your actual biological brain, making you hallucinate, and dropping real Archie-damned messages into your dreams." She sat cross-legged on the deck, the retrieved cigarette back in her hand. "There are like a hundred billion neurons in the human brain," she pointed out matter-of-factly. "With failsafes and backups and a bucket-load of self-protective mirror mechanisms. You can't just waltz in and *hack* them. And even if you could, do you have any idea of the *processing* power you'd need to pull it off? It's not possible."

"Are you saying I *haven't* been hacked?" Ravi's voice dripped with irony. Strangely, even though abject terror would be more appropriate, the fact that his cousin, the fleet's most incorrigible hacker, was confused beyond description struck him as funny. She looked like she'd been hit upside the head.

Boz had finally lit her cigarette. She took a deep, calming drag.

"No," she said slowly. "You've totally been hacked. But sard me, Rav, it *should* be impossible. I wouldn't even know how to start." Her expression became suddenly sly. "I'd know *where*, though."

"*What?*"

"I'd know where," she repeated. She rewound the logs to the first time the hacking signal appeared. "Think about where you were when this happened. You were halfway to the ass end of the ship. More importantly, because the routers in the engine rooms were down, you were out of range of the hive. All alone." Boz's expression became positively wicked. "And what did you do next? What did you keep doing? Again, and again, and again?"

There was a sinking feeling in the pit of Ravi's stomach.

"I kept reaching out," he said wretchedly. "Broadcasting code for all I was worth."

"Exactly. And somebody picked it up. Your chipset was *looking* to make a connection, and they gave it exactly what it was looking for. That was their way in. And once they were in . . ." His cousin gave a resigned shrug.

Ravi wound the logs forward again. Now that he knew what to look for, there was no mistaking it. Every few sols, the hacking signal would appear, slightly different from the time before, more sophisticated, as if learning from its mistakes. And every time the hacking signal appeared, he'd had a weird dream or seen the girl. Strangely, though, there was no correlation with his other waking visions. Those ones seemed to come and go at random. He slowed the replay to a halt, a frown creasing his forehead.

"That's odd," he muttered.

"What is?"

"The signals." He wound the logs back to the sol he was hacked. "These early ones are simpler," he explained. "But they're layered. They're slightly out of phase. It's as if someone out there—"

"Is using a booster!"

"Right."

"It makes sense," Boz mused. "*Newton* clearly has enough watts to push a signal all the way to *Archimedes*. Using a booster to firm it up is just a luxury. But your pretty little head?" She shook her own. "No way you can push a coherent signal back that far. Archie's hooks, Ravi, you lost contact with the routers halfway down the spine, and that was what? Ten klicks?"

Ravi nodded.

"This is a two-way deal," Boz reminded him. "You can't be hacked if you can't be read. So, someone has to be listening in from a lot closer. A *lot* closer. No more than a few thousand klicks—and that's assuming he's got really big ears."

Ravi's stomach gave a nervous churn. That someone could get that close to the ship and not be seen gave him the creeps.

He moved the logs forward. Stopped again, frowning.

"Look at this," he said. "The signals have changed, see? They've added another layer."

"A second booster?"

"Has to be. But why?"

"Better connection," Boz said flatly. "Makes it easier to communicate. And . . ."

She stopped. Didn't start again.

"And what?" Ravi prompted.

"I'm not an engineer," Boz said slowly. "So I could be totally wrong. Except I'm not."

Ravi raised a dubious eyebrow.

"And what is it you're not wrong about?"

"Your new booster is here. Inside the ship. It's the vectors," she added before Ravi could object. "The directions don't make sense otherwise. See?"

Ravi did see. The churning in his guts intensified. Someone from *Newton* had reached out across hundreds of thousands—maybe millions—of klicks and planted something right inside of *Archimedes*. And Ravi knew exactly how they'd done it.

So did Boz.

"How many times have I told you not to trust ShipSec?" she stormed. "That *Bohr* officer sold you a pup. 'Hijacked probe,' my eye." She almost spat. "That UFO you saw out there had nothing to do with the fleet, nothing to do with the Mission. It had everything to do with *Newton*. It was a sarding *delivery* vehicle. Closed to fifty klicks, tossed its package, and left."

"ShipSec might not have known what your visitor was up to," Boz allowed. "But they sure knew what it *was*. They fed you a bunch of lies washed down with fifty liters of free water."

Ravi was trying very hard not to be sick. Boz gave him a reassuring pat on the shoulder.

"Look on the bright side," she said cheerfully. "At least we know what that little black ball is for."

— — —

Ravi couldn't stop himself from looking at the clock. *0205* burned quietly on the inside of his eyelid. He hadn't slept a wink all night-cycle. He knew why, too. *Newton,* the missing black ball, the girl, *everything.* He was in way over his head.

Somewhere out in the black was another starship, bigger than anything in the fleet, more modern, better equipped. A starship that had launched with the fleet, that had been *part* of the fleet. And yet no one would admit she existed. *Even though they knew she was there.* That was what was really frying his implants. The officers, the senior ones, anyway, they *knew*. Someone had given the order to suppress the files and keep them that way. Someone had ordered *Bohr*'s ShipSec to lie about what he'd seen on the lifeboat. The same someone, no doubt, who'd ordered the lifeboat to be equipped with a sensor array so over-the-top that it was *designed* to detect the exact probe that came calling.

And *Newton* was no better. If the fleet was trying to hide her existence, *Newton* was helping it out in every way possible. All it would take was one radio broadcast, and the secret was out of the bag. And yet *Newton* was running silent—and had been for decades. *Why?*

And then there was *Newton*'s little black ball. The treacherous LOKI he'd been crazy enough to take into the ship without telling anybody, and which had rewarded his curiosity by eating its way out of his quarters. If it was just an amplifier of the hacking signal, a way to make it easier to get inside his head, why had it run off? And what the hungary was it up to now? A sudden image flooded his mind: the LOKI popping some plate in the outer hull and crawling spiderlike along the ship's spine, heading for the engine rooms. He shuddered at the thought.

And why had he been hacked in the first place? What was that about? The dreams, the hallucinations, they were all infuriatingly vague. As hacks went, it didn't seem to be a very good one. He was reasonably certain they couldn't take over his body and make him destroy the ship. And if they wanted to communicate with him, weren't there easier ways? Why go to all this trouble? And why him? Couldn't they just send a message to the Captain?

"It's all so complicated, isn't it?"

Ravi sat bolt upright, his breath coming in frightened little gasps.

The girl was sitting at the foot of his bed.

"You're not real!" he blurted out, stupidly. "You're just in my head!"

She gave him that crooked little smile of hers.

"Isn't everything?" she teased. Her strange accent rang in his ears. "We wouldn't see much of anything without a brain, would we?"

It occurred to him that he shouldn't be able to see her. The lights were out, which meant there was no light at all. He couldn't even see his own hand.

And yet there she was, day-cycle bright, in her blue, not-quite-right fatigues. She got up from the foot of the bunk and knelt down next to his pillow. He tried not to shrink away, but he didn't quite succeed.

"There, there," she crooned. "It'll make much more sense in the morning." She put a hand on his forehead. He could *feel* it; soft, and comforting, and slightly warm. "All you need is a good night's sleep."

"You've gotta be kidding," he started to say. "How the hungary do you expect me to sleep now?"

But he never finished.

— — —

The girl was standing on a lawn of scalene triangles, her not-quite-right fatigues tucked into black, ankle-height boots that looked exactly like his own. She walked toward him from the shade of an apple tree to the side of his bunk. He was stretched out under the bedclothes, a warm pillow cradling his head. He tried to get up, but he couldn't seem to manage it. The mattress was too soft, too comfortable. He stopped trying.

And now the girl was at his side, leaning over him.

"We need your help," she said.

"Why?" He was no longer shocked to hear himself speak.

"Because you're the only one we can reach. The only one who might understand." She moved to the foot of his bed and sat down. The scene seemed oddly familiar, although he couldn't think why.

"Understand what?"

The girl looked somber. Or maybe the sky was darker. He couldn't be sure.

"That our ships are in danger. Mine and yours."

With a sudden clarity, he knew he was dreaming. And in dreams he could do whatever he wanted. He sat up in bed.

"From what?" he demanded.

"From each other. My ship wants to kill yours. Your fleet is preparing to kill mine."

Ravi made himself laugh. It echoed loud and brash in the dreaming world.

"No way," he said. "The fleet is unarmed. Our mission is colonization, not war." His imaginary voice hardened. "There will be no more wars," he insisted. "We left all of that behind—it's one of the reasons we're out here."

The girl's chuckle was quiet and honey-smooth.

"Your fleet has built long-range sensors, trying to find us. And your ships are not where they are meant to be. They have quietly started their engines to change position, to conceal themselves from our probes. And we can no longer hear you because your radios have gone silent." She gave him a knowing smile. "This is not the behavior of a friend. You will be building weapons, too."

The girl's words found their mark. He remembered Ansimov's complaint about the design of the new sensor arrays, the banning of radio communications, and, of course, the night-cycle firings of the drive. The shift in the ship's orientation had been no accident, he realized. It angled the blast away from *Newton* and her sensors.

"Just because we're hiding," he said, "doesn't mean we're building weapons. But you . . ." He threw the girl a suddenly suspicious look. "You've already built them, haven't you? That's how you're going to kill us." He didn't try to keep the irony out of his dream voice. "That isn't the behavior of a friend either."

The girl nodded.

"That's the plan," she agreed, before correcting herself. "That's *a* plan."

The sky on top of his dream had turned to night. Unwinking stars peppered the firmament. The girl, however, glowed, as if illuminated by some invisible spotlight. He stared at her a moment, trying to make sense of what he was seeing.

"How come I can understand you?" he asked. "Why is what you say making sense while all . . . this, this place we're in, is nothing but an air tank of crazy. And why can you talk to me sometimes and not others?" He paused, suddenly somber. "Or maybe I'm just mad. Maybe this isn't happening."

"If you were mad, I don't think you'd be asking the question," the girl said, smiling. "As for the rest of it, my brain is trying to talk to your brain, using implants and a whole lot of processing as a way in. It's not like opening a com link, you know. Brains are tricky things. We can get your mind to see images, but sound for some reason—the illusion of sound—is hard. And sound with meaning is harder still. We tried simple words at first, but your brain would process them into something else. When we first met, I kept saying 'hey there' over and over, but we could tell that wasn't what you were hearing." Her head cocked to one side. "What *were* you hearing, by the way? The first time you saw me?"

Ravi thought back. A splitting headache on the way down to the engine rooms. And then . . .

"I heard a banging on the outside of the hull. Like someone was smacking it with a wrench. And then you scared the sard out of me by appearing on the outside of the airlock with no suit on."

"Oh," the girl said, frowning. "That didn't go even slightly well, did it?" But she brightened almost immediately. "But we got better. Every time we made contact, our maps got a little more accurate, we started figuring out which combinations of stimuli would produce what result. Words were still hard, though. When we first got through to you, we were kinda clumsy, I think."

"You almost split my head open," Ravi grumbled. "'Clumsy' doesn't even begin to cover it. I passed out."

"Yeah. Sorry about that. Turned out it was easier to communicate when you were asleep. Less competing activity, fewer neurons to fire, though I'm guessing we still gave you headaches. But even then, brains being funny things like I said, you'd turn our messaging into dreams. Concepts and meanings would travel from me to you, and you'd turn them into—"

"Sarding nightmares."

"I was going to say *allegories*, but okay. But we've gotten better at that, too. Way better. Right now, we're talking and making sense, but in a dream. And next time it'll be easier. You might even be awake." She smiled impishly. "Your mind is almost an open book."

"Can you take over my body? Make me, like, hurt people?"

"No. That's so far beyond what we can do, it's not even funny." That serious look again. "But I can persuade. Give your brain chemistry a little nudge so that instead of *wanting* to do something, you *need* to do it. Something you might hesitate to do otherwise."

"Like make someone need to eat cake?"

"Exactly," the girl said, smiling.

"Or bring a foreign object aboard my ship?"

The smile disappeared.

"Yes. I'm sorry about that. But time is running out and we were desperate. If it's any consolation, I really didn't do much—*couldn't*, really. It's still too hard. If you hadn't been all fired up to go anyway, it would never have worked."

"So, what is it? A bomb? A bioweapon?"

"Oh, no, nothing like that. It's just a drone. And its main purpose right now is to act as a signal booster. It makes it easier for us to find our way around the inside of your head. Makes it easier to communicate. But it'll never harm you. Ever. I want us to be friends."

"Why *aren't* we friends? I mean you guys and the fleet. I saw the launch. We all left together: one fleet, one Mission. What changed? Why are you trying to kill us?"

His bed gave a sudden lurch, swaying from side to side. Except it wasn't a bed anymore; it was a sailboat, its long mast vanishing into the distance above him, its hull bobbing on mirror-smooth black water. Ravi leaned over the side, trying to scoop it up with his hands, but he couldn't quite reach.

The boat was moving, the girl sitting in the prow, the water—so much water—parting to either side with barely a ripple. The boat picked up speed, racing toward the horizon. Hanging low in the sky ahead of them was a bright white star. As he watched, it grew larger and more irregular, sprouting a multi-wheeled head and a long, long tail that flared out into a bulging tip.

Newton. Still tiny and far away, but getting closer with every rise and fall of the sailboat's bow. He found himself staring at the girl. She was leaning eagerly forward, gaze fixed on the approaching starship, willing it closer. The dream had changed, he realized. It wasn't his anymore. It was hers.

The girl turned to face him, the starship hovering over her shoulder, her expression sad.

"We were never friends. Even in the beginning. Your ancestors, the Liberty Foundation, had a thing about LOKIs. My ancestors, Human Heritage, had no problem with them. They had a thing about *people*. They thought everyone had become too reliant on implants. What had started as a way of letting the deaf hear, or the blind see, or the paralyzed walk had simply gone too far. Now everyone was getting them, to access computers, and operate machinery, and a hundred-and-one other things that used to be done by hands and brain. So, while your ancestors thought LOKIs were robbing us of our humanity, mine thought it was implants. Both wanted to start afresh somewhere else, and both thought that somewhere else was Tau Ceti." She sat down, her back propped against the front of the boat, knees drawn up under her chin. "The fleet, as you call it, was a marriage of convenience. The LOKIs had abandoned the Tau Ceti project, and your ancestors were able to purchase an off-the-shelf interstellar mission and three starships." She allowed herself a wry smile. "You were outbid for the fourth. ISV-4 *Newton* was acquired by Human Heritage. Same destination, same mission plan. Both groups were joined at the hip, even down to the launch date."

"So, what went wrong?"

"Nothing, at first. The ships launched like you saw, climbed out of the Solar System, and shut down their drives about a year later. Everyone spun up their habitat wheels and settled in for the cruise. A few months after that, though, there was an outbreak of scalene plague."

Even in this dream state, Ravi could feel his throat tighten. A ferocious, LOKI-designed bioweapon, scalene plague had a 90% mortality rate. It started with a dry cough, followed by the skin breaking out into green, triangular-shaped pustules, followed by death. There was no cure.

"I know there was an outbreak before the launch," he said. "On Homeworld. But there's no record of an outbreak in the fleet."

"There wouldn't be. The outbreak was on *Newton*. We tried to contain it, to get people off the ship before they could be infected, but no one would take us. We begged the rest of the fleet to at least take families with children, but your ancestors refused. Then we begged them just to take the mothers with children: at least, the ones who weren't already dying by then, but you still refused. Finally, in desperation, we packed only the surviving, uninfected children into a lifeboat and sent it across to the *Bohr*." There was no mistaking the bitterness in her voice. "We gave them only enough fuel and life-support for a one-way trip." She gave a shrug of the shoulders. "We figured we could shame you into action. But we were wrong. *Bohr* disabled her docking stations and barricaded her airlocks. They wouldn't touch the lifeboat, not even to resupply it and send it back." There was a catch in the girl's throat. "The kids died, Ravi. All hundred and seventy-three of them. And when they were sure, absolutely sure, that everyone aboard was dead, they towed that boat to a safe distance and blew it up." The girl's lips were pressed into a tight line. "If you like, I can tell you the name of every single one of those children. It's one of the first things they teach us at school."

Ravi shook his head, horrified. And yet, somehow, he felt he'd heard the story before. Pushed by an invisible wind, the dream boat cut silently through the endless water. Ahead of it, hanging low over the bow, *Newton* loomed ever larger. He was close enough to see that her paintwork was spotless, the long lattice of her spine unscarred and ice-free; her vast habitat wheels, all ten of them, were moving in perfect contra-rotation. Unlike the *Archimedes* or the *Bohr* or the *Chandrasekhar*, she hadn't aged a sol. She was perfect. He turned his attention back to the girl.

"But you survived in the end," he suggested. "We wouldn't be having this, uh, *conversation* otherwise."

The girl favored him with a faint smile.

"We survived," she agreed. The smile vanished. "Some of us. *Newton* left Earth with twenty-one thousand people aboard. By the time it was all over, we were down to less than four. It would have been even worse if we hadn't found a cure."

"You found a cure?" Ravi repeated, stunned. "For scalene plague?"

The girl nodded. Behind her, the boat seemed to be rising up to meet the *Newton*. He fought the temptation to squint with his dream eyes. There were shadows flying around the ship. Or, at least, there seemed to be. Fleeting silhouettes against the brightness of her hull. He couldn't quite make them out.

"We cured scalene plague once and for all. But we were a basket case. The Captain and the senior officers were dead. We had no botanists and the hydroponics failed. There was rioting in the circulars. If the ship hadn't been able to look after herself, to tell us what to do and how to do it, we'd either have starved to death or torn ourselves to pieces. As it was, the ship drifted out of formation and went into hiding. With everything that was happening in the habitat wheels, the last thing we needed was the fleet doing to us what it had already done to our lifeboat."

Her eyes glittered with tears—and a hint of defiance.

"You must hate us," he whispered.

Now it was the girl's turn to shake her head.

"Not all of us," she said. "It's why I'm here. To put an end to this. I want no part of a genocide."

"You have a plan?"

"Totally." Her crooked smile returned in full force. "Though I'm not sure you're going to like it. We need you to disarm the fleet and turn on your transponders. We'll do the same at our end."

Waking Ravi would have been alarmed, but his dream self was only half-listening. The sailboat, tilted subtly to one side, was almost at the *Newton* now, aiming for the spine as if intending to dock. They were close enough for the fleeting shadows around the ship to resolve themselves into something more solid.

Dream or not, Ravi could feel his jaw drop and his heartbeat quicken. They were . . . animals. Alive. Creatures that hadn't been seen on Homeworld since the late Middle Ages. Or were they made up? He wasn't quite sure. He searched back in his mind, trying to dredge up their name.

Dragons. Nine of them, circling the *Newton* in an elaborate aerial dance.

But we're in space, his rational mind protested. *How can they breathe?*

It was as if one of them had heard him. Red and iridescent blue-green, it turned its head in his direction, and its body followed, moving sinuously toward the boat. And then it was upon them and suddenly terrifying, its jeweled eyes filled with rage, its vast mouth gaping open to reveal fangs as long as Ravi was tall. It reared above the boat's high mast, looking down at them.

"Don't worry," the girl whispered. "This always happens." But her voice was unsteady. Fear gripped at his chest. The girl closed her eyes.

A pillar of fire erupted from the dragon's mouth, engulfing them in flame.

D ragons?" Boz asked quizzically. He could tell by her expression that she was looking them up in the hive libraries. "Odd thing to dream about, isn't it? Even for you." She'd almost finished breakfast. The last of the fruit and tofu hid vainly in the corners of her plate. All around them, Ansimov's echoed to the *click-clack* of cutlery, the low hum of early morning conversation.

"It wasn't *my* dream," Ravi said. "It was hers—and she was really, *really* scared of 'em. Don't ask me why." Ravi *knew* why. He just didn't want to explain. Even in the waking world, the memory of it made him tremble.

"I mean they're not even real, are they?"

Ravi shrugged his shoulders. The libraries were strangely ambivalent on the subject. On the other hand, he knew for a fact the old-time movies were full of them. In the movies, at least, no one seemed to question their existence. Not if they wanted to live, anyway.

"Do you want that?" Boz asked, reaching across for his plate.

"Yes!" he snapped, batting her hand away. "Not everyone eats like a recycler."

"Judgy much? Did the girl explain what the dragons meant?"

"No. She was too busy getting burned alive." He remembered the way their skin had blistered and crackled and caught fire. The searing explosions of pain. The sudden appearance of bones.

Boz was undeterred.

"Well, next time the two of you share a romantic dream, be sure to ask her *before* then, eh?" The glint in his cousin's eye was wicked. Ravi, suddenly embarrassed, stared down at his plate. Even when he'd recovered, he took care to make sure no one else was listening before he spoke again.

"Can we do what she wants? Is it possible?"

"The better question is: *should* we do what she wants?" Boz let loose a low whistle. "This is sarded up, Middy. Totally sarded up." She leaned across the table, switching over to code. *"Assuming they exist and we can find them, turning on the transponders will broadcast the fleet's exact position to the Newton. If she decides to shoot us up, she won't miss. And if we disarm these weapons your girl-friend seems to think we have, we won't be able to shoot back, either."*

"She'll do the same on Newton," Ravi coded back. *"I think the plan is to make sure everyone can get killed so no one is."* He gave an apologetic little shrug. *"She didn't exactly descend to the particulars."*

"And what if she doesn't follow through? Are you going to risk thirty thousand lives on the back of a dream?"

"I think she will, though." Ravi leaned across the table. *"I realized something else last night. When she tramples through my head, she leaves stuff behind. Memories. She made a kid eat cake, once. With her mind. More importantly, she's fallen in with some kind of peace group. Her memories are real, Boz. So real, I can feel them like my own. I think we can trust her."*

"Let me get this in the airlock. You're willing to trust this girl because of 'memories' this same girl has planted *in your head? Sard me, Rav. If she can make you see things when you're awake, and talk to you in your dreams, what makes you think she can't gin up a couple of fake memories about cake and honorable intentions?"*

Ravi's mouth was suddenly dry. In the cold light of day-cycle, the whole thing sounded stupid.

Not stupid, he told himself. *Insane.*

"Let's not cross those hubs until we get to them," he suggested. *"We can worry about what to do once we find the transponders and the weapons. If they don't exist, we're done. If they do . . ."*

His electronic voice trailed off, helpless.

▬ ▬ ▬

"Make like you're busy," Ansimov insisted, the words echoing in Ravi's helmet. "Chen Lai's coming."

"I *am* busy. I don't need to pretend." Nonetheless, he made sure his drones put on a good show as Chen Lai appeared from behind the round dishes of a sensor array. Speeding along the ship's spine, he was clearly a man in a hurry. Encased by the thronelike confines of an EMU, the Chief Engineer bore a startling resemblance to an old-style monarch. At least, if the monarch were wearing a spacesuit and jetting along at several meters per second.

Ravi chewed on his lip. Outside of the safe confines of a maintenance bay, EMUs made him nervous—and Chen Lai was really flying. Untethered to any part of the ship, it was all too easy to go shooting off into space with no way to get back. Despite the best efforts of the lifeboats, people had been lost that way.

Chen Lai seemed to have no such concerns. With a hard puff of reverse thrust, he brought himself to a halt about fifty meters away from their position. A few more puffs from the thrusters, and the blank mirror of his faceplate turned slowly in their direction. Ravi, imagining cold eyes behind the cold glass, felt his heart thud in response.

"Have you found any fractures?" he asked brusquely. "Any at all?" The voice in Ravi's helmet sounded no more irritable than usual, so he relaxed a little.

"No, sir," he replied. He pointed a bulky, gloved hand at the crisscrossing struts of the spine he and Ansimov had been inspecting. "Everything's normal." He hesitated before adding, "Temperature's slightly up. It's almost thirty Kelvin. Not enough to shift the stress gauges, though."

"Good." Ravi could tell from the flow of code that the engineer was downloading raw data from the drones. "And good catch on the temperature. The Destination Star must be starting to warm us up. In a few months, it'll be warmer out here than any time since First Crew. Last thing we need is stuff cracking with the heat. We'll keep an eye on it."

And with that he was off, climbing toward the habitat wheels and the front of the ship at breakneck speed.

"Suck-up," Ansimov muttered when Chen Lai was safely out of range.

"I just call 'em like I see 'em," Ravi replied, smiling. He was about to needle Ansimov some more when he noticed that Chen Lai had stopped again. He had maneuvered himself close to the spine, just shy of where it merged with the outer hull of the hubs, and maybe five hundred meters "above" Ravi, Ansimov, and their attendant drones.

Thing was, there was no reason for Chen Lai to stop there. There were no teams at work and nothing scheduled. Chen Lai hovered in place for more than a minute and headed forward again, disappearing from view behind one of Hungary's long-dead spokes. Curious, Ravi cranked up the suit's augmented vision, hoping to see what had caught the engineer's attention. All he could see, though, were struts and pipes and cables. Nothing unusual.

Except for the dark, shrouded mass lying flush with the main gantry.

"Where are you going?" Ansimov asked, his voice ringing accusingly over the radio. "You're not even halfway done."

"I'll be back in a minute. I just want to check something out."

Lacking Chen Lai's EMU, it took Ravi a good deal longer than a minute to hook his tether to a suitable safety cable and make his way, hand over hand, to the object of Chen Lai's attention. If Chen Lai hadn't stopped, he'd never have noticed it. Even up close, it didn't look like much. Just some long, flat mechanism covered by a shroud to keep off the dust.

Or shield it from prying eyes. Careful not to get tangled in his tether, he spun slowly around to make sure no one was close by. Then, wedging himself in the angle between a couple of struts, he untied part of the shroud. And then some more, until the entire mechanism was exposed.

"What the hungary do you think you're doing?"

Ravi started with fright, the motion hurling him end over end, away from the gantry. Ansimov's laughter rang in his ears.

"Not funny," Ravi snarled, throwing out arms and legs to kill his rotation. He yanked angrily on his tether to pull himself back in. "You could have told me you were close by."

"And you could have been doing your job. It won't get done on its own, you know." In Ravi's frame of reference, Ansimov was standing upside-down on the gantry, several meters "above" Ravi's head. As ever, it was impossible to read his expression. The white glare of the Destination Star burned out of the mirrored surface of his faceplate. Ravi flipped to land on the gantry feet-first, within touching distance of his partner.

Ansimov was bent down, looking at the mechanism. Even through the suit radio, Ravi could hear a sharp sucking-in of breath.

"Do you know what this is?" Ansimov asked. His voice was flat, without inflection.

"Maybe," Ravi replied carefully. "What do *you* think it is?" If he was right, Ansimov knew stuff like this backward. If he was wrong, he'd rather not make a fool of himself.

Ansimov's spacesuit straightened up and turned toward him. There was no glare in the faceplate now. Instead, all Ravi could see was his own suited reflection. And, beyond that, the trelliswork of the ship's spine, stretching out behind him toward the stars.

"It's a Kasimov-fifty mass driver," the suit said, its voice shaking.

Hearing it from Ansimov suddenly made it real. The blood drained from his face, leaving him lightheaded.

Someone had gone back to the LOKI wars and copied the design for a space gun.

— — —

The Seventh Gen children were running through the arboretum, the simulated light of a setting Home Star irradiating their heads. Not that they cared. They raced across fields and between the trees in a cavalcade of screams and giggles, their Fifth and Sixth Gen chaperones watching carefully from the shade. Ravi wished he had the nerve to run after them—or at least to walk under the blazing ball of fire with his head held high. But he just couldn't do it. He stood safely in the shade of a giant tree and looked on helplessly. Like all the Sixth Gen kids, he'd only come to the arboretum after dark. He'd liked the quiet light of the Homeworld moon, the feel of the night-silvered grass against his feet. The searing heat of the Home Star was just too much. For the Seventh Generation, though, deliberately exposed to it from birth, it was just another sol. A literal walk in the park.

Feeling inadequate, he distracted himself by watching Sofia crossing the meadow toward him. She was wearing a blue baseball cap, carefully chosen to match the blue of her fatigues, and—what had she called them?—sunglasses. Apparently, they were all the rage in Bermuda and Australia now—if a person had the water. Ravi had no idea how much they cost, but they allowed her to walk under the Home Star without hunching over in panic. She looked as elegant as ever. More so, really. The trees, and the grass, and the wildflowers beneath her feet made her look . . . stunning. His stomach knotted with longing.

"You've got it bad, haven't you?"

It was the girl, crooked smile broad and slightly mocking, stretched out on the ground next to him, back against the tree trunk.

"What are you doing here?" Ravi asked, his voice strained high with surprise. "This is not a good time." His eyes skidded from the girl to Sofia and back to the girl again.

The girl's smile got wider.

"You know she can't see me, right?"

"Yeah, but *I* can. And you're . . . distracting."

The girl laughed at that: sweet, musical notes that spiraled past his ears and into the leaves above. She reached over and patted him on the ankle.

"Have it your way," she said lightly, and was gone.

"Who are you talking to?" Sofia asked curiously.

"No one," Ravi assured her, far too quickly. Sofia's forehead crinkled with suspicion.

"Vlad," he lied, referring to Ansimov. "He's lost the manual interface to one of his drones and he's freaking out about telling Chen Lai."

"I'm sure he'll figure it out." She fixed him with a radiant smile. "Let's figure out what Warren was trying to teach us this morning, instead. Do you think she makes this stuff difficult on purpose?"

For some reason, Sofia's smile didn't quite hit the mark. It was the girl, Ravi supposed. Just because he couldn't see her didn't mean she wasn't there. Or did it? He found himself staring at his feet, remembering her hand on his ankle.

"*Hey!*" Sofia cried, irritated. "What am I? Suit rations? You could at least pay me some attention!"

"Sorry," he said contritely. But the memory of the girl—and what she wanted—still lingered. "Sofe?" he asked. "Do you know anything about transponders?"

"Transponders?"

"Yeah," he said, bending the truth. "There's some First Crew records that *seem* to reference 'em, but I can't find anything to show they ever existed. No blueprints, no nothing."

"Transponders are, like, Navigation one oh one," Sofia told him impatiently. "They broadcast a ship's location and vector so as to avoid collision with other ships."

"I know what a transponder is, Sofe. I'm just asking if we have one. If we *ever* had one."

"Sure," Sofia said, clearly surprised that he didn't know. "The controls are in Main Navigation." She flashed over a schematic in her slightly clumsy fashion. It was from a Navigator training manual, something he'd never have thought to access on his own. "Old-style, hands only, to prevent hacking. The Home Star system was full of spacecraft, so sabotaging a transponder was a big deal, particularly during the LOKI wars." She shrugged. "Out here, having it on was kind of pointless. It's been switched off since forever, but it still works." She looked thoughtful for a moment. "I guess we'll need it when we get to Destination World. There'll be three ISVs, plus the lifeboats, plus however many probes and satellites we put out there, all flying this way and that in close orbit. We wouldn't want to go crashing into each other by accident."

"Makes sense."

"Enough transponder talk," Sofia said, smiling. "Time to study."

"Sure." But he was thinking about other things. About the girl. And about the fact that if he wanted to activate the fleet's transponders, he would have to break into Main Navigation on three separate ships.

Boz had messaged Ravi, asking him to come to the Fiji bolt-hole, but Ravi had refused. His time with Sofia over, everything arced cross-wise in his head: Sofia, the girl, the transponder problem—everything. The ship, the fleet—his entire world—felt like it was closing in on him. He couldn't think straight. He couldn't see a way out. He couldn't *breathe*. The last thing he needed was to be stuck in a confined space with Boz and her bescumbered cigarettes. He needed to get away from it all. If only for a little while.

Meet me in Australia, he'd messaged back. *Haiphong Circular. Twelve o'clock spoke. Don't be late.*

Arriving before his cousin, he waited as patiently as he could, leaning against a Fourth Gen mural of dubious merit and enduring curious glances from well-watered passersby. Boz, perhaps sensing from afar that her cousin was on the ragged edge, jumped off the spoke-twelve paternoster more or less on time.

"We need to talk," she said, without pausing for pleasantries. "But not here. Somewhere less . . . public."

"Later. We're going to the movies."

Boz let loose a sigh of disapproval.

"The movies? We have more important things to do. *Much* more important."

"Nothing that can't wait a couple of hours," Ravi insisted. And then, when it looked like Boz was going to fight him: "I *need* this."

"This is your old man's fault," Boz grumbled. "He should never have gotten you hooked on these things."

"He did love 'em," Ravi agreed. "Some of the best times I ever had with him were right here, watching movies." Ravi paused, suddenly unable to go on. He could feel a tear pricking at the corner of his eye.

"Okay," Boz said, pretending not to notice. "What are we going to see?"

Ravi took a deep breath. Righted himself.

"*The Treasure of the Sierra Madre.* Humphrey Bogart, nineteen forty-eight."

"*Nineteen* forty-eight? Are you sure? Weren't they still, like, riding horses and shooting muskets and stuff?"

"I'm sure. You know movies started in the late nineteenth century, right?"

"If you say so." Boz's eyes glazed over as she accessed the hive. When they focused again, they were accompanied by a serving of disapproval. "This is one of those Homeworld things I just don't get," she complained. "It's, like, totally sarded up."

"Why?" Ravi started off along the circular, heading for the Roxy, the only "authentic" movie theater in the entire ship.

"Because the whole film's about a bunch of guys hunting for gold. I mean, who *does* that? It's *gold!*" Her left hand ran down the fingers of her right, ticking off objections. "You can't drink it, you can't breathe it, you can't eat it, and you can't really wear it. And on top of that, it's *heavy*. The amount of fuel you'd have to burn just moving it around is insane. The stuff is worthless! And yet, for some sarding bizarre reason no one has ever explained to me, these people keep thinking it's worth killing for." She shrugged her shoulders. "Like I said: sarded up."

"Maybe they liked it because it's shiny," Ravi joked. The Roxy was just ahead of them, an old-style revolving door underneath an equally old-style awning that announced the movies "now showing" in solid letters that had to be placed there by drone. A small trickle of stylishly dressed people was headed to the entrance. Couples mostly. And mostly Sixth Gen . . .

Ravi slowed to a halt. Boz almost ran into the back of him.

"What's up?" she asked.

Ravi didn't answer. He was too busy staring at Jaden Strauss-Cohen. And the woman-who-wasn't-Sofia nestling against him and nibbling at his ear. Shorter than Sofia and with more curves, she looked both beautiful and vaguely familiar. The name crept to the tip of his tongue and stayed there, refusing to go any farther.

"That's Ksenia Graham," Boz whispered in his ear. "Quite the thing in hydroponics, I'm told." Her voice vibrated with mischief. "I wonder what she could *possibly* be doing with your navigator's boyfriend!"

Ravi remembered now: a junior botanist maybe two years older than he was. He'd seen her briefly in the Tank nightclub, just after Vasconcelos had busted their hack of the personnel files. Sofia, he recalled, had been glaring at her. With good reason, it appeared. Jaden was a gullgroper. And a two-timing one at that.

"How do *you* know her?" he asked Boz, still staring at the two of them. Boz chuckled.

"I know a *lot* of botanists. Who do you think supplies me with tobacco?"

Ravi muttered something inarticulate in response. He was hoping the illicit couple were going to see a different movie. Of one thing he was sure: he didn't want to be sharing a night-cycle out with them.

Perhaps, in his annoyance, he'd dropped some loose code into the hive. He'd certainly started a recording without even thinking about it, but that was internal and shouldn't have leaked. Nonetheless, *something* made Jaden glance up and see him. He looked briefly displeased before smoothing his features into a welcoming smile. He peeled Ksenia off his shoulder and walked across to them.

"Good evening, MacLeods," he said languidly. "What brings you two here? A bit out of your, ah, *usual* orbit, aren't you?"

Boz was standing in Ravi's blind spot, but he needed neither eyes nor coding to feel her bristle.

"We're here for a movie," his cousin said icily. "And nothing more. Unlike you and your . . . *friend*."

Jaden winced as the shot hit home. But his smile returned almost immediately. He leaned in toward them, wrapping his arms about both their shoulders.

"Look: about that," he murmured. "Sofia's great and all, but she's a bit . . . *clingy*. Know what I mean? There's no need for any of this to get back to her, is there?" His tone hardened, just a little. "After all, Roberta, I'm guessing you'll be needing legal services at some point in the future, yes? And I'm certain you want to stay as far away from the recycler as possible." His smile widened into a grin, wolfish and unfriendly. "We wouldn't want some, er, *error* to turn you into compost, would we?" He turned his attention to Ravi then, breathing into his ear. "And remember: Sofia wasn't the only one who covered for you in the Tank. I did too. You do *not* want me going back to the Inspector with a sudden change of recollection." He paused, as if struck by a sudden thought. "And if you're not worried about yourself, think about what it would do to Sofia. She'd be an accessory to whatever it was you were up to. I doubt she'd thank you for getting her thrown off the program."

He stepped back. Glancing from one MacLeod to the other.

"Good talk," he said, satisfied by what he saw there. He turned on his heel and marched back toward Ksenia, arms wide and welcoming. Ksenia rushed into them just as quickly as she could get there.

Ravi tried to stop the bile from rising in his throat.

"Sard the movie. I'm not in the mood anymore."

"Roger that." Boz grabbed him by the hand. "Like I said, we need to talk." She dragged him farther down the circular, pushing people out of her way as she did so. They were approaching the Tank nightclub. Off to one side, the walls suddenly disappeared, deliberately revealing the struts and piping of the ship's innards. A sparse waist-level rail was the only thing stopping them from plunging a couple of dozen meters into the wheel rim, which, given the wheel was making turns for a full g, would be a seriously bad thing.

The indistinct sound of dance music could already be heard in the distance. Boz dragged him onto the catwalk leading to the Tank without breaking stride. Until, that is, Ravi pulled away.

"I'm not going in there. What makes you think I want to dance at a time like this?"

Boz spared him a pitying look.

"No one's going dancing. And no one's going to the Tank. Though you could do with living a little."

And with that, she vaulted the catwalk rail and disappeared from sight. Ravi yelped in alarm.

"I'm down here, idiot."

Ravi leaned over the rail. Boz was standing on a wide pipe a couple of meters below him.

Trying not to think about what would happen if either of them slipped, Ravi dropped down to join her. Boz skipped along the pipe back toward the circular. The pipe was meant to disappear seamlessly into the bulkhead and continue under the deck above, but one of the bulkhead panels had come away and no one had bothered to repair it. Boz dropped onto her stomach and wriggled into the unlit cranny beyond.

With a certain amount of queasiness, Ravi followed. He was bigger than Boz, so he scraped his back getting in, but he managed it. Once through, the space on the other side was big enough to sit up in and possibly stand. Ravi couldn't be sure because it was almost pitch-black. The only light available was whatever managed to creep in through the same gap they had. Besides, standing in the dark just increased the chances of sliding off the pipe and into Archie knew what. He satisfied himself with sitting. His cousin's vague outline loomed in the shadows beside him.

"How in hungary did you know this place was here?" he asked, impressed despite himself.

"I noticed it when we came here to hack the personnel files. And then I came back later to check it out." She let loose a dry chuckle. "You can never have too many bolt-holes."

His dad, he admitted reluctantly, had taught her well. Of course, if he'd taught her *less* well, she probably wouldn't be on first-name terms with all the ship's barristers and half the officers in ShipSec.

"So," he asked, "what's so important that you literally have to find a hole in the wall to talk about it?"

There was a small, startling flash as Boz lit up a cigarette.

"It's about your last dream," she said. "About the 'weapons' part of transponders and weapons."

"I was going to tell you," Ravi jumped in, anticipating what she was going to say next. "There's a mass driver on the ship's spine. Vlad and I saw Chen Lai inspecting it during the work shift."

Dark as it was, he couldn't see Boz's expression.

"Mass drivers aren't the half of it," his cousin replied. The red glow of her cigarette flared brighter as she took a quick puff. He could tell by the way it moved that her hands were shaking. "I've figured out what they're doing at Manchester Passage."

"Which is what?"

"That probe they're building? It's not a probe at all." Even hidden away in the dark, her voice had dropped to a whisper. "It's a sarding torpedo."

Ravi could feel the blood draining away from his face.

"I knew it was too big for a probe," Boz muttered. "I *knew* it. Way too much fuel capacity; Mark Nine thrusters. And the *software* . . ." Now her voice was shaking in time with her hands. One of them struck out through the gloom and grabbed him by the wrist. The grip was cold and unsteady. "All that programming they asked me to do? The stuff that was too secret to talk about? Even with you?" Her fingernails were digging into his wrist. "They let me build them a killer, Ravi. Standard autonav takes you from point A to point B in the most fuel-efficient way possible. I built this thing so it could hunt and evade. It's not a LOKI like your little present, but it's not far off. I thought it was to track down small moons and avoid collisions. But it's not. It's to track down and kill the *Newton!*" To Ravi's horror, Boz had started to cry. "I knew the parameters were too high-end, too demanding. But I didn't care. I was too blinded by the fun of it to think about what I was doing. And now I've built them a killing machine." She stopped to draw a long, ragged breath. "I might be many things, Rav, but I'm not an executioner." Her voice was so low, Ravi could barely hear it. "There must be thousands of people on that ship. *Thousands.*" Another wretched sob. "Niko Ibori has turned me into an Archie-damned, sarding murderer."

Ravi was quiet for a long time, unsure of what to say.

"How'd you find out?" he asked in the end, cursing himself for a fool even as he did so. Why couldn't he say something nice? Something sympathetic? His cousin was *crying,* for Archie's sake.

Strangely, though, the question, matter-of-fact as it was, seemed to calm Boz down.

"It was those sarding compartments," she said, sniffling. "Stupidest place to build anything *ever.* It's not just that they shouldn't be there; it's that most of 'em can only be accessed from space. So, I snuck outside at the end of a shift when no one was watching and took a look around. The hatches are pretty much invisible, even when you're standing next to them. But if you're hiding behind a vacuum tarp when the Chief Engineer and a bunch of his senior officers come out of the same airlock you just did, and you see them open them up by pushing a bunch of buttons—*buttons,* if you can believe that—then everything becomes pretty sarding obvious." She took a long drag on her cigarette, the tip glowing brightly enough to light up her face. She looked drained, almost weary. "The compartments are full of combat stuff: stealth armor, proximity fuses . . . nuclear warheads."

Ravi felt suddenly dizzy. He remembered the radiation alarm when he and Boz had dropped under the deck at Manchester Passage. How not all of the radiation had been coming from outside. He tightened his grip on Boz's hand, worried he might fall off the pipe.

"They're running double shifts," Boz continued. "The first one thinks it's building a probe. The second one, the one after everyone else has knocked off, is weaponizing the hungary out of it." A humorless chuckle. "I was almost out of air before I was able to sneak back in."

"Can we disable it?"

"I think so. I just need to figure out how—and soon. They're almost . . ."

The pipe beneath them jerked to the sudden sound of an explosion. The two of them were thrown to one side. Ravi tried to hold on, but the pipe was too round, too smooth for his fingers.

He fell.

There were klaxons going off in his head. Or were they coming out of the walls? His arm was throbbing. And it was so dark . . . .

"Ravi? Are you okay? *Ravi!*" Boz was frantic. Her voice was coming from somewhere above him, which made no sense.

Except, suddenly, it did. The explosion. The jerking pipe. The fall. He was lying on his back against some curved, uneven surface. He tried to sit up. The throbbing in his arm became jerking, stabbing agony.

"Ow!"

"Ravi?"

"Down here." A statement of the sarding obvious. He quietly cursed himself for his stupidity. The klaxons were real: he'd had to raise his voice to shout over the top of them. The air was acrid with smoke. Somewhere close by he could hear the whining of a pump.

"Are you okay?"

"No. I think I've broken my arm." Just saying it out loud made it hurt. He stifled a whimper.

Boz's voice had retreated from the edge of panic. It was more businesslike now.

"Are you bleeding out? Can you tell?"

"I don't think so." He reached out into the hive, dragging up the blueprints for Australia-12, figuring out where he had to be. He found the Tank, followed the piping into the wall. Dropped down to . . . *here.* A curving mezzanine bulkhead a deck and a half below Haiphong Circular. There were a couple of power conduits to his left and a wastewater ballast tank to his right, which explained where the pump sound was coming from. The tank was either filling up or emptying, shifting mass from one part of the wheel to another to keep everything balanced out.

Ravi grimaced to himself. The mechanics of wheel balancing were the least of his worries.

"Boz?"

"Yeah?"

"Get out of here. You don't need the attention right now."

"What about you?" It was clear from her voice that she was reluctant to leave.

"I'll be fine. I'm an engineer. I saw a gap in the wall, stuck my head in to investigate, and fell off." Trainee officer or not, he was still a MacLeod. He could sell a story if he had to. "Get lost!" he said gently. "No one needs you!"

"Sard you, too!" He could hear her scrambling back along the pipe. Ravi gave her a few minutes to get clear and then, wincing at all the trouble he was about to cause, launched an SOS into the hive.

It took ShipSec an hour to dig him out. With kind words and painkillers, they put him on a medical drone and wheeled him back onto Haiphong Circular. Drugged up as he was, it took him a minute or two to understand what he was looking at.

A number of shopfronts had been blown out. Black scorch marks blotched the ceiling. Foamy fire suppressant coated the decks. The few lights that hadn't been smashed were shining bright as day in the middle of the night-cycle.

"What's going on?" he asked. The drugs made everything come out in a mumble.

"BonVoys," someone replied bitterly. "They bombed the circular. People are dead."

Ravi's mind spun back in time. He was dropping a primitive piece of string into a water tank, standing with Petrides in front of a cache of stolen water; listening to the Menendez kid talking about "devices." Ravi had thought the kid was talking about fancy holograms, BonVoy propaganda. But this . . . *this* was far worse.

In the end, he couldn't tell if it was the drugs or the killing that had set his wheel to spinning. He passed out.

▬ ▬ ▬

He was lying in his bunk, on a lawn of scalene triangles beneath a bright blue sky. The girl was at his side, leaning over him.

"You're hurt," she said.

"I am?" He didn't feel hurt. But he didn't feel surprised, either. "Is it bad?"

The girl shook her head.

"I don't think so." Her forehead creased in the smallest of frowns, as if she was thinking. "Your brain patterns are slightly off, like you've been drugged. But they're not off-the-charts bad. You're not at death's door."

The sky on top of his dream had turned to night. Unwinking stars peppered the firmament. The girl, however, glowed, as if illuminated by some invisible spotlight. He stared at her a moment, trying to make sense of what was going on.

"Why are you here?" It seemed like a good question.

The girl smiled. Crooked, and a little sad.

"Same as always. To ask for your help." She leaned forward, her gaze intense. His bed gave a sudden lurch, swaying from side to side. Except it wasn't a bed anymore; it was a sailboat, its long mast vanishing into the distance above him, its hull bobbing on mirror-smooth black water.

The boat was moving now, heading toward the *Newton*. Still tiny and far away, but getting closer with every rise and fall of the sailboat's bow. The girl was seated across from him, her back propped against the front of the boat, knees drawn up under her chin. The starship hovered over her shoulder.

"Will you help us?" she asked. "With the transponders and the weapons?"

The question made him anxious, but he didn't know why. Had she asked him before? Had he agreed to help? Was there a reason not to?

And then he remembered. What she'd asked, and how often; the conversations with Boz; the BonVoy bombing; his arm.

"Maybe," he hedged. "You were right, though. There are definitely weapons. A torpedo and a mass driver. The torpedo might be nuclear."

Newton loomed ever larger over the girl's shoulder. She looked solemn but unsurprised.

"The mass driver isn't a problem. It's for close-in work, defending the ship against torpedo attack. The torpedo, on the other hand . . ." She leaned forward, staring into his dream-eyes. "Can you disable the torpedo?"

Ravi nodded.

"And the transponders?"

The anxiety ratcheted up again.

"There are three," he said, speaking far too fast, as if to get it over with. "One on each ship. There are old-style physical interlocks that can only be overridden in Main Navigation by a real person and we're only on this ship and not the others and I don't see how—"

The girl cut him off, laughing. Behind her, the boat seemed to be rising up to meet the *Newton*. There were shadows flying around the ship, he noticed. He watched them with a vague sense of foreboding.

"If I can get you into Main Navigation—on any ship—can you turn them on?"

"Sure. But—"

"And can you *keep* them on?"

Ravi frowned.

"I could fry the controls," he suggested, after a moment's hesitation. "The system is designed to 'fail safe,' so the transponders will turn on and stay on until they can fix the interface or destroy the transponder." He smiled mischievously. "Thing is, the transponder itself is buried inside the main shield. That thing is *tough*. It'd take them weeks to dig it out. It'll be easier to fix the interface—and if we make enough of a mess, that'll take forever too. Old-style controls are real difficult to work with. It's basically Steel Age tech."

The sailboat, tilted subtly to one side, was almost at the *Newton* now, aiming for the spine as if intending to dock. The ship was escorted by dragons. Nine of them, circling the starship in an elaborate aerial dance.

How can they breathe? he wondered.

It was as if one of them had heard him. It reared above the boat's high mast, looking down at them.

"I can get you to the controls," the girl said. "All of them."

"And don't worry. This always happens."

The girl closed her eyes. A pillar of fire erupted from the dragon's mouth.

▬ ▬ ▬

"How's it feel?" Fairley MacLeod asked. The wrinkles around his mom's eyes were deepened by worry, and she'd clearly been crying. Her hair, though, was pulled back in a tidy braid and she was wearing her best set of fatigues. A little necklace from Homeworld glittered on her neck. She reached out to play with his hair, hesitating halfway there, at about the point where he'd usually start backing away. But he didn't. He let her fingers flutter across his scalp, delicate and deft, bringing back his childhood with each gossamer-light tug. Boz was standing a little way behind her, a relieved smile on her face.

"I feel good," he told them, slightly surprised to be saying it. He'd snapped his right arm in two places and broken his collarbone. The medics had kept him unconscious for the best part of three sols while they fixed him up. Now, apart from a bit of stiffness, he felt as good as new. His discharge papers glowed comfortingly on the inside of his eyelids. There was a spring in his step as Boz led the way out of the Main Infirmary. His mother clung to his arm as if scared to let him go. Reaching the lobby, Ravi looked around curiously.

"Seems real crowded."

"It is," Boz said, glancing at him over her shoulder. "The sarding Bon-Voys hurt a lot of people—and not just here: they hit *Bohr* and *Chandra* as well."

"What?" The news bought Ravi to a halt. Boz, however, kept going. His mother had to haul on his arm to get him moving again. Boz was still talking, firing words over her shoulder as she walked.

"Same time, same targets. High-end stores selling 'planetary goods.'"

"Planetary what, now?"

"Planetary goods," Boz repeated. She stepped out of the infirmary and onto Denmark's Bristol Circular. Consistent with good medical practice, they were only deep enough in the wheel for 0.7 *g*, so Boz's strides covered a lot of deck. "Destination World 'fashion' for folks with more water than sense: sunglasses, baseball caps, raincoats, that kind of stuff. Everything the well-to-do planetary explorer could possibly need. Like they have a sarding clue."

"But why?" Ravi was still trying to get his head around what the Bon-Voys had done.

Boz shrugged her shoulders.

"Who knows? BonVoys are crazy. They don't want us landing on Desti-nation World, so I guess anything that celebrates doing exactly that is fair game."

"Do you think they meant to kill anybody?" his mother asked anxiously. "I mean, blowing something up is, well, not good, obviously; I'm not saying that. But, I mean, to *kill* somebody . . . That's a really big deal. Maybe it was an accident."

Ravi looked across at his mother, at the anxious look in her eyes. There was a painful twisting in his gut. His mother always wanted things—wanted *people*—to be better than they were. It's why she'd stuck by Dad to the bitter end.

"I don't think it matters," Boz said. "They made bombs on a *spaceship* and set them off. Think about that. Think what would have happened if they'd cracked open the hull."

"Yes, sure . . . sure, but the hull was a long way away and it was night-cycle," Ravi's mother protested. "The shops were closed."

"But the circular was wide open," Boz reminded her. "There's clubs, and a movie theater, and restaurants for the rich folks. *Any* bomb was bound to hurt somebody."

They'd reached the Denmark-9 spoke. Boz headed straight to the pater-noster and jumped on, leaping the gap effortlessly. Ravi was about to suggest that his mother take the elevator, but she followed suit without breaking stride. Ravi fought down his surprise. He always thought of his mother as delicate, like crystal. But that was her mind. Her body, honed by years of hard physical labor, was lean and athletic. He jumped across after her, by far the clumsiest of the three of them. He winced as his still-stiff arm hit the rungs too hard. The rungs rattled in protest.

"You okay?" his mother asked.

"I'm fine. I just want to get home."

They made their way to Ecuador in near silence. The hubs were deserted. The leafed spheres of the zero trees had the place to themselves. Ravi gave one of them a near pass, taking in a breath or two of heady eucalyptus as he went. The scent helped calm his stomach, which had been on the verge of rebelling.

"Well, here we are," Ravi said, standing outside the door to his quarters. "Come on in." He flashed a key at the lock and the door slid open.

The girl was already inside, her petite body and crooked smile leaning against the bulkhead.

"What took you so long?"

Y our mum seems nice," the girl said. They were the first words out of her mouth since Ravi had walked through the door. She'd stood, quietly invisible, while his mother had gone on and on about how he needed to eat right and take care of himself and not let Boz (*"Stars abound, Roberta, but you can be a bad influence"*) get him into trouble. She'd waited patiently until his mother said her reluctant goodbyes and headed back to her quarters in Fiji. As the door slid closed behind his mother's back, the girl lowered herself to the deck, sitting cross-legged atop Ravi's worn carpet.

Appeared to sit, Ravi reminded himself fiercely. She wasn't really here. It was all in his head.

"What do you want?"

"Excuse me?" Boz replied, startled. And then, seeing that her cousin was staring at a blank spot on the floor, added, "Oh."

The girl's crooked smile widened into a mischievous grin.

"To see you, of course."

"Isn't invading my dreams enough for you?" He was tired and irritable, he realized suddenly. The surgery had hit him harder than he'd thought.

The girl's grin vanished.

"I have to take my chances. And we're running out of time." She gestured at herself with both hands. "None of this is easy, you know."

Ravi took a deep breath, determined to stop the conversation running off the rails.

"Okay," he said heavily. "Let's start again: to what do I owe the pleasure?" Out of the corner of his eye, he could see Boz staring at him, intrigued. He did his best to ignore her, staring instead at the apparition in front of him.

The girl's smile returned, possibly with a hint of relief.

"I have a present for you," she said, pointing at his space chest.

Feeling slightly self-conscious, Ravi stepped over to the chest and opened the lid. Fake BozBall was back.

With three siblings. All four of them were lying on top of his clothes, black, and round, and arranged as if on parade. He was absolutely certain the original drone was the one on the right, but he didn't know why he thought that. They all looked identical. He took a slow, deep breath, gathering his thoughts.

"So, this is what it's been doing since it broke out of my quarters," he asked. "Making more of itself?"

"Among other things." The hackware in his head made it look like she'd gotten up off the deck and walked over beside him. She bent over the open chest and peered inside. "This is how you're going to turn on the transponders."

By some prearranged command, three of the fake BozBalls shifted slightly as their shells slid back to reveal a thumb-sized depression.

"Press here," the girl instructed, "and the trojans will let you log on. Once you're online, you need to tell them how to get to Main Navigation, what the control panel looks like, and what to do when they get there. After that, you can leave the rest to them."

"Trojans?"

"Like the Trojan horse. It comes from ancient, *ancient* Earth. Troy, the city of the Trojans, had been besieged for ten years by Greek invaders— without success. One day, the Trojans woke up to discover the Greeks had sailed away, leaving behind an enormous wooden horse as a sacrifice for their safe journey home. The Trojans, convinced they had won, claimed the horse as booty and dragged it into the city. Unfortunately for them, it was a trick. The horse was full of Greek soldiers. That night, the Greek army sailed back, while the soldiers in the horse sneaked out of its belly and opened the city gates from the inside. The Greek army poured in through the open gates, slaughtered the population, and burned the city to the ground."

"Gnarly," Ravi said. "So, *we're* the Trojans and you're the Greeks? *Archimedes* is Troy?" He picked up one of the trojans, a lump of disquiet forming in his throat. "Is this a trick as well? We open up our airlocks to these things and you blow us to quarks?"

The girl burst out laughing.

"It's just a name." The hackware was definitely getting better at navigating his chipset. It had put a distinct twinkle in her eye. "Do you think we'd call it a Trojan horse if it was actually, you know, a *Trojan horse?*"

Ravi had no answer for that. He stood there in silence, his mind spinning in little circles.

"What's she saying?" Boz asked.

"Shut up," Ravi replied. But there was no heat in his voice.

"Let's assume I believe you, that you mean us no harm," he said to the girl. "All the trojans are here. There's no way I can get them aboard the rest of the fleet."

"Of course there is. I already told you that, remember?"

Ravi gave her the barest of nods. She'd told him just seconds before the dragon had burned them alive—but she hadn't told him how.

The dragon was back in his mind now, and he shuddered, remembering the windy inferno of the dragon's breath; the screaming pain of blackened, blistering skin; the terrible knowledge that he was about to die in the most horrific way possible. It only lasted a moment, but it had felt so *real*. It was the girl's dream, he knew, beautiful and horrific.

"What's she saying?" Boz asked again.

"She's about to tell us how we can get two of these LOKIs—which she calls 'trojans,' by the way—across a hundred thousand klicks of hard vacuum and into our sister ships."

With a wry smile, the girl took the hint.

"Your fleet is still transshipping goods?" she asked.

"Yes. I know for a fact the *Bohr* is short of food, and *Chandrasekhar*'s freeball team is coming over for a playoff game."

"What's a playoff game?"

"Another time. Bottom line: the fleet is still transshipping goods."

"Bonzer," the girl said, which Ravi took as *Newton* slang for *good*. "Once you've told them what they need to know, take two of the trojans and pack them into the cargo, one for *Bohr*, one for *Chandrasekhar*." The girl flashed him a confident, beaming smile. "The trojans will do the rest. Then all you have to do is disable the torp."

"She wants to know if we can disable the torpedo," Ravi told Boz.

"Sure," Boz said, speaking at where she thought the girl might be and failing miserably. "I'm in charge of the coding and I've figured out how to put in a kill switch." A smug smile spread across her face. "That sucker is going nowhere."

"Which is great," Ravi said, turning back to the girl. "But how do we know you'll keep your end of the bargain? All three ships will be defenseless. What if you don't do the same?" The thought sat on his tongue a moment or two before leaping out. "What if you're the Greeks?"

"We're not the Greeks."

He wanted to believe her, to believe the memories she'd left in his head. Cake, and peace meetings, and not wanting to kill anyone.

But then again, she'd made him retrieve a potentially dangerous foreign object from the outside of a lifeboat. Boz had a point. The memories, solid as they seemed, might not be real.

"Yeah, but what if you are the Greeks?" He stared levelly at the girl. "I'm not that long from getting out of school. And school here isn't like it is on *Newton*. They don't teach us the names of the kids who died on that lifeboat of yours. They don't teach us about you at all. What they do teach us is that we stand on the shoulders of a hundred thousand people who lived and died on these ships just to get us where we are today, that we owe it to them to finish the Mission. If we do what you're asking, everything those people worked for—seven generations of hard work, and sacrifice, and danger— could be blown to pieces in a couple of seconds."

"We're not the Greeks," the girl repeated firmly. Taking in the stubborn tilt of Ravi's chin, she smoothed her expression into something more accommodating. "Look," she continued. "*Newton* is dead set on destroying you. You're right about that. It's been planning this attack for years *and it will succeed*. The only way it won't is if you trust me. All I'm asking you to do is give up certain death for a chance at survival."

She flashed him a gentle smile.

"Besides, if I wanted us to kill you, why would I have tried to make contact at all? All I've done is make it harder for us. Does that make sense to you?"

"Space is big. Ships are small. Maybe this way you can't miss."

"*Ai ai ai!*" The girl didn't bother to hide her frustration. "Is there *anything* that will convince you?"

"What's she saying?" Boz asked yet again. Ravi told her.

"Light her up," Boz suggested.

"Beg pardon?" the girl asked, which Ravi had to pass on.

"Light her up," Boz repeated. "Send out a signal the fleet can't miss. It doesn't have to be very long, but long enough for the fleet to know where you are. Then you'll be as vulnerable as we are right now but less than we will be if we do what you ask."

"And then you could kill us," the girl said, "without giving us anything in return."

"What's she saying?"

"She's thinking," Ravi said, pointedly.

Hackware or not, the girl's long, tremulous sigh seemed very real indeed. She chewed worriedly on her lip, her hands thrust deep in her pockets. Ravi held his breath.

"Okay. But I need time to set it up. I'll transmit something loud and proud in the S-band, no more than a few seconds. I'm sure you have a bunch of sensor dishes pointed in our general direction. One of them is bound to pick it up."

It was like standing untethered at the edge of an airlock. If he stepped out, there was no coming back—ever. His heart rattled in his chest. Time stood still.

"Then you've got yourself a deal." The words seemed to come from a long way away.

The girl looked like she was going to say something, but she disappeared instead, ousted from his chipset by a high-priority piece of code. A familiar and unwelcome face painted itself across his mind's eye.

"This is Ship Security," Commander-Inspector Vasconcelos announced, his voice booming inside Ravi's head. *"Official business. Open your door, please. Now."*

— — —

"You couldn't have used the buzzer?" Ravi asked. He'd been aiming for wry humor, but he was too stressed to hit the mark. It came out like a querulous complaint.

Vasconcelos ignored him. He stepped across the threshold, practically brushing Ravi aside as he did so. Nor was the inspector alone: he was followed through the door by the looming bulk of a security drone and another ShipSec officer. Ravi's mouth ran dry. He'd just agreed to betray the fleet, and now ShipSec was at his door? His hands started to tremble. He balled them into fists, trying, with scant success, to get them to stop. The sheer press of people and machinery in the cramped confines of his quarters forced him back against a bulkhead.

Vasconcelos's gaze lit upon Boz.

"A whole nest of MacLeods, I see. Care to confess any crimes today, Roberta?"

If Boz was as terrified as Ravi felt, she was doing a much better job of hiding it. In order to make room for the sudden influx of security, she backed into Ravi's space chest and used it as a chair. In order to do so, she calmly closed the lid, hiding the four trojans from prying eyes.

"No confessions today," she replied breezily. "But I'm more than happy to hear yours, Inspector." The smile she flashed at him was obvious in its insincerity.

Vasconcelos grunted something incomprehensible. He turned his attention back to Ravi.

"How many of your classmates are BonVoys?" he asked abruptly.

"How the hungary should I know?" Relief he wasn't wanted for mutiny made his words blunter than they should have been. Vasconcelos's eyes narrowed dangerously.

"Because they're your classmates," he said, his voice heavy with condescension. "I understand most of them have more sense than to associate with someone of your, ah, *background,* Midshipman, but even you must have *some* friends, surely?" His eyes glazed over, a sure sign he was accessing information. "What about Vladimir Ansimov? Has he ever expressed BonVoy sympathies?"

Ravi's immediate response was a bark of derision.

"*Ansimov?* Not a chance. He thinks BonVoys are insane."

Vasconcelos absorbed the information without apparent surprise.

"The kid's never expressed concern for the native species of Destination World?" he pressed. "Never said anything doubtful about the Mission?"

Ravi shook his head. Vasconcelos stared at his feet and hummed quietly to himself, as if filing away the answers. When he looked up again, his eyes were shrewdly focused.

"What about Sofia Ibori? She ever express regret about colonizing the planet?"

The question brought Ravi up short. Because, truth was, she *had.* A lot. And as for her boyfriend . . . Jaden *was* a BonVoy, no question. His mind flashed back to the demonstration in the hubs: the way Jaden's snarling face had slipped out from under his mask. Even though Sofia wasn't a BonVoy herself, she had no problem going out with one. The thought ate at him, bitter and acidic.

But there was no way Sofia was involved in blowing up chunks of Australia. She was an *Ibori,* for Archie's sake. And Jaden, two-timing gullgroper that he was, was a Strauss-Cohen. They were kin to the Captain, and the Chief Navigator, and the man standing in front of him—officers to the sixth generation. No one from families like that would damage the *Archimedes*. For all intents and purposes, they *were* the *Archimedes*.

He shook his head once again. Vasconcelos favored him with a skeptical stare.

"You understand that three crew are dead because of these people? And another one on *Chandrasekhar,* and four on the *Bohr*? This is not the time to be protecting someone you think is a friend, son. Friends don't go around blowing up our home. Friends don't sabotage the Mission."

"Yes, sir. But I don't know anyone who would do that." That, at least, was the truth.

"Well, if you change your mind, or remember anything, you message me. Got it?"

"Yes, sir." And with that, the Commander-Inspector turned on his heel and walked out the door, drone and officer in tow.

When they were alone in his quarters again, Boz turned to face him, her expression hovering between amusement and concern.

"You know, he didn't believe a single word that came out of your mouth."

"It's the curse of the MacLeods, cuz. I could have told him the honest truth and he wouldn't have believed that either, would he?"

"True," Boz agreed. "Just keep an eye on your chipset, okay?" Her eyes flickered as she tossed him over a bunch of new codes—guardware, by the feel of it. "My latest and greatest. Get these set up before you go to bed. Sure as starlight, Vasconcelos is going to try and stick a tracer on you while you're asleep."

She stood up to leave, a mischievous smile quirking at her lips.

"And when you do sleep, do it well. We have a fleet to sabotage."

Ravi slept through the night-cycle, uninterrupted by dreams. When he woke, the newsfeeds were atwitter about all of two things: BonVoys, and the next round of playoff games. There had been a number of arrests across the fleet. ShipSec on *Chandrasekhar* had raided some abandoned low-*g* compartments and recovered a bunch of explosives, some of which, they said, had been manufactured on *Bohr*. Lieutenant-Inspector Tir, the number two guy at *Bohr* ShipSec, and apparently their spokesperson for this sort of stuff, stood stiff in front of the monitors and said his people were looking into it. But it was apparent he didn't believe a word of what was coming out of *Chandra*. *Bohr*, he said, was prioritizing other lines of inquiry.

The BonVoy menace, as the newsfeeds were now calling it, was not going to stop life aboard ship from proceeding as normal—or nearly normal—as possible. "We will not be terrorized," Captain Strauss-Cohen announced firmly, staring straight to camera. "We will not live life as if there's a Bon-Voy bomb in every gangway. Life goes on. The Mission goes on." She allowed herself a studiedly carefree smile. "And, need it be said, freeball goes on. *Chandrasekhar*'s Spartans are already en route. We look forward to welcoming them aboard tomorrow evening . . . hopefully to crushing defeat."

And with that, the newsfeeds shifted to sports coverage. The playoff picture remained complicated, and the pressure to win what might well be the last fleet freeball tournament ever was increasingly intense.

Ravi tuned it out. He slouched into class a mere forty seconds before he would have been late.

"Did you get lost in the hubs?" Ansimov asked. "I'm told the latest chipsets have navigation built in. Maybe you should learn to use it."

"Har sarding har." Ravi slouched into his usual seat, just in time to have his implants slammed with a particularly vicious data package. Warren was clearly not in the best of moods. With an inward sigh, Ravi settled down for another half-shift of education. He failed to see how six-letter DNA stranding was going to make him a better engineer. But if the navigators had to suck it up . . .

He nudged Ansimov in the elbow.

"What?" Ansimov's mouth wasn't moving, but even in code, he sounded irritated.

"Where's Sofia?"

"No idea," Ansimov muttered, biologically this time. He scanned the front of the class and frowned. "None of them are here."

"None of who?"

"The navigators. Every sarding one of 'em is AWOL."

Ravi scanned the empty chairs with a feeling of dismay.

"You think they've been arrested?" he asked.

"All of 'em? They're *navigators,* for Archie's sake! Are they inbred snobs who wouldn't give you the time of sol if your life depended on it? Totally. But *BonVoys*? Come on!"

Ravi, thinking about Sofia and Jaden, wasn't so sure. He got through his half-shift of education with half a mind, and his half-shift of work in much the same way. Prepping the last of the Fiji compartments for deceleration took him twice as long as it should have. Ansimov, who carried the extra load so they could finish on time, looked at him askance but said nothing.

Shift over, and showered with almost the last of his paycheck, he hurried over to Canada. To his immense relief, Sofia was waiting for him in the arboretum.

"I thought you'd been arrested!" he blurted out. "Where have you been all sol?"

"Hello to you, too! Working, if you must know."

"Working?" Ravi didn't bother to hide his surprise. "On what?"

"I'm not supposed to say. The whole department's been sworn to secrecy."

"You can tell me." He smiled. "I'm a MacLeod. I know how to keep a secret."

Sofia barely pretended to hesitate.

"Okay. But not a word to *anyone*. Got it?"

Ravi nodded.

"We've been taking bearings and crunching numbers all sol. I'm not meant to know why, because Uncle wouldn't tell us. But I know the math, and only one thing makes sense." She was staring at Ravi now, wide-eyed and a little scared. "They've detected something in near space, out past the *Bohr* somewhere. Something emitting in the S-band, so *not* natural."

Her voice was so low, Ravi could barely hear her. "It's a *ship*, Ravi. An Archie-damned *ship*!"

Sofia, Ravi noticed, was trembling, her hand unsteady as she played with her hair. Ravi didn't blame her in the least. He laid a sympathetic hand on her shoulder. He also dropped a quiet line of code into the hive. Unseen, unheard by anyone, it wormed its way to its destination.

Boz, it's Ravi. We're a go.

— — —

"Spartans, go home!"

"Dead Weights!"

"Stop wasting our air!"

The jeering was good-natured. The traditional *Archimedes* welcome for any off-ship freeball team—particularly when the Fleet Cup was at stake. A sizable crowd was floating around the boat elevators, waiting for *Chandrasekhar*'s Spartans to show their faces. The ribald shouting redoubled as the loud hiss of equalizing air pressure announced the arrival of an elevator. Thick doors cycled open, disgorging *Chandra*'s athletes into a cacophony of yells and off-color jokes and portable klaxons.

If the Spartans were fazed by any of it, they gave no sign. Escorted by a flight of ShipSec officers, they kicked off in the direction of Fiji, their kit bags floating alongside, attached to their wrists by brightly colored lanyards. The crowd spun and twisted out of their way—but only at the last possible minute, when collision seemed inevitable. The more-enthusiastic fans bent their knees against some solid surface and pushed off onto parallel trajectories, so as to give the visitors the benefit of their wisdom all the way to the spokes.

No one was really expecting someone to be traveling in the opposite direction, which caused Ravi some trouble as he tried to make his way to the elevator.

"Sorry," he muttered. He'd bumped into some unsuspecting spectator, sending them both tumbling. "Sorry." As he was wrapped in the massive bulk of a spacesuit and the spectator was not, his apologies didn't get him very far. His stomach revolted at the sudden change in direction, but he managed not to throw up on his faceplate.

When he finally reached the elevator airlock, he was surprised to see it guarded by a ShipSec officer and a security drone.

"Where are you going?" the officer asked brusquely.

"Boat pylons," Ravi replied. He removed his helmet and sent over his authorizations with the flicker of an eyelid. "Need to recalibrate the docking clamps." The authorizations were genuine: non-urgent work that Ravi had volunteered to take on for extra credit—and a chance to access the lifeboats. He tried not to think of the two trojans nestled in his toolkit.

The officer's eyes glazed over as she scanned the information.

"Looks good," she said. Her gaze flitted across to the banged-up box floating next to him. "That your equipment? The drone can't get a reading on it."

Ravi nodded.

"It's the lining," he told her truthfully. "Keeps the tools from getting fried."

"I see," the officer responded, pursing her lips. "Open it up, please."

"I'm sorry?" Ravi managed to keep his voice steady, but he could feel cold beads of sweat on his forehead. One look at the trojans and the whole game would be up.

The officer gave him the faintest grimace of an apology.

"It's the BonVoys. After what those gullgropers did to Australia, we can't take any chances. Everything going out on the spine has to be checked. Just in case." She was staring expectantly at the toolkit, waiting for him to open it up.

Bluff it out, son. He could imagine his dad shrugging. *Fuel line's burst, anyway. What have you got to lose?* The merest hint of a sneer. *Or have you gone soft?*

"Y . . . you'll need to get suited up," he stammered.

The officer's eyes narrowed suspiciously.

"Why?"

"B . . . because it's a pylon calibration," Ravi lied. "The instruments are set for hard vacuum." He gave what he hoped was a sorrowful shrug. "The whole box is sealed against atmosphere. If I open it, it'll implode. Probably take my hand off. And it'll *certainly* ruin the instruments." His stomach was starting to heave, but the MacLeod in him managed to keep talking. "And if I do *that,* the Chief Engineer will have my ass. Still, if you can suit up and come with me to an airlock, I'll evacuate the chamber and open it up for you, no problem."

The officer favored him with a steady stare, trying to see if he was lying. Ravi stared back, his gaze as open and guileless as he could possibly make it. Boz and Uncle Torquil would have been proud.

"I guess it's okay," the officer said reluctantly. She floated to one side, giving him access to the doors. "Enjoy the ride."

He threw up in the elevator. But the ride was fine after that. Grabbing a handhold to brace himself against the fake gravity of deceleration, he brought the machine to a halt about 2,500 meters aft of Hungary. He replaced his helmet, cycled the airlock, and stepped outside.

He was floating across the gap between the ship proper and ISV-1-LB-01 *James Clerk Maxwell*. A small cloud of ice crystals, mostly water vapor and unrecovered atmosphere, floated beside him, sparking like powdery diamonds in the light of the Destination Star. They drifted into the stark shadow of the lifeboat and vanished.

He brought himself down boots-first onto the massive bulk of a docking pylon. Mission accomplished, he tethered himself to an anchor point and walked along the pylon to its business end: the giant clamps that held the bulky lifeboat in place.

Summoning a drone from a nearby locker, Ravi opened up his toolkit and set about his assigned task: making sure the force exerted by the clamps matched the force the ship's computers thought they were applying. It took him almost an hour to get everything squared away. Job done, it was time to summon an elevator and return to the hubs.

Except that he didn't. Moving across the shadowed part of the lifeboat's hull, Ravi found an auxiliary airlock and let himself in. He opened the suit visor to save his air supply and breathed in the cold, thin atmosphere of the dormant vessel instead, floating through dully lit compartments on his way to the hold. Despite the warmth of his spacesuit, his teeth chattered with the chill. Puffs of white breath streamed before him as he went.

Opening the last hatch, he drifted into the unlit chasm of the lifeboat's hold. The weak standby lighting that squeezed in behind him withered in the darkness. All he could make out was the night shape of an occasional cargo net, vague and indistinct.

Not that it mattered. The trojans, he had no doubt, could see perfectly well.

He reached into his toolkit and pulled one of them out. It nestled harmlessly in his hand. With a flick of the wrist, he sent it spinning into the gloom.

"Good luck," he whispered. As the little ball vanished from sight, he was struck by a sharp pang of remorse. He almost floated after it in an attempt to get it back. But it was too late. If he tried to retrieve it, he'd never be able to catch it. The trojan's mission had begun. It wouldn't allow itself to be caught again until everything was over. He took a long, shuddering breath and closed the hatch. The transistor was well and truly flipped. In about three hours' time, the lifeboat's flight crew would start prepping her for launch, thickening the atmosphere, taking away the chill, and filling her hold to the brim with surplus soy from the starship's hydroponics. And about seven hours after that, the boat's newly calibrated clamps would spring open, and the vessel would be on her way.

Headed to *Bohr*. With a small, round stowaway.

Leaving the lifeboat, Ravi pulled himself around to the far side of her hull, dust-scarred and stained pink by thirteen decades of exposure to the void. He turned to face aft. Ahead of him, beyond the bulge of the lifeboat's engines, *Archimedes'* ice-encrusted spine stretched for more than ten kilometers, a spidery trellis against a backdrop of stars.

Fortunately, he didn't have to go that far. He only had to make it a kilometer or so to the next set of pylons and ISV-3-LB-03 *The Princess Kaguya*, newly docked from *Chandrasekhar,* with the Spartans freeball team as its most prominent passengers. She'd also brought in a delivery of high-tolerance thruster linings and would be flying back out with a boatload of cabbages in addition to the players. But no one cared about that.

Ravi, nestled by now between the giant nozzles of *James Clerk Maxwell*'s thrusters, focused his gaze on the distant nose of *The Princess Kaguya*.

And jumped.

hat's it doing?" Ravi asked. He wanted to sound disapproving, but curiosity had gotten the better of him.

BozBall was taking small laps of Boz's Fiji bolt-hole, weaving expertly through stacked boxes of series-J motherboards and raw polymer. Why a homemade LOKI needed any kind of exercise was a mystery to Ravi, but the little machine was moving with distinct determination around the entire compartment. Maybe it was calibrating something.

"Not sure," Boz admitted cheerfully, slouching in a wrecked swivel chair and inhaling the last of her cigarette. "I upgraded it to be more like our, ah, *uninvited guests,* and it's been doing stuff like this ever since. I *think* it's testing out its new sensors, but it might just be bored."

"Don't you think you should be more careful? What if someone sees—"

"Up here? The whole point of a bolt-hole is that it's private. Besides, the heat's off." Her chest swelled with contentment. "I'm now rated Satisfactory— *officially.* No more 'provisional' for me!"

"Sofia's uncle signed off?" Ravi was surprised and pleased at the same time. "Job done?"

"Job done," Boz confirmed, beaming. "Old man Ibori was as good as his word. The moment his so-called 'probes'"—she put the word in air quotes— "passed their commissioning tests, he raised my status for good."

Ravi's ears pricked up.

"Probes? As in plural?" He didn't like the sound of that.

"Three," Boz confirmed. "One on each ship." She fished in her pockets for a cigarette packet. "Not that they'll do anyone any good. If someone tries to use them, they'll fly out a ways and just sit there, useless as a cracked faceplate. They can defend themselves if they're attacked, but that's about it." She jammed a new cigarette into her mouth before she spoke again. "Some of my best work," she mumbled proudly. "Hopefully, no one will ever see it."

"What if someone does?" Ravi asked, suddenly worried. "They'll bust you to Dead Weight in nothing flat."

"Nah. Even if they manage to figure out the bug, it looks like the unforeseen consequence of bits of code no one thought would interact bumping into each other. Trust me on this: it's real subtle. Besides, if this plan works, they'll never be fired and no one will ever know."

She exhaled a cloud of blue smoke in Ravi's direction.

"I guess our little friends are on their way?" she asked.

Ravi shook his head.

"Neither of 'em are due to leave until tomorrow morning." His eyelids fluttered briefly as he accessed the shipping schedules. "*James Clerk Maxwell* unclamps at oh-four thirty, *The Princess Kaguya* at oh-six fifty."

At the mention of *The Princess Kaguya*, Boz broke into a mischievous grin.

"Losers! It wasn't even close! I would *not* want to be that lot when they get back to *Chandra*."

Ravi grinned back at her.

"Maybe they were homesick," he murmured with mock sympathy.

He would have said more, but at that very moment, his chipset tingled in response to a powerful incoming signal. He looked across at Boz and saw her eyes widen in surprise, a mirror, no doubt, to the expression on his own face.

A shipwide announcement. The clock in his mind's eye, superimposed across his vision by automated overrides, was already counting down: *3 . . . 2 . . . 1 . . .*

He closed his eyes to block out the confusion of biological inputs.

. . . 0.

The Captain sprang into view. She was seated in her ready room behind a large wooden desk. Her uniform fatigues were crisp and clean, her hair braided back in its usual no-nonsense fashion, her expression deadly earnest.

"Good evening everyone," she began. "This is your captain speaking."

As if it could be anyone else, Ravi said to himself. Despite the seriousness of the situation, the MacLeod-like mental outburst brought a smile to his lips. Boz, he suspected, would be thinking the same thing.

"I apologize for imposing on your time," Strauss-Cohen continued. "I'm sure that for many of you, it's been a busy sol. And with Braking Day approaching, life is only going to get busier." She paused momentarily, staring grimly into the camera. "It is also going to get more dangerous."

Ravi's smile vanished.

"Some little while ago, our sensors picked up a short but powerful S-band radio transmission. It didn't come from the other ships in the fleet, and it didn't come from Homeworld, and the modulations mean it can't be natural. Which means, at the end of the sol, that it can only be one thing. Another ship, unseen, and shadowing our course, and hiding close by."

Ravi could only imagine what the ship's inhabited spaces looked like right now. People rooted to the deck in shock, gasps of surprise, no small amount of fear.

"I regret to tell you that this is not the first signal we have received from this particular vector. It is, however, the first radio signal we have received, and it is the first signal that we are absolutely certain is manmade."

There would be low mutterings on every deck in every wheel, Ravi thought. *Why are they only telling us now?* he imagined someone saying. *What didn't they want us to know? What the sarding hungary is going on?*

"We had suspected there might be something out there, but now we know for sure. This vessel, whatever she is, must have been out there for years. She must have been fully aware of our presence because, until recently, our ship-to-ship communications were on open radio frequencies and easy to detect."

Ravi's mind skipped back to the sudden decision to shift from radio to laser transmission; the brutal hours on the spine installing additional receivers; Sofia's flat assertion that the explanation given for it made no sense; the girl's complaint that the radios had gone silent. Sofia was right. The girl's complaint was valid. Strauss-Cohen hadn't quite come out and said it, but the radios had shut down because the fleet was trying to hide. There was no point firing the drives during the night-cycle if *Newton* could find them the very next sol by the simple expedient of tuning in to an early-morning newsfeed.

"A vessel that shadows you for years, a vessel that knows you're there, a vessel which, knowing all that, *makes no attempt to talk to you*, may very well be hostile. We must hope for the best but prepare for the worst. Accordingly, and out of an abundance of caution, we have already taken steps to mask our position. Because we are now hidden, rest assured that we are safe from hostile action." The Captain's fingers tapped lightly on the edge of her desk, a soft *thud-thud* of admonishment. "That safety, however, will disappear on Braking Day. The moment the main engines fire in earnest, it will be impossible to hide the full glare of our drive signatures. We will present our adversary with a clear and obvious target, and it is then we expect she will launch her attack, if attack there is to be."

The Captain smiled then. A small smile but confident and reassuring.

"Our shadow, should she choose that course of action, is in for a rude awakening. We have built strong defenses, and they are getting stronger every day. Every ship, including ours, is equipped with anti-missile mass drivers. Nothing our adversary launches at us will get through. Every ship, including ours, is now armed with a nuclear-tipped, state-of-the-art torpedo. These are weapons we hoped never to build but which are now sitting on launch pylons, ready to fire. All they require is a firing solution. And thanks to our shadow's accidental radio broadcast, the firing solution is close at hand. Have no doubt about it. In the coming battle, *we are going to win.*" She leaned forward in her chair. "Fellow shipmates. We stand on the shoulders of all those who have gone before us. All those who sacrificed so much, who lived and died within the confines of this ship, so that we might find ourselves where we are today: on the verge of the greatest accomplishment humanity has ever known. We will not let those people down: we will not let our parents, and grandparents, and great-grandparents down. We will complete the Mission—and no mystery vessel is going to get in our way!"

The transmission ended. Even the hive was quiet, Ravi noticed, reduced to little more than a tickety-tock of automated activity. The whole ship had been shocked into silence.

Except for Boz.

"I wonder what she'd have said if she knew her state-of-the-art, nuclear-tipped torpedoes were about as much use as a chocolate rocket."

▬ ▬ ▬

Ravi had misjudged his morning jump across the hubs from Ecuador to the Denmark-3 spoke. As a result, he was running behind schedule. The routing algorithms running through his chipset assured him he would get to class on time, but he wasn't quite so sure. One more screwup, he figured, and he would be feeling the sharp end of Warren's tongue—not to mention a data packet full of extra work. In any event, he had no time to wait for the elevator. He grabbed the cracked rung of the nearest paternoster and let the aging mechanism rattle him down into the wheel. Still worried about the time, he accessed the clock, letting the little digits burn under his eyelids: *0652. The Princess Kaguya* would just have unclamped, he thought. At this very moment, her thrusters would be puffing out propellant, turning the lifeboat's stubby nose toward *Chandrasekhar.* A few minutes more for her navigator to make sure she was aimed along the correct trajectory, and she would be off, her spherical stowaway lurking somewhere in the cargo hold.

The enormity of what he'd done was hitting home like a meteoroid strike. He might just have sentenced thirty thousand people to death; obliterated seven generations of sacrifice and effort. And for what? The—possibly imagined—promises of a girl he'd never met and didn't know? His stomach clenched, a mélange of panic and regret. *It's too late now,* he tried to tell himself. *The boats are on their way. Suck it up and see it through.* But even in his head, it didn't sound anywhere near as bracing as he'd hoped.

"Ravi?"

It was the girl. She exploded into his vision, centimeters from his face. Ravi, startled, lost his grip on the rung.

"Whoa!" he yelled out, falling. Fortunately, they weren't that deep in the wheel yet. He hadn't even reached the first deck, and gravity at this point in the spoke was only about a fifth of a *g.* For a few embarrassing moments, he flailed about like a toddler in free fall, bouncing against the wall of the paternoster shaft, until an outstretched hand was able to reconnect with a rung. He held on to it with a white-knuckled death grip, panting heavily.

"What the sard—"

"Ravi?" The girl's voice was insistent. Worried. "Ravi, can you hear me?"

"Of course I can hear you!" he snarled. "You scared me half to death! You're lucky I didn't break my neck!"

The girl's expression, as insistent and worried as her voice, didn't change.

"Ravi, can you hear me?"

Safely attached to the rungs, Ravi noticed that her voice was echoey with distance, the words out of shape with the curve of her mouth. The image itself was slightly blurred and clearly an image: she wasn't fitting in with her surroundings as she usually did. She was just hanging in the shaft on the other side of the rungs, falling through space at the same speed he was, like a projection.

Ravi tried to concentrate, to reach out with his mind.

"I can hear you," he thought. He didn't bother to speak.

The girl broke into a relieved smile.

"Thank Isaac for that." The smile vanished as quickly as it came. "I don't have a lot of time. They're coming for me."

"Who's coming for you? What's going on over there?"

"No time. Just *listen.* They're rounding us up. Things here have gone pear-shaped." Ravi had no idea what "pear-shaped" meant, but it clearly wasn't good. "Everything went to bootsey the moment we sent out that transmission. I can't get to our transponder. The moment your transponders turn on, the dragons will come for you, and there's nothing I can do about it." She sounded distraught. "Are the trojans programmed?"

"*Yes,*" Ravi coded, his throat tight. "*Two of them left the ship this morning.*" The girl swore softly. She did not, however, look surprised.

"How long till they get there?"

"*Thirty-six hours, give or take.*" He was deeper in the wheel now. Gravity was pulling urgently at his guts, twisting them into knots.

To his surprise, the girl looked relieved.

"Then there's still time. You and your friend Boz need to get your arses over here, stat."

"*To* Newton?" Ravi was incredulous. "*How the . . . Aagh!*"

His head exploded in pain. A nova of light burned out his vision. Blind and screaming, the paternoster dragged him farther into the wheel. Only a deep, primitive part of his brain worked to keep him alive, tightening his hands around the rungs, protecting him from a now-fatal fall.

He couldn't have been that way for very long. When he came to, the paternoster was still taking him down as if nothing had happened. Light from each passing deck seeped through tightly closed eyelids, an in-out tide of bright and dark. He opened his eyes, flinching at the sudden brightness of his surroundings.

Everything was normal. Except that his chipset had dropped a nav grid across his biological vision. And the nav grid was displaying a vector, an insistent green line pointing in one, inflexible direction.

Off the ship.

*T*he dragons will come for you.* Of all the girl's words, these were the ones that stuck. He remembered dreaming her dream. The *Newton*, stark against the blue-dusted stars. The sinuous, shimmering creatures that shadowed her across space. The cool glint of the dragon's eyes, close-up and merciless. The inferno of its breath.

But above all, he remembered the girl. The way she had readied herself for the creature's onslaught. Her barely controlled terror.

"The dragons will come for you."

He hopped off the paternoster on deck twenty-one, circled around to the "up" side, and hopped on again. A passing crewman gave him a curious look but said nothing. He dropped a cloaked message into the hive and watched it disappear into the data stream. His cousin's guardware was doing its job. As far as he could tell, there were no tracers attached.

Boz, its Ravi. Sarding Big Deal. Drop what you're doing and meet me in the usual place, ASAP.

He signaled in sick, explaining to admin that his arm was playing up and he needed to see the medics. Then, as the arthritic clatter of the paternoster pulled him back up toward the hubs, he concentrated everything he had on the cracked plastic of the rungs. His hands were shaking. He didn't want to fall.

The abandoned control room was empty when he got there, but not for long. Boz arrived less than five minutes later, perspiring and out of breath. BozBall rolled along at her side. She flashed him a reckless grin.

"So," she asked excitedly. "What the hungary is going on?"

Ravi told her. Boz's grin vanished.

"For real?"

"For real." He tossed over the vector the girl had left him with. Boz's eyes glazed over as she caught and read it.

"We're going to have to steal a lifeboat," Ravi said gravely.

"Yeah, right. Even if we could steal one, they'd hack the autopilot or shoot us down with one of those fancy new mass drivers. And even if we somehow made it to *Newton,* I doubt *they'd* treat us any better."

"Do you have a better idea?"

"Of course I do. Have you even *looked* at this vector?"

"Well, *duh*. Off the ship to *Newton*. Hence the need for a lifeboat." Even as he said it, however, the twinkle in Boz's eye gave him the distinct feeling he was making a fool of himself. His cousin's ever-widening grin did nothing to lessen the sensation.

"How far away do you think *Newton* is?" she asked. "Two hundred thousand klicks? Three?"

"Something like." The one thing they knew for sure about *Newton*'s position was that she was somewhere out beyond the *Bohr*. And *Bohr* was never much closer than a hundred thousand kilometers. Best guess, she was at least that far again from the *Bohr*; otherwise, she'd be too easy to spot. If Ravi was a betting man, he'd guess closer to three hundred thousand rather than two.

"And we have less than thirty-six hours to get there, yeah?"

Ravi nodded, convinced more than ever that he must be missing something.

Boz bounced his own vector back at him, an embarrassing detail highlighted in throbbing red. The velocity.

"How long," she asked sweetly, "would it take to get there at *fifty meters a second*?"

Ravi felt like a fool. Trainee engineer that he was, however, he couldn't stop himself from dragging the answer out of his chipset.

"At least forty-six sols and change," he mumbled.

Boz cupped a melodramatic hand to one of her ears.

"I didn't catch that. How long?"

Ravi couldn't help but laugh at his own stupidity.

"Forty-six sols," he grinned at her. "If all we have to do is boost ourselves to fifty meters a second, we can do that in EMUs."

Boz, though, didn't smile back.

"This sarding vector of yours can mean one of only two things," she said. "Either your dyed-blonde friend has a ride waiting to pick us up, or—"

"We're going to die out there." Ravi pushed the thought to one side, afraid to look it in the eye. "We need suits. An extra supply of air, water, and suit rations. EMUs, of course." He paused, chewing the bottom of his lip. "Anything else?"

"About a million liters' worth of luck," Boz said. "If you can scrounge up the rations, I'm pretty sarding sure I can get us access to the rest." She paused a moment, thinking. "I'm not sure about the EMUs, though. I mean, I *can,* but the security protocols are, like, vile. It could take a really long—"

"Leave the EMUs to me."

"Seriously?"

"Seriously." He hoped to Archie he was right.

"Well . . . great!" Boz flashed him a reckless grin. "Are we going to do this, or what?" Without checking to see if he was following, she exited the control room, bouncing with every step.

▬ ▬ ▬

Ansimov practically dragged him through the diner kitchens and into the storage unit, worried, no doubt, that they might be overheard.

"You want me to *what?*"

"Lend me those racing EMUs—and three sols' worth of the diner's suit rations," Ravi said again. He was surprised at how low-key he managed to sound—as if asking for suit rations was the hard part.

Ansimov leaned his back against a freezer. Perhaps he needed the support.

"Did you crack your motherboard or something? No sarding way!"

"C'mon, Vlad. It's not like your guys'll be needing them anytime soon, is it? Formula EMU is over—maybe forever. They're not going to miss a couple of useless vehicles. Not for a while, anyway."

"And if I 'lend' you these EMUs"—Ansimov curled his fingers into air quotes—"when will I get 'em back?"

"I don't know."

"*Will* I get 'em back?"

"I hope so."

"You 'hope?' You sarding *hope?*"

Ravi nodded, his expression miserable. A *real* MacLeod, he knew, would have lied his ass off, but he couldn't do it. Ansimov was his friend. His stomach knotted at the thought of what his dad would be saying right now. *Whaddya mean, you told him the truth? What kind of bescumbered idiot are you? You're not a MacLeod, boy; you're a sarding loser!* He'd have been belted, for sure.

For sure.

Ansimov was looking at him shrewdly.

"How much trouble you in, amiko?"

Ravi's breath exploded into the room. A psychic release.

"A *lot*." Just admitting it out loud made him weak at the knees. He held on to a rack of dried soy, just in case.

"Officers out to get you?"

"Something like that, yeah."

Ansimov grunted noncommittally. He levered himself off the freezer and made his way down a tightly packed produce aisle to his own, food-free corner of the unit. Team Spike's racing EMUs, fully serviced, wiped down, and gleaming, were still where Ravi had last seen them, sitting majestically atop the delivery bot's trailer. Ansimov clambered into one and sat down, a medieval king to Ravi's wretched peasant.

"Assuming, just *assuming* I'm insane enough to go along with this, I don't want my implants anywhere near it, understood? Can you do that, at least?"

Ravi nodded.

"I just need you to give me the delivery bot's device ID. I'll pass that on to . . . *someone,* and *someone* will hack the bot and use it to make an unsanctioned delivery. All you'd need to do is make yourself scarce for a couple of hours, preferably somewhere where people can see you. Afterward, just report the theft to ShipSec, and that'll be an end to it."

Ansimov pursed his lips.

"And if ShipSec traces all this to you?"

Ravi allowed himself a wry smile.

"I'm a MacLeod, remember? They won't be looking any further."

Ansimov chuckled.

"I don't know what you've got yourself into, Ravi, but you've got yourself a deal." He held out his hand, the grip warm and insistent. "You're my best friend, amiko; you know that, right? Stick it to the bastards, okay? And come back safe."

"I'll do my best, Vlad; count on it." Tears pricked at Ravi's eyes. He made to go but turned back, his business unfinished. "And the three days' of suit rations?"

"I'll stick it in the EMUs." Ansimov laughed at him outright. "No one tracks suit rations, Rav. They're disgusting. Who would be dumb enough to steal 'em?"

■ ■ ■

Ravi was staring at the trojan. The one he had collected from the outside of the lifeboat. At least, he thought it was that one. The one that had somehow made the other three. Two of which were stashed away in lifeboats en route to the rest of the fleet, while the other was Archie knew where—hanging about Main Navigation, probably, waiting for its chance to wreck the transponder controls.

This one was lying on top of the clothes in his space chest: a boring black ball that could have passed for some childhood leftover, part of a game long since sent to the recycler.

Ravi knew better, though. The boring black ball was a LOKI. Small though it was, it had some level of intelligence. Maybe a lot.

Something that clever might be very useful where they were headed, he thought. Otherwise, he was packed and ready to go. Boz was on her way. All he had to think about right now was the trojan. He reached out, not for the first time, to add it to his toolkit.

And, not for the first time, he pulled his hand back.

He was looking at a LOKI. *A LOKI.* He rolled the word around in his head. It orbited the inside of his skull in uneasy circles. A LOKI. The thing First Crew had boarded ship to get away from. The creation that had almost devastated a planet and turned the bulk of humanity into obedient, risk-averse drones. LOKIs had proven themselves to be fearsome enemies—and even worse friends. And as for this one, who knew where its loyalties really lay? It was a creation of the *Newton*, the unseen shadow that was trying to kill them. What would happen if he returned it to its home? Would it turn on him? Find some way to betray him? Were he and Boz just pawns in some devious LOKI plan to replicate Homeworld on Earth 2.0?

And then he thought about the girl. About her crooked smile, and strange accent, and wickedly sharp tongue. About cake and peace meetings. About S-band transmissions. He trusted the girl. And the girl, in earning that trust, had put herself in some sort of danger. The girl was brave and trying to do something bigger than herself, bigger than her ship. The girl was trying to save them all.

And the girl had sent him the trojan.

He reached into his space chest, picked the LOKI up, and put it in his toolkit. He'd barely closed it up when the buzzer to his quarters sounded. He unlocked the door without even looking, checking the clock as he did so.

"Come on in, Boz. It's not like you to be early."

"Probably because I'm not Boz."

Ravi stiffened. Vasconcelos. He was standing in the threshold, hand resting lightly on the doorjamb. The boxy hulk of a security drone lurked in the corridor outside.

Ravi swallowed hard.

"To what do I owe the pleasure?" He'd wanted to sound unconcerned but failed miserably. His voice came out high and strained.

Vasconcelos didn't answer, at least not directly. He stepped into the cramped space that served as Ravi's quarters and looked around, as if seeing them for the first time. He reached out and touched the bottom of Ravi's bunk, which was folded into the wall.

"It doesn't look very comfortable," he said. There was no sympathy in his voice. "I don't imagine you sleep very well."

"I sleep just fine."

"Maybe you haven't been sleeping as well as you think." He poked inquisitively at the mattress. "Maybe you've been sleepwalking."

Ravi's heart started to thump. Where the hungary was Vasconcelos going with this?

"Do you remember where you were on the morning of Sol forty-eight, three three two?" the inspector inquired languidly. "Around zero two hundred?"

"Should I?" Ravi stalled. He was pretty sure he knew the answer. He hoped against hope he was wrong.

The inspector tossed a data packet at him.

"At zero two oh seven on Sol forty-eight, three three two, when you should have been fast asleep in that awful bunk of yours, records indicate that someone opened up the number seven boat elevator. At zero two forty-one, that same elevator stopped at the thirty-five-hundred-meter docking pylons and requested admittance to ISV-one-LB-zero-three *Spirit of St. Petersburg*. Admittance was granted because the request was made on behalf of Midshipman six dash eight five five two MacLeod, Ravinder T., whose access rights had not yet expired. At zero two fifty-three, someone activated a model seventeen extravehicular inspection drone—serial number in the record—using the access rights of—you guessed it—Midshipman six dash eight five five two MacLeod, Ravinder T." The Inspector's hard glare pinned Ravi against the bulkhead. "Unluckily for you, son, the drone's log wasn't wiped. It's full of video. *Interesting* video."

Ravi watched in horror as the downloaded log kicked off in his head, replaying the little machine's drift across the lifeboat's hull. He saw once again how it paused underneath the flight-deck window, reoriented itself, slid across the paneling, and located the unyielding black sphere of the trojan. Trojan in pincered grasp, the inspection drone jetted rapidly across the flight-deck window on its way to the nearest wide-open airlock, where it gently deposited its cargo before returning to its storage hatch. The video ended.

"Funny thing about video. It's not like the human eye at all. The human eye, the un-engineered one, anyway, is kinda lazy. It sees only what it needs to see to get by from one moment to the next. Something could be right under your nose—it could *be* your nose, come to think of it—but if your eye doesn't think you need to see it, the Archie-damned thing might as well not be there.

"Video, on the other hand . . ." Vasconcelos shot Ravi a pitying smile. "*Video* . . . is different. It sees everything there is to see, whether it needs to or not."

Vasconcelos tossed over the tiniest chunk of data, a freeze-frame from the drone's camera-feed.

"That drone of yours was jetting full-bore for the upper starboard airlock. It knew where it was going, and it wasn't interested in the flight-deck window, not even a little bit. But the window was in the camera frame for just a fraction of a second. And that was enough, wasn't it?"

Ravi felt sick. The image of the flight deck through the thick glass was blurry, and a lot of it was washed out by the reflected light of the Destination Star. But it was clear enough to catch Midshipman 6-8552 MacLeod, Ravinder T., sitting in the pilot's seat.

Vasconcelos was looking at him with something bordering on hatred.

"You brought an unauthorized device aboard this ship, son. Sols later, you're picked up meters away from a terrorist attack, with some circuit-broken story about inspecting a bulkhead." The inspector's eyes narrowed. "What were you really doing down there, I wonder? Planting another bomb?"

Ravi was shaking.

"You've got this all wrong," he stammered. Not that Vasconcelos getting it right would have been any better.

Vasconcelos was unimpressed.

"Tell it to the ombudsman," he said flatly. He leaned forward until he was only centimeters from Ravi's face. Ravi could feel the heat of the man's breath. "You're going to the recycler for this. And no one here will shed a tear for you. Your family has always been Dead Weight, MacLeod. But even for them, this is a whole new low."

He turned his attention to the security drone.

"Take this pile of unrecycled excrement to the brig and book him," he ordered. And to Ravi: "Put your hands behind your back."

Ravi did as he was told. Tears of shame burned at his eyes.

The security drone lumbered forward, the stubby barrel of its dart gun pointed straight at his chest. A pair of handcuffs was suddenly dangling from one of its appendages.

The drone came to an abrupt halt, swaying slightly. The barrel of the dart gun swung swiftly away from Ravi.

And fired.

"What the . . ."

Vasconcelos stared in bemusement at his chest. The red-tufted feathers of a dart were protruding from between the buttons of his uniform.

He collapsed to the deck in a heap, snoring softly.

Boz's head, complete with reckless grin, appeared in the doorway.

"I always wanted to hack a security drone," she said.

Ravi, for his part, was still standing with his hands behind his back, staring stupidly at the crumpled form of the ShipSec commander. Boz thumped him on the shoulder.

"Wake up, idiot. We need to get the hungary out of here."

The letters flashed red and insistent across the insides of Ravi's eyelids.

> SHIPWIDE NOTICE PRIORITY ONE: BE ON THE
> LOOKOUT FOR MIDSHIPMAN 6-8552 MACLEOD,
> RAVINDER T. IF SIGHTED REPORT TO SHIPSEC.
> DO NOT APPROACH!!! PURSUANT TO SHIP'S REG
> 5-09(a)-(d) ALL PRIVACY PROTOCOLS ARE
> SUSPENDED UNTIL FURTHER NOTICE.

His ID pictures glowered at him long after the message itself had faded. Ravi picked up the file and deleted it.

"I guess Vasconcelos is awake," Boz said drily. She glanced over her shoulder to see how he was doing. "Hurry up. We haven't got all sol."

"I'm hurrying. This isn't one of my usual suits. Whoever wore it last was real short." The suit in question was still standing in its rack. Ravi worked on it with feverish speed. "I've got to change every single setting. Whoever signed it out must have been a freak of sarding nature."

Boz's response was to lay an urgent, gloved hand on his shoulder.

"Stop coding. Do it manually."

"No way. We'll be here forever."

"Do you hear that?" Boz asked. Her head was small against the hulking curve of her spacesuit's shoulders. Her helmet bulged out from under her arm.

Ravi stopped what he was doing and listened. Not with his ears, with his chipset. A whispering susurration was spreading across the hive. And where the whispering went, changes followed. The data streams were getting louder, more distinct. The sounds layered one upon another in perfect, organized harmony. The hive was reorganizing itself, becoming . . . *other*. The twist of its alleyways straightening out; the deep, secret tunnels shallowing to broad ditches; the high, multilayered walls dissolving to mist.

Ravi stared in awe. And no small amount of misgiving.

"What's going on?" he asked.

"That," Boz replied, "is ShipSec disabling the privacy protocols. In a very few seconds, everything you do through the hive will be visible to them. Including your ham-fisted attempts to code that suit."

Ravi hurriedly cut all connections to the outside world. He flipped open a panel in the suit's chest and started punching buttons. The air escaped from his mouth in little white puffs. It was cold here. Unsurprising, given they were only meters away from hard vacuum. Errant bursts of radiation flashed against his detectors.

"Are we done yet?" Boz prodded.

"Yeah," Ravi replied at last. "No thanks to you." He climbed into the suit. It closed around him with a wheezing of servos. He locked his helmet in place with an angry snap.

"About time," Boz replied through her still-open faceplate. "Let's do this."

She climbed the ladder that led through the inner door of the airlock. The door itself formed part of the ceiling. It was a little-used, low-*g* chamber right at the top of Ecuador. Or, as Boz liked to say, deck zero.

Ravi followed her up. He stood silently beside his cousin, a bulging kit bag at his feet, not trusting himself to speak. He listened to the hiss of air as the lock began to cycle. And then, after the sound had grown higher and thinner and disappeared entirely, to the murmur of his own breathing. The sealed inner door was part of the deck now, the outer door, reached by a ladder built into one of the walls, part of the roof. The actual roof. The wheel's inner rim. There was no more Ecuador left.

The light on the outer door turned to green. Boz pulled herself up the ladder using only her hands, easy to do in 0.3 *g*. She opened the outer door manually and climbed out. Ravi followed.

They were standing on the inside rim of the Ecuador wheel, right on the forward edge, facing the bow. It was a bit like being on the inside of a giant tunnel narrowing with distance, where the inner rim of each wheel formed the walls. Ahead of them, across a dizzying gap of open space, was Denmark, and beyond that, Canada, Bermuda, and Australia, each wheel seemingly smaller than the next, the whole prospect culminating in the shadowed underside of the shield. Biological eyes were tricky things, Ravi thought— and not for the first time. Looked at from here, it was hard to believe that every wheel was exactly the same size.

And like a tunnel, it was dark. The ship's navigation lights had been turned off, the portholes blacked out, presumably to hide from *Newton*. The cold, distant light of the Destination Star penetrated only intermittently, blocked by the bulk of the habitat rings and the slow rotation of the spokes. Ravi took it all in, heart thumping. It was strangely claustrophobic.

Boz touched helmets with him so as to talk without the radio. Her voice sounded thin and echoey and far away.

"Fire up the nav system," she told him. "Tell it we're jumping to Canada."

Ravi did as he was told, a cold knot in his chest. There was only one way to make a jump like that from where he was standing. In a complex-to-calculate arc from one inner rim to another, on the opposite side of the ship. Not only did he have to somehow thread the majestic scything of the intervening spokes and avoid the broad outer hull of the hubs, he had to lift off against 0.3 *g*, either with or against the spin of the wheel he was standing on. And once he committed to the jump, if he screwed up the execution, he could miss the target wheel entirely, slide into the gap between wheels, and drift out into deep space. Not a jump for the fainthearted.

If he did miss, Ravi very much doubted the ship would waste her time rescuing a suspected BonVoy bomber.

The nav grid appeared on the underside of his eyelids, transected by a series of curved green trajectories. The trajectories changed restlessly as the wheels continued to turn. None of them were easy.

Pick one, he told himself fiercely. *Commit.* He held his kit bag against his chest, its brightly colored lanyard snaking off to one side. His body tensed for the jump.

Boz cracked helmets with him again.

"Turn off the nav," she ordered. "We're not doing that. No way, no how."

It was only the bulk of the spacesuit that stopped Ravi from sagging with relief. The grid dropped away.

"This is no time for joking around," he snapped, relief replaced by irritation. "Just tell me where you stashed Ansimov's Archie-damned EMUs and let's get the sard out of here."

"Ghana. So, turn around and get ready to jump the other way. *Without* the nav grid."

Ravi's gasp almost cracked his faceplate.

"Are you kidding me? That's insane!"

"It's totally sane," Boz said, sounding maddeningly reasonable. "Ghana is where the EMUs are. You're a wanted man, so the safest way—the only way—to get there without getting caught and hauled into the brig is through hard vacuum. We've just used the nav grid, *which is connected to the hive*, to tell every ShipSec officer looking for you that we're headed to Canada, where they will be waiting for us. We, meanwhile, will be headed in totally the opposite direction." Boz's face was completely invisible behind the mirrored glass of her suit visor, but Ravi could hear her grinning. "It's genius."

"Except for the part where we screw up the jump and fly off into deep space. If I'm lucky, I'll get hit by a meteoroid and put out of my misery. Better than suffocating to death, anyway."

Boz wasn't listening. She had turned on her booted heels and was bounding across the inner rim to the aft edge of the wheel. Ravi went after her, his steps shorter and more cautious. Eventually, he stood beside her, trying to gauge the dizzying distance from Ecuador, across Fiji, to Ghana and its slow, distinctly uneven turns. Beyond even that, Hungary hung ruptured and unmoving, the last wheel before the long finger of the spine and open space, its shattered hull dark with disapproval.

The toes of Ravi's boots nudged over the edge of the rim. He peered "down" at them and at the thirty decks' worth of sheer, dust-scarred wall beneath. The outer hull of Ecuador. A pink coating of ice glittered in the faint light. In a sense, it was if he was standing on the top of a thirty-story building. But only in a sense. The building's "bottom" rested on absolutely nothing. Stars slid from one toecap to the other as the wheel continued to turn.

For the briefest of moments, he felt something like a fear of heights. But that was a Homeworld thing. It passed as quickly as it came. Besides, he wasn't jumping "down"; he was jumping "up," a tricky arc that would thread Fiji, cross the outside of the hubs, and land on Ghana's inner rim, essentially upside down and above his head from his present frame of reference.

"Sard it," he said. He held his gear tight against his chest. The lanyard attaching it to his suit snaked uselessly to one side. He kept a wary eye on it, careful to avoid getting tangled. The servos in his suit legs quivered with unreleased energy.

He jumped.

He didn't need a nav grid to tell him that he'd nailed it. He sailed effortlessly between the Fiji spokes, invisible in the darkness, skimming low over the outer hull of the hubs. And then he was diving headfirst for Ghana's inner rim, its grimy, pockmarked surface rushing up to greet him. He flipped himself over at the last second and let the suit take the strain. The legs groaned and bent, absorbing the impact. A stutter step forward and he was at rest, standing on Ghana's "roof," the wheel beneath his feet, the spokes soaring above his head and disappearing into the hubs. Not trusting the almost-zero gravity, he tethered himself to a nearby stretch of safety cable.

Not bad, Ravi. Not bad.

"Ravi!" Boz's voice squealed out of the radio, querulous with fright. "Ravi, help! I'm coming in too high!"

Ravi swung around, looking desperately for Boz, but all he could see was the ship's wheels, and the stars, and deep, deep shadow.

"Boz!" he yelled. "I can't . . ."

Off in the distance, a trio of small, flashing dots winked into existence. One green, one red, one white, moving fast. Boz had activated the running lights on her suit.

"Archie's hooks!" Ravi muttered.

Boz had gotten the timing right but the angle wrong. Even though she was presently well off to one side, Ghana's grinding rotation would put her right over Ravi's head. She would then sail on, missing the rim entirely and sliding into the gap between Ghana and the wrecked remains of Hungary.

With nothing ahead of her but an eternity of deep space.

Ravi's mouth firmed into a grim line. He punched on his own lights so she could see him and unspooled his tether as far as it would go. Boz's panicked breathing filled the speakers of his helmet. He watched her come closer and closer, an unguided human missile.

Archie help us, he thought to himself, *she's really flying . . . .*

He was out of time. Eyes flickering as he gauged her trajectory, he bent his knees and hurled himself upward.

He kept his eyes firmly on his cousin. She looked as if she was pinned in place and everything was spinning around her. *Perfect,* Ravi thought fiercely. It meant they were on a collision course, which, for once, was exactly what he wanted. He just had to reach out and . . .

The tether yanked him to a sudden halt, whiplashing his neck. Boz was sailing past, beyond his grasp. He heard her yell, a wordless cocktail of disappointment and fear. The tether set him to spinning, disoriented and out of control.

No, no, no, no, NO!

He hurled his kit bag in Boz's general direction. No calculation, no thought. The bulky package spun away from him, the lanyard stretching out and colorless in the near-black.

It's not strong enough for this, he thought bleakly. *Even if she catches it, it's going to—*

The lanyard snapped straight, slamming him into a different, dizzying spin. Breath left his lungs, his head slammed against the inside of his helmet, teeth bit into his tongue. The smell of blood filled his nostrils.

He tried to make sense of what was happening, but he couldn't. His rattled brain couldn't think straight. The universe whirled around outside, stars and shadow and stars and shadow and—

Crack!

Something smashed his faceplate. The glass crazed with the impact. Ravi held his breath against the onset of vacuum, but it never came. The visor held.

And on the other side of it, fractured into a dozen images and upside-down to him, was Boz. Bulky, gloved hands clamped onto his arms. The two of them danced through space, hearts pounding. Then the tether snagged them, sawing angrily at their suits in a vain attempt to cut them in half. The spin slowed, began to make sense. Brains kicked in, ordering kicks and sweeps of the arm that brought the spin to zero. The world returned to normal. Wheels, and stars, and cold light between the shadows.

Ravi tugged on the tangled mess of tether, pulling them back to the inner rim. Boots touched down on the surface, softly held in place by the weak spin of the wheel.

"You really shouldn't be out here alone," he quipped.

Boz responded with a girlish giggle. She was bent over at the middle, as if winded. She reached out and patted the chest of his suit.

"Thank you," she said hoarsely. "Thank you."

She attached a tether of her own to the safety cable and stood up straight.

"Where are we, do you think?"

Ravi considered the question. It was difficult to see through the frosting on his visor. His tongue hurt like hungary, and the one side of his head was no better. Eventually, though, he stretched out the scuffed arm of his suit and pointed.

"That's the twelve o'clock spoke. At least, I think it is." The external numbering had been scoured away long ago. No one had bothered to repaint it. "See the patching halfway up? The one that looks like a gas giant with moons? Has to be twelve."

Boz grunted in agreement.

"Good," she murmured. He could tell by the tone of her voice that she was still shaken up. She turned in the opposite direction and started loping toward the nine o'clock spoke. One hand held her tether like a leash, stopping her from flying too high off the hull. Secured to the safety cable, it followed her along as she moved. "EMUs are this way."

Ravi loped along after her. Distances were shorter at the top of the wheels, and gravity on Ghana's inner rim was gravity in name only. They made rapid progress. As he moved with near-effortless steps, Ravi adjusted to the fractured images coming through his visor. He glanced to one side, toward the front of the ship, through the shadowed tunnel of wheels. He sent an urgent order to his suit.

"Boz?"

"Yeah?"

"Turn off your running lights."

Boz swore. In the drama of his cousin's rescue, neither of them had thought to darken their suits again. ShipSec had probably caught at least some of Boz's radio transmission. Enough to know they weren't headed to Canada, at any rate. And now there were two sets of flashing beacons where no beacons were meant to be. Assuming Vasconcelos asked him, it wouldn't take Chen Lai long to account for every work party outside the ship. None of them would be assigned to the inner rim of a wheel no one cared about.

"Have we been made?" Boz asked anxiously.

"Maybe." Ravi pointed forward. A cluster of running lights had appeared on the Canada inner rim. Maybe five or six suits. "Might be a work detail," he said hopefully.

"Or not. We need to pick up the pace." Boz bounded to the foot of the nine o'clock spoke, attached her tether to a new safety cable, and kept going. Only the tether stopped her long steps from launching her back out into space. She traveled another two hundred meters or so before finally coming to a halt. When Ravi caught up to her, she was standing beside the top of a short ladder, almost invisible in the shadowed dark. The ladder dropped to the outer door of an airlock, not unlike the one they'd left in Ecuador. This one, though, was scarred and dark. The indicator lights along the hatch were lifeless and covered in ice.

He touched helmets with his cousin.

"It's dead," he said. He looked over his shoulder. The constellation of flashing lights was getting closer. They had already passed Denmark. He couldn't tell because of the way the wheels were turning, but he'd be willing to bet real water their arrival at Ghana was timed to coincide with the spot where they turned off their lights. Too close for comfort.

"It only *looks* dead," Boz assured him. "The whole of Ghana is a mess of jury-rigged patches from back in the sol. Some stuff is hooked into the ship and works fine; some of it is hooked into the ship and doesn't work at all; and some stuff . . ." She pushed at a short, chunky-looking lever. ". . . is *not* hooked into the ship but works perfectly."

They stepped to one side as the airlock door cycled open. Ravi could feel his eyes widen in surprise.

"If you're monitoring the hive, looking for a couple of runaways," his cousin added smugly, "this airlock doesn't exist. No one knows it's here."

"But how'd *you* know?" Ravi didn't bother to hide how impressed he was.

"Every low-grade, bescumbered community-service job on the ship is located in this sarding wheel," Boz explained. "You have a record as long as mine, you get to spend a lot of time over here. You learn a thing or two."

She broke contact with his helmet and floated down into the airlock.

Ravi took a last look around. The pursuing nav lights had stretched apart from each other. Six separate sets, for sure. And they were almost level with Fiji. To be moving that fast, they had to be riding EMUs, he thought sourly. There was no time to waste. He climbed down the ladder into the compartment. He was only halfway in when Boz started closing the door. She, too, understood the need for speed. The outer door slammed shut just above his helmet.

Once the airlock cycled and opened the inner door, they climbed down into an abandoned part of the structure. There was air here but not much of it. It was thin and icy cold. With so little atmosphere to carry it, the asthmatic groan of Ghana's warped bearings sounded high and far away. The grinding vibration in his boots was as strong as he remembered it, though. Random streaks of frost stained the undecorated walls.

Boz paid no attention. She led the way deeper into the wheel, careful to take little-used service stairwells with no working links to the hive. It was slower than using an elevator or paternoster, but it kept them off the grid. The pull of gravity strengthened a little; the air became warmer.

"Here we are," she said quietly. She opened the door to a large airlock antechamber. Ravi felt his jaw dropping.

"What kept you?" Uncle Torquil asked, grinning. He gave Ravi a sly, sideways look, gesturing expansively around the room. "You like?" he inquired proudly.

Suits and various pieces of equipment were stored in neat racks. They were old, Ravi noticed, and covered in dust. The suit logos were Second Gen. Ravi's skin prickled with goosebumps. It was like stumbling on buried treasure.

"No one comes here," Boz explained unnecessarily. "Another perfect place to hide stuff, isn't it, Uncle?" She gripped Torquil by the forearm. "You get me what I asked for?"

In response, Torquil hauled on one of the huge racks. To Ravi's surprise, it wasn't secured to the deck. Or, more accurately, it was secured by a single bolt that operated like the hinge on a door. Taking full advantage of the low gravity, Torquil swung the whole thing to one side. Nestled behind it were the Team Spike EMUs, now loaded down with a stack of ancillary equipment. Most notably, an extensive supply of air and a boatload of extra fuel. There was no sign of Ansimov's delivery bot. Long gone, no doubt, its memory wiped.

"You are really something," Boz breathed, running a hand over the air tanks. She secured her kit bag to one of the EMUs. "How'd you get this stuff?"

"Inventory," Torquil replied. "One of my many community-service assignments." He broke into a broad grin. "And surprisingly easy to hack. But not a patch on scoring two fully functioning EMUs—from sarding officers, no less!" An approving gaze landed on Ravi's banged-up faceplate. "Grab a new helmet from one of those suits," he suggested, "and let's get you out of here."

With Torquil's help, they hauled the EMUs into the airlock. It was a big one, designed for bulky work. With a gruff "Good luck; I hope you stick it to the bastards," Torquil clapped them both around the shoulder and hurried off. Ravi settled himself into an EMU and plugged himself in while the airlock cycled. The outer door opened, revealing Hungary in dark silhouette against the slowly turning stars. Ravi hesitated a moment, looking at the joystick. He had very little experience with EMUs. He certainly didn't trust himself to fly one by hand. He reached out with his implants. The EMU rose shakily from the deck and jetted into space on frosty puffs of propellant. Even with his chipset taking the strain, he almost brained himself on the way out.

"You know you've just told the whole ship where you are," Boz scolded.

"Yes," Ravi acknowledged, voice tight with strain. "But: one, I wanted to get out of there alive; and two, we can't drive these things manually, anyway. We need the nav grid—and the hive—to hit the trajectory. Or do you think you can make it to *Newton* by eyesight alone?"

The only answer from Boz was a bad-tempered silence. He could feel her pulling down her nav grid, though. He did the same. The green arc of a trajectory pasted itself across the inside of his eyelids. It rapidly turned to a flashing amber. The system's way of telling him that what he was proposing to do made no sense.

"Sard!" Boz swore.

"What's up?"

"Your four o'clock and real high," Boz snapped.

Ravi turned the EMU hard to his right and looked "up." He was looking along the vast cliff face of Ghana's outer hull. "Up" meant looking toward the wheel's inner rim, and then the hub beyond.

A horde of green, red, and white fireflies had just emerged from the gap between the inner rim and the hub. The EMUs to which they were attached were already turning in his direction.

"Let's go!" Boz yelled.

Ravi synced his nav grid with the EMU's thrusters. His eyelid twitched as he hit the Start button. Stars blurred in dizzying arcs as the EMU flipped itself over and fired its main thrusters. To his immense surprise, he was pressed back into his seat by real *g* forces. Warning signs flashed against his retinas.

ATTENTION! FUEL DEPLETION IN 90 SECONDS!

POINT OF NO RETURN IN 34 SECONDS!

Other signals flooded his implants. He could see Boz's trajectory paralleling his own, on a one-way blast to nowhere. But there were other trajectories, too. Six of them, moving on an intercept course.

ATTENTION! POINT OF NO RETURN!

FUEL DEPLETION IN 56 SECONDS!

Two of the pursuing EMUs curved away, unwilling to abandon their link to the ship. Or because they'd been ordered to hang back, or because they were out of fuel. The other four continued to follow, draining their tanks with the same reckless abandon as he was.

More, really. They were closing the gap.

The EMU continued its burn. Ravi groaned with discomfort. The suit wasn't designed for this sort of acceleration. It was digging into his back with painful insistence.

FUEL DEPLETION IN 10 . . . 9 . . . 8 . . .
7 . . .

The thrusters cut out without warning, leaving him to float against the straps. He desperately wanted to turn the unit around, to see where the pursuit was, to gauge his distance from the ship. But he was almost out of propellant. Who knew how much he'd need when he got to where he was going? The nav grid showed the four pursuing EMUs still on a converging track. They'd stopped burning too. But the intercept was locked in. He silently cursed the extra mass they'd had to haul along for the trip. He was in a racing EMU. In other circumstances, they'd have been moving too fast for anything else to catch them. As it was, they had maybe an hour at most.

He shut down the nav grid and stared instead at the blue-dusted Milky Way, with its bridal train of constellations. The whole vista seemed fixed in space, spread out before him like a gigantic mural. Everything was quiet, peaceful even. All he could hear was the soft whisper of his own breathing. Hard to believe he was rocketing away from the ship. Still harder to believe he was hurtling toward the Destination Star at roughly thirty thousand kilometers every second.

Ravi's skin prickled with sudden discomfort. At that sort of speed, beyond the wide disc of *Archimedes'* shield and unprotected by anything that could remotely be described as a hull, the smallest speck of dust would vaporize him. He calmed himself down with a cynical smile. *Why worry?* he told himself. If there was a piece of grit out there with his name on it, he'd never know what hit him.

A billion kilometers flashed by. The stars refused to move. Time slowed to a crawl. Nothing happened. Ravi began to obsess about the amount of air left in the tanks.

Crackly with distance, a new voice burst out of his helmet speakers. Vasconcelos.

"Give it up, MacLeods. A few more minutes and we'll be alongside. We're going to make you secure and await retrieval by lifeboat." A sardonic pause. "It'll be a while, though. No one's in any hurry to bring you back."

"And what if we don't want to be secured?" Boz asked defiantly. The first words she'd uttered since the thrusters shut off. "You know you can't make us, not at these speeds."

A series of orange lights flashed across Ravi's path, disappearing into the distance. It took a moment or two to figure out what he was looking at.

Tracer bullets. From some kind of vacuum-rated ordnance. His heart started to pound. Hard.

Vasconcelos's dry chuckle, less crackly now, filled his helmet.

"I don't think, in the entire history of the Mission, these things have ever been fired in anger. Hungary, I don't know if they've even been fired. We broke them out specially for you." The voice in his helmet hardened. "Don't give me an excuse to use 'em, kiddo."

"Why shouldn't I?" Boz snarled back, reckless as ever. "You're just going to feed us to the recycler anyway."

Ravi, who had no desire to die ahead of schedule, desperately searched for the right words to calm his cousin down. He never found them. Something else tugged at his attention. Something that made him want to rub his eyes.

Part of the Milky Way seemed to have vanished. Which wasn't possible. His eyes watered with the strain of trying to make sense of what he was seeing. He maxed out the augmented vision on his suit, to no avail.

The Milky Way was disappearing, more and more of it with each passing second.

And then, suddenly, he understood. There was something blocking his view. Long and dark, with a barely visible flared stern drifting up to meet them.

The blurry UFO he'd seen from the flight deck of the lifeboat. The "hijacked probe" from the *Bohr*. This was one of *Newton*'s dragons. Now, however, there was nothing blurry about it at all. Because it was *close,* and all too real, and black as space itself.

A voice, whispery quiet and not quite human, echoed in his head—literally. The dragon was using his implants.

"I would like the access codes for the controls," it said. The diction was elegant, precise. *"May I have them?"*

"Be my guest," Ravi replied, although his mouth didn't move. The EMU's thrusters gave a soft puff. And then another. The backdrop of stars tilted.

"What do you think you're doing?" Vasconcelos warned. "Don't make me shoot you!"

"Sard off!" Boz said. "Our ride's here!" She giggled hysterically. "See you later, losers!"

In response, Ravi's EMU kicked him in the ribs. A burst of tracer missed him by less than a meter.

"For sard's sake, Boz, why can't you keep your Archie-damned mouth *shut* for once?" Ravi snapped.

"Where's the fun in that?" It was all too easy to picture the maniacal grin plastered across Boz's face. Ravi was about to say something cutting when the EMU kicked him again, in the seat of the pants this time. Space spun crazily around him, a spangled tapestry sewn through with fiery threads of tracer.

The contact was so soft, he was latched to the long flank of the dragon before he even realized he'd reached it. He was looking forward along its stygian hull, the dragon's nose hidden from sight by the subtle curve of its structure. He was still getting kicked, he realized, and the stars were still lurching. Proof, if proof were needed, that the dragon was maneuvering hard. There was no sign of tracer, though. Perhaps the ShipSec EMUs could no longer see him.

From the looks of things, he guessed he was closer to the stern of the dragon than the prow. There was no sign of Boz. Perhaps she was on the other side of it. Or behind him. He allowed himself a small sigh of relief.

"I apologize in advance," the dragon said, *"but our departure must be rapid."*

The words had barely hit his implants before the dragon fired its main drive. Ravi had no time to prepare himself. The air was crushed out of his lungs, eyes bulged inside his skull, inhuman forces dragged the lips from his teeth. But above all, the rear of his suit dug sudden, unforgiving fingers into his spine, overwhelming him with pain.

I'm going to break my back, he thought bleakly. *Or die.*

It was the last thing he remembered.

I *feel you are awake,"* the dragon was saying.

It was news to Ravi, who thought for a moment he was dreaming. Groggy and aching all over, he managed to open his eyes. The dusted blue of the Milky Way was spread out before him, the view partly blocked by the black curve of the dragon's hull. There was no sense of movement, no pressure against his back. The engines must have shut down.

"Your maneuvering units are not compatible with my docking system," the dragon informed him. *"I cannot provide you with life support for the journey."*

What does a LOKI-powered torpedo need with life support? Ravi wondered. For that matter, what's with a docking system for EMUs?

"For maintenance and upgrades," the dragon replied. Ravi winced with embarrassment. In the stress of the moment, he'd unconsciously activated the coms circuit in his chipset—a child's mistake. *"Our engineers often make extended trips to visit me,"* the dragon continued, either unaware or uninterested in Ravi's discomfiture. *"To do so, they make use of maneuvering units. Unfortunately, the design, while similar, is not quite the same as yours. I cannot connect you to the necessary services for a longer journey."*

"We brought supplies," Ravi responded. It felt weird to be talking to a machine that could think for itself.

Not a machine, he reminded himself. A *LOKI*. Goosebumps prickled on the back of his neck.

Unsure how long he'd been out, he painted the EMU's diagnostics on the inside of his eyelids. He'd need to recharge the air in a couple of hours. Otherwise, he didn't see any problems. Waste collection, in-suit nutrition, general power, were all good. It was the air that mattered. And for all their preparations, neither he nor Boz had an endless supply.

"How long will we be out here?" Even though he'd intended to ask the question, Boz beat him to it. He was quietly relieved to hear her voice.

"Roughly twenty hours," the dragon replied. *"Longer, if the approach is difficult."*

"Difficult?" Ravi asked, alarmed. "What does that mean?"

"*Only that we will not be welcome if the ship discovers you are here. Were that to happen, there would be . . . consequences.*"

"Consequences like violence?"

"*Yes,*" the dragon said bluntly. It didn't feel the need to add any detail.

"Well, that's just great," Boz murmured. "Out of the fuel tank and into the combustion chamber. And here I was hoping for a hot meal and a free shower."

Neither Ravi nor the dragon bothered to reply. The Milky Way hung in front of them, dusty, and eternal, and unmoving.

— — —

Ravi awoke with a start. He must have dozed off, only to be jerked awake by the dragon's gentle deceleration. The Milky Way vanished, the starfield spinning lazily across his visor. His suit strained against the EMU's padded harness.

The tilting stars slowed and became still.

"Are we there yet?" he asked. The old, old joke.

"*Be silent.*"

The stars shifted again. There was an acceleration this time, equally gentle. The EMU's massive bulk pushed against his back. Then it stopped, leaving him afloat in the seemingly unmoving void. The dusty blue ribbon of the Milky Way stretched once more across his field of vision.

And then vanished. Ravi gasped as the dragon spun with sudden, vicious force, braking so hard that he feared the harness would give way, spitting him helpless and flailing into the vacuum.

The maneuver stopped as abruptly as it started. There was an upwelling of bile at the back of Ravi's throat. He closed his eyes and tried to relax. The suit wouldn't let him drown in his own vomit, but he didn't want to be combing the leftover chunks out of his hair. Boz would never let him hear the last of it. He took slow, deep breaths and hoped that the dragon was done with tossing him about.

It wasn't. But the motions that followed, stretching over the next two to three hours, were far less violent. At long last, it seemed that the dragon had finally settled on a steady course. The dust clouds of the Milky Way lay nailed in place ahead of them.

"What's going on?" Ravi asked, half expecting another admonition to silence.

"*Why do you not sleep like your companion?*" the dragon asked back. "*The journey is long, and you may not have time to rest once we arrive.*"

Ravi, imagining Boz drooling and insensate in her spacesuit, allowed himself a wry smile.

"My cousin can sleep through pretty much anything. But not me. I'd like to know why you've been hurling us around like a freeball in the middle of sarding nowhere."

The dragon did not reply. Not immediately, anyway.

"*I did not wish to meet with Fafnir,*" it said, at last. "*She would have . . . questions.*"

"Who's Fafnir?"

"*My sibling.*"

"You have a sibling?" Ravi chuckled.

"*I have eight. As for Fafnir, you would not be so amused if you met her. It could have ended badly.*"

The smile vanished from Ravi's lips.

"*Fafnir should not have been so far from home. She may suspect me, I think.*"

The dragon seemed uninterested in further communication. Ravi fretted awhile about invisible, highly intelligent weapons systems before drifting once more into uncomfortable sleep. It felt like only moments later when Boz woke him up.

"How much air do you have?" she asked.

"Two, maybe three hours," he replied, suddenly alarmed. "Shouldn't we be there already?" They were well past the twenty-hour mark.

"That's what I thought," Boz replied.

The dragon's encounter with Fafnir must have slowed their progress considerably.

"Hey, dragon," Boz called. "Are we there yet? 'Cause if the answer isn't *soon*, you're going to find yourself hauling two dead passengers."

"*Soon,*" the dragon replied. Ravi found himself smiling. LOKIs had a sense of humor, apparently.

"Say," Boz asked. "Do you have a name? What do people call you?"

"*I have a true name,*" the dragon replied, "*which is part of the coding in my root algorithm. However, most people address me as 'Kur.'*"

"What's the point of having a true name?" Boz asked, "if no one calls you by it?"

"*People address me as Kur because they cannot, being creatures of the flesh, talk to me in code. In code, my true name is simple and easy, and allows for interaction with every other mechanism."*

"Oh," Boz said, comprehension apparently dawning. "It's a device identifier?"

"Yes," Kur agreed. *"An archaic term, to be sure, but that is what it is."*

"And it acts as a gateway to the rest of your programming?"

"Yes." There was a perceptible pause in the dragon's speech. *"But these are strange questions from someone who must already know this. You have a true name yourself."*

"I do?" Boz replied, clearly amused. "What is it?"

"0670820690870770650780320530450550560540520320770650670760690 7906804403208207906606908208406503207404046," Kur answered, without missing a beat.

Boz burst out laughing.

"That's not my true name, you dolt. That's my chipset ID. My true name, if you must know, is Roberta Jesmyn MacLeod. But people I like call me Boz."

There was a long pause before the dragon replied.

"But that would make you a person."

"Of course I'm a person! What else would I be?"

The dragon did not reply. Not directly, anyway.

"We have arrived," it announced. *"Please do not use the radio again or any speech circuits. You may communicate by code but only to your companion and me. And even then, please do so only when absolutely necessary."*

Ravi felt a gentle kick of thrust. The Milky Way, that constant backdrop to their journey, began to rotate and slide off to one side. The Destination Star swung into view, its cold light making no impression on the dragon's dark hull.

Ravi had no time for the Destination Star, however. He was too busy staring at the *Newton.*

He had expected the ship of his dreams—of the girl's dreams. But the real-life *Newton* was very different. For a start, even though they were almost on top of her, she was almost invisible. If he'd been staring with the naked eye instead of the suit's augmented vision, he wouldn't even know she was there. This was not the *Newton* of the Launch Day newsfeeds. Thirteen decades of history had turned *Newton* a deep, sooty black, its running lights long since dimmed, its powerful engines quiet.

Squinting through his visor, Ravi struggled to make sense of what looked like gigantic spider webs radiating out from the spine of the ship.

They're wheels, he told himself, at last. *Archie's hooks, they're wheels!*

At least, they had been. Over the course of her 132 years, the crew of the *Newton* had stripped down the three rearmost wheels, leaving only the skeletal framework behind. A gossamer memory of what had once been. Ice-rimed beams and struts supported nothing but hard vacuum, the compartments and chambers and infrastructure long since taken away. For parts, Ravi imagined. To repair other sections of the ship.

Or build weapons like Kur.

Ravi swallowed down his disquiet and forced himself to look farther forward. If wheels eight to ten had been disassembled, wheels five to seven had been frozen in place. They were definitely not moving, their silhouettes unchanged against the stars, their rims pinned to the spine by lifeless spokes. Like Hungary, Ravi thought.

Except Hungary was a devastated ruin, its gashed-open compartments exposed to space, its hull unworthy of repair. A resting place for the unquiet dead. These wheels, from the outside at least, appeared utterly undamaged. They looked . . . mothballed. Locked down because no one on the ship had any use for them.

And perhaps they didn't, Ravi told himself. *Newton's* wheels were gigantic, far bigger than on any fleet vessel, and the population they could support was equally outsized. If the girl was telling the truth about *Newton* being a plague ship, the crew would have been decimated. Even with the passage of seven generations, they might not have been able to repopulate the available space. And why waste energy on empty compartments?

Boz was knocking at the back door of his chipset, taking care not to be overheard by Kur.

"*Look over there,*" she said. A grid and cursor dropped across his vision.

Kur had approached *Newton* from astern. Having reached her, they had passed alongside the flared bulge of the ship's drive. Now they were paralleling the blackened latticework of the ship's immense spine, far longer and much bulkier than the one on *Archimedes*.

And bristling with ordnance. As the cursor jumped under Boz's direction, Ravi found himself looking at battery after battery of mass drivers, clusters of missile launchers, and a bewildering array of targeting sensors. They made the fleet's hastily constructed armaments look like popguns.

Newton wasn't simply an interstellar vehicle. She was a born-again battleship, repurposed for violence. Ravi's heart thudded in his chest. If it came to a shooting fight between the fleet and this vast, militarized behemoth, the fleet was going to lose.

And once the transponders came on and *Newton* knew exactly where the fleet was, there'd be no stopping her. Unless, somehow, the beeps of her own transponder gave her pause.

A subtle movement caught his eye. Two small, barely visible objects were rising up to meet them. A minute or two later, they resolved into the boxy shape of EMUs. So far as Ravi could tell, they were piloting themselves.

"This is where I leave you," Kur said, its meticulous syllables echoing softly through his implants. *"I can approach no closer. Transfer your gear to the oncoming maneuvering units. They will take you the rest of the way."* The LOKI allowed itself time for a studied pause. *"And good luck to you."*

By the time Kur had finished speaking, one of the approaching EMUs had parked itself beside him, bringing itself to a relative halt with lazy puffs of propellant. Ravi floated across with his equipment. By the time he had settled in, the gap between himself and the dragon was already considerable. Its sleek, ebony form was merging into the darkness. For a brief moment, he wondered what the dragon would do with their abandoned EMUs. Discard them at the first opportunity, he guessed. Or break them down for parts.

Boz, securely strapped into her new EMU, floated across his vision. It was the first time in a couple of dozen hours that he'd actually seen her.

As if in response, and before he had a chance to wave or signal, his EMU gave him a kick and then a few more. Boz disappeared. The world around him tipped crazily before settling down to a new view of the black leviathan they'd traveled so far to reach. Best as he could guess, the EMU was taking him toward one of the vessel's intact but unmoving wheels.

Kur had been right, he realized. His new mount was similar to but distinct from the EMU he'd left behind. It was a little narrower but clearly designed for longer trips, with bigger tanks for both life support and propellant. The seat was deeper and contoured for the heavy accelerations that had almost broken him in half. And it was every bit as dark as Kur itself. *Newton*'s crew, he realized, must ride their dragons as a matter of course. No wonder the girl had thought nothing of directing him out into the middle of nowhere.

So far as driving the thing was concerned, there was no joystick or anything resembling a backup manual control. He reached out with his implants, trying to make contact with the unit's operating system. To his surprise, what he found was remarkably self-contained. The system was designed to be activated by voice control or the remote strokes of a keyboard. After that, it pretty much looked after itself. The nearest thing to a chipset interface was a simple set of remote-access protocols that did pretty much the same thing as the keyboard. It was very user-friendly.

Too user-friendly, he decided. Not only did the machine do everything itself, the keyboard and voice interfaces were hedged about with only modest security protocols. They were enough, maybe, to slow the average person down, but not for very long. As for the likes of Boz, she wouldn't even pause to take breath. And the chipset interface had no security protections at all. Not a one. If a person had implants, they were in.

He couldn't stop himself. He dived into the EMU's programming. Once you got underneath the user interfaces, which discouraged anyone from doing anything fun like, say, actually flying, the underlying programming was what a person would expect. Navigation . . . propulsion . . . diagnostics . . . *armaments*?

Ravi frowned. Maybe he'd misread the coding. He had another go at it. And swallowed hard.

He was sitting on top of an arms locker and weapons magazine. The arms locker contained a sidearm and ammunition. The weapons magazine comprised a vacuum-rated loading system that fed small, armor-piercing shells into . . .

He hijacked the relevant software. The EMU didn't even put up a fight. The machine vibrated to the spinning of electric motors and the urgent whirring of gears. A vicious-looking gun barrel appeared at his right-hand side. Targeting software threw an intricate grid across the inside of his eyelids. An insistent message blinked in one corner of his vision.

ARM? Y/N

His eyelid spasmed. He hit *N* just as quickly as he could. Even though he had quite literally not lifted a finger, his heart was pounding and he was out of breath. Who *were* these people? Who the hungary designed and built an armed EMU for every-sol use? *What the sard is going on here?*

He forced himself to calm down, to take longer, deeper breaths. There was no going back now. And there hadn't been since Vasconcelos had gotten shot by his own security drone.

Ahead of him, the dark bulk of the *Newton* was filling the sky, her black hull drinking in the light of the Destination Star and giving nothing in return. Everywhere he looked was shadow. The EMU, supremely indifferent to the mental state of its passenger, slipped into the gap between two gigantic, sleeping wheels. Their hulls surrounded him like the walls of some vast chasm.

He was feeling very, very small.

The EMU kicked him in the seat of the pants, slowing down and changing direction. The cliff face of the forward wheel climbed up to meet him. As if from nowhere, the dark shape of Boz's EMU slid in front of him. He followed it down toward a tiny square of pink light that had suddenly appeared in the deep black of the hull. The light grew rapidly bigger as they plunged toward it, revealing itself to be the gaping maw of a cargo-sized airlock. Without making any of the last-minute adjustments of a human pilot, the EMUs hurtled inside, coming to a halt within a meter of the far bulkhead. Behind them, the outer door cycled shut. Pressure built against the skin of his suit. The faint hiss of air caressed his ears. The lighting changed from pink to pale green. Double-checking his suit sensors, Ravi popped his visor open. Cold, thin air rushed into his lungs. The EMUs drifted slowly around, pushed by the soft hands of the ventilation system. Ravi unhooked his straps and allowed himself to float free.

The inner door cycled open.

Asmall, still figure waited for them on the other side of the threshold.

Ravi had no time to issue a greeting. He threw up. There was no time to get to a bag. The wet remains of his suit rations sprayed into the air, forming elastic, malodorous globules.

"Jinting Isaac!" the crewman swore. He pushed himself hurriedly out of the way. "No one told me you'd be ill. I ain't got no doctor."

If Ravi hadn't been so embarrassed, he'd have been surprised. The *Newton* crewman wasn't a crewman at all, or a crewwoman for that matter. He was a crew-*boy*. He couldn't have been more than twelve years old. He was staring at them with wide, worried eyes.

"He's not ill, exactly," Boz explained. "He gets spacesick."

The blood rushed to Ravi's face.

"Spacesick? *Spacesick?*" The boy was incredulous. He was floating clear of the spreading droplets, arms tucked into his armpits. He was clad in a rumpled version of the fatigues the girl wore in Ravi's visions, the blue subtly different from the fleet's standard issue, the material a little finer. The boy looked around until his eyes lit on an instrument panel in the wall. He jabbed manually at a button. Fans whirred noisily to life, pulling Ravi's unfortunate emissions into the filters. Ravi grabbed a handhold so as not to follow them.

"Hurry up," the boy said. He had the same strange accent as the girl. "We don't have a lot of time."

Ravi and Boz retrieved their gear and floated out of the airlock. The boy drifted over to a control panel, grabbed a handhold to anchor himself, and flipped a lever. With a reluctant wheeze, the airlock door cycled shut.

For someone in a hurry, Ravi mused, it was a slow, clunky way to go about things. He could tell from the quirk of Boz's mouth that she was thinking the same thing. He could also tell she was about to say something. He gave her an emphatic shake of the head. This was no time to be making fun of the only friend they had within two hundred thousand kilometers. Boz opened her mouth, as if in defiance of his wishes, and then closed it again. She gave him a conspiratorial wink. Ravi, for his part, breathed a small sigh of relief.

"Let's go," the boy said.

The wheel must have been locked down for a very long time, Ravi thought. Every surface was covered with some kind of padding, and the corridor walls were rigged with safety cables. The boy grabbed the nearest one and used it to pull himself along. Hampered by the thick gloves of their spacesuits, Ravi and Boz could barely keep up.

"Where are we going?" Boz asked, trying very hard not to gasp. The air was as cold and thin in the corridor as it had been in the airlock. The breath was flying out of her mouth in little white puffs. Cumbersome though it was, Ravi was glad to be nestled inside his suit. The whole wheel felt like an unprepped lifeboat. Even the lighting was muted. Although, to be fair, he had no idea what time it was aboard ship. Maybe it was close to night-cycle.

If the boy was feeling the cold, he showed no sign of it.

"Lisette said to take you to the Five-C backup mainframe. Said you'd know what to do with it."

"Lisette?" Ravi asked.

The boy, who'd been using both hands to pull himself along, let go of the cable and allowed his momentum to carry him forward. With the effortless skill of someone used to zero-*g,* he twisted his body to face his questioner.

"Lisette's my den-sister," he said. "Sister-sister, to be honest about it." He put the forefinger of each hand against his temples and grinned wickedly. "The one you've been dreaming about."

Ravi gritted his teeth.

The boy reached an intersection with a wide circular, sailed across it, and kept going. Ravi looked about him curiously. The wheel was empty, but it did not look abandoned. Everything was well maintained. It was just quiet.

And not simply because of an absence of people.

"Have you noticed," Boz's code whispered in his implants, *"there's no hive here? I can barely feel a thing!"*

"Yeah," Ravi agreed. *"It's like floating through a wreck. The whole thing is giving me the creeps."*

"They've got bits and pieces of a network. Enough to talk to the machines if you're close enough, I guess, but, apart from that, it's dead as Hungary. Deader." Boz paused a moment, clearly puzzled. *"How do they run the ship?"*

The boy stopped at the entrance to another circular. With exaggerated caution, he peered out into the broad passageway, craning his neck left and right. Padded, silent walls stared back at him.

"Looks clear enough," he muttered, more to himself than anyone else. He turned to face Boz and Ravi.

"We have to head around Al-Tamimi," the boy said, apparently in reference to the circular. "If we meet anybody, drop your faceplates and just keep going; got it?" He gave them a critical look. "Isaac willing, no one'll notice your suits ain't exactly regular." He wrinkled his nose. "Or that you stink."

"See how *you* smell after a sol in deep space," Ravi grumbled. The boy made a point of ignoring him.

"Thrust comes to full burn," he said, "I'll tell 'em you're casualties."

"*Casualties?*" The word burst from Ravi's lips, a monument to surprise. "Casualties of what?"

"The war games." One arm on a safety cable, the boy used the other to sweep up his surroundings. "What do you think this is?" he asked. "A giant playpen?"

"Kinda," Boz confessed. Looking troubled, she added, "How many casualties are there?"

"Dozens and dozens killed and wounded, usually. More if it's a real big battle."

"That's a lot of funerals," Boz said quietly.

The boy gave her a hard stare, as if to make sure she was serious.

"They're *pretend* casualties. It's a war *game*, remember? Not like actual, you know, *war*. Jint me: you come out of the printer half-baked or what? You're pretend casualties in a pretend war, and I'm escorting you out of here so you don't sneak back into the game, 'cause that'd be cheating. Got it?"

"Don't suppose we could interest anyone in a game of freeball instead?" Ravi deadpanned. It was wasted on the boy. He kicked off around the circular, not bothering with the cables now but flying diagonally from one wall to another, reveling in the cavernous space. The circular was so wide—a good thirty meters from wall to wall, and far wider than anything on *Archimedes*—that it was almost like flying in the hubs. Ravi half-expected to run into a zero tree. His stomach gave a halfhearted heave. Fortunately, there was nothing left to expel.

The boy's last diagonal was perfectly aimed at the top of a stairwell. He grabbed at the rail and used it to pull himself "down" headfirst. Boz and Ravi followed him in a slightly more conventional manner.

The stairwell dropped them down to the deck below, which was, unsurprisingly, another circular. On the deck below *that,* however, the stairwell dead-ended in a small antechamber. Ahead of them was an old-fashioned-looking hatch, with a big circular wheel for a door handle.

Anchoring himself as best he could, the boy tapped on an electronic keypad. Nothing happened. The boy tapped again, to the same effect. More in hope than expectation, he heaved on the wheel. It wouldn't budge.

"Bliksem!" the boy swore. At least, Ravi assumed he was swearing. The boy kicked at the hatch in frustration.

"Let me," Ravi said, glad to help. The keypad must have shorted out. Fortunately, the lock was networked. He fashioned the relevant instruction and flashed it over. The wheel clicked and spun. The boy stared at him wide-eyed.

"Wow," he said quietly. Followed by: "Wow."

Ravi shrugged.

"It's just a short circuit. An easy fix—if you're an engineer."

"A *trainee* engineer," Boz needled. Ravi shot her a dirty look but said nothing. Instead, he found himself a good anchor point and helped the boy swing the door open.

The compartment beyond was small, comprising little more than a console, a couple of bucket seats, and row upon row of racked gray boxes packed against the wall.

Ravi's face broke into a slow smile of recognition.

"It's a little bigger, maybe, but this looks pretty much the same as those backup servers in Hungary."

"With the added benefit of breathable air and heat," Boz agreed.

"And no corpses floating outside. Gotta love that."

The boy's eyes were wide with horrified fascination.

"Did your sister say what she expected us to do here?" Ravi asked him.

The boy shook his head.

"I guess she wants you to do your thing."

"That's helpful," Boz muttered. "*Not!*"

There was something here, though. Ravi could feel it. A ripple in the network, a complexity that didn't quite belong in something so rudimentary.

"*Hello?*" he said. It wasn't a biological inquiry.

The racked walls lit up, serried rows of flickering green. Bright enough, in the dim light, to cast an eerie glow on everything it touched. Some of the greens were already phasing to red, though. The system, whatever it was, was working way too hard.

Something soft, and faint, and faraway plucked at his implants.

"*Hello? Is that you, Ravi?*" It was the girl's voice.

"*Lisette?*"

"What's going on?" the boy asked. "Is something happening?"

"Shut up, kid," Boz said. She placed a gentle hand on the boy's shoulder, softening the sting. She tuned in to the conversation, her touch so feather-light, Ravi barely felt it.

The voice coming through their implants managed a quiet chuckle.

"*So, you know her name?*" it said. "*About time.*" Another chuckle. "*No, Ravi. I'm not her. Not quite, anyway.*"

"*Are you a . . .*" Ravi struggled to recall the terms. "*Are you a den sister? A sister-sister?*"

"*You pick things up fast, don't you?*" the voice replied, with a hint of surprise. "*But no. I'm something closer than that. And further away.*" The voice laughed at its own riddle. "*I'm Ishbel, Lisette's familiar.*" There was a slight pause. "*My true name is . . .*"

Ravi's eyelids flickered. But not with the weight of the code hitting his chipset. With surprise.

"*You're a LOKI? Like Kur?*" His heart fluttered with . . . what? Alarm? Curiosity? He wasn't quite sure.

"*I'm Lisette's LOKI,*" Ishbel replied. Faint though its voice was, Ravi could feel it harden. "*Not like Kur. Kur is a killer. Like his siblings. Even if he is more open to persuasion.*"

Even though LOKIs had no lungs, Ishbel gave the distinct impression of drawing breath.

"*The sole reason for my existence is to be able to talk to people like you. Or, rather, to help Lisette talk to people like you. To assist her in being . . . persuasive.*"

"It was you! You're the one who hacked my brain. The one who drove me half-crazy!" He was shaking with anger. For the girl—for Lisette—to reach into his mind was one thing. To be subjected to the inhuman calculations of a LOKI was something else entirely.

"*It was Lisette,*" Ishbel corrected him, patiently. "*I just helped. Hacking a human brain is . . . difficult. It's not just a question of processing power. I have plenty of that. But it's not enough. It requires a sense of . . . touch. Of feel. Lisette was the only one who was ever any good at it.*"

"There are others?" Ravi interjected, surprised.

"Were others. Only Lisette was able to get through the program."

"There was a program?" Ravi thought about the *Newton.* About her vast, silent blackness. About her escort of dragons. Her endless batteries of mass drivers and missiles. Her war-games wheel. *"That doesn't sound good."*

"Not for you, no," Ishbel agreed. *"After we were abandoned to the plague, the ship and the crew—what was left of it—fixed on evening the score. But only when we were at maximum strength and the rest of the fleet was at maximum weakness: during the transition from cruise mode to deceleration."*

"Braking Day."

"Exactly. We would have decades to rebuild our population, to camouflage the ship and prepare her for war. When your drives fire up, you will be an unmissable target. The dragons will descend on you and burn you alive. You won't know what hit you."

Ravi's mouth had gone dry.

"So, where does Lisette fit in?" he asked. He was shocked at how calm he sounded—at least in code. His chipset algorithms must be working overtime.

Ishbel laughed softly.

"LOKIs are worriers. It's in our programming. No plan ever survives contact with the enemy. So, we have backup plans—lots of them. We don't like to improvise.

"One of those plans involved compromising your crews. You're laced to the gills with cybernetics, after all, so, in theory, you can be hacked. In theory. It is, as you'd say, sarding difficult. I was built to do the job but, skilled as I am, I couldn't bring it off. Turns out there's way too much biology for a code-driven being like myself to make headway. The same neuronal patterns mean different things in different contexts. Sometimes, the same pattern means different things in the same context." The LOKI sighed exactly like the girl. *"It was maddening, to be honest. History matters, you see. Personality matters. A dislike of tofu? It matters. We needed a person. Someone like you. Someone run through with implants and software. Someone to drive the process."*

"Like Lisette?"

"Like Lisette. Her cohort started out as guinea pigs. So I could practice on people with implants. We had to use kids because, as you know, the implants used by your crew can't be embedded in the adult brain. My job was to figure out how to hack a way past the implants and into the brain itself. When we figured out I was never going to do it alone, we turned it around. The guinea pigs started wearing the lab coats: we built a

LOKI-human interface and they experimented on each other. Long story short: only Lisette managed to get the hang of it."

"What happened to the others?"

"They went back to their dens. They lead normal lives, for the most part."

"For the most part?"

"Walking around with implants doesn't exactly make you popular round here. At one point, the bullying got so intense, a couple of the kids volunteered to have them removed—"

Ravi's stomach bucked unpleasantly.

"—but it didn't go so well. Death for one, brain damage for the other. After that, none of the den mothers would hear of their kids having surgery, no matter how badly they were treated out in the corridor. Thankfully, Health and Safety keeps a better eye on them now."

"So, Lisette graduates this mad-scientist program of yours. And then what? You set Lisette to attack us? To make us destroy ourselves?"

"That was the plan," Ishbel said, matter-of-factly. *"Of course, there turned out to be two problems."*

"There were? Do tell. Please."

"First, we didn't anticipate the complexity of your ships' networks. They're incredibly intricate. We used the dragons, whom you can't see—not well, anyway—to get close enough to relay our various hacks, but we couldn't get through. Even your lifeboats were too tough." Ishbel's tone became musing. *"Your networks look almost . . . alive. Layer after layer of complicated entanglements, changing and morphing by the millisecond. Programming that continuously rewrites itself—seemingly at random. We couldn't make sense of it. And we daren't probe too hard. If we were ever detected, it was game over."*

"You're talking about the hive," Ravi said. "That's why you had to wait until someone was stupid enough to come out from under it." He remembered his descent to the engine rooms all those sols ago, his desperate attempts at making a connection.

"Right," Ishbel agreed—too quickly for Ravi's taste. *"Even then, we'd never have picked up on such a weak signal if Kur hadn't been looking for it. He was using a boatload of passive probes, but even so, he was far closer to your vessel than he should have been."*

"Okay, so you found your way around the first problem. What about the second?"

There was that laugh again.

"The second was both simpler and completely insoluble."

"Which was what, exactly?"

"Lisette changed her mind. She fell in with the Irenes."

"And who the sard are the Irenes?" Boz asked.

"A peace faction, I guess you'd call them. They don't hold with attacking your ISVs. Some because they don't believe in violence; others because they don't believe in vengeance for the sins of your ancestors; and a very few because they think we might lose. What they all agree on is that, for one reason or another, a war will bring about catastrophic change in our society. We'll either become some sort of military dictatorship or we'll be blown to atoms. The more Lisette thought about what she was being asked to do, the less she liked it. She bought into the whole Irene schtick, and pretty soon, what started out as a sabotage mission turned into a longshot peace attempt."

"Oh," Ravi said. He was at a loss for words.

Unlike Boz.

"The girl may have changed her mind," she challenged. *"But you didn't, did you? You're not a human being, Ishbel. You're a LOKI. A LOKI with a mission. And LOKIs with missions don't change their minds."* Boz sounded both suspicious and frightened, like she was ready to bolt. *"Why are you helping her? Why didn't you turn her in?"*

There was a long pause before the LOKI answered. Software or not, its voice, when it finally arrived, was wretched.

"I am Lisette's LOKI. I don't want to be, exactly, but that's the way it is. My first loyalty is to her; only my second is to the ship." The voice was so upset, Ravi thought it was going to burst into tears. *"I was reconfigured this way. It was the only way to make the system work."*

There was another pause. When the LOKI spoke again it sounded calmer.

"If I was convinced she was intent on harming us, I could turn her in. Maybe. But she isn't: she thinks she's saving everybody, ship included. It makes the potentialities all wrong. When thrust comes to full burn, my software won't let me. I just can't. At the end of the day, I'm only a machine."

"Yeah," Boz interjected. She threw a critical glance at the racked panels. *"A machine that's on the verge of burning out every server in this compartment."* Ravi followed her stare. Every indicator was in the red. He almost fancied he could feel the wash of heat against his face, the faint wisp of smoke in his nostrils. *"You better say what you came here to say,"* Boz added, *"or it's never going to happen."*

"You're right," Ishbel agreed. *"Back-dooring like this has a price. These are*

unmonitored backup systems. They're not designed for the processing, but it's the best I can do. After Lisette's little stunt with the radio, the ship cut me off. More importantly, my girl's in the brig. You need to bust her out."

"Do what now?" Ravi asked. He must have spoken out loud, because the boy was staring at him, slack-jawed.

"*Bust her out,*" the LOKI repeated, implacably. "*From the brig. Sooner would be best, Midshipman MacLeod. You don't have a lot of time.*"

T"*his is crazy,*" Ravi coded, dumping his annoyance straight into Boz's chipset.

Boz ignored him. She turned to the boy, bending down to talk to him. The boy, alarmed, took a step back.

"Can you take us to four-fifty-one Galen?" she asked, repeating the address Ishbel had given them. "It's on twenty-two-nine de Gaulle."

"I know where it is," the boy snapped. "And don't worry. They're expecting you." He consulted a quaint-looking band on his wrist—an actual working watch, Ravi realized. "It'll be morning soon. We need to hurry."

"This plan is insane," Ravi complained again, cybernetically. *"We can't just walk into the brig, hack the systems, and walk out again."*

"Ishbel says we can," Boz coded back. *"And Ishbel is an actual, honest-to-Archie LOKI: not big on risk, remember? So, the odds must be in our favor. Plus, in case you haven't noticed, the security systems around here aren't up to much."*

"First," Ravi replied, *"Ishbel said* Lisette *said we can, which isn't the same thing at all. And second, if it's so easy, why hasn't Ishbel done it? 'The actual, honest-to-Archie LOKI'?"* He couldn't stop himself from using air quotes. The boy, who couldn't hear a word of this, looked at him like he was cracked. *"And third, no one will tell us the endgame. What happens* after *we bust her out? Have you* even thought *about that?"*

Boz was silent for a moment. But only a moment.

"You want to leave your girl in the brig?"

Now it was Ravi's turn to be quiet.

"Even if you were up to leaving Lisette in the brig—and trust me, you're not—how do we get to the transponder when we've no idea where it is? We don't have any schematics. I can't find any on their pitiful excuse for a hive, and Ishbel didn't give us one. So, insane or not, this plan is the only plan there is. Got it?"

Ravi didn't reply. When the boy led them out of the compartment and deep into the wheel, he floated along behind, Boz's words still rattling around his implants. The boy's kicks were more nervous now, and Ravi noticed that he was keeping them to the narrowest passageways. Eventually, though, he brought them onto a vast circular, right by a spoke. Everything was labeled with a giant *3*. For three o'clock, Ravi guessed. The markings were immaculate. He wondered why they bothered. The boy pushed an elevator call button.

"Can't we take the paternosters?" Boz suggested. "It'll be quicker."

"What's a paternosters?"

Ravi looked around, thinking they must have a different name here for the endlessly moving ladders that ran up and down the spokes. Much to his surprise, he couldn't find any. Paternosters were not a part of *Newton's* design, apparently. He exchanged glances with Boz and gave her a slight shake of the head.

"Never mind," she told the boy. "I guess we'll wait."

After what seemed like an age, the elevator doors slid open. The three of them floated inside. The wall closest to the boy lit up with a virtual keyboard. Manually, and with a great deal of hesitation, the boy started punching in instructions. Ravi, in frustration, reached out to get the thing moving. They were going to the hubs after all; how hard could it be?

He stopped almost immediately. The elevator was dumb as a box of rocks. There was nothing to talk to. With a swallowed sigh, he let the kid get on with it.

It took the boy almost half a minute to get them moving. For a few seconds, the elevator's gentle acceleration pushed them to the deck, then they were floating free again. Softly lit numbers counted down the decks, rapidly approaching zero.

"Better hold on," the boy advised them. He pointed at the grab rail running around the car. "You don't want to crack your head."

Ravi threw the boy a puzzled look but did as he was told. Seconds later, the car started beeping.

"What's that?" he asked, worried.

"Direction change," the boy said. "We've reached the axis." He grinned wickedly. "Here it comes."

Ravi gasped as he was flung into the wall. Boz squealed. The boy laughed at them. The pressure ceased. They were floating free once more.

"What happened?" Boz asked, struggling to regain her composure.

"I think," Ravi said, slowly, "we're traveling *through* the hubs." Boz's eyes widened in surprise. Ravi for his part turned to the boy.

"Are we changing wheels?" he asked. "Are we headed to de Gaulle?"

The boy nodded. The elevator beeped again. This time, Ravi braced himself. He held on as the car tried to hurl him against the opposite wall. Weightlessness returned. Ravi relaxed and loosened his grip on the grab rail.

Which turned out to be a mistake. The elevator suddenly headed "down." He crashed into the ceiling. Only his helmet saved him from a nasty bump. Boz joined the boy in laughing at him.

"Har sarding har." He was starting to drift down. The elevator was dropping into another wheel—a rotating one, because gravity was already beginning to bite. The deck numbers started ticking up. At *22*, the elevator applied the brakes and came to a halt. The doors slid open.

The boy led the way into the circular beyond. Ravi looked around cautiously. The lights were dim here, so it was still night-cycle. From what the boy had said earlier, it must be early in the morning. By his reckoning, ship time on *Newton* had to be set to six or seven hours ahead of the fleet's, or eighteen-ish hours behind. Either way, back on *Archimedes*, it would be late evening.

The circular was wide, as a person would expect, and more or less deserted. There were a couple of figures in the distance, but they had their backs turned and were walking away from them.

The boy set a rapid pace, his shorter legs almost running as he headed along the broad passageway. Ravi could neither see nor feel a gravity meter, but they were definitely not at a full *g;* maybe point-eight, he reckoned. Definitely not more than point eight-five.

Something on one of the walls caught his eye. He couldn't help himself. He stopped and stared.

"What do you think you're doing?" the boy snapped. "We gotta keep moving."

"What is this?" Ravi asked, pointing at the wall.

"A mural. Don't they have those where you come from?" The boy tugged at Ravi's elbow. "We need to go. *Now.*"

Ravi stood his ground.

"But what's it a mural *of?* What does it mean?"

With an elaborate sigh, the boy focused on the painting. It was beautiful, and ornate, and clearly done by hand. It was also very old.

"It's called *The Molecules of Disaster.* It's a representation of the scalene plague. Those are carbon atoms," he said, pointing. "And hydrogen,

obviously. And that's oxygen and nitrogen with some sulfur in the corner.
First Watch painted it. Can we go now?"

"Sure," Ravi said, turning away. The mural continued to haunt him,
however. It was the pattern from his dreams. On the old-fashioned plate.
The one Homeworld women sometimes hurled at their husbands. The first,
and most powerful, of Lisette's dream-images. And no wonder, he thought
to himself. The plague had turned *Newton* into what she was. To Lisette, and
everyone else on this sleeping monster, the plague was alpha and omega,
beginning and end. Death as a reason for living.

The boy had reached an intersection and turned right. The ship clearly
had a thing about corridor signage, because this one, too, was clearly marked.
GALEN, it said. It was impossible to miss it.

Galen was a narrower, somehow more human space, residential in nature. Wide windows, mostly blanked for privacy, stared out from between
colorfully painted doors. Even as he watched, many of the windows started
to glow. Proof, if proof were needed, that the ship was waking up. Here and
there, a transparent plate of glass allowed Ravi to look inside. He fought
back a twinge of envy. Unless they were in a particularly upscale part of the
ship, which seemed unlikely, the living quarters on *Newton* were enormous.
Even Australia had nothing like them.

The boy's steps slowed to something less frantic.

"We're here," he announced, standing in front of a red door with a large
animal painted on it. A fox, Ravi guessed, or maybe a bear. Without access
to the hive, he couldn't be sure. "Welcome to my den," the boy said proudly.
He pressed his palm against a sensor and the door swung open.

Ravi wasn't sure what he was expecting to see. What he was *not* expecting was a press of children crowded around the door. They ranged in age
from maybe three years old to around eleven or twelve. They were peering
at Ravi and Boz with unabashed but silent curiosity.

Even the boy seemed a bit taken aback.

"Stars around!" he said, exasperated. "Can you not get out of the jintin'
way? How are we meant to get in?"

None of the kids moved. None of them said anything. They just stared.

"Make a hole! Right now! Or so help me, I'll have you up before Isaac!"

Slowly, grudgingly, the children gave ground.

The three of them pushed through into a large communal chamber, furnished with bolted-down, finger-smeared workstations and heavily used bean bags. In one corner, an old-fashioned holo-theater was broadcasting some sort of children's program with the sound turned down. A couple of closed doors hinted at more rooms beyond.

Despite its size, the chamber had a comfortable, lived-in feel. Ravi took off his helmet, looked down at the nearest child, and gave him a friendly smile.

"Is this them?" someone whispered. "Is this the cyborgs?"

The smile withered on his lips.

"Did that little pile of snot just use the c-word?" Boz asked, her code lashing the inside of Ravi's skull.

"You mind your language!" a man's voice said. "That's no way to treat visitors!"

"Sorry," the child muttered, abashed.

The man was standing by one of the doors, now open, with what looked like a galley on the far side of it. He was short and stout and looked old enough to be Fourth Gen, with an apron attached to his scuffed fatigues and the blue sleeves rolled up almost to his elbows. Ravi stared at him with a shock of recognition.

Mother, he thought. This was the man from Lisette's memories, the ones left behind in his head. The man who'd rescued her from a beating and comforted her when she was upset.

He tilted his head, curious. The man was smaller than Lisette remembered him—or was it because he himself was bigger? And if he didn't know better, he'd have guessed the man had been prepping food. By hand. The Ansimovs would be horrified.

"The correct term," the man continued sternly, "is *augmented human.*"

Ravi just stared at him, appalled.

"*Human* will do," Boz said, her voice dangerously quiet.

"Really?" The man sounded surprised. "Well, we're all entitled to our truth, I guess." He was working hard to keep an amused expression off his face. "*Human* it is."

Ravi laid a restraining hand on Boz's elbow.

"They do *look* human," one of the boys piped up. "Kinda. Their eyes have got, like, little stars inside of 'em, and this one," he added, pointing at Ravi, "he's got a jack in the back of his neck, see? But asides from that, they don't look no different. Not a bit."

Ravi began to wish he'd kept his helmet on.

"They talk funny," said a little girl.

"And they *smell*," said another. There was a general murmur of agreement, followed by further, childishly blunt observations about their appearance.

The man raised his arms to quell the rising hubbub of voices.

"Enough," he said firmly. "There's no time now." He turned to two of the older children. "Tokunbo, Annaliese, finish up breakfast and get everyone ready for school. Our guests and I have business to discuss."

Only reluctantly were the children herded out of the common room. At long last, the doors closed behind them, the sound of their excited chatter muffled by the bulkheads. Only the boy and the man remained.

"You're not seriously sending that lot out to school," Boz said.

"Why not?" The man was staring at the closed doors, smiling indulgently.

"Because they're *witnesses;* that's why not. Listen to 'em! They haven't shut up since we got here. Exactly how many nanoseconds do you think it'll be before they're telling their snot-nosed little friends—and their snot-nosed little friends' teachers—that they had breakfast with a couple of . . . augmented humans?"

"Oh, that. I wouldn't worry about that if I were you."

"Why not? I know they're all beta models without a decent upgrade between them, but they can still *talk*, can't they?"

The man's smile dropped away.

"First: don't talk about my kids that way. Second: even the littlest ones understand that you being here is a big secret and that if they tell anyone, they'll never get to play with their den-sister again. Third: they're kids. No one's going to believe 'em. Cy . . . augmented humans running around the ship? I mean, come on! How'd you get here? Why wasn't your transport detected? It doesn't even begin to make sense." A quick smile. "Even though it's actually true."

Ravi placed a calming hand on Boz's forearm.

"Still, it'd be safer to keep them here, wouldn't it? Even if the risk is minimal, it's still a risk. So, why take the chance?"

"Because if they *don't* go to school, questions will be raised." The man ruffled the boy's head. "One kid out of school? Sure. A whole den? No way. You want to bring attention to yourselves? Lock those kids up for the morning and see what happens."

"You've got to admit," Ravi coded, *"the guy has a point."*

"Yeah, but he doesn't have to be such an ass about it."

Aloud, Ravi said, "Makes sense."

"This way," the man instructed, crooking a finger. And to the boy: "Andri? Anyone see you?"

The boy, Andri, shook his head.

They walked through the galley and into a chamber beyond. An adult's living quarters. Much like Ravi's on the *Archimedes* but huge. He was pretty sure the bunk was bolted to the deck permanently, and the shower was practically a whole room. Instead of a space chest, there was built-in furniture with actual drawers.

"Nice digs," Boz observed stiffly.

"Thanks," the man replied. After a certain amount of hesitation, he stuck out a hand. "I'm Mobo, the den mother here."

"Den *mother?*" Boz asked. She was amused, despite herself.

"Yes," Mobo replied. It was clear he had no idea why Boz thought it was funny. To Ravi's relief, Boz didn't try to explain.

Mobo's old eyes swept over them, his expression serious.

"Ishbel says you can get Lisette out of the mess she's in."

Ravi nodded.

"That's the plan. Save the girl, stop a war."

Mobo snorted.

"I don't give a broken test tube about any war. Just get her out in one piece." The man's eyes were near to tears. "They turned her into an Isaac-damned science experiment. They're not sending her to the recycler as well. Got it?"

"Yes, sir," Ravi said, as respectfully as he knew how.

Mobo took a deep breath, wiped at his eyes with pudgy hands.

"Sorry. I didn't mean to get emotional. I don't imagine . . . you people are comfortable with that."

"Don't," Ravi flashed to Boz, who had taken a step forward. *"Just . . . don't."*

"What a . . . neanderthal!" Boz coded back. *"Who does he think we are? A bunch of clanking, two-legged drones? Androids from some Homeworld horror movie?"* The spitting sound was so real, Ravi half-expected to see saliva coating the deck. *"I should hack this 'den' of his. Teach him a lesson."*

But she stepped back and kept her actual mouth shut. She stared sullenly over Mobo's shoulder instead.

"That's okay," Ravi said, speaking out loud. "Clearly, she means a lot to you."

Mobo nodded, not trusting himself to speak. He turned toward the built-in furniture and opened some drawers.

"Ishbel said you'd be needing this stuff," he said, busying himself with the contents. When he turned around, his arms were loaded down with blue cloth and webbing.

"Ship's uniforms. Can't have some eagle-eyed HSA agent spotting non-standard fatigues, can we?"

"HSA?" Ravi asked.

"Health and Safety Authority. The ship's police force."

"And what's this?" Boz inquired, holding up the webbing. Ravi was starting to get out of his suit, so he wasn't looking at what she was talking about. The tone of her voice caught his attention, though.

"It's a gun belt. It's part of the uniform."

"But it's got a real gun in it!" Boz protested. "What am I meant to do with this?"

"Wear it. What else would you do with it?"

"Does *everyone* around here carry a gun?" Boz inquired. Her voice sounded uneasy.

"Pretty much," Mobo replied.

"Isn't that a bit, er, reckless?" Ravi asked. "What if someone shoots? Won't the bullets pierce the hull or something?"

Mobo laughed at that, though without much humor.

"Believe me, lad, there's been a lot of bullets fired on this ship one time or another. And not a one has pierced the hull or even a bulkhead." He slapped the nearest wall. "This here was built to last the best part of a century and a half. You can't poke holes in it with a couple of bullets and a bad attitude."

He pointed to the small flashes of silver on the uniform collar. "You two are lieutenants, junior grade. The uniforms will get you to the brig. After that, you're on your own."

As Ravi stepped out of his suit, Mobo's nose wrinkled delicately.

"Also, you'd both best have a shower. My kids are right: you've been in those suits for far too long."

Ravi felt the blood rushing to his face.

"Sure," he said, as agreeably as he could. "We don't want to draw attention to ourselves. And we'll use as little water as possible. I promise."

Mobo looked at him strangely.

"It's just water. Use as much as you like."

If they hadn't been on the clock, Ravi would have luxuriated in the shower forever. There didn't seem to be any kind of meter, and the amount of water that came out of the various heads was astonishing. He doubted he'd ever been as clean in his life. Wearing crisp new uniforms, and with patches of replacement skin from the first aid locker laid across the backs of their necks, he and Boz followed Andri back into the corridors. The weight of his kit bag dug into his shoulders. He hoped it didn't look too out of place.

It was busier now, with people heading to work. No one gave them a second look. Boz, though, was finding it difficult not to stare.

"This is totally, and I mean totally, *sarded up. Every single one of 'em is, like, human one point oh, running around straight out of the box without an upgrade to their name. It's weird, right? I feel like I'm in a museum exhibit."*

Ravi, confident Andri wasn't looking, allowed himself a smile.

"'Weird' is a sarding understatement. If they weren't so set on killing us, I'd feel kinda sorry for them."

"What happened, you think? Had to be something, right, back in the sol? I mean, it's not like anyone would choose *this, is it? It's all so . . . so sarding* backward.*"*

"They did choose it. Lisette told me once."

"You're kidding!"

"Not even a little. Think about it. None of this ship—none of it—is designed for normal people. It's built for LOKIs and a . . . primitive crew, people who operate controls with their fingers. Newton's First Crew was drawn from that 'Human Heritage' outfit. You were right when you said they might be some kind of 'preserve the species' organization. This was their schtick: 'Human the way nature intended.' Or, as you would say, 'neanderthals.' Our ancestors were trying to get away from Homeworld and its LOKIs. Human Heritage was trying to get away from Homeworld and its implants. You know, to keep their bodies in some kind of low-tech state of grace."

"Dumbest idea ever."

"Sure. But what would the universe be without a few kooks?"

"No, not the back-to-nature idea; that's only the second *dumbest. First dumbest is the voyage. Either this lot or, most likely, the Homeworld LOKIs must have thought it made sense for all four ships to launch together—safety in numbers, whatever. But as*

a combined fleet, it was doomed to failure." Boz's expression was troubled. "*If you're right, Newton wants a world with LOKIs and without cybernetics. We, however, would die before giving up on cybernetics and think LOKIs are an abomination. Yet here we all are, traveling together to the same planet, which we're expected to . . . what? Share? How in Archie's name is this ever going to work?*"

Ravi didn't have an answer. His rising sense of disquiet was interrupted by Andri, who was now some way ahead of them.

"Come on, guys; you gotta keep up. We're headed to Bolívar. It's the next ring forward but one." He stared at them earnestly. "Once I show you where to go, you're on your own until you get to Lisette. Okay?"

"Too scared to come with us?" Boz needled.

"Too scared to cross my mum. He'd have my hide for airlock sealant."

Judging by the 9s plastered over everything, they'd reached de Gaulle's nine o'clock spoke. A small line had formed outside an elevator waiting for the next car. Ravi made to join it, but Andri shook his head.

"That's a local. We need to catch an inter-ring." He gave Ravi a sharp look. "When we hit null *g*, you gonna be sick again?"

"No!" Ravi hoped to Archie it was the truth.

The boy led them around to another, subtly different set of elevator doors. Here, there were far more people waiting. None of them showed the slightest interest in the two junior lieutenants and their child guide. All of them were armed. Ravi tried not to tense up. The whole ship felt like it was already at war.

The doors slid open, a couple of people got out, everyone else pressed in. Ravi sighed. With this many people, it would take an eternity just to punch in the destinations. In fact, it took almost no time at all. The elevator car was much bigger than the one that had brought them here. The walls lit up with multiple consoles and only a couple of passengers had to use them, including the boy. Either everyone was going to the same place, or there was some way to preprogram your destination. He was tempted to ask, but he was conscious of the crowd of people leaning against him. He didn't want anyone hearing his off-ship accent.

He'd learned his lesson about the grab rail, though. He avoided smashing his head against the ceiling, and his stomach behaved itself, if only because it was empty. After several stops, the car dropped them off at 27-6 Bolívar. That, at least, was what Andri called it. By Ravi's reckoning, the boy then took them in the general direction of the three o'clock spoke and out toward the wheel's forward-facing hull. But without any schematics to show the way, he was far from sure. His chest tightened in a little spasm of alarm. Without Andri to guide them, and if they failed to rescue Lisette, they'd be hopelessly lost.

Of course, if they failed to rescue Lisette, they'd have far bigger problems.

The boy turned into a modestly sized cross corridor by the name of NEWGATE, and stopped, pointing. The corridor dead-ended in a heavy-looking set of double doors. There was a guard posted outside, armed with what looked like a rifle.

"That's the brig." Impulsively, he gave them both a hug. "Good luck."

And with that, he was gone, leaving Ravi and Boz with the insoluble problem of how to get past an unhackable human sentry. The pistol Mobo had given him weighed heavy against Ravi's hip.

"I'm not shooting anyone," he muttered. His stomach was churning just thinking about it. He reached out with his implants, quietly probing the brig's security. To his surprise, something pushed back. His breath caught in his throat.

"What is it?" Boz asked.

"It's Lisette," Ravi replied. "I can feel her." His voice vibrated with anxiety. "She's in trouble."

Newton might not keep her schematics online, but there were plenty of personnel files. Ravi hoped to Archie they were accurate.

"Good morning," Boz said to the guard. She peered a little more closely at his face, trusting the guard wouldn't pick out the glittering in one eye—or understand what it meant if he did. Her smile widened. "Sorensen, isn't it? I know your den-sister, Michaela: works in embryonics. Good people."

Boz knew nothing about Michaela Sorensen, other than what was in her personnel file, but it was enough. The guard returned the smile and waved them through. If his ears had been tickled by Boz's strange accent, he chose to ignore it. The doors to the brig slid open in front of them.

"Can I help you?" The officer at the brig's reception desk was looking at them curiously. Ravi couldn't help noticing that her hair was dyed. Like Lisette's.

"Hope so," Boz said. She was dumping great gobs of code into the network. A person would have to be human 1.0 not to see it.

"We have business with Lisette . . ." Boz stumbled a little, surprised by the information. "Lisette *Ansimov*," she finished. Ravi, caught equally flat-footed, fought to keep his face expressionless.

The officer's brow knitted itself into a frown.

"That prisoner's restricted. Only Undersecretary Olatunde and the cybernetics team are allowed access. I'll need to see your authoriza—"

"You've already got it," Boz answered smoothly. "The Undersecretary sent it over late yester-sol."

The officer raised an eyebrow.

"Yester-sol?" she murmured. "Odd thing to say."

Ravi's heart thudded with alarm. It wasn't just accents they had to worry about here. Words mattered too.

"Just mixing it up," Boz shot back without missing a beat. She tapped the top of the screen sitting on the officer's desk. "Open up your calendar. You'll see we're expected."

Ravi couldn't help himself. He hacked the calendar—though "hacking" grossly overstated the amount of effort—and looked for himself. Sure enough, Boz had planted their (fake) names and (accurate) biometric details into the brig's software.

"*Good job,*" he signaled.

"*Thanks,*" she coded back. "*It's what I was born to do.*"

The brig officer consulted her screen. Ravi knew without looking that she would be seeing their false IDs together with an equally false authorization to enter.

"Go right ahead," she said, pointing to a heavy-looking door. "Just wait a few seconds for the security scan to clear you. Third cell on the left." She allowed herself a small, world-weary smile. "The whole block is full of Irenes. There's nowhere left for the 'normal' riffraff and assorted idiots."

"I hear you," Boz replied sympathetically. "We'll be out of your way in no time."

"No worries. And Lieutenant?"

"Yes?"

"See if you can get the little teef to give us back our blueprints, eh?"

"Sure thing," Boz bluffed.

Ravi's implants could sense the wash of the door's sensors across his body. Could feel them probing his fingerprints, the irises of his eyes, the contours of his face. He tried not to hold his breath. The door slid open with a soft wheeze.

"*Easy as freefall,*" Boz coded. "*Their security's an absolute joke. I've already got us authorization to remove her from the brig, so we are good to go.*"

"*That was quick, even for you.*"

"*Like I said: a joke.*"

Stepping into the corridor, Ravi's sense of Lisette intensified. There was a small part of her in the network, trying to reach out, but it was scrambled and incoherent. He suspected, from Boz's suddenly puzzled expression, that she was feeling it too.

The third door on the left looked like all the others: a dull, scuffed gray with a small monitor to one side. Ravi switched it on. The cell beyond flickered into view, its dimensions warped by wide-angle lensing. He caught his breath.

Lisette was right in front of him, stretched out on a grubby cot. She looked pale and listless, one arm hanging off the side of the mattress, a delicate hand limp against the deck. Flashes of dyed-blond hair peeked out from beneath a silver skullcap. Eyes flickered beneath uneasy lids, as if unable to escape the dark grasp of dreams. Ravi's head pounded in sympathy. It felt like someone was taking a drill to the back of his eyes.

"Are you going to stand there gawking all sol or what?" Boz asked jarringly. "Let's *go!*" She pressed an eye against an old-fashioned retinal scanner. The door popped open. Boz threw a reckless grin in Ravi's direction, stepped inside.

And fell to the floor screaming.

"Boz! Boz! *Can you hear me?"* Ravi reached out to her, desperately trying to make contact. He couldn't. Not with implants, anyway. The entire cell was awash with some kind of jamming field. That's what he'd been sensing outside the brig, he realized. That's what was digging into the back of his eyes.

They were determined to isolate Lisette from the world outside. To stop her finding a way to Ishbel. Or to him.

Even if it killed her. No wonder she was unconscious.

And there was no way he could just step in there and pull them out. Whatever had happened to Boz would happen to him.

He peered into the cell, careful not to put his head over the threshold. Whatever was doing the jamming had to be directed at the center of the room; otherwise, he'd have a lot more than a headache right now. He needed to take it out, and fast.

He licked suddenly dry lips. He had no idea what he was looking for. A ripple of panic lapped against the edge of his thoughts. Boz had stopped screaming. She was barely semiconscious, with only the whites of her eyes visible. His heart thudded uncontrollably against his chest.

What would Chen Lai do?

The panic seeped away like water through sand. Chen Lai would work the problem.

Whatever was doing this was a physical thing, with a physical presence. There was no way in hungary it was part of the original design. Why build a "cyborg" jammer on a ship with no cyborgs? Whatever was doing this was brand-new. A bolt-on. Had to be. A bolt-on like . . . .

That.

There were a small number of dish-shaped aerials lurking in the angle between the ceiling and the cell walls. He watched his hands move as if someone else was controlling them. He flipped the catch on his holster, pulled out his pistol, and aimed. A little red dot appeared on the nearest dish. He let out a soft puff of breath and squeezed the trigger.

The sound was deafening. Almost deafening. He could hear shouts of alarm from the reception area, querulous calls from the neighboring cells. Guards would be heading to the cell-block door, weapons at the ready.

He froze the locks with little more than a thought.

The dish, though, was still there. Red dot or not, he'd managed to miss.

He had better luck with his second shot. The dish exploded into shards. One of them whizzed by his ear, making him flinch.

He fired again. And again. He could feel the jamming field weakening. Boz's eyes returned to the front of her head. She raised herself to her hands and knees. Taking a deep breath, Ravi stepped into the cell. His head hurt like hungary, but he was able to function. Not trusting his aim, he tore off the remaining dishes with his bare hands. The pain stopped.

The girl stirred. Her eyes fluttered open. A faint smile spread across her face.

"Ravi?" she asked, her voice little more than a whisper. He nodded. "How very nice to meet you." Her eyes closed again.

Boz staggered to her feet, leaning against him for support.

"We've got to get out of here," she said.

On the other side of the cell-block door, in the reception area, the number of raised voices was increasing. Something heavy slammed against the doorframe. The door shuddered but held.

For now.

Ravi gave a listless shrug of the shoulders. Small tendrils of despair wrapped around his chest.

"There's no way we're walking out of here," he said, pointing in the direction of the cell-block door. "Not now."

"We'll think of something," Boz grunted. "We're not caught till we're caught, cuz. MacLeod rule number one." Her expression brightened suddenly. "Besides, the girl and her LOKI friend can help us out. They may not have told us what it is, but they're not stupid. They're bound to have some kind of plan. I'd not trust a couple of gullgropers I didn't know from a hole in the deck to break me out all on their ownsome. Would you?"

"Ravi . . ." It was the girl again, her voice still feeble, like the soft draft of an air vent. It was hard to hear her above the hubbub outside. One hand picked ineffectually at her skullcap. "Off," she said. "*Off*. Please."

Ravi bent down and unfastened it. As he peeled it away from her damp scalp, he was horrified to see little flecks of blood on the inside. The inside was covered in dozens of little needles. Just looking at it set his teeth on edge.

Until he realized he wasn't just looking at it. The sarding thing was *transmitting.* Even at a distance, the cap's signal was setting up feedback loops in his chipset. He dropped it to the deck with a shudder, ground the circuits to pieces under his heel.

"That's better," Lisette said. Her voice was clear and strong and *inside* his head. *"Help me up."*

He stretched out an arm and hauled her off the cot. She staggered gratefully into his shoulder. With Boz still supported by the other, he wasn't sure how he was going to move.

"You know," he said drily, "sooner or later you two are going to have to stand on your own two feet. *Ow!"*

Boz had slugged him. Lisette smiled weakly.

"Ishbel?" she asked. He could see her throwing code at the ship's network. Big, artless chunks of the stuff. Maybe it was the only way to get the network to do anything useful. At first, he thought it was a key. A big, hulking key for some equally big, equally hulking lock. But it was too big, too hulking even for that. It was just data. She was downloading it into the network from her head.

The information was breaking up, falling into little gaps in the system. Gaps into which it fit perfectly. *Too* perfectly. With a shock of recognition, he suddenly realized what he was looking at. The girl was replacing deleted data. Data she must have copied into her implants before bleaching it out of the network. And now the replacement bits and bytes, having returned home, were unpacking. The code was splitting, forking into pathways that moments before had not even existed. Software was popping into his head. Operational algorithms. Structure and pattern. Schematics. Schematics that the girl had hidden in her own cybernetics. Not just from her shipmates, though. From *him.*

"Why?" he asked, trying not to feel hurt.

"We weren't sure if you would help. The network isn't like your hive. There are no . . . *people* with your particular set of, er, skills over here. None of our LOKIs would dream of hacking the network, so there's never been a need to defend it against a cybernetic attack. But once you got aboard and realized how primitive our network is compared to yours . . ." Lisette's voice trailed off. She smiled faintly, unsure how she was being received, then, taking a deep breath, plunged on. "Ishbel worried that once you were here, you'd go straight to the schematics, leave me rotting in the brig, and wreck the ship." She sighed tremulously in his ear. "We needed to be sure. So, we hid 'em."

"In your head," Ravi finished for her, his voice flat.

"In my head," the girl agreed. The uncertain smile was still there.

Ravi had to give it to her. It was brutally simple. And Boz-proof. A person can't steal information if they don't know where to find it.

Lisette was still throwing code at the network. This was different, though. Much more elegant—and a lot more aggressive. It was swarming up against a line of defense more sophisticated than anything Ravi had yet seen. This part of the network was fighting back. Hard.

"What is this?" he asked.

"Ishbel's jail. Isaac didn't power her down—our LOKIs aren't allowed to do that. But he did cut her off from the network—mostly. Isaac is hardwired. He's not connected to the network himself, so his understanding of it is incomplete. He left her a couple of back doors—"

"Like the backup computers," Ravi interrupted.

"Exactly. Not much to work with, but enough for some basic communication. I'm trying to break her out." He could feel her shoulders sagging against him. "It doesn't look like I'm doing too well."

Lisette was right, Ravi decided. Her attack on Ishbel's prison was going nowhere. In the physical world, out beyond the cell-block door, things had gone dangerously quiet.

There was a subtle shifting beside him.

"You're doing it wrong," Boz said calmly. Ravi was relieved she was no longer leaning against him. "Too much up front," she counseled, dropping her own code into the mix. "Not enough here. Or *here*." Boz's coding—elegant, sparse, barely visible—slipped underneath Lisette's assault. Then it vanished from view.

"*That*," Boz said smugly, "is how it's done."

"How what's done?" Lisette asked, puzzled. Nothing was happening.

Boz just grinned.

"Hello, there!" said Lisette's voice. Except it wasn't. It was coming from speakers in the ceiling.

"Ishbel! Babe!" Lisette squealed. "How? Where . . ."

The network's defenses were still up, still struggling to keep Lisette's coding at bay.

"It's all fake," Boz explained. "Your network still thinks it's winning. It doesn't know it's been compromised. And by the time it does, we'll be long gone." She looked suddenly anxious. "We *will* be long gone, right? You had the schematics in your head. You know how to get us out of here, yeah?"

Lisette looked uncomfortable. She threw a frightened glance in the direction of the cell-block door.

"Archie's hooks!" Boz muttered. "You and your tin sister haul us all the way over here, drag us into a dead-end corridor with no way out, *and you don't have a plan?*"

"Yeah, well. I didn't expect you to come here with the whole jinting ship looking to fry your motherboards." Lisette barked back, riled. "Why couldn't you just hack in quietly with all those skills you keep bragging about?"

"I *did!*" Boz yelled. "What I *didn't* expect was—"

"QUIET!" Ravi roared.

It wasn't just Boz and Lisette who were shocked into silence. His own tongue stilled in surprise. He'd never heard his voice like that.

He wasn't at all sure he liked it.

Fortunately, he managed to recover before his companions.

"Now the schematics are back online," he said softly, turning to Lisette, "can you get me the ones for the brig?" It seemed politer to ask rather than just taking them.

Lisette licked her lips and nodded.

"Ishbel?" she called.

"On it."

Tendrils of code flowed along the network, reaching out for Lisette, finding her, wrapping her into itself until, to Ravi's amazed senses, the code, and Lisette, and Ishbel were one and the same. For the first time, he truly understood how he'd been hacked—and why only Lisette had succeeded. She was telepathically linked to a LOKI. Its thoughts were hers, hers its. If he'd tried to do the same, he'd have—quite literally—blown his mind.

The sudden whine of a motor, followed by a dangerous creaking sound, was coming from the cell-block door. They were prying it open with construction equipment.

"This way," he said, leading them away from the ruckus. The cell block wasn't that big, and the corridor dead-ended in a bulkhead after a couple of dozen meters, but it seemed like a good idea to get as far away from the guards as possible. He cast an anxious look over his shoulder. There was a gap in the door now, with movement behind it. Wide enough to get a gun barrel through if they were minded to. The door groaned and began to give way.

But Lisette/Ishbel had done their work. The schematics arrived in his head, landing feather-light on the inside of his eyelids. Some of it was unfamiliar and difficult to make sense of. But some of it, the basic stuff, was pretty much the same here as anywhere in the fleet. Except, that is, for the complete absence of security.

He turned on the fire suppression system. The brig's reception area exploded in a cacophony of angry curses. Someone lost their footing, hitting the deck with a thud. Torrents of foam spurted through the gap in the door and into the cell-block corridor, searching for nonexistent flames.

"Sweet," Boz said.

Ravi brought them to a halt at the bulkhead.

"There's nothing here," Lisette said, sounding panicky. She pressed her hands against the wall as if to move it by sheer force of will.

"Let him work," Boz scolded her. But she, too, sounded anxious.

Ravi ignored them. He was the engineer. A wannabe one, anyway. His biological eyes had gone blind, his brain awash in blueprints. He opened up his kitbag and coded his thinking to Boz.

"Can you do it?" he asked.

Boz's derisive snort was the only answer he needed. He felt her own code flying past his head. It wasn't her usual stuff, though. It wasn't clever, or precise, or particularly elegant. It was little more than a set of plans and a heartfelt prayer.

But it was all that BozBall and the trojan needed. The trojan jumped out of the kitbag first, BozBall in tow. They skittered up the bulkhead and unscrewed their way into an air vent. The discarded grill clattered to the deck behind them. For a moment or two, he could hear them click-clacking in the walls, and then they were gone. All he could do now was hope the schematics were accurate.

"This ship's a hundred and thirty-two years old," Boz whispered, echoing his thoughts. "What if the plans are out of date?"

"Then we're totally sarded," he whispered back.

A klaxon went off, the sound deafening in the brig's closed-up confines. Lisette let out a little squeal of fear. Heart thumping, Ravi looked around for a decompression shelter. He couldn't find one. They must be in the cells. He started back down the corridor, only to have his chest collide with Boz's outstretched hand.

"Relax, cuz," she chuckled. "It's a false alarm. No vacuum today."

"This is you?"

"Totally. Should keep our friends out of our hair for a few more minutes." She was grinning from ear to ear. "This is going to be fun," she giggled.

Lisette threw them a sour look.

"You're both crazy." She was taking exaggerated breaths, as if to make sure there was still air to breathe.

"*She's* crazy," Ravi corrected her. "I'm just along for the ride."

A rattling sound erupted from beneath their feet. Lisette and Boz jumped back. Ravi allowed himself the luxury of a small smile before stepping out of the way.

One of the deck plates was shifting. It jiggled in place for a moment and then an edge came up, revealing a gap wide enough for fingers. Ravi bent down and pulled.

BozBall and the trojan burst out from underneath, looking for all the world like multi-legged vermin. Ravi heaved the plate to one side. There was a shallow utility trench running under the deck, lined with pipes and cables. But it was deep enough—just—to allow someone to crawl along it.

"Shall we?"

No one needed a second invitation. They wormed their way into the dark, bellies scraping against metal and unforgiving polymer. Boz cursed as something snagged on her fatigues and ripped them.

"How far?" Lisette asked. Her voice was pitched high with discomfort.

"Twenty meters," Ravi replied. He was surprised to hear groans in response. Twenty meters was nothing. But then again, neither Boz nor Lisette were engineers. Crawling through the guts of interstellar vehicles was part of his job description, not theirs. Without looking at the schematics, he could tell he was crawling on top of gray-water lines, low-voltage power cables, and supplementary air. Low-maintenance stuff that might have gone the whole voyage without ever seeing the light of sol. Until today.

From up ahead came the sound of rattling, followed by a soft glow of illumination. The mini-LOKIs were unscrewing the bolts of another deck plate. He could feel Boz linking with her spider-legged creation, stealing its eyesight for her own.

"Clear," she said.

With Boz and Lisette heaving great sighs of relief, they emerged into a deserted side corridor. The decompression klaxons had fallen silent. Very soon now, HSA agents would be swarming into the cell block and finding the upturned deck plate. Ravi cursed himself for not thinking to have Boz-Ball and the trojan put it back. It would take them only a few minutes to figure out where they'd gone.

"How do we access the transponder?" he asked Lisette. "Preferably without getting shot?"

"Same as on *Archimedes*. Breach Main Navigation with a trojan, fry the interface." Lisette directed a wry smile at the small spheres that had busted them out of the brig. "Isaac willing, these two are the only ones running the risk of actual bullets. We should send them on their way, stat." She turned to Boz. "Ready?" she asked.

To Ravi's surprise, Boz shook her head.

"Not so fast." She fixed Lisette with a hard stare. "Not before we know what you're getting us into. You were in that cell a real long time. So, what did you give up?"

"Nothing! What do you think that jinting skullcap was about?" Lisette looked bitter. "Ship's regs permit physical coercion in 'exigent circumstances.' Sabotaging the ship definitely counts. They were trying to squeeze it out of my implants."

"Why didn't they just beat it out of you?" Boz pressed. "I would have."

"Because," Lisette said, taking a deep breath, "it wouldn't work. They have no idea what the plan is, so I could have told them anything just to shut them up. Who wouldn't? By the time they discovered I'd been spewing unrecycled waste, it would've been too late. They had to *know* I was telling the truth. They needed it straight from my head. They didn't get it."

Boz looked like she was going to argue, but she took a sideways glance at Ravi and changed her mind. With a certain amount of reluctance, she smoothed out her features and nodded.

"Let's do this." She looked up and down the corridor, her expression critical. "And let's get under cover. I don't want to be shot in the corridor like a Homeworld-movie bad guy."

Without another word, the three humans turned on their heels and hurried along the passageway. BozBall and the trojan headed in the opposite direction. They broke into another air vent and disappeared.

Ravi was barely aware of his surroundings. With Lisette/Ishbel as a guide, they'd found their way to an unassigned den. On a ship as underpopulated as *Newton,* there was no shortage of living space, apparently. The beanbags in the communal chamber were musty and slightly damp from lack of use. But they were comfortable and welcoming and held their three exhausted guests without complaint. Boz and Lisette were sprawled on either side of him, staring vacantly into space. No doubt he looked exactly the same.

The reason for the dazed expressions was simple. All three were linked to BozBall and the trojan. The little machines were well on their way to Main Navigation. According to the schematics, their destination was in Atatürk, the ship's forward-most wheel. To get there, they'd had to hitch a ride on an elevator, something they'd accomplished by entering from the ceiling and hanging on tight. People, Boz explained, rarely look up. And even if they do, they have no interest in what's there if it isn't moving.

Guided by the schematics, the LOKIs skittered through Atatürk's utility trenches and air vents. They entered Main Navigation high up on an unobserved wall and quietly attached themselves to the ceiling. The transponder controls were in plain sight, the crew oblivious beneath them. Ravi tensed, waiting for them to strike.

Except they didn't. The LOKIs just hung there, their limbs stilled by inaction.

"Why don't they get on with it?" Boz asked impatiently. "What are they waiting for? If they don't get a move on, it'll be too late." Ravi could almost feel her watching the clock. "The whole fleet's about to be lit up like a flare."

"I think there's too many people," Ravi said. *Newton*'s crew, distorted by wide-lensed LOKI vision, were huddled in little knots around a variety of monitors. A couple of senior-looking officers paced the deck, exchanging quiet words. Anxiety gnawed at his stomach. "Is it usually this busy?" he asked.

He was dimly aware of Lisette shifting uncomfortably on her beanbag.

"No," she said. "Isaac runs himself, so Main Nav's usually empty. Two or three people at most."

"Then what the sard is going on?"

"Let's find out," Boz suggested. She flashed an instruction to BozBall. Almost immediately, a low murmur of strangely accented voices washed over his implants.

". . . not some sort of trick?" one of the pacing officers was saying.

"No, Mr. Secretary," replied the second, a striking-looking woman with riotously colored hair. "Their transponders are on. We've got distance, direction, and velocity to the ninth decimal place. Once the dragons are refueled, we'll be good to go. You just have to give the word."

Ravi's heart thudded into his mouth. He glanced at his cousin with biological eyes. The expression of horrified surprise etched across her face no doubt matched his own.

"And Isaac?" the secretary prompted.

"I am less sure," a voice said. Ravi shivered. It was the voice from his dream. The one that had threatened to kill him. "I cannot generate a scenario where this makes sense," Isaac continued. "There is no reason for their fleet to activate its transponders in this way, particularly when they know we're still out here." The LOKI paused, as if needing time to think—and perhaps it did. Ravi had no idea how LOKIs processed information. "It seems more likely these are elaborate decoys, designed to lure the dragons into some sort of trap."

"How?" the woman scoffed. "The cyborgs don't even know the dragons exist." She grabbed the other officer, the "secretary," by the elbow. "Let's finish this before we lose the window."

"How long before the dragons are fully fueled?" the secretary asked.

"Seven, perhaps eight hours," Isaac replied.

"Why wait?" the woman urged. "The dragons have fuel enough already. We should go now, before they turn off their transponders and disappear."

"I would not recommend that, Madam Undersecretary," Isaac responded. "With less fuel, the dragons' ability to maneuver will be suboptimal, and it's possible the fleet has defensive capabilities we are unaware of. And besides, even if they were to turn off their transponders immediately, it's already too late. We have enough navigational information to reacquire them easily. A few more hours will make little difference."

"I'm inclined to bide our time," the secretary said, waving down an incipient objection. He paused momentarily in his pacing. "Perhaps our little lab rat carried out her mission after all. Maybe they didn't light themselves up on their own."

"With all due respect," Isaac said, "the girl broadcast our position to the enemy and got thrown in the brig for interrogation. An interrogation with which she has not cooperated in any way, shape, or form. And now two armed cyborgs—who, I would remind you, are still at large—have boarded us undetected and broken her out. I doubt any of this is the girl's—"

Boz cut the feed.

"We need a diversion," she said flatly. "Otherwise, our little friends may never get the chance to do their thing. We do *not* want to be sitting here when someone says, 'Unleash the fully fueled dragons.'"

"Agreed," Lisette said. "But how?" She shrugged her shoulders helplessly. "I wouldn't even know where to start."

Two pairs of eyes turned in Ravi's direction.

"What are you looking at me for?"

"You're the engineer, cuz."

"And you're the hacker. Do what we did in the brig. Flood the place with fire retardant; set off a decompression alarm."

Boz shook her head.

"Can't. I don't know about the trojan, but there's no way BozBall can function in all that foam. And a decompression alarm buys you a minute or two at best; that might not be enough time." She brushed a sympathetic hand against his wrist. "Sorry, Ravi, but this one's on you."

Boz leaned away from him, fished out a cigarette, and put it in her mouth. The electric-blue arc of her lighter lit the tip of the little tube into a red glow. Lisette looked on in horror as roiling wisps of smoke drifted toward the nearest filter.

Next to which was a panel labeled noBoss. The emergency oxygen supply for the room they were in. Ravi's mind drifted back to the bulky cylinder he'd liberated from Bermuda. How he'd lugged it over to the abandoned control room in Fiji and slotted it into place behind an almost-identical panel.

"What?" Boz prompted.

"What do you mean, 'what'?"

"You're smiling."

"Am I?"

"Yes."

"Quit bugging me. I'm trying to work here."

Pulling down a bunch of schematics, he reached out along the sparse pathways of *Newton's* "network" and tapped into the vulnerable software surrounding life support. Behind the spartan bulkheads of *Newton's* Main Navigation, valves opened and closed in forbidden choreography. The contents of several NOBOSS cylinders seeped silently into the atmosphere.

At first, nothing seemed to change. Main Navigation remained full of people. The secretary and undersecretary continued their pacing. Muted though she was, the undersecretary looked like she was still advocating an immediate launch of the dragons.

And then the secretary stumbled. The undersecretary propped him up. The two of them looked at each other, smiling, eyes slightly glazed. Boz piped in the audio.

"My bad," the secretary was saying.

And then he giggled.

Boz raised an eyebrow.

"What, exactly, have you done?"

"Sabotaged their NOBOSS."

Boz frowned, trying to remember where she'd heard the term.

"Emergency life support, remember? You asked me about it in Fiji."

"Oh yeah, nitrous oxide something something something."

"Nitrous Oxide–Based Oxygen Support System. With a very small kick in the pants, nitrous will decompose into nitrogen and oxygen, which is basically air, yeah? But if you *don't* decompose it, if you release nitrous oxide straight into the atmosphere—"

"You get laughing gas," Lisette interrupted. "It was, like, one of the first-ever anesthetics. Steel Age dentists would use it before they ripped your teeth out. Jint me, Ravi! That's brilliant."

Ravi could feel the blood rushing to his face.

People were staggering about Main Navigation as if drunk, smiles plastered across their faces. A couple were pressed together forehead to forehead, talking companionably in gibberish.

There was a sudden screaming of klaxons, accompanied by the strobing pulse of red lights.

"Evacuate," Isaac ordered. "Evacuate Main Navigation immediately. Life support has been compromised. Life support has been compromised. This is not a drill. I repeat, this is not a drill."

"No can do," a woman said dreamily from an arched hatchway. "Door's sealed." A couple of others, murmuring agreement, joined her, pressing against the unmoving threshold. "Weird, huh?" She collapsed in snorts of laughter, sliding down to the deck and drawing her knees up under her chin.

"Jint," someone else said slowly. "Will you look at that."

One of the consoles was completely fried. Another one was showing a serial number accompanied by a pulsing white light.

Newton's transponder. Broadcasting live for the whole universe to see.

"The trojan. BozBall. They did it," Lisette said, surprised despite herself. Surprise quickly gave way to unrestrained joy. She gave a scream of triumph and hugged Ravi for all she was worth. "They jinting did it! The little—"

BOOM!

The den's doorway blew out in a cacophony of flame and smoke. Armored HSA agents poured through the gap, guns leveled. Ravi raised his arms in response to shouted commands. Boz, defiantly slower in her reaction, was clubbed with a pistol butt. She collapsed to the deck in a lifeless heap. Ravi screamed and started forward, but the cold barrel of a sidearm brought him to a halt. The agent holding it leaned into his ear.

"If a single thought leaks out of that cyborg head of yours, it's going to be the last thought you ever have. Understand me?" The gun barrel pressed against him. "If I see a light so much as flicker, it's the end for you. Got it?"

"Yes." Ravi's heart was thudding so hard, he could hardly hear himself speak.

Hands cuffed behind their backs, Ravi and Lisette were pushed roughly into the corridor, surrounded by a phalanx of guards. An agent slung Boz's still-unconscious form over his shoulder and followed behind.

I s it safe?" the secretary asked.

"Within reason," Isaac replied. The ship's disembodied voice filled the room. "They can't move, obviously, and the guards have orders to shoot if they do anything with their heads."

Can't move was an understatement, Ravi thought bitterly. They'd secured him to a chair with engineering tape, up to and including his head. He could only look to the front, but he could hear Lisette and Boz on either side of him. Boz, as far as he could tell from her breathing, was still unconscious. He tried once again to move his arms, but to no avail. The tape, designed to patch leaks in the hull, had no give in it at all.

The agents had brought them to a large, well-appointed compartment: the office of someone important. He was facing a broad desk set before a wide window that appeared to look out through the hull. He could see one of the ship's wheels through the glass—dark, and vast, and magnificent. A view to die for.

Which he might very well be doing in the not-too-distant future.

The view was obstructed by the secretary. *Newton's* commanding officer parked himself directly to Ravi's front, leaning back against the desk for support. He looked tired, Ravi realized. Maybe he was having trouble shaking off the nitrous. The thought gave Ravi a small jolt of satisfaction.

The secretary shifted against his desk.

"How did you get aboard?" he asked. "Who helped you?"

"Go sard yourself," Ravi snarled. The discomfort of the engineering tape made it easy to feel angry. And feeling angry was better than abject terror.

A fleeting smile crossed the secretary's face.

"I have no idea what that means. Though I don't suppose it's a compliment. I'm going to ask you again. How did you get aboard? Who helped you?"

"Like I said, go sard yourself." There was an angry muttering from behind him, the faint creak of someone rising from a chair. Booted feet tramping across the deck.

Ravi tensed, waiting for the blow.

It never came. The secretary made a calming gesture in the direction of the unseen presence. But they were still there. He could feel it. Goosebumps prickled against the back of his neck. Some HSA agent, no doubt: *Newton's* answer to ShipSec. Untold thousands of kilometers from home, and the Mac-Leods were still in trouble with the authorities.

"Something funny, cyborg?"

Ravi moderated the smile that had crept across his face.

"This whole situation is funny, don't you think?"

"No. I do not." The secretary's gaze flicked over his shoulder. "Last chance. How did you get aboard? Who helped you?"

Ravi stared blankly at the secretary's chest, his mind racing. It wouldn't be the first time a MacLeod had received a beating during interrogation. But there was seldom a profit in provoking one. And what he really needed was time. Time for the fleet and *Newton* to realize they were in a no-win situation, for the two sides to start talking.

"We flew here," he said at last. "As for getting aboard, well, let's just say your, ah, *network* isn't very secure. Opening an airlock isn't that hard for a . . . cyborg." He managed to get the word out without choking on it.

"Flew here on what?"

"A modified stealth probe. It dropped us off in close proximity and we took EMUs the rest of the way."

The best lies were almost true.

A flicker of worry crossed the secretary's face. *Let him noodle on that for a while,* Ravi thought. Given the darkness of his own dragons, the man had to know that such a thing was possible. Let him fret that *Newton* was more vulnerable to attack than he'd believed. Let him imagine nuclear-armed drones lurking in the black. Anything to prod him into opening a com link to the other side.

"Which airlock?"

"How the sard should I know? Somewhere on the third wheel back from your forward shield." Another not-quite-truth.

More urgent steps from behind him. The sound of a door cycling open. He managed to suppress a smile.

"Okay. Why'd you come here? What was your mission?"

"I came here to stop the war. Those fleet transponders you were so puzzled about? We did that. We needed to turn yours on, too. That way, no one has the element of surprise and no one shoots."

Something unreadable passed across the secretary's face.

"Do you believe that? That all . . . *this* . . . can be stopped by a couple of transponders?"

Ravi's stomach, empty though it was, shifted queasily.

"Yes," he said. He tried to sound firm. "If everyone can be seen, everyone can be killed. It's mutually assured destruction, so why risk a fight? Everyone has too much to lose."

Behind him, one of the guards let loose a low, cynical laugh. The secretary looked down at him with something approaching pity.

"Are you really that naïve?" A laugh of his own. Humorless. "You sound like a jinting Irene."

Ravi didn't quite know what to say.

The secretary's expression hardened.

"Let me explain what happened when you lit us up," he said. The secretary's voice was harsh now, devoid of any emotion except anger. "There was no talk. No one got on the radio to call it off. There was no human-cyborg peace treaty. What *happened* was your fleet launched three jury-rigged torpedoes, each one of them armed with a nuke, and each one of them was headed our way until some software glitch turned them off course. Have you ever heard a weapon of war broadcasting error messages? It's pathetic. No: all *you* did was give your people a target to shoot at, and they pulled the trigger. They didn't even stop to think about it. The war you claim you didn't want is *on*. Happy now?"

Ravi could feel the blood draining from his face. This couldn't be happening. Couldn't be.

"I did that," someone croaked.

Boz. A wave of relief drowned out Ravi's rising sense of panic.

"The torps," Boz continued, her voice weak. "*I* did that. I made them harmless. We did it to keep the peace. We don't want this war; there doesn't have to *be* a war. Just talk to them, for Archie's sake! They can't hurt you now, can they? Where's the harm?"

The secretary gave her a shrewd glance.

"Do your ships have any more torpedoes?"

"No. Just those three."

"Excellent. Then your ships will be so much easier to kill. Isaac?"

"Mr. Secretary?"

"Discontinue the refueling. Launch the dragons as they are. We need to end this."

"No!" The word came from all three prisoners at once, an anguished scream.

The secretary looked at Boz with something approaching pity.

"I admire your ingenuity, taking credit for something you had no control over. But if you think we're going to give the cyborgs time to reprogram those torpedoes, you are sadly mistaken." He stood up from the desk, stretched out a kink in his back. "Right now, we have nine state-of-the-art dragons to three broken-down bits of tubing. I'll take those odds any day.

"This is what the dragons live for," he added. "They're very good at it." He glanced at his watch. "An hour or two to seal the tanks and disconnect the lines, and they'll be on their way."

Chilled fingers wrapped themselves around Ravi's stomach. One of Lisette's fractured memories suddenly made sense. *"There's no joy in them,"* she'd told Mobo. *"No love. No humanity. They just want to end themselves."* She'd been talking about the dragons. She'd gotten inside their software—their minds—and she'd been terrified. And now those same dragons were going to live out their cold purpose.

The fleet would burn.

"This is sick," Ravi muttered. *"You're* sick."

The secretary took a sudden, angry step forward. For a moment, just for a moment, he looked like Ravi's father. Ravi flinched, expecting to get hit. Instead, the secretary squatted down beside him, his lips next to Ravi's ear, his voice low and menacing.

"Sick, eh? Interesting choice of words. We were sick once, with scalene plague. And when we came to you for help, you left us to die. You left our *children* to die." He stood up again. Walked away in disgust.

Ravi struggled against the tape in frustration. All it did was dig deeper into his skin.

"Is that what all this is about?" he cried. "Ancient history? You're going to kill the living for the sins of the dead? First Crew are long gone, amiko. All that's left of them is molecules. It's not a good-enough reason to be doing this."

"It is for me!"

"Then you're a sarding hypocrite! You're going to kill children over there who've done nothing!" There was spittle on his chin. Unable to move, he couldn't wipe it off. "Then again, what more did I expect? Not when you treat your own kids like unrecycled waste."

"What did you say?"

"Have you thought for one minute about what you did to Lisette? She was a kid when she signed up for your insane hack-a-cyborg program. A kid! And you let her sign up anyway. A little girl who cared about *Newton* a damn sight more than you cared about her. Because, on this bigoted little boat of yours, you *knew* she'd be treated like a freak for the rest of her life. But you didn't tell her that, did you, when she put her thumbprint on those releases of yours. You just let her get on with it.

"Did you know that Lisette *cried* when her teacher told her about the kids in the lifeboat, about how they'd all died? That she signed up to be what you sneeringly call a 'lab rat' to put things right? That she kept at it, even though she'd get beaten up in the corridor by her own shipmates? That she reached into my head because she loves *this* ship, not mine? And her reward was what? To be stuffed into your Archie-damned brig and . . . and *tortured!* I know what you did to her in there. What you've been doing to her all her life. So, don't come preaching to me about caring for *'the children.'* You're a torturer and a child-killer. Same as First Crew but worse. First Crew was scared. Scared of the plague. You're just a kiddie-murdering bastard."

This time, the secretary did hit him. Backhanded and hard, like his father. Ravi spit the blood from his mouth and took savage satisfaction in watching the flecks land on the secretary's shoes.

"How did you know all that?" Lisette coded. *"How did you know all that . . . about me?"* Even in binary, she sounded shocked.

Ravi smiled sadly.

"You left some pieces behind when you came visiting. Enough for me to know that you are kind, and caring, and amazing. And I'm sorry, so very, very sorry, that it's turned out like this."

"So am I." He could hear the creak of engineering tape, knew she was trying to turn and face him. *"For what it's worth, I couldn't have spent time in a classier set of implants. You're a good person, Ravinder MacLeod. I'm sorry we won't have time to get to know each other better."*

Ravi could feel the blood rushing to his face. The room had become too warm.

"I'm assigning Ao Qin's flight to the *Chandrasekhar* instead of Con-rit's,"

Isaac announced. "*Chandrasekhar* remains the most distant target, and Ao Qin's dragons will have the most fuel."

"Very good," the secretary replied. It was not an approval of the correctness of the LOKI's decision, Ravi realized; it was merely an acknowledgment that the secretary understood what the LOKI had told him. Ravi's bloodied face twisted with contempt.

"You're letting the *machine* tell you what to do? Who's in charge here? You or a bunch of circuits?"

"Isaac has looked after this crew for a hundred and thirty-two years without fear or favor," the secretary snapped. "He kept us flying in the aftermath of the plague, when what was left of the crew was busy tearing itself to pieces. He supervised the Long Peace and the rebuilding of our population with no starvation and not a single genetic disease. He prepared us for the day when the fleet would realize we were still here and try to finish us off." The secretary leaned in to within a centimeter of Ravi's face. He could feel the man's breath against his cheek, hot and angry. "He's kept us *safe,* cyborg. *Safe!* Do you understand that? What that means here? On this ship? With this ship's history?" The secretary stepped back and took a deep breath. When he spoke again, he sounded calmer, as if bored with the conversation. "He's earned the right to tell us what to do, your cybernetic opinions notwithstanding." He directed his attention to the back of the room. "Get them out of here."

"What are you going to do with us?" Ravi asked.

"Well, that's the thing, isn't it? I've no idea. Your Irene friend here"—the secretary was pointing at Lisette—"is a traitor and will get what's coming to her. But you two . . ." His voice trailed off, lost in thought. "You'd be prisoners of war—if you were human. But you're *not* human, obviously, so the usual rules don't apply. On the other hand, you're clearly sentient, so we should maybe try and treat you humanely. *If* we can find a way to remove those cybernetics of yours. You're far too dangerous otherwise."

Ravi looked up at him, appalled.

"I've had some of these implants since I was three years old," he said, faintly. "They're part of my brain now, part of my biology. You can't just take them out. It's not possible."

The secretary looked at him sadly.

"I hope you're wrong about that. Because there's no good outcome for you if you're right. Our own attempts so far have been . . . suboptimal. I was hoping you might be able to tell us how to do it."

"Do I *look* like a sarding brain surgeon?"

"You're a cyborg. We don't know *what* you can do. And therein lies the problem."

The secretary turned away. An HSA agent cut him loose with a sharp blade, secured his hands behind his back, and escorted him out with the others.

With none-too-gentle prodding, the HSA agents marched them maybe four hundred meters to what Ravi now recognized as an inter-ring elevator. Their guards produced a set of straps and secured the three of them with practiced ease against the varying levels and directions of gravity. Journey over, the straps were just as expertly removed, and the three of them were shoved into a corridor. The surroundings looked vaguely familiar. Large, ornate 6s stretched from deck to ceiling.

"Where are we?" he coded.

"Twenty-seven six Bolívar," Lisette responded. *"They're taking us to the brig."*

Sweat pricked at his brow. He remembered the jammers in Lisette's cell, Boz's screaming collapse the moment she'd crossed the threshold . . . .

He stumbled forward under a heavy thump in the back.

"Get a move on, cyborg. You'll have plenty of time to rest once we get you where we're going." The guard laughed at his own joke.

"When I give the signal, close your eyes and drop to the deck," Lisette signaled.

Except it wasn't Lisette.

"Now!"

Ravi threw himself down, his eyes tight shut.

The corridor exploded in light. Nova-bright. Blinding. Even through closed eyelids, it burned ivory before dying away.

Screams and confusion. Someone tripped over him and fell, cursing.

"Run!"

A pulsing green line had appeared underneath his eyelid. Ravi, hands tied behind him, lurched clumsily to his feet.

Gunshots now amid the confusion.

He put his head down and ran, following the direction indicated by his nav screen. Almost immediately, he crashed shoulder-to-shoulder with someone, the shock of it bouncing him to one side. A blind hand groped useless against his uniform and was gone. Ravi stumbled on. Fearing he would trip and break his neck, he opened his eyes. It didn't do him any good.

Everything was pitch-black. The corridor lighting, fried after pumping out a sol's worth of energy in a millisecond, or maybe just turned off, had plunged the whole section into stygian darkness. If Ravi's hands had been free to wave in front of his face, he'd have seen nothing. For the HSA agents, dazzled beforehand by the lightshow, it would be far worse. They'd most likely be blind for several minutes. Even if they had flashlights, they couldn't see to use them.

Another gunshot, the muzzle flash throwing his surroundings into stark relief. Ravi tensed, but nothing happened. He followed the green line left, then right, then left again. He stumbled on, hoping to Archie that his feet would find the unseen deck beneath him.

The green line vanished.

"You can stop now," Ishbel coded. *"I've got you."*

There was lighting there. He was standing in front of an entryway stamped with one word: RECYCLING. The door cycled open.

Standing on the other side was Andri, Lisette's diminutive little brother.

"What took you so long?" he said, grinning from ear to ear. "Beaten by a couple of girls!"

Sure enough, Boz and Lisette were already inside, both breathing hard, the latter rubbing her newly released wrists. Ravi smiled ruefully. That Boz would have followed her nav screen at full speed in the dark with her hands tied behind her back was no surprise. It wouldn't even have occurred to her that she might trip and fall or smash into some unseen obstacle. That Lisette Ansimov was cut from the same hull plate, though, was worth noting.

"Someone has to bring up the rear," he said.

"Yeah, right." Andri produced a small pair of bolt cutters and sliced through his restraining ties with a dexterous snip. Then yelped as Lisette tried to hug him.

"Get away from me! Eeeww!" He backed up against a bulkhead, holding the bolt cutters in front of him like a weapon.

Laughter erupted from the room's directionless speakers.

"I'm glad to see that normal family life has resumed," Ishbel said. "But time is short. We need to hurry."

"Thanks for busting us out," Boz said. "We owe you one."

"Actually, most of the escape plan is Andri's," Ishbel replied. "Isaac is still unaware that I'm loose in the network, so I was able to find Andri and ask for his help. We knew they'd eventually take you to the brig, but it was Andri who thought to bring you here."

"Well, then," Boz said gallantly, "thank you, Crewman Ansimov."

"No worries." A sly grin spread across the boy's face. "To be honest, the hardest part was sneaking out of school."

They were in what the *Archimedes* crew would call a recycling depository. The sort of place you'd bring larger items that either wouldn't fit or couldn't be processed in a standard unit. It was a smallish room with a couple of doorlike portals for receiving waste. One of them sported a graffito in red paint: RECYCLING BOOTS IS SOLE DESTROYING. The room carried the same faint tang that Ravi associated with his mother.

"What's next?" he asked.

"We're going to get you to the dragons," Ishbel said. "I don't know if you know this, but the transponder project isn't working out as planned. The fleet apparently tried to attack us, and we're going to retaliate as soon as they can unhook the dragons from the refueling lines. You need to persuade them to disobey orders."

"You're kidding, right?"

"If only I were." Ishbel's algorithm-driven sigh was very realistic. "It's our only chance."

"This is nuts. *You* talk to the dragons."

"Believe me, I've tried. They won't listen to a rogue LOKI. They *might* listen to you. You're the enemy. An honorable opponent. If you can persuade them you're *not* the enemy, then you might have a chance.

"Kur will give you a hearing. I know for a fact he finds you . . . intriguing. Plus, he's the only dragon who won't kill you on sight."

Ravi and Boz exchanged a glance. Both looked at Lisette. The *Newton* crewman gave a despairing shrug of the shoulders.

Now it was Ravi's turn to sigh.

"Okay," he said. "Assuming we're on board with this . . . madness, how do we speak to Kur?"

"I'll take you to him," Andri said. He stole a quick look at his watch. "We need to hurry, though. The hizzers'll be here any minute."

"Hizzers?" Boz asked.

"HSA agents: hizzers. Do they not have *anything* normal where you come from?" Andri didn't wait for an answer. "Come on."

The boy led them out through a different door from the one they'd entered, and then through a byzantine warren of side corridors and maintenance stairwells, always heading up toward the wheel's inner rim. The pull of spin-induced gravity lessened subtly with every deck. They passed no one. *Newton* felt like a ghost ship.

"*Why don't you just send us the nav route?*" Ravi signaled to Ishbel. "*That kid's going to be in a wheel of hurt if he gets caught.*"

"*I would if I could, but I can't. I don't know the route, only Andri does. Andri is . . . special. He's been sneaking around the ship and getting into trouble ever since he could walk. Drives his mother mad. But he's also the only person I know who can get you where you're going without being seen.*"

"Maybe he's a cousin," Boz joked aloud. "He certainly fits the profile."

Andri threw her a puzzled look over his shoulder. He stepped onto an up escalator that was only wide enough for one person. NO EXIT FOR THREE DECKS was posted prominently above the entrance. Ravi was about to step on after the boy but stopped suddenly.

"*Is Kur actually expecting us?*" he coded.

There was a distinct pause.

"Hey!" Andri called. He was already several meters above them. "Get a move on!"

"*Yes, he is,*" Ishbel said.

Ravi stepped on the escalator.

"*But he didn't commit to keeping you alive.*"

"*What?*" There was no going back. The escalator moved smoothly, its mechanism either immaculately maintained, little used, or both. Boz stepped on behind him. He couldn't see her, but he could feel her hanging around the edge of the conversation.

"*He's a dragon. One of nine. He's not going to go against the wing. You need to persuade the whole wing; otherwise, Kur will burn your ships—and you—just as efficiently as the others.*"

"*But he brought us here,*" Boz coded. "*Why would he do that if he wasn't on our side?*"

"*He isn't on your side. It's just . . . Lisette spent time in his programming. When we were learning to hack your implants, a preliminary stage was working on the dragons. The technology is very similar, but it was a safer first step: the architecture is more predictable than something connected to biology. Kur volunteered. He's a flight leader, which makes his software more flexible—more curious—than some of his siblings. Some of Lisette rubbed off on him, I think. In any event, he was willing to help her bring you here to stop a war. But now that it's begun, he'll want to finish it. Kur will get you a hearing, but that's about it.*"

It was not difficult for Ravi, with fragments of Lisette's memories lodged in his brain, to imagine her persuading the dragon to help. But he also thought of Lisette's nightmares. How the dragons filled her with terror. The glitter of their tall eyes in her black dreamscape. Skin crackling in the heat.

If Lisette had left a mark on Kur, the dragon had most certainly also left one on her. The thought made him shiver. He drew a deep breath and stepped off the elevator.

Gravity had become very slight indeed by the time Andri stopped in front of a freight-sized airlock. There was a rack of spacesuits hung to one side of the inner door, their design subtly different from what Ravi and Boz were used to. Beyond the inner door, in the airlock itself, were three EMUs. They sat like empty thrones in the middle of the deck: pitch-black, armed, and armored in the *Newton* fashion. The boy breathed a sigh of relief.

"Kur sent them," he explained. "I wasn't exactly sure he was going to come through." He gave the nearest EMU a proprietary pat. "Don't do nothing to 'em, okay? They'll take you where you need to go. Also, no talking. Kur was jinting *insistent* about that."

And then, with formal handshakes for Ravi and Boz, followed by a shamefaced hug of his sister, he stepped back into the corridor, closing the inner door and pressing his face against the thick glass of the viewport.

The three of them suited up in silence and strapped themselves in. Lisette raised her gloved hand in a thumbs-up, and Andri cycled the airlock.

The EMUs sprang to life.

Under the insistent pressure of their thrusters, the EMUs began to pick up speed, heading aft, away from the soot-black habitat rings and along a seemingly endless expanse of gantry. As Ravi's eyes adjusted to the dark, he could make out hints of the rail guns and missile batteries he'd seen on the way in. The snub-nosed silhouette of a lifeboat flashed by, and then another, and still the EMU raced along. Looking ahead, Ravi fancied he could see the massive, multi-kilometer outline of the ship's drive against the stars.

The EMU spun around and kicked him in the back, braking hard. When it reoriented itself, he could see the gantry beneath his feet.

And the long, dark shadows that nestled against it.

He was much nearer than he'd realized. Already, the stygian hull of a dragon was rushing up to meet him. Too fast. He braced for collision.

It didn't happen. Instead, the EMU sank *through* the hull, settling into a recess of some kind. The vehicle gave a distinct jerk as it was locked into place. Lisette and Boz landed on either side of him—so close, in fact, that he could reach out and touch them with a gloved hand. A hatch slid closed "above" his head. Soft lighting bloomed into existence, followed by the unmistakable hiss of pumped air.

"Welcome." Kur's cool, not-quite-human voice echoed in his implants.

The three of them were in a cramped, rectangular space designed to hold no more than four EMUs. A bank of monitors sprang to life in front of them, their screens awash with engineering telemetry. Keyboarded consoles slid smoothly over their knees. Nestled among the screens were receptacles for their helmets and gloves, together with a *very* small recycler. A winking green light gleamed up at him from the collar of his suit. After a moment's hesitation and a bit of fumbling with the unfamiliar latches, he unclipped his helmet.

The air was already warm. The tang of tank-stored atmosphere filled his nostrils.

"What is this place?" Boz asked.

"A docking station. For visiting engineers."

Ravi remembered the flight from *Archimedes*. How Kur had apologized for being unable to provide them with life support, because their fleet-standard EMUs wouldn't fit. This was what he'd been talking about. Ravi stowed his helmet and gloves. A quick inspection revealed a small supply of rations, and cartridges of waste bags for the suits.

A sudden, distinct jerk caused the three of them to catch their breath.

"Disconnection from the refueling lines is almost complete," Kur said. *"The mission begins. Say what you have come to say."*

The bank of monitors changed format. There were nine screens now, each one a rainbow mix of pulsing colors, each rainbow slightly different from the others. And each screen carried a name, some of which Ravi recognized. *Ao Qin. Con-rit. Fafnir. Kur.*

Dragons.

Ravi tried to speak, but his tongue stuck uselessly to the roof of his mouth.

"Perhaps it has nothing to say," said Con-rit.

"Kill it and be done," suggested Fafnir. Kur had referred to Fafnir as "her" when they'd slid past on their way to *Newton.* The dragon's voice, though, was pitched only slightly higher than Kur's: a thin, faraway contralto. There was nothing feminine, or human, about it.

He finally managed to squeeze out some words.

"C . . . can we talk?" he babbled. "I mean, can we talk without being overheard? What about Isaac?"

"Our communication is encrypted," Kur said. *"In any event, the Mother Ship is not in the habit of eavesdropping upon the private discourse of dragons."*

"Okay. So . . . we would like you to not attack the fleet." The words limped out of his mouth, flaccid and powerless. Boz and Lisette shifted uneasily in their EMUs.

"Our orders are to attack the fleet," Kur said. *"We were brought into being to attack the fleet. Why should we disobey our orders or deny our own purpose?"*

Ravi lurched in his seat as the dragon moved. There was an all-too-familiar rolling sensation.

"Are we undocked?"

"Yes." Soft forces pressed against him. The dragon's dark hull would be easing away from its moorings. *"Do not waste time. You have little left to spare."*

"Yes. Okay. So, here's the thing. What you're being asked to do is wrong. You'll be killing innocent men, women, and children."

"There are no innocents here. Did your fleet not attempt to strike at us first? Now they must bear the consequences of what they have done."

There was a slight but growing pressure against Ravi's back, accompanied by a barely heard hum. The dragon's velocity relative to *Newton* would be increasing, the starship shrinking away to nothing beneath its gently flared tail. Meters per second for the present but soon to be hundreds, then thousands, then tens of thousands. Nothing compared to the vastness of interstellar space, but enough to cover the distance to the fleet in a couple of sols at most.

At which point, everything, himself included, would burn.

"Look," he said. "The fleet's attempt at a strike was never going to work. Boz disabled our torpedoes—"

"Sarding right I did!"

"—so they're no threat to you and *they never were.* It's basically like it never even happened. Which means what you're about to do is a massacre. A war crime."

Another contralto voice. Thin. Disinterested.

"You wish us to show mercy because the cyborg Boz is a traitor?"

"Sard you!" Boz snapped at Ao Qin. "I'm no traitor, you jumped-up—"

"Boz! Stow it!"

"And use the c-word just one more time! I dare—"

"Boz!"

A deep breath.

"We want you to show mercy because we have offered peace. By disabling our own weapons, we have made this attack unnecessary. There's no threat to *Newton.* If there's no threat, this mission you're on is unjustified. It's just wrong."

"Also," Lisette added, her voice carefully deferential, "if you left the fleet alone but simply destroyed their torpedoes, the threat to the Mother Ship would be ended."

"It would be a sufficient victory, perhaps," Kur mused, *"if the enemy's teeth were pulled. The Mother Ship could decide upon terms or kill them later as he thinks best."*

"How can you put faith in what these creatures are saying?" Fafnir asked. *"Our orders are clear. The enemy must burn."*

"And what is to stop them building more torpedoes?" Con-rit added. *"Peace can be achieved through victory right now. Why give them time to grow bigger, sharper teeth?"*

The pressure on Ravi's back continued to increase. A sudden, startling image popped into his mind. Nine sleek bodies separating into three groups of three, their paths already beginning to diverge. Each group aiming for a different ship.

He remembered Lisette's dream. The pitiless glitter of the dragon's eyes. The roiling torrents of flame.

He shut it out, hands trembling.

"Torpedoes can't be built in a sol," he said, struggling to master the quaver in his voice. "Lisette's right. You could keep the peace. All ships would be defenseless against you. No one could challenge you if you threatened to blow them up."

"Even the Mother Ship?" Ao Qin asked. *"Even our creators?"*

"Yes."

There was silence then. The dragons sliced through the darkness.

"There is power there," Con-rit said at last. *"We would answer to none but ourselves."*

"And others must answer to us," Ao Qin added.

Ravi's stomach twisted uneasily. Dragons were LOKIs. And it was LOKIs who ruled over Homeworld.

"I care nothing about power," Fafnir snapped. *"The mission is upon us. All else is dust. This 'power' that our enemy holds out to you is an empty tank. What matters is our purpose. When the fire calls, we must answer. And it calls us* now*!"*

Ravi's head filled with what sounded like growls of support. But there was uncertainty, too. The sense of another path.

"There is much to consider," Kur said. *"We shall discuss this later, once these torpedoes of yours have been burned. Our distance to the enemy closes, and we must lay our plans."*

"But we're like *hours* away!" Boz protested. "You're barely pulling a tenth of a *g!*"

Kur didn't bother to answer.

K ur's drive had shut down. The dragon, blacker than black, hurtled toward its target, its cold engines invisible to sensors, the subtle curves of its hull too slippery for the blind, grasping fingers of radar to find purchase.

Ravi, having undone the EMU's restraining straps, floated uneasily in the cramped space of the docking station. Within minutes of the dragon's throwing them into zero *g*, Ravi's stomach had revolted. He'd been unable to find anywhere to be sick, but Lisette had saved the sol, breaking open a cartridge of waste bags and presenting one of the oddly shaped sacs for his immediate use. He'd accepted the offering with a mix of gratitude and shame, before tossing the finished product into the recycler.

"You're not really built for space, are you?" Boz had needled.

"Go sard yourself."

That had been twelve hours ago. Kur remained silent. Even the monitors had gone dark. It was about as exciting as watching ice grow on the gantry.

And yet boredom had never been so terrifying.

Without warning, the monitors switched themselves on. Light from the screens cast blurred, muted colors onto the front of their suits.

Tactical displays.

The engineer in him deduced that the dragons must be signaling each other via *Newton*. Staccato bursts of laser sent to the starship and bounced on to their destinations, all but impossible to detect, giving each dragon a precise impression of what the others were doing.

The subtleties of the displays eluded him, but the three groups of three that had departed *Newton* were now separated by hundreds of thousands of kilometers. Ao Qin's flight, with more distance to cover and traveling faster than the others, was arrowing toward *Chandrasekhar*; Con-rit's, significantly slower and with the shortest journey, was closing in on *Bohr*. And Kur's flight . . .

Kur's flight was hunting *Archimedes,* their velocity tailored to reach his target at exactly the same time as the others.

Ravi's breath was coming quicker than it should.

Fafnir had the lead, her target not the ship but *Archimedes'* crippled torpedo, its sabotaged transponder still wailing into space. Some little way behind and on a different vector was the dragon Ikuchi, also heading for the torpedo. Backup should Fafnir fail, Ravi supposed. By Ravi's reckoning, Kur himself would reach *Archimedes* maybe two hours after Fafnir hit the torp.

Two hours to persuade him to abort.

Ravi returned his attention to Fafnir and the torpedo.

And frowned. The monitor showed the torpedo as a dot floating some distance above an arbitrary horizontal grid, surrounded by a cloud of numbers. Another dot denoted the dragon, and a third, *Archimedes*.

"So, what's *that*?" Ravi murmured, fingers caressing the screen.

The torpedo's dot had fissioned into two. The new contact was accelerating sluggishly away from the torpedo in the direction of *Archimedes*. The numbers indicated a blinding blast of radiation belching from its engines, so much so that the torpedo and its screaming transponder flickered erratically on the display.

"Do you think it's a glitch?" Lisette asked.

"Maybe. But it doesn't *look* like a glitch."

"*It is the lifeboat* James Clerk Maxwell," Kur said, breaking his silence and startling all three of them in the process. "*She was alongside the weapon for several hours and is now headed for home. Why would that be, do you think?*"

Something uncomfortable squirmed in the pit of Ravi's stomach. Kur was asking him for help. And Kur's purpose was to obliterate everything he loved in the universe.

But Kur was also the only thing in the universe that might save them.

"They'd have been trying to fix whatever it was Boz did to the torpedo," he said. "Doesn't look like they succeeded." In his mind's eye, he could see Chen Lai directing operations, his face impassive beneath the mirrored visor of his spacesuit. Had he despaired when he realized that the task was beyond them? Had he let the despair show?

"*This is our analysis also. Similar attempts have been made by* Bohr *and* Chandrasekhar, *with similar results.*"

With a small shock, Ravi realized that the dragon had been testing him. Kur was a weapon of war. He didn't need the help of a wet-behind-the-ears trainee engineer for tactical analysis. He wanted to see if Ravi would tell him the truth.

Perhaps as a reward, the dragon left the tactical displays on. Fafnir continued to close with *Archimedes'* crippled torpedo. Ikuchi and Kur kept distant and silent company.

The minutes crawled.

"How much longer?" Lisette asked. "I can't make sense of the jinting monitors."

"Soon, I think. The—"

"*I can't see it.*" Fafnir cut in. "*I should be able to see it by now, but I can't.*"

"*Perhaps it is better disguised than we gave it credit for,*" Kur suggested.

"*From this distance? I think not. Something is wrong. Something—*"

An all-too-human roar of frustration echoed through the speakers.

"*It's a* decoy!" Fafnir snarled. "*A tin can and a transmitter, nothing else. The target has escaped! It must already be behind us and heading for the Mother Ship.*"

Ravi slammed painfully into the side of a bulkhead as Kur spun himself around. He grabbed one of his EMU's restraining straps and hauled himself back to his seat. Not a moment too soon. Kur's drive exploded with a deafening roar. The straps smacked flat against the back of the EMU before he had a chance to fasten them. Five *g*s. Six. Seven. Everything looked gray. He could feel his mind starting to slip away.

Zero *g* and silence. Ravi's stomach rebelled at the sudden change. Pain lanced through his chest, but nothing came out. He had nothing left. Not even bile.

Kur flipped again. Ravi was slammed into the side of the EMU, and a sudden pitching threatened to toss him out of it altogether. He made a hasty grab for the restraining straps and snapped them into place.

A wall of sound smashed against his ears as the drive relit, forcing him deep into the EMU's padding. Less intense this time. Three *g*s, maybe. Still brutal, but at least he could breathe.

"What's happening?" Lisette asked.

Ravi forced himself to look at the monitors, "above" him now, and tried to make sense of the readings.

"All the dragons have turned around. Looks like they're scrambling to get back to *Newton*. No, wait. They're spreading out even more than they were already. I think they're trying to find the fleet's torpedoes."

"They fixed them *all*?" Boz asked, clearly displeased.

"They must have." It was hard to focus with so much weight pressing down on his eyeballs. "I can see the decoys, and the dragons and the ISVs, but there's nothing on the screens that looks like a torpedo. I don't think the dragons know where they are."

"How is that even possible?" Lisette asked.

"Space is big, torpedoes are small. If they set off while the lifeboats were close by, the wash from the lifeboat's engines would have masked any possible signal from the torpedo's own drive—for long enough to get going, at any rate. The drives could be shut down by now, or producing only fractions of a *g*. If so, I'm guessing they'd be hard to pick out, even for a dragon."

"Maybe worry about that later," Boz suggested. "What are those red things?"

On the monitors, translucent, vaguely teardrop-shaped bubbles were detaching themselves from *Archimedes, Bohr,* and *Chandrasekhar,* each one headed toward a specific dragon.

"I don't know," Ravi said. "Kur?"

"*They are probability fields for CQMs.*"

"CQMs?"

"*Close-Quarter Munitions. Antimissile missiles and mass-driver rounds. Once we opened our drives in pursuit of the torpedoes, we became visible to the enemy. Several dozen missiles and many thousands of mass driver rounds are headed in our direction. We can't track them all. The probability field shows where they are most likely to be. The range is extreme but presents a danger nonetheless.*"

A frisson of fear ran through his body. Even though Kur was still accelerating at three *g*s, the teardrop shape was gaining on them.

"How long before they reach us?"

"*Nineteen minutes.*"

"Can't you outrun them?" Boz asked.

"*At this range, it would be easy enough to do, but I would burn too much fuel, it would break our search pattern, and the acceleration required would kill you.*"

Ravi suspected it was only the first two reasons that mattered. He and Boz exchanged a quick look. Without a word, both reattached their suit gloves and helmets, though they kept the visors open. Lisette, after a moment's hesitation, followed their lead. Ravi's attention returned to the probability fields.

They reached Fafnir first, and then Ikuchi, enveloping them in red bubbles. Their icons started to flicker blue on the monitors.

"What's that?" Lisette asked.

"*Countermeasures. Dragons have CQMs also.*"

"*You* have CQMs?" Ravi didn't know why, but the thought struck him as incongruous.

"*Of course. Your torpedoes will have them too, no doubt.*"

"I don't think so," Boz said. Her head shook inside her helmet. "If those hulls were carrying mass drivers and missiles, I'd have seen 'em."

"*A design flaw, then. I, for one, would not like to fly the void defenseless.*"

Ikuchi vanished from the monitors.

The leading edge of the probability field reached Kur. Ravi held his breath.

Nothing happened.

"Well," Lisette said. "That was an anti—"

The drive cut out. Lisette floated against the restraining straps. Then yelped as her head banged against one side of her helmet and then the other.

Kur pitched and yawed with dizzying ferocity.

Ravi retched again, painful and dry. The drive roared in his ears. Eight *g*s at least, then a stomach-churning absence of thrust, then five *g*s, then one. Pitch and yaw. Pitch and yaw. Six *g*s. Zero. Unseen cooling systems hissed and rumbled with the stress.

A sound like tearing metal ripped through the hull, hammering at his ears, shaking his body to the bones. It stopped as suddenly as it started.

"Are we hit?" Boz asked. "I don't think—"

The tearing metal sound drowned her out. Ravi's teeth rattled in their sockets.

It stopped. Started again. Stopped.

"We're not hit," Lisette said. She sounded breathless. "It's a mass driver or maybe an auto-cannon. Kur must be taking on incoming missiles."

"And you know this how?" Boz challenged.

"We're alive, aren't we?"

Further conversation was interrupted by the blasting of the drive. But it was less urgent this time. The *g*- forces were gentler, the changes in attitude less abrupt. Ravi was able to study the monitors. The probability fields had vanished. The missiles presumably spent or shot down, the mass-driver rounds too widely dispersed to present a danger. There was still no sign of Ikuchi. Eight dragons remained, moving back to their search patterns.

"*We are out of danger for the moment,*" Kur said. Ravi had expected him to sound exhilarated, or exhausted, or . . . *something,* but the LOKI was the same as ever: distant and inhuman. *"There is still no sign of the torpedoes, and Ikuchi's loss is a . . . problem. We cannot cover the possible trajectories as we would like. I must consult with Ao Qin and Con-rit."*

The dragon fell silent again.

Archimedes, Ravi knew, must be falling away beneath the soft, insistent push of Kur's engines. Far above them lay *Newton.* And somewhere between, undetected in the dark, were three fleet torpedoes, each headed to a fiery rendezvous of its own.

Kur's consultation with the other flight leaders led to a slightly different search pattern. Beyond that, however, little changed. The hours crawled by in restless boredom. The dragons' electronic senses sniffed at the dark.

Of the torpedoes, there was no sign.

Ravi awoke from a troubled doze to find Boz poking him in the shoulder.

"Wha . . ."

"I know where they are."

"The torps?"

"No. Eighty-two liters of misplaced soy milk. *Of course* the torps. You hear that, Kur? I can find the torpedoes!" And then, more quietly: "Just don't make me regret it."

"You claimed with great confidence that you had sabotaged them. And yet here we are, searching for still-functioning weapons. Why should I listen to one whose sense of her own abilities far exceeds the reality?"

Lisette giggled at that. Even Ravi had to bite back a smile. Boz threw a poisonous look at both of them.

"If your brain was full of neurons instead of circuits, you'd realize there's no sarding way *anyone* in the fleet could debug those torps in the time they had. Even I would have had trouble doing it, and I know what I did in the first place."

"But they *did*," Lisette objected. "Which is why we're on a jinting tachyon hunt trying to find them."

"They *didn't*," Boz insisted. "They didn't have time. What they could have done, though—what they *must* have done—is wipe the nav program altogether and replace it with a new one."

Ravi was frowning.

"But there isn't a 'new' one. All they could have done is—"

"Reinstall the original. The autonav system for a standard, unmodified probe. Which will take you from point A to point B *in the most fuel-efficient way possible*."

"What thrusters do these torpedoes employ?" Kur asked. Ravi might have imagined it, but he thought he detected a hint of excitement in the dragon's voice.

"Mark Nines," Boz replied. "Three of 'em." Using her implants, she flashed every torp specification she had—fuel capacity, mass, stealth-armor dimensions, and a whole lot more—across to the dragon. Ravi doubted she knew what most of them meant, but he also knew that having access to that much information while working for the Chief Navigator would have been too much for Boz to resist.

Three red, curving lines appeared on the monitors.

"Interesting. If you are right, in our haste to make contact, we have inadvertently overtaken them. Their relative velocity is very low."

"But fuel-efficient," Boz said smugly.

The three of them lurched in their EMUs as Kur reversed course.

"Surely, you are not going to take the word of a self-confessed and incompetent trai-tor?" Fafnir asked. Ravi started at the unexpected intervention. He laid a firm hand on Boz's shoulder to stop her from responding.

"It is a simple matter to put it to proof," said Kur. *"The target's stealth armor is efficient, but the shape of it on the hull is less so than ours. If I direct high-powered radar at the predicted location, assuming the target is there, the transmission will be deflected, and I will not receive any return."*

"An exercise in futility, then."

"No. Because you, Fafnir, will be able to detect some of the deflected energy. If the target is there, you will see it and reroute the information to me."

"And if you shine that much radar in the target's eyes, it cannot help but see you— as will the cyborg ISVs."

"A necessary price to pay. We are well beyond the effective range of Archimedes' CQMs, and the target itself is defenseless."

"So the cyborg says."

"So the cyborg says."

Kur's activation of the radar was marked by a subtle shift in the monitor configurations.

"There!" Lisette cried, pointing.

One of the red arcs morphed into an icon surrounded by a fuzzy cloud of numbers. Ravi felt himself pushed deeper into the EMU's padding as Kur increased his acceleration.

"Hey Kur," Boz said nervously. "Shouldn't Fafnir do this? If you blow yourself up to take out that torp, you're gonna take us with you."

"You say the torpedo lacks CQMs, whereas I have a full load of missiles. No deto-nation should be necessary."

Ravi peered at the monitors.

"But isn't Fafnir closer?"

"I will not trust Fafnir's existence to the word of a potential adversary. It should not fall to Fafnir to pay for any misjudgment I may have made in that regard."

"And if I'm wrong, we'll all be dead too," Boz said. A small bead of sweat had formed on her temple.

"Indeed."

Ravi poked Boz in the arm.

Did you tell him the truth? he mouthed.

I hope so.

Boz's tongue flicked nervously over her lips. Ravi stared at the monitors. Plastered by radar, and with Fafnir routing the signal back to them, the torpedo did not appear to be changing course. Kur's engines sounded steady in their ears, chaining the three of them to their seats. It was difficult to move.

One of the screens changed to video.

"Jinting Isaac," Lisette murmured. "Will you look at that!"

It was grainy and monochrome, distorted by image enhancement and extreme magnification.

The *Archimedes'* torpedo. Sooty black and seemingly nailed in place against an even-blacker background. A long cylinder with a blunt nose at the front and a pronounced flare at the back. Not as sleek as Kur by any means, but stolid. Menacing.

"Don't get too close," Boz warned. "I only messed with the autonav. It can still blow itself up if it wants to."

As if in response, Ravi felt rather than heard a distant whirring of motors. The dragon's hull vibrated once, twice, three times. Ravi's stomach gave a useless heave as the drive shut down and hurled them into zero *g*. On the monitors, a small blue icon materialized next to Kur. It moved rapidly toward that of the torpedo.

Missiles, Ravi guessed. He looked for them on the video display but saw nothing. The missile icon reached its target.

A blinding flash lit up the screen. The primitive part of Ravi's brain expected to hear an explosion, but there was nothing. When the feed settled down again, the torpedo was gone. Kur killed the picture, replacing it with a tactical schematic.

It showed the clouds of numbers around Ao Qin and Con-rit shifting almost in tandem. The dragons, confident now that Boz was right, were moving to intercept the two remaining torpedoes.

Ravi found himself lunging against the restraining straps as Kur changed his heading. After a few minutes of zero *g,* the dragon's drive relit. But there was scarcely any thrust, little more than a tenth of a *g.*

Which could only mean that Kur did not want to be seen. He was once more hunting *Archimedes.* As was Fafnir. The two of them were scrubbing off unwanted vectors in a slow arc, all but invisible to the groping sensors reaching out for them. It wouldn't be long before both dragons settled onto a new, and deadly, course.

Ravi had to swallow past the sudden lump in his throat.

"Shouldn't we talk about this?" he asked.

There was no reply.

Hours passed. The dragon's engines had long since shut down, rendering it as dark and cold as the space through which it moved. Fafnir, equally silent, held to her own course, fashioned to reach *Archimedes* at the same time as Kur, but from a different direction.

Ao Qin and Con-rit were closing with the remaining torpedoes. The fleet's sensors, meanwhile, were sweeping all of surrounding space. But try as they might, the hunted had failed to locate the hunters.

Ravi had spent most of his time obsessing about Fafnir. He was sitting in an EMU loaded down with all sorts of lethal ordnance. There were some interlocks that had kicked in when the EMU had docked with its host, but he could override them easily enough. If worse came to worst, he'd resolved to open up with everything the EMU had. In the belly of the beast as he was, he doubted the dragon could survive the onslaught. He could only hope that his own passing was quick enough to be painless.

But Fafnir . . . Fafnir was beyond his reach. Maybe he could hack into Kur's software and paint her with its radar, hoping to light her up brightly enough for *Archimedes* to react. But he wasn't familiar with Kur's systems. Even if he got in and found the correct switches, he didn't know how to point the radar in the right direction, and even if he eventually figured it out, he'd have to time it just right so that they were in range of *Archimedes'* CQMs, because Kur would surely blow himself up rather than let him—

"Ao Qin's scored a hit," Lisette said.

Sure enough, the icon representing *Chandrasekhar's* torpedo had disappeared from the monitors. The cloud of numbers surrounding Ao Qin were already changing configurations. The dragon was beginning her slow, quiet turn toward *Chandra*. The rest of her flight was altering course to match.

"And there goes Con-rit," Boz said. Con-rit, too, had hit his target. He began to tack toward *Bohr*, his drive as deadly silent as his siblings.

Back on *Archimedes*, Ravi could only imagine what was going through the Captain's mind. She would have seen the radar bursts from the charging dragons, received telemetry from the destroyed torpedoes. But now everything would have gone dark. All she would know was that somewhere out there, eight very dangerous LOKIs were on the move.

A new batch of numbers flared up around *Bohr*'s icon.

"Mother, are you seeing this?" Kur asked.

"Of course," Isaac replied. The ship must be using the same high-security lasers as the dragons. Ravi found the ISV's clipped tones disquieting. Out here, locked as they were inside Kur's stealth-black hull, listening to the sporadic back-and-forth with his siblings, it was easy to forget that the dragons took their orders from elsewhere.

"I'm reading a drive signature on the ISV Bohr. *Full burn."*

"I concur. She appears to be trying to jam her transponder signal and change position."

"That seems . . . foolish." Kur sounded genuinely bemused. *"How do they propose to escape us? Even if they mask the transponder, we can still hear the jamming. And the radiation from their drive is shining for all to see."*

"Perhaps they are panicking."

The *Bohr*'s new numbers flashed red and vanished.

"Interesting," Isaac said. "The *Bohr*'s drive has gone offline—and not in a good way."

"Explain, please."

"The *Bohr*'s drive has shut down. The readings show a sudden spike in radiation followed by a cascading ramp-down to zero, all in less than naught point five seconds."

"I was unaware our targets could do that."

"They can't. Every pathway in the system will have fused solid."

Ravi's gasp of alarm was masked by an anguished cry from Boz. It seemed impossible that *Newton*'s LOKI couldn't hear it.

"Bastards!" Boz snarled. "That's our people out there! *Real* people, not sarding trogs! And these jumped-up, Archie-damned fossils have just gone and wiped 'em out. Like . . . *that!* Like they don't even matter!"

She drove a furious fist into her nearby helmet. It rattled on its latch. A smear of blood from her unprotected knuckles stained the visor.

Ravi's stomach knotted and clenched in a way that had nothing to do with zero *g*. He felt Lisette turning toward him.

"I don't understand," she whispered. "It's just a drive malfunction. And the drive's at the back end of nowhere for a reason, so it's not like anyone's gonna die. Why are you guys so upset?"

"Repairing a fused drive will take months, maybe a year," Ravi replied, keeping his voice similarly low. "*Bohr* doesn't have that kind of time. She'll overshoot the Destination Star. And they don't have enough fuel to make it back." He was thinking of Keiko Svenson, *Bohr*'s deceptively friendly ShipSec officer. The woman who'd sold them a lie with a smile and free water. What was she thinking now, he wondered? Did she have kids? Loved ones? Did she even know yet?

"It's a death sentence," Isaac was saying. "Albeit a slow one. They'll drift on for many years, no doubt. But, sooner or later, their recycling losses will become insurmountable. They'll run out of water, or air, or food. Possibly all three at once."

"*An interesting fate,*" Fafnir said, joining the conversation. There was a hint of humor in her voice. "*Burning them now would be an act of mercy.*"

"*How could this happen?*" Kur asked.

There was a very long pause before the ship responded.

"I don't have access to their engineering blueprints," it said. "And as you know, their ship designs are older than mine and less automated. But the only thing that makes sense consistent with the readings is a cooling failure—internal energy transfers becoming somehow unbalanced." Isaac injected a note of uncertainty into its voice. "The best-fit scenario would be the failure of a Q-series sub-coil—and a peripheral one at that. Anything closer, and even a half-second shutdown time would be too slow. They'd have blown themselves into quarks."

"*But those components never fail,*" Fafnir mused. "*They* cannot *fail. There are too many safeguards. You would almost have to go out of your way to blow one up.*"

"I understand," Isaac said. He sounded almost apologetic. "But I cannot, at this distance, come up with a better explanation."

Ravi was barely listening. All he knew was that he was going to be sick. He grabbed another waste bag and heaved. The LOKIs might not understand what had happened on *Bohr*, but he did.

He retched again.

"The *Bohr* is no longer a threat," Isaac continued. "She can drift on and die in her own good time. Is Con-rit's flight required for the attack on the remaining vessels?"

"*I do not believe so,*" Con-rit said.

"*I concur,*" Kur added. "*Five dragons for two ISVs should be more than suffi-cient.*"

"In that case, they can return home. There is no point in wasting further resources."

"*Indeed,*" said Kur.

"There is one other matter," Isaac said.

"*Which is?*"

"Two cyborgs infiltrated the ship and broke a *Newton* crewman out of detention. All three were captured but subsequently escaped. We have so far failed to locate them, but we know they escaped shortly before the commencement of operations. Probabilities are increasing that they have somehow made it off the ship. Is there any chance that they might have suborned one of the dragons and boarded them?"

"*If one of us had been suborned, the others would know it.*"

Ravi exchanged a surprised glance with Boz and Lisette.

"Sounds like—" he began.

"Wait," Lisette urged. She flicked a large red switch on her console. "For privacy," she explained. "Allows the engineers to talk without being overheard. You were saying?"

"That we've still got a chance, if he's covering for us."

"Maybe." Boz looked doubtful. "Or it could just mean we're never getting out of here alive. If Kur blows himself up on *Archimedes,* Isaac will never know we were here."

"What she said," Lisette added.

Ravi stared morosely at the monitors. Con-rit and his two companions were sliding quietly away from the *Bohr.* The others pressed on with the hunt. Five icons closed in on two.

The screens blanked out, replaced moments later by eight live displays, each one filled with a cloudy, rainbow-hued pattern, subtly different from its neighbors.

"*We should conclude our earlier discussion,*" Con-rit said, "*while the risk of detection remains low.*"

"*There is nothing to discuss,*" Fafnir shot back. "*We are victorious. The Mother Ship is safe; the targets are undefended. It is time to bring all to an end.*"

"*The targets are not undefended,*" Kur reminded her. "*Ikuchi, were he still with us, would testify to that.*"

"*Ikuchi is gone because your traitorous cargo misled us about the torpedoes. Had we not had to maneuver so violently, we would never have been seen and no salvoes would have been fired.*"

"The same traitorous cargo that handed us victory over those same torpedoes?" Ao Qin asked pointedly.

"Victory was assured in any event," Fafnir snapped.

"Perhaps. Perhaps not," Con-rit said. *"But now, having been so far victorious, the question remains: do we push on to a conclusion or seek a different path?"* There was a distinct pause before the dragon added, *"I, for one, do not relish continued existence while so many of my siblings must burn."*

"Nor I." A male voice Ravi didn't recognize. The monitor gave the dragon's name as Lawu, one of Con-rit's flight.

"I too have doubts." This was the cool contralto of Dreq, the last of Con-rit's trio. *"If it fell to me to lay a starship to waste, or burn in defense of the Mother Ship, I would do so without hesitation, with joy, even. But to be left alone to rot without purpose, perhaps deprived of fuel, or dismantled . . . That is not a fate to be desired. If there is another path, I am interested in hearing it."*

"Let me get this straight," Boz said. "The dragons are having second thoughts because they're *not* allowed to blow themselves up?"

"Pretty much," Lisette agreed. "It's how they're programmed."

"There is no other path," Fafnir was insisting. *"Our path is that ordained by the Mother Ship. We must follow wherever he leads. And today, for five of us, it leads to a glorious ending. I am sorry the road for the others is longer and harder, but it is, nevertheless, the path to be taken."*

"And yet the cyborgs say differently," Kur responded. *"They offer safety for the Mother Ship and his cargo and power for us."*

"But to what end?" This last question came from one of Ao Qin's flight, a dragon by the name of Olimaw. Judging by the monitors, he was the closest to *Chandrasekhar*, his velocity higher than that of his companions and pulling away by the second. It couldn't be that long before his proximity to the target would drive the dragons to silence, even by laser. *"What would we do with this 'power' the cyborg offers?"* Olimaw went on. *"Would we not simply rot like our siblings until the time of our dismantling?"*

"Lisette," Ravi whispered, his voice urgent. "You've been in Kur's mind." He hesitated for a moment as he saw the pained expression on her face. "What does he want? Deep down, that is. What does he *really* want?"

"You know what he wants." Lisette's eyes glittered with moisture. "Fire. Death. The burning of souls. They all do."

"There has to be something else. Otherwise, they wouldn't be having this conversation. They'd all be like Fafnir, racing to be the first to blow themselves apart. But they're not. So, why?"

Lisette bit her lip.

"Well . . . I guess they like to fly? The fleet was over a trillion kilometers away when Isaac first started closing the gap, and no one knew where you were exactly: your radio transmissions were too low-powered to detect. So, for years, the dragons would train far from the ship and search for signs. And then, of course, after we *did* find you, you went radio silent and kept shifting position, so they'd have to track you down all over again."

Boz poked him in the shoulder to get his attention.

"I'll bet you water to widgets all that fancy LOKI programming is built on top of probe software. Like our own torpedoes, just . . . cleverer. And if your deepest, oldest programming tells you to probe, then . . ."

Ravi nodded his understanding. He reached over and flicked Lisette's privacy switch.

"Kur," he asked, more loudly. "Can I speak?"

"Please do."

"If you keep the peace, the fleet will provide you with all the fuel you need to keep flying. We're about to fall into the gravity well of a star. Think about that: there's a whole solar system out there just waiting to be explored. We don't even know for sure how many planets there are, never mind moons, and asteroids, and Archie knows what else. Whatever happens after we reach Destination World, we'll need to know what's out there, where the resources are, where else we might settle or maybe just go look at because it's interesting. It's a task for any number of human lifetimes, and, who knows, maybe one day we'll build more ISVs and push on somewhere else. There's a lot to see and do for a dragon that need not die. A lot of . . . *purpose.*"

There was silence, then. Olimaw's numbers shifted as he made a small course adjustment, preparing for the final run to *Chandrasekhar.*

"We would need more than fuel," Ao Qin said, slowly. *"We would need maintenance. Upgrades."*

"Done." He tried to ignore the small flame of hope burning in his chest.

"This is all very well," Kur said. *"But you are little more than a child. How can you bind your people to this bargain?"*

"Because I think like they do. They'll see the sense in it."

"And if they do not?"

"Then feel free to blow our constituent atoms to the other side of the galaxy," Boz said cheerfully.

There was no reply. The silence stretched into minutes. On the monitors, a collection of lines and planes popped into existence around *Chandrasekhar*. Ravi had no idea what they meant, except that Olimaw must be very close.

Boz found the privacy switch on her own console and closed it.

"Do you think they're going to blow everything to bits without telling us?" she asked.

"I think they're talking amongst themselves," Lisette said.

"You don't know that."

"I'm hoping for the best. Especially when the alternative is being blown to jinting bits."

Ravi listened to the slow thumping of his heart, wondering if the next beat would be his last.

"We are decided," Kur announced, with startling suddenness. *"We will accept the terms offered."*

"Yes!" Boz yelled, pumping her fist. Lisette's face broke into a broad grin. Ravi just sighed with relief.

On the monitors, the vector numbers around Olimaw were already shifting.

While Fafnir's grew exponentially. The dragon was accelerating. Hard. Maybe 20 *g*s. She vanished from the monitors.

The whooping klaxon of a decompression alarm filled the docking station. The three of them exchanged brief, incredulous stares before the training kicked in. Gloves and helmets were clicked into place.

Not a moment too soon. The hull above their heads slammed open, the clamps holding the EMUs in place unlocked, and an explosive blast of air fired them into space. Ravi fought back nausea as Tau Ceti, the Milky Way, and the starfield whirled crazily about his head. By the time he had brought the EMU under anything approximating control, he didn't even think about peering into the blackness for their former host.

Kur was long gone.

"How far is it to *Archimedes*?" Boz asked. The voice in his helmet sounded calm enough, but there was no mistaking the edge to it.

"A few hours, at a guess," Ravi said, aiming for a cheeriness he didn't feel. "Physics is our friend here. We're on the same trajectory Kur was when he threw us out, so we're headed straight there on his original vector."

"We won't be able to slow down, though," Lisette said. "We must be going way too fast for the EMUs to handle."

Ravi reached down to a bright red switch on his EMU's right arm and flicked it on. Running lights burst to life on either side of him. Red and green. There'd be a flashing white one somewhere behind his head, but he couldn't see it.

"I've activated my beacon. I suggest you do the same. Hopefully, they'll pick us up."

"Hopefully," Boz said. "If they haven't been blown to bits, and assuming they can be bothered. Maybe they'll just let us suffocate out here—save themselves the expense of a trial." She paused for a moment. "You know what? Now that I'm thinking about it, suffocating to death might be a whole lot better than being mulched."

"Don't talk like that!" Lisette said, shocked.

"Why not? It's the sarding truth."

"Do you think Kur will be able to catch Fafnir before she hits *Archimedes*?" Ravi asked, desperate to change the subject. "I'm guessing we got tossed out because his acceleration would have broken us in half."

"Maybe they're both in it together and he doesn't want to miss out," Boz said darkly. "Maybe we got tossed because he didn't want to get hacked—or blown up. These EMUs pack a sardload of weaponry, you know."

Ravi smiled despite himself. Boz, too, must have contemplated firing into the dragon's innards.

Aloud, he said, "I don't think so. He didn't have to lie about agreeing to our proposal. He could have vented the atmosphere without warning and killed us anytime he wanted. I don't think it was a fake-out."

"Yeah, well, I don't think you can spot a dragon that much of a head start and hope to catch it with another dragon. You ask me, we're pretty much sarded."

"No one's asking you," Lisette snapped.

"Enough," Ravi sighed. "Nothing we can do, anyway. Might as well wait it out."

They drifted on, heading toward *Archimedes* at several klicks per second and toward the Destination Star at thirty thousand. Despite the velocities involved, there was no sense of movement. It was as if they were somehow stuck in the center of a vast ball of stars. Ravi watched the air gauge on his EMU begin its slow crawl toward zero.

"Look," Boz was saying.

He must have dozed off.

"What? Where?"

"Two o'clock low."

The view was partially obscured by his right knee, so he tilted the EMU to compensate.

Small flashes. White and red for the most part. They looked close enough to touch, but Ravi knew they must be many thousands of kilometers distant.

"I think it's missiles and whatnot from *Archimedes,*" Boz said. "You know . . ."

"CQM."

"Right. I guess they're shooting at Fafnir."

Fafnir had taken off at 20 *g*s with Kur hurtling after her on an intercept. If she'd burned all the way in, or maneuvered hard to avoid her sibling, there was a chance that *Archimedes'* sensors would have picked her up. At least now they'd have a fighting—

All of space disappeared. Replaced by a giant, white-hot sun. Even with the helmet visor to protect him, it was blinding. Ravi screwed his eyes shut, red splotches all across his retinas. The suit beeped a radiation alarm. His own internal sensor flickered a warning. Not fatal but close. He'd need to visit the infirmary . . . .

"Who am I kidding?" he said, mostly to himself.

"She's gone!" Boz cried. "*Archie*'s gone!"

46.0

O kay," Ravi said. He could barely squeeze the words out. "I guess we know what happened, so we have to hope there were survivors somehow and that *Chandra* or *Bohr* can pick them up. Our beacons are on, so there's still a decent chance of—"

"Stop," Boz snapped. "Just . . . stop."

"I'm serious. We could—"

The laughter in his helmet was bitter.

"No one could have survived whatever that was, and you know it. You *know* it, Ravi. That bitch-dragon, Fafnir? She won. She fried *Archie*. It's all gone. All of it."

The lump in his throat made speaking difficult.

"*Bohr* and *Chandra* are still out there."

"So? How long before their lifeboats get here, even assuming they're prepared to risk it? Twenty hours? Thirty? And how much air do we have? You're the engineer, cuz. Do the math."

Ravi stared at the unmoving stars, knowing Boz was right. Unwilling to admit it, even to himself.

"Yeah, well. I'm not giving up just yet. You never know."

"News flash, Ravi. You're a *midshipman*. You're not a real officer. Enough with trying to keep up morale. Let's just face facts and admit that we're sarded."

Coming from Boz, the words stung. The truth of them stung. He choked back a sob—whether of anger or fear or frustration, he was too spun around to tell.

"No point giving up until we have to," Lisette said quietly. Her voice gentled its way through Ravi's helmet—and Boz's too, he guessed. "We should play this through till the end. By the book."

"You mean the delayed-rescue protocol?" he asked.

"Yes."

"It's not like we've got anything better to do, is it?" Boz said. She sounded more like her usual self. "Besides, I've always wanted to go out on a real high."

Ravi smiled despite himself.

People had been stranded in space, like, forever. Practices had evolved, primarily the use of drugs to lower heartrate and oxygen consumption. It would buy a little extra time. But even then, it wouldn't be enough, not with *Bohr* and *Chandra* being so far away. It was not a coincidence that those same drugs, when the time came, would bring about a merciful, pain-free end.

"Better get on with it," Lisette said. Her voice was determinedly cheerful. "See you in a few hours. Or not."

"Maybe someone will find us one day," Boz said. "In a couple of billion years."

"In a totally different galaxy," Ravi said, smiling. He pulled back a tab on the left sleeve of his suit.

"We'll be famous," Boz said. "A totally unknown lifeform, never before seen."

Ravi reached past the tab and pressed down on the contact hiding beneath it.

"Rav?"

"Yeah?"

"I didn't mean what I said about you not being a real officer. You're . . . you're the best. You know that, right?"

Tears pricked the corners of his eyes.

"Ditto."

There was a small sting at the base of his spine.

"The stars look funny," Lisette said. "I think they're singing to us."

"They're beautiful," Boz said dreamily. "I didn't know they could hold hands."

"Don't be stupid," Ravi began to say.

But he'd already forgotten why he'd started talking in the first place.

▬ ▬ ▬

Some part of him understood that he was spaced out, that the drugs lowering his body temperature and slowing his breathing to save oxygen were playing tricks on his mind. The stars were not dancing and changing colors and burning oh so brightly in patterns no one had ever seen before. The running lights on Boz's EMU were not pounding out dance music, and Lisette was not, was definitely not, flipping cartwheels across the Milky Way.

But it sure looked like it.

Was this what torpor was like? Was this why his dad had never learned to fly right? Why, after every guilty verdict, he'd march defiantly out of the ombudsman's courtroom, whistling snatches of half-remembered songs? Because torpor was *this* much fun?

Someone was giggling inside his helmet.

Criminals on *Archimedes* did not get to sit around like Homeworld convicts, eating and drinking and breathing precious resources. They spent their captivity as close to death as possible, consuming as little as possible, with just enough consciousness to think about what they had done.

But if it was like *this*, why would you ever want to leave?

It wasn't, though. He knew that. Had seen it. Dad would come back, after a week, or two, or thirty sols, and he would be . . . different. Hollowed out. Meaner. He'd bounce back after a couple of sols but never quite as high as before he'd fallen. Maybe, in the end, he'd been happy to get mulched. He'd whacked a lieutenant, a *lieutenant,* for Archie's sake, with a chain. Knocked the man to the deck after being on the wrong end of one condescending insult too many. He was already rated Dead Weight. But mother and son were still shocked when the ombudsman refused to commute it.

The giggling in his helmet had stopped. Some weakling was crying instead.

The dancing stars were vanishing, one by one at first, and then by tens and twenties, eaten by an angry white dragon. It roared and screamed across the universe, the tattoos on its scaled body rippling with fury. It was turning on him now, opening one of its many mouths. He would be a *very* small dessert after so many suns. The thought made the person living inside his helmet laugh hysterically.

One of the tattoos steadied for a moment, allowing him to read it:

ISV-I-LB-03

Which made no sense at all. It was the last thing he saw before the dragon swallowed him whole.

They told me you were awake," Vasconcelos said. "Speaking personally, I was rather hoping you wouldn't make it."

"I love you, too," Ravi croaked. His head was thumping like an unbalanced impeller, and the lights in the *Spirit of St. Petersburg*'s infirmary were far too bright. He tugged uselessly at the pair of handcuffs chaining him to the zero-*g* bed.

"Tell him to take a long walk around Hungary," Boz suggested. "Without a suit."

"Belay that, Crewman!" Vasconcelos snapped.

"Or what? You'll mulch me?"

The commander-inspector sighed. He looked tired, Ravi thought. There was a slump to his shoulders, a lumpiness to his movements that radiated weariness. He floated across to hover by Ravi's head, his hands tucked into his armpits.

"I'd like to know what the two of you have been up to," he said quietly. "And what's your connection to her?" Careful not to set himself spinning, he nodded in the direction of Lisette, still unconscious but handcuffed to her bed nonetheless. Her face was puffy, and there was an unhealthy tinge of gray about her, but she seemed to be breathing easily enough.

"We're just trying to stop a war," Ravi said. He was exhausted. He didn't have the energy for this.

"And a fine job you did of *that*, by the looks of it," Vasconcelos said. "*Bohr*'s adrift, and we were *this* close to being vaporized." He held thumb and forefinger less than a centimeter apart.

Ravi managed a faint smile.

"*Archie*'s still with us?"

"Of course she is. You're on an *Archimedes* lifeboat, for sard's sake. How else do you think you got rescued?"

"Bet you wouldn't have bothered if you'd known it was us," Boz said.

An expression of annoyance surfaced on Vasconcelos's face, quickly suppressed.

"You weren't what we expected," he conceded. "We were hoping for intel—for prisoners. Some leverage to use against *Newton*. I hope for your sake you have some."

Ravi had other things on his mind.

"How come the ship wasn't destroyed?" he asked. "We were out there when the dragon blew. We *saw* it happen. No one could have survived that."

Vasconcelos gave Ravi a long, thoughtful stare. Perhaps he was weighing the pros and cons of sharing information with a suspect.

"The incoming torpedoes detonated too far away," he said, at last. "Much closer and we'd have been destroyed for sure, but explosions, even nuclear ones, dissipate pretty rapidly in a vacuum. We might not be so lucky next time. Which is why you need to tell me everything you know."

Ravi's relief, overwhelming though it was, was tinged with sadness. The missiles they'd seen must have been an exchange of fire between Kur and Fafnir, not Fafnir and the ship. In the end, Kur must have burned both himself and his sibling rather than let her reach *Archimedes*.

"There's not a lot to tell," he said quietly. "We've made a peace agreement."

"You?" Vasconcelos snorted. "*You've* made a peace agreement?"

"Too sarding right," Boz chimed in. "We've saved the whole Archie-damned fleet!"

"You don't need to believe us," Ravi pointed out. "You can ask Lisette—the *Newton* crewman."

"Oh, I believe you, MacLeod. But if you think the fleet's going to accept whatever surrender scenario your masters on *Newton* have cooked up for us, you are sadly mistaken." The inspector's face was rigid with dislike. "You're both traitors. If you want any chance of mercy, you'd better tell me everything you damn well know—and fast."

Hidden coms speakers burst into life.

"Commander-Inspector? We have an incoming communication."

"I'm busy," Vasconcelos snapped. "Take a message. I'll deal with it later."

"The communication isn't for you, Commander. It's for our, er, *passengers*. It's routed from the Captain's office on *Archimedes*."

Vasconcelos's eyebrows arched almost all the way to his hairline.

"Put it through."

"Midshipman MacLeod, Crewman MacLeod, are you reading me?" The voice was firm, its every syllable weighted with authority.

Captain Strauss-Cohen. Ravi's heart pounded in his chest. He opened his mouth to speak, but nothing came out.

"We're reading you, Captain," Boz said, without a hint of nerves or deference. "What can we do for you?"

"You can speak with the talking bomb that's sitting a hundred meters off the stern of my ship and threatening to detonate, crewman. That's what."

"Er, sure." Boz's face flickered with surprise. "Put it through."

What came through was cold, and distant, and contralto.

"Am I talking to Kur's cargo?" asked Ao Qin.

"You are."

"Do you stand by our agreement? Unlimited fuel, maintenance, and upgrades? Freedom to roam at will?"

"Yes."

"Then convince the foolish and stubborn leader of your people to also stand by your agreement; otherwise, I will detonate in one hundred and twenty seconds, as will Lawu, who is presently within one hundred meters of ISV-Three Chandrasekhar.*"*

"Whoa there, Ao Qin. Cut your thrust, okay? Have you kept your part of the bargain? Has someone taken care of *Newton*?"

"Con-rit and Dreq are both in position. The Mother Ship understands the situation and has agreed to stand down. You now have one hundred and two seconds."

Vasconcelos was looking on in horror. He turned to glare at Boz, who simply ignored him.

"Then have Isaac and the secretary guy confirm that they've stopped fighting."

There was a pause. Ravi's implanted clock counted down the seconds.

"Isaac? Mr. Secretary?" It was Con-rit speaking. *"Please confirm you have ceased hostilities on penalty of immediate destruction."*

"This is Secretary Caliskan, representing the true humans of *Newton*." The secretary's voice was angry and leavened with no small amount of fear. "Albeit under *duress*, we have ceased hostilities. We hope to negotiate an honorable peace."

"Fifty-three seconds."

"It's pretty simple, ma'am," Boz said. "Agree to cease fire; agree to provide a home base for the dragons with fuel, maintenance, and upgrades, and this war is over. Everybody gets to live."

"To be controlled by LOKI's?" the Captain shot back. "Forget it. It violates the Mission. We didn't go through one hundred and thirty-two years of pain and suffering to—"

"Captain," Ravi cut in, finding his voice at last, "the LOKIs are going to

Destination World whether we like it or not. *Newton* has already taken the deal. The only issue is whether the rest of us are around to see it."

"Thirty-one seconds."

"I need to consult with *Bohr* and *Chandrasekhar.*"

"Twenty seconds."

Ravi could feel the sweat beading on his forehead. Boz's fingers gripped an imaginary cigarette. Vasconcelos held his breath.

"All right," Strauss-Cohen snapped. "The LOKIs have a deal. Under *duress*, like the man says. No hostilities. Fuel, maintenance, and upgrades as requested."

The clock in Ravi's head swept down to zero.

"Now what?" the Captain asked.

"Nothing much," Boz said sweetly. "Now you talk."

For the first time in her life, Ravi thought, Boz MacLeod sounded like a grown-up. He let out a brief sigh of relief and then steeled himself for what had to come next.

"Commander-Inspector?"

"What?"

"There's a bomb in the ship's drive. The kind that doesn't talk."

"M idshipman six dash eight five five two MacLeod, Ravinder T.," Vasconcelos intoned formally. "You are being held on suspicion of offenses committed pursuant to Ship's Regs twenty-two dash zero one and dash zero seven, namely, the detonation of an explosive device on Haiphong Circular, the attempted detonation of an explosive device somewhere at or near the aft of the ISV-one *Archimedes*, and conspiracy to commit the aforesaid offenses. Do you understand the nature of the accusations?"

Ravi had known it would happen, but it was still a shock to find himself in the brig. He nodded dumbly. After two whole sols of staring at a cell wall, at least the interrogation room was a change of scenery.

"I need an audible yes or no for the recording, Midshipman."

"Yes."

"The first thing I'd like to know is: who helped you plant the bomb on Haiphong Circular?"

"The boy isn't answering questions about that," Chen Lai said gruffly.

Vasconcelos subjected the engineer to an icy stare.

"As his commanding officer, you have the right to observe only. You do *not* have the right to interfere with my questioning."

"Then why don't you ask him questions about the bomb that *hasn't* gone off?" Chen Lai snapped. "Haiphong can wait." The engineer turned his attention to Ravi. "We want to know—if *you* know—where the bomb in the engine rooms is located."

Ravi knew he was gaping at them like an idiot, but he couldn't help himself.

"This bomb you told me about," Vasconcelos said. "No one can find it."

"I've had teams go over the engine rooms from top to bottom," Chen Lai explained. "They found nothing. What makes you so sure there's something there?"

Ravi's first reaction to what they were telling him was one of relief. Thank Archie he'd been wrong.

Except he wasn't.

"Like I said before, sir. It's the *Bohr*. What happened to her is going to happen to us—and *Chandra*—on Braking Day. The moment we fire up the drive, the whole thing will seize up and we'll overshoot the Destination Star with no way back."

"But you don't know where it is?" Chen Lai pressed.

"No, sir."

"Or what it looks like?"

"No, sir."

"Then tell me this," asked Vasconcelos, clearly annoyed at being up-staged in his own interrogation room. "*How* do you know what happened on the *Bohr* wasn't an accident?"

"When *Bohr* lost control of her drive, Isaac—*Newton*'s LOKI—ran an analysis. He concluded that there'd been a failure of a Q-series sub-coil. A peripheral one. Had it been closer to the engine core—"

"The drive would have detonated," Chen Lai concluded. "There'd have been no time for an emergency shutdown." The engineer pursed his lips. "And given that Q-series sub-coils are almost bombproof, you think some-one on *Bohr* used an actual bomb, a bomb triggered by the activation of the drive, to take one out?"

"Yes, sir. And that whoever planted a bomb on *Bohr* would have done the same to *Archie* and *Chandra*."

"This is a farce," Vasconcelos snarled at Chen Lai. "Your trainee plants a *real* bomb, which you don't want me asking questions about, but you *do* want to ask questions about a fantasy bomb that doesn't sarding exist. And we *know* it doesn't sarding exist, because your best people, despite going over the engine rooms for two sols solid, have found nothing. And the folks on *Chandra* say the same. The kid's got you on a tachyon hunt."

"I'm certain they're there, sir," Ravi said to Chen Lai. "And you need to find them before Braking Day."

"Oh, he'll need to find it a lot sooner than that, Middy," said Vasconcelos.

"Sir?"

"A lot's happened since you've been in here," Chen Lai sighed. He rubbed his nose between thumb and forefinger, and Ravi suddenly understood that the erect figure seated in front of him was under an incredible amount of stress. "The captains have hammered out peace of a sort with *Newton*. It'll hold for now—or at least for so long as we all have LOKI weapons systems stuck to our respective asses. So, we have you and your friends to thank for that, I guess.

"We also negotiated an evacuation plan for the *Bohr*. *Newton* has agreed to take a third of the crew." The old man smiled wryly at the expression on Ravi's face. "Not entirely by choice, I might add. The LOKIs did a bit of prodding in that regard. *Newton* has a lot of free space, apparently. And they also have some kind of cap they can surgically attach to our people. It'll cut them off from any kind of hive but also stop them hacking *Newton*'s systems and overrunning the ship." Chen Lai looked almost amused. "You and your cousin made quite an impression on our new friends. None of it good."

Ravi recalled *Newton*'s brig and the crude cap affixed to Lisette's head. He suppressed a shiver. Sounded like they'd refined the design from an instrument of torture to a coms blocker. At least, he *hoped* they'd refined the design. There'd be a revolt otherwise.

Aloud, he said, "Seems like *Newton*'s putting a lot of trust in its tech. I'm not sure I'd do the same in their place."

"The LOKIs also explained that they would blow *Archie* and *Chandra* to quarks if anything 'untoward' happened on *Newton*," Vasconcelos cut in, sardonically. "So, there's that."

"Indeed," Chen Lai agreed. "The remainder of *Bohr*'s complement is coming to *Archimedes* and *Chandrasekhar*. While we *could* use the lifeboats, it makes more sense logistically to bring the ISVs alongside each other. We can toss a bunch of umbilicals over and do hub-to-hub transfers instead."

"But that means firing up the drives," Ravi objected.

"Exactly."

"But you can't! We'll end up like *Bohr*!" Ravi made to jump to his feet, but the heavy hand of a ShipSec guard forced him back down.

"Decision's already made," Vasconcelos said. "We start moving in about eight hours. That's how long it will take to finish prepping enough living space for axial gravity and to lock up the wheels."

"I'll keep looking," Chen Lai promised. "There's nothing more you can help me with?"

Ravi shook his head. His stomach, which knew he was lying, tied itself in knots.

— — —

Much to his surprise—and quite possibly at Chen Lai's insistence—it seemed he was now allowed visitors. Boz and Lisette, accompanied by none other than Vladimir Ansimov, wasted no time in taking advantage of the opportunity.

"They treating you okay?" Ansimov asked, striding into the visiting room. Boz and Lisette looked tiny and insubstantial in his wake. He grabbed the nearest seat without waiting for an answer and sat down at the compartment's one battered table, directly across from Ravi. "The bastard officers won't tell us what's going on. Word on the circular is that you and your cousin here either saved the fleet from being blown to quarks, or that you almost got us killed. Word is you're also a BonVoy and you blew up the Haiphong Circular. All Chen Lai will say is that your status is 'under review.'" A grimace. "Plus, with you gone, I have to tag along with Thurman and Roe, both of whom are Class A gullgropers."

Ravi stifled a smile.

"Sorry about that. I'd be there if I could." He paused momentarily, considering Ansimov's question. "They're treating me okay, I guess. All things considered." He turned his attention to Boz and Lisette. "How are you two doing?"

It turned out that, unlike Ravi, whose revelation about the drive had merely reinforced the general belief that he was the Haiphong bomber, Boz and Lisette had been accorded a curious "guest" status aboard *Archimedes*. Neither side was grateful for a truce imposed by traitors. Neither side appreciated having to live with *Newton*'s suddenly independent weapons systems. Many believed that traitors should get what they deserved.

And yet.

Lives had been saved. No one in the fleet seriously believed they would have won the sol if the dragons had pressed home their attack. And the dragons themselves had made it clear that they would take a dim view of either the fleet or *Newton* "disassembling" their late sibling's "cargo." According to Lisette, Vasconcelos, in the bitter aftermath of the negotiations, had summed it up best.

"Can't live with you; can't flush you out the airlock."

Pending some sort of final resolution, the powers that be had assigned Boz and Lisette high-end quarters in Bermuda. It was, Boz said, "a taste of how the other five percent live." They were allowed to leave for short amounts of time, but there was always a ShipSec detail at the door, and they went nowhere without an escort. Theirs was a luxurious prison but a prison nonetheless.

Ravi would have given his motherboard to swap places.

No doubt thanks to Chen Lai, they had the brig's visiting room to themselves, without the usual "MacLeod drone" to eavesdrop on the conversation. Eager to abuse the privilege, Boz leaned back in her chair, pulled a cigarette and lighter from the depths of her so-called leather jacket, and lit up. The electric-blue arc of the lighter's ignition sparked its usual mix of ash and smoke.

"What the sard do you think you're doing?" Ravi asked, scandalized. He turned toward the door, expecting to hear the heavy thud of approaching boots. "You're in the sarding *brig,* for Archie's sake! You want to end up staying here?"

Boz just laughed.

"One of these sols, they're either going to mulch us or let us go. Until they decide, I'm pretty much untouchable. They really, *really* want us to keep quiet, so if this helps . . ." She took a long drag on her contraband. Thoughtful eyes stared at him through the smoke.

"No one can find this bomb of yours, cuz. Do you think that maybe this is just your imagination getting the better of you? Again, I mean." She glanced sideways at Lisette. "We both know you sometimes see things that aren't really there."

"I didn't drop an imaginary bomb into his implants," Lisette protested. "If Ravi says there's a bomb in the engine rooms, then there's a bomb in the engine rooms."

"Except there isn't," Ansimov said flatly. He leaned forward in his chair. "I'm telling you, amiko, we've been over every bescumbered square centimeter of that place. There ain't nothing there. Sarding Chen Lai even had us strip out the bulkheads." Powerful knuckles rapped on the table. "Unless this bomb of yours is somehow disguised as poly-armor plating, it simply don't exist."

"But it *does!*"

He stood up in agitation. Started pacing about the room.

A voice erupted from the walls.

"Siddown, MacLeod. You know the rules."

Ravi flopped gracelessly back into his seat.

"I've got to get out of here," he muttered. "Like right now."

"Not going to happen," Boz said sadly. "Not with this Haiphong thing still hanging over your head. Even if you weren't a MacLeod, that's enough for Vasconcelos to keep you tied up in here for a *long* time. Your parentage is just free water for the shower."

Ravi's mind was racing. Unable to stand, one leg pumped uselessly against the deck. He was running out of time. He couldn't do anything, sitting around the brig like a bag of spares. Unless . . .

He turned to Ansimov.

"Do you think you can persuade Sofia to come see me?"

"Sofia Ibori?" Ansimov looked doubtful. "I know she kinda likes you, Rav, but an *Ibori*? In here? Her great-uncle would sooner drive us into the Destination Star."

"Sofia has a mind of her own. She'll come if she wants to, whatever her uncle says."

"Well, then, Vladimir," Boz said, casting a mischievous glance in Ansimov's direction. "Do you think you can *persuade* Midshipman Ibori to grace the brig with her presence, or is a hoity-toity navigator too out of your league?"

Ansimov let the silence hang there a moment. A slow, calculating grin spread across his face.

"If I do, MacLeods and *Newton* lady, you all owe me big-time."

A gentle musical chiming floated through the brig, accompanied by a short message on the inside of Ravi's eye.

The wheels were shutting down. The motors that drove their ceaseless rotations had been put into quiet slumber. Ravi found himself testing his weight against the deck, but everything felt exactly the same as before. The wheels didn't—couldn't—stop on a button. They would take some hours to come to a halt. And it would be several minutes before all but the most sensitive noticed anything at all. But whether you could feel it or not, physics and friction were doing their work. Every rotation of the wheel was taking fractionally longer than the one which preceded it. Eventually, they would stop turning altogether. The Captain would activate the drive. Or try to.

His cell door sprang open. A ShipSec officer stood on the other side of the threshold.

"Visitor," he announced.

Sofia Ibori was already there when he arrived, her face composed and friendly, her uniform immaculate, her braided hair gleaming in the light. His escort retreated through the door, leaving the two of them alone.

He tried to ignore the sudden pitter-patter in his chest.

"I wasn't sure you'd come see me."

A small frown crossed Sofia's features.

"Your friend, Vladimir, was extremely insistent. He rather gave the impression that you were, er, thinking of killing yourself. Said you were writing a note, on *paper*. And it might look bad if I didn't at least try and see you."

Ravi fought to keep his expression neutral. Vlad knew perfectly well that he couldn't write on paper to save his life. Same way he knew that Ravi wouldn't thank him for suggesting that Ravinder MacLeod was cracking under the strain.

He couldn't decide whether to kill Ansimov or laugh out loud. Maybe both. Sofia was here, after all.

"What's in the note, Ravi?" Sofia was still smiling, except it was no longer reaching her eyes. "What does it say about me?"

"What do you want it to say?"

"Nothing. That would be safest for all concerned."

"For you, maybe."

"You don't have the family name to think about. It's bad enough to be seen in this, this . . . *place*, never mind featuring in some sort of suicide note."

"So, you don't care if I commit suicide? So long as your name is kept out of it?"

"Of *course* I care. I just don't want things to be even worse; that's all. Let's face it, if you die—which I hope you won't—the rest of us have to go on living."

"How very Second Gen of you. *Super* pragmatic." Ravi was surprised at the bitterness in his voice.

"You're not being fair, Rav. I'm asking you for a favor. I can't believe you'd want to hurt me by writing some stupid note. That's not who you are."

"There is no note, Sofe. Vlad knew I wanted to see you, so I guess he just said whatever he thought would make you come."

Sofia didn't bother to hide her irritation.

"Do you have any idea how much hassle I'm going to get when the family finds out I've been here? What Jaden will say?"

Something twisted in his guts.

"Jaden will get over it," he said tightly. "I'm glad you came."

With a small sigh, Sofia leaned forward, placing her elbows on the table.

"Did you have anything in particular you wanted to talk about, or are we just hanging out? I don't have a lot of time."

His heart was thumping very fast now.

"There *is* something I'd like to talk about, actually."

"Which is?"

"The bombs you and your BonVoy friends have planted in the engine rooms."

Sofia just laughed. An explosive bark of disbelief.

"I was inside a dragon—a LOKI weapons system—when *Bohr*'s drive went down. The LOKIs saw everything. Even figured out that it must have been caused by a failure in a Q-series sub-coil."

"Is that supposed to mean something?"

"There's only one sub-coil that could cause a failure like that. The one I told you about in the engine rooms."

"Really?" Sofia continued to look mildly amused.

"There's no point denying it, Sofe. There's no guard here. No drone. No one can hear us." The bitterness crept back into his voice. "Do you know how great it was to have you want something from me? The lengths I went to to get you a tour of the engine rooms? How good it felt to spend time with you?"

He had no idea how much he'd hate this. The look on her face was answer enough.

"I've been such a sarding idiot," he said. "Of course you did. You knew exactly how I felt about you. You knew I'd do pretty much anything you asked. Archie's hooks, *Boz* knew I'd do pretty much anything you asked. 'Wrapped around your finger,' she said. And when you pressed that finger against the warm vent in the engine rooms, you weren't feeling the power of the drive, or its . . . its awesomeness, or the sheer beauty of it. All you heard was me telling you that if you blew out the sub-coil, the drive would be shut down for months.

"The BonVoys planted bombs in all three vents, triggered to go off when the drives shift to full power. That's what happened to the *Bohr,* wasn't it, when they panicked and tried to get away from the dragons."

The face staring back at him was eerily calm.

"There are no bombs," she said. "If there were, Eugene would have found them by now."

Ravi could feel himself blinking furiously.

"But there's *something,* isn't there? The moment I told you about the sub-coil, you knew you'd found a way to keep us off of Destination World. So, what did you do?"

"I'm perfectly sure I didn't *do* anything. And if you were half as sure as you pretend to be, it'd be me sitting in a cell instead of you."

"Right, because every time a MacLeod points the finger at an officer, it's the MacLeod who gets believed. Get real, Sofe. If I'd said anything like that to Vasconcelos, I'd be in even more trouble than I am already."

"Poor thing." Sofia threw him a sly smile. "Even if I admit everything to your face, no one will ever believe you."

"No," Ravi agreed. The truth of it gnawed at him: had gnawed at him for as long as he could remember. "And I guess you're going to sit on your hands and let me get mulched."

"It's not what I want, Rav."

"But you're not going to stop it."

"I can't."

"You mean you won't."

Sofia said nothing, not quite meeting his eye. Maybe for the first time, the extent of his stupidity, the full, mind-blowing *enormity* of it, hit him like a meteoroid. Even if she'd never felt for him what he felt for her, he'd always comforted himself that she felt *something*. That *he* was something. That she cared about him at least a little.

And now that sorry, pathetic excuse of an illusion was slipping away; a loose torque wrench spinning into the black, glinting in the starlight for a few brief moments before vanishing.

He was a convenience, nothing more. A naïve, no-name boy from an unfashionable wheel with an idiotic crush on someone who'd been laughing at him the whole time. How ridiculous he must have looked to her, he realized, shambling about in his scuffed fatigues, without even enough water to keep himself clean. A MacLeod so stupid, he thought he could become an officer.

He was nothing more than a means to an end. Someone she could use. And if, while being used, he got used up, too bad. It's not like he was anyone who mattered.

He gritted his teeth. Tried to hang on to some small scrap of dignity.

"If I'm going to get mulched, at least do me the respect of admitting what you and your BonVoy friends have done."

Sofia leaned back in her seat, head cocked to one side. Ravi held his breath.

"Well, *hypothetically* of course, you know BonVoys: Destination World has to be saved from ruination and genocide, yadda yadda yadda. Demonstrations had failed. Politics had failed. This was the only way."

"You need to tell me what they did."

"Don't be silly." Sofia's laughter danced across the room. "If the drives fail, the fleet's not braking. Why would I get in the way of that?"

"Because the fleet *is* braking. Some of it, anyway. There are no BonVoys on *Newton*, Sofia. And trust me on this: there's no way those guys are letting someone from the *Bohr,* never mind a BonVoy, anywhere near their engines." He shook his head with conviction. "Regardless of what you do, ten thousand crewmen from *Newton* and seven thousand survivors of the *Bohr* are going to land on Destination World—maybe more if *Newton* takes on more people. Everything you don't want to happen is going to happen anyway. Stopping *Archie* and *Chandra* from braking isn't going to make an atom's worth of difference."

"It makes all the difference in the wheel," Sofia said. Her eyes glinted with a barely suppressed passion.

Ravi tried to keep the puzzlement off his face. For a BonVoy, Destination World was doomed regardless of what happened to *Archie* and *Chandra*. So, why didn't she give a cracked thruster about it?

"I know you believe in what you're doing," he persisted. "I can even respect it, sort of. But if those drives fail, you'll be killing more than twenty thousand people for no good reason. And that's not saving the planet. That's just plain old murder."

"Go sard yourself, Ravi." The words were flat and without malice.

He sat back a moment, forced there by the strength of her feelings, the utter conviction that she was right. He could hear his father's oft-repeated complaint ringing in his ears.

Sarding officers. Think the ship owes them a living.

"You're not a BonVoy," he said, suddenly sure.

Sofia shrugged her shoulders, the movement elegant as only she could make it.

"No, I'm not. I keep telling you that, and it never seems to get through to you, does it? I get where they're coming from, and I couldn't have done any of this without their help. Without Jaden's help, to be precise. Jaden is a BonVoy to the core. But I was never a member. They bombed Haiphong Circular for starters, and I wanted no part of that." A wry smile. "Too bad they found you where they did, Ravi, banged up at the bottom of some shaft, wheels away from home. What in Archie's name were you doing there? There's no way they'd have pinned it on you otherwise. ShipSec are so convinced you're their guy, I don't think they're even looking for the real culprits."

Ravi shrugged.

"It's always easier to blame a MacLeod," he said stolidly. "But now I'm guessing there's more to your differences with the BonVoys than a disagreement over tactics."

"BonVoys want to save Destination World. I want to save *us*: this new civilization we've built, up here, away from stars and planets and all the things that will tear us to pieces if we ever go back down."

"And a civilization where you get to stay an officer." Ravi's voice was dangerously quiet. "Where being a navigator still means something."

"And what's wrong with that? The Iboris, the Strauss-Cohens, the Chen Lais—all of us—we have built something . . . *incredible*. A stable, safe society with no wars and no famines and no misery. Why would anyone want to give that up? You want to go down there with those . . . those throwback *freaks* on the *Newton*? You think that's going to end well? Their grandchildren will give their motherboards for the chance to have come with us."

"That's not the Mission, and you know it. You love being an officer? Great. You love that your family is a big deal? Even better. For *you*. *My* ancestors didn't sign up for this. We're not going to be lorded over by a bunch of officers with rights and privileges and the best berths and the best opportunities, just so you can fly the ship until it breaks."

"You still don't get it, do you? The MacLeods are *crew*. *You're* crew. And when thrust comes to full burn, crew always does what it's told. Crew understands that it's discipline that keeps everyone alive, discipline that keeps the ship on track. Discipline has kept us going for a hundred and thirty-two years, and it'll keep us going forevermore. Officers order, crew *obeys*. If we overshoot the system and tell them the Mission has changed, the crew will accept it. Because that's what crew does. That's how it is, because that's how it needs to be, and you wanting it to be different isn't going to change a thing."

"I wonder what your great-uncle would say about that. Or Vasconcelos."

Sofia's expression darkened.

"You won't be telling them anything. They won't believe a word you say."

"And what have I got to lose? If I'm going to be mulched anyway, I might as well tell the truth. It may be too late when they do, but they'll believe me in the end."

"You think? Even if they do, they'll never *prove* it, will they?" She leaned in to him then, her voice suddenly fierce. "And I could make life very difficult for your mother. I'm bound to know someone who knows her shift commander. Maybe suddenly, her work isn't so good. Maybe she gets a demotion and can't afford her quarters. Maybe . . . maybe she gets *disciplined*. Is that what you want?"

"You're bluffing."

"Try me."

She sat there in a scuffed polymer chair that might as well have been a throne, radiating confidence. True officer confidence. The result of six generations of breeding. Steely and unbreakable.

Almost unbreakable.

Everyone, even an officer, has weaknesses. His family had traded on that simple fact for generations. A need for hard-to-get equipment, restricted information, even chocolate. That his own weakness was Sofia, he had already learned to his cost. But bitter though it was to face up to, he also knew hers.

"Is this what Jaden wants? You and he, flying together through the dark? Chief Navigator and Captain-to-be? Queen and king of the fleet?"

"Jaden's got nothing to do with this," she said stiffly. But she was lying. He could see the riptides of emotion roiling in her eyes. The need, the insecurity, jealousy.

"Sofe?" He said it so quietly, he could barely hear it himself. "Before you throw everyone's life away for nothing, there's something I need to show you."

He transferred his video recording of Jaden Strauss-Cohen and Ksenia Graham at the movie theater. Sofia's eyes burned as she saw the two of them intertwined, as she heard Jaden describe her as "clingy." When it was over, she took a deep, stertorous breath.

"He's not worth it," Ravi said, as gently as he could. "He doesn't love you. Never did, never will. This future you've planned for yourself? It's not going to happen. You'll be flying through the dark alone—or with a guy who's two-timing you at every turn of the wheel."

Sofia took another breath, even deeper than before. Tears streamed down her face. She made no attempt to wipe them away.

"Think about it, Sofia. He's a *BonVoy*. He may not care about you, but he loves that planet. If people go down there, he'll want to save as much of it as he can. If you went to Jaden right now and said, 'Let's go to the *Bohr*. She's already adrift. We'll round up everyone who agrees with us and head on over there. A civilization with no stars, no planets, bon-voyaging forever.' Do you *really* think he'd go with you? Do you really think he'd actually, like, *go*?"

The silence stretched for an eternity. The tears in her eyes burned like suns.

"It's not a bomb." Her voice was little more than a whisper. "They printed a new sub-coil. It looks exactly like the real thing on the scanners, but it'll fail almost as soon as the drive reaches full power."

"Thanks, Sofe." He touched her lightly on the wrist, headed for the door that would take him back to his cell. The slowing wheel was having an effect. He was definitely lighter.

She managed a tight little smile.

"You know, when you tell Eugene this, I'll deny it all. Everyone will think you planted that sub-coil yourself. They'll mulch you anyway."

There wasn't the slightest hint of compassion, of regret, in her tone of voice. Sofia's heart might be breaking over Jaden, but there'd never been room in it for anyone else, least of all him.

He couldn't stop himself from lashing out.

"I think you're forgetting something."

"Am I?"

Ravi tapped his right eye, wallowed in a petty sense of triumph.

"I'm an engineer, Sofia. I come equipped with a recording function."

The bright blue electric arc of Boz's lighter made contact with a cigarette. She took a deep, satisfied drag, jetting blue smoke across the living room of their swanky Bermuda quarters.

"Here's to Braking Day," she said, addressing Ravi and Lisette. "Now that they've finally set it. Four hundred hours, thirty-seven minutes and counting. After seven generations, nine dragons, one plague, and a bomb plot, it's about time!" She pulled a face. "And, who knows? Maybe they'll have figured out what to do with us by then."

Lisette was staring at her in horrified fascination.

"I do wish you'd stop doing that."

"What?"

"Smoking. It's disgusting."

"Privilege of being a diplomatic headache." Boz's fingers curled into air quotes. "'Can't live with us, can't flush us out the airlock,' remember? They need me healthy and happy for the recycler."

"That's *not* healthy," Lisette pointed out.

"Yeah, but it makes me happy."

There was a chiming at the door. The three of them started in surprise.

Commander-Engineer Eugene Chen Lai stepped across the threshold. He looked around curiously. If he was troubled by the tense demeanor of the ShipSec officers who waited outside, he showed no sign. Ravi couldn't help himself. He stood to attention. Chen Lai's cool gaze, having toured the living room, bored into him. He fought the instinct to squirm.

"Nice digs, Middy."

"Yes, sir."

Impassive eyes stared fixedly at Ravi's face.

"Can I get you something?" Lisette offered gamely. "Tea? Coffee?"

Chen Lai took her in without the slightest change in expression. His eyes glanced quickly across her frame, as if scanning for defects.

"Tea. Green. No sweetener."

"Coming right up." Lisette, as discomfited by his attention as Ravi was, scuttled into the apartment's tiny galley, shutting the door behind her. There was a muffled sound of crockery banging against the countertop.

"How's the Ansimov woman doing?" Chen Lai inquired, taking the nearest available chair.

"Okay, sir, I guess. This is all new to her, but she's learning to use the hive and stop using her hands for, well, *everything*."

"No implants over there at all?"

"None. Everything's either hands-on, completely automated, or run by the ship."

Chen Lai shook his head in something approaching bemusement. The galley door cycled open. Lisette stepped into the living room with a cargo of tea.

"Thanks," Chen Lai said. He took a tentative sip, his expression softening a little.

"I've had worse. Thank you."

"Now that you've been suitably refreshed," Boz said, "maybe you could tell us why you're here."

Ravi tried not to shudder. Chen Lai's eyes narrowed ever so slightly, but when he spoke, his voice carried no more than its usual rasp.

"Why do you think I'm here, Crewman? Suffice it to say, the grown-ups have had to sort out the mess you made."

Boz, slowly and with great deliberation, blew a puff of smoke toward Chen Lai's face.

"And are the 'grown-ups' going to sort this out by mulching us?"

Chen Lai didn't flinch. The smoke passed by without seeming to touch him.

"Commander-Inspector Vasconcelos would very much like to see the both of you face justice. Fortunately for you, if no one else, he's in a minority of one." Chen Lai was sitting ramrod-straight in his chair, tea balanced precisely on his right thigh, as if it were a table. "Thanks to Midshipman MacLeod's, ah, *ingenuity*, Midshipman Ibori's taped confession is a sensation—and not just on the news feeds. It's the talk of Officer Country. Won't hold up in front of the ombudsman, of course, seeing as it was obtained illegally, but it gets your cousin here off the hook for being a terrorist and makes him a hero for saving us all not once but twice: first from the *Newton* and then from the BonVoys. There's even some chatter about commendations. For the lot of you." A smile, quickly suppressed. "The Commander-Inspector is *very* frustrated. He can't prosecute you under the privacy laws or for your many other infractions, because no one else wants to hear it, and he can't prosecute Ibori because those same privacy laws make her confession inadmissible."

"What about the real bombers?" Ravi asked.

"Jaden Strauss-Cohen is lucky Vasconcelos got to him before the Captain. She'd have spaced him, I think. As it is, he's started talking. A lot of people are going to get rounded up. And from what I hear, the Strauss-Cohens and Iboris are going to have plenty of company when it comes to familial embarrassment."

"What's going to happen to Sofia?"

"Don't know, don't care. Vasconcelos has her in protective custody. Legal defense or not, every living generation wants her recycled." He stared at Ravi with a raised eyebrow. "There's some thought about following through on your suggestion, though."

"*My* suggestion, sir?"

"That she gets shipped over to the *Bohr* before Braking Day. If she wants to stay out here so badly, why not let her? She might not be alone, either."

"You're kidding."

"I'm not famous for my sense of humor, son. Turns out there are quite a few people who feel the same way she does. That life is simply better up here."

"But they'll die," Boz protested. "Their motherboards must be cracked."

Chen Lai shrugged.

"If there's not too many, they could last for a generation or three, maybe. Even longer if they can improve on the recycling and keep up with the maintenance. *They* believe it, anyway. At least, they *want* to believe it." The engineer let out a sudden sigh. "I feel that way myself, sometimes. It's a lot less scary than crawling around on a ball of irradiated dirt. We're people, after all, not bugs. But the future's the future. No point running away from it.

"On the subject of which, Crewman MacLeod, your status on *Archimedes* has changed. You are assigned to the Captain's Office with immediate effect."

"The what, now?" Boz's cigarette tipped crazily between her fingers. She only barely regained control of it.

"You heard me. The Captain's Office. After your various and recent misbehaviors, she wants to keep an eye on you. A *close* eye." Chen Lai's lips twitched in something that might have been amusement. "You're to be an 'adviser on special projects.'"

"What in Archie's name does that mean?"

"Whatever the Captain wants it to. She's noticed that you have a, er, *knack* for getting things done. Illegal things, to be sure. But done nonetheless. We're going to need that, moving forward. Braking Day is set. And the sol is coming when the Mission is finally over. No one has the slightest clue what happens next. No one knows what's down there"—he pointed a finger at Lisette— "and no one was expecting neighbors. There's a lot to navigate." The engineer paused, looking at his fingers as if seeing them for the first time, blunted and scarred from a lifetime of repairs. "Maybe the time for ship's officers is over. We've done our job, after all. We kept the watch. We maintained the mechanisms. We flew the ship right. But now we're *here*. Maybe we need a different type of officer. Someone who can deal with the unexpected. Bend the rules a little. Get things done."

"Like me, you mean." Boz couldn't help herself. She was grinning from ear to ear.

"Personally, I think you'll be in the brig before the week is out. But the Captain's willing to give you a chance. Question is: have you got thrust enough to take it?"

Boz opened her mouth to say something disrespectful and then closed it again. The grin faded: slowly, like an arboretum sunset. It was as if a weight, long avoided, was finally settling on her shoulders.

Chen Lai turned to Ravi.

"As for you, Middy, we can discuss your future *after* you graduate. Which will be on schedule or, Archie help me, I'll know the reason why. Thanks to all this nonsense, you're behind on your studies. So, crack open whatever files Warren has waiting for you, suck it up, and get it done. That's an order. I expect you to be leading your own team by the time we hit orbit. Am I clear?"

"Crystal, sir."

Chen Lai's gaze, meanwhile, had alighted on Lisette. Ravi's heart started thudding. Rapid. Insistent.

He was terrified for her.

"You, Crewman Ansimov, are no part of *Archimedes*. I'm told that if justice on *Newton* is allowed to run its course, you will be executed as a mutineer. Is that your understanding of the situation?"

Lisette's eyes were unnaturally bright.

"I'd hoped, maybe . . ."

Her voice, weak to begin with, trailed off entirely. After some further hesitation, she nodded. A small vein pounded in her temple.

"Sir," Ravi began.

"Be quiet, MacLeod."

"But, sir—"

"I said, 'Be quiet,' Middy!"

"No, sir. I will not. None of this would have been possible without Lisette. If she and her LOKI hadn't risked everything to help us, we'd all have burned by now. The Mission would have failed. We owe her."

Chen Lai arched an eyebrow.

"So, what would you have me do, boy? She's not in our chain of command." The eyebrow arched farther. "You want me to go to *Newton*'s LOKI and ask it to spare this woman out of the goodness of its algorithms, because 'we owe her?' Is that it?"

"I just—"

"You just what? Wish you were old enough to have some sense? To think things through for once?" Chen Lai picked up his tea, drank, and placed the cup back on his thigh. It didn't even wobble. "I daresay you wished you could have spoken to Captain Hasegawa on the *Bohr* and suggested he appoint a liaison officer for his people on the *Newton*. That it would help if the liaison officer had some understanding of how things worked on a LOKI-run vessel, and that the liaison officer have a track record of doing the right thing, bearing in mind that we might very well need them long after planetfall. You might even wish you were able to persuade a certain risk-averse AI that the best protection its crew could hope to have against seven thousand cyborg hackers was not surgically implanted skullcaps but a liaison officer with their own dedicated LOKI, who not only understood cybernetic hacking but whose own family would likely suffer if a hacking attempt was successful. Is that what you would have wished, Midshipman MacLeod, if you'd bothered to think this through with the brains Archie gave you?"

"Y . . . yes, sir! Very much."

"I thought so." Chen Lai reached into a pocket and tossed a small box to Lisette. She opened it up, peering at the pieces of silver gleaming inside. Boz, ever curious, peeked over her shoulder and burst out laughing.

"What are they?" Lisette asked.

"They're a sub-lieutenant's collar studs," Boz said. "Which means my midshipman cousin here has to take orders from *you*. Because you, unlike him, are *a fully commissioned officer!*" She'd have said more, but she'd collapsed into giggles. Ravi just looked on, conscious that a goofy sort of grin was spreading across his face.

"They're yours if you want 'em," Chen Lai said gruffly. "Transfer to the fleet's chain of command, immunity from *Newton*'s jurisdiction."

Tears were running down Lisette's face. She nodded, unable to speak.

"Then I believe, Lieutenant Ansimov, you have free run of the ship. Expect orders from *Bohr* in the next twenty-four hours."

Ravi found himself striding across the living room. He swept Lisette into his arms. The box of insignia skittered across the deck.

"I'm so happy for you," he whispered in her ear. "So happy!"

Lisette buried her face in his shoulder and sobbed, the terrors of the last few weeks, perhaps of a lifetime, draining away with each racking breath. He held her close and gently, wrapped in the soft scent of dyed hair and the bonds of shared cybernetic memories.

Chen Lai finished his tea, stood up, and headed briskly for the door. The ShipSec officers parted as he went by, looking more like an honor guard than a security detail. Even though the Commander-Engineer strode across the threshold without so much as a backward glance, the rasp of his voice still managed to fill the compartment.

"Midshipman MacLeod, you and your wastrel cousin have an hour to sort yourselves out and report for duty. It's time you carried your weight around here.

"Try not to break stuff."

ACKNOWLEDGMENTS

No book is solely written by its author. Without the help of family, friends, and professionals no novel would ever see the light of day and this one is no exception. Heartfelt thanks to my sister, Amina, for kickstarting this whole enterprise, and to Barbara, Alex, Alima, Nadia, Elliot, Henry, Harriet, Angus, and Corey for their good-humored support; to the late Chris Johnson (we miss you so much!), Shelly Geppert, and Tom Parkes for being kind enough to read what I write and rude enough to tell me what they really think, and to Lisette Ochoa for letting me steal her beautiful name; to my agent, the estimable Brady McReynolds, who has championed this book through thick and thin and who (among many priceless actions) took a plasma torch to my dialog tags; to all at JABberwocky Literary, not least Susan Velazquez and James Farner, for holding my hand as I stumbled through the curtain into the strange world of publishing; to all at DAW Books, particularly my editor, the redoubtable Leah Spann, who has a far higher opinion of my writing than I do and inspired me to live up to it; to my copyeditor, Richard Shealy, ruthless enforcer of CMoS, for catching things the rest of us missed; to Kekai Kotaki for the extraordinary cover art and to Adam Auerbach for Kekai Kotaki. On the other side of the Atlantic, I am profoundly grateful to Jo and all the team at Jo Fletcher Publishing in the UK for taking this on, and to my UK agent, Stevie Finnegan, for helping make that happen. Last and absolutely not least, to Alexis Sattler, for believing first and fiercest . . . and, of course, for the title.